W9-AWB-079

SAVAGE . . .

He moved. Striding toward her, where she lay.

She leaped up at last, standing defensively beside the bed. But it made no difference. He reached out for her, caught her wrist, wrenched her into his arms. His chest was bare and she felt the fevered heat of it burning through the thin white fabric of her nightdress.

"You've no right," she began brokenly. "You can't come here like this—"

But he had. And he didn't speak a word, just captured her face between his two palms, found her lips with his own. Forceful, passionate.

Savage . . .

"You were just in my room," he told her huskily. "What did you come for?"

"To say good-bye," she whispered.

"No. The truth."

"I came . . ."

"For me. For this . . ." His mouth covered hers again. Demanding, heated, passionate, undeniable.

Heather Graham

CAPTIVE

A TOPAZ BOOK

TOPAZ
Published by the Penguin Group
Penguin Books USA Inc., 375 Hudson Street,
New York, New York 10014, U.S.A.
Penguin Books Ltd, 27 Wrights Lane,
London W8 5TZ, England
Penguin Books Australia Ltd, Ringwood,
Victoria, Australia
Penguin Books Canada Ltd, 10 Alcorn Avenue,
Toronto, Ontario, Canada M4V 3B2
Penguin Books (N.Z.) Ltd, 182–190 Wairau Road,
Auckland 10, New Zealand

Penguin Books Ltd, Registered Offices:
Harmondsworth, Middlesex, England

First published by Topaz, an imprint of Dutton Signet,
a division of Penguin Books USA Inc.

First Printing, August, 1996
10 9 8 7 6 5 4 3 2 1

To Kate and Chris Ryan, Linda and Dean Ryan, Sharon Spiak and Carl Litwin, and Kathryn Falk and Kenneth Rubin—thanks for lobster at Chumley's, steak at Le Bar Bar, brown beer at Jekyll & Hyde, coin-op machine parties, and so many other great times. Thanks for making business pleasure, and for giving me one more reason to be so very grateful for what I do for a living.

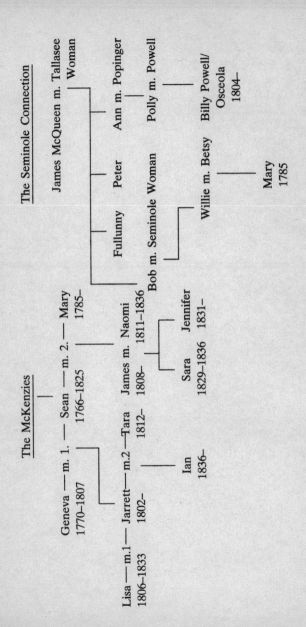

CAPTIVE

Prologue

The Hostage

The Florida Territory
Early fall, 1837

She was dead. Almost dead. So close to dead that she could nearly taste the metallic silver of the blade that threatened her throat, feel the hot stickiness and choke on the pulsing red spill of her own blood ...

But then a harsh, deep cry went out, shattering the air. The warrior about to murder her paused. The blade did not touch her throat. The cry, the shout of command that had broken through the carnage, had been so fierce that it stilled even the jubilant sounds of pillage, murder, and glory from the savages who had so recently won their battle and now set upon their victims, some stealing rings and trinkets, some giving the coup de grace to maimed and anguished men, some seeking murder, some seeking scalps.

The shouted cry stopped them all. It had all been cacophony; the day was suddenly and incredibly still. Teela stared up at the warrior, who seemed to have frozen in motion. A fierce warrior, one with blunt-cut ink black hair, an all but naked bear-greased body, and mahogany eyes that impaled her with hatred. One who had wanted her life. She stared back at him, hating him equally.

Enough. She didn't know quite what was going on— why the sudden ringing command of one warrior should stop this carnage—but she had endured enough. She'd not been part of a U.S. Army war party. She had only been on her way to leave this savage place. So savage, even in its beauty. Even now, as the sun fell, the sky was streaked with a rainbow of golden colors, yellows, oranges, crimson. The sun would fall soon, and the moon and the stars would rise and cool breezes would blow away the heat.

And she would most probably still die as the darkness blanketed the wild, raw, beautiful land . . .

Perhaps she was in this wretched danger because most of her escort had been chosen from men who had often served beneath her stepfather—hardened, ruthless soldiers who had prowled these swamps for endless months now, and battled the Seminoles and others on their own wild lands. Not perhaps—most certainly it was so. Few whites were hated by the Indians as much as Michael Warren. That hatred extended to the men who served him.

And, so it seemed, to his daughter.

And perhaps she knew full well in her heart that the soldiers had often been as cruel and rapacious as any "red" man could be. Perhaps she could not even blame the Indians for their hatred of her father and anything and anyone that he had touched.

But she had brought them no harm. And a few of the men on this escort service had been nothing more than green boys, too young, too innocent, to deserve such a death in the wilderness. Dear God, she did not deserve such a death in the wilderness!

"Bastard!" she cried suddenly to the warrior who still held her by the waves of her hair. She kicked into his gut and groin with all of her strength, desperate to be freed from him, even if it would be for nothing more than the last few seconds in which she might draw breath.

He gave out a cry. A furious cry of deep masculine pain, and to her relief and fleeting pleasure, his hand eased its death grip from her hair as he doubled over with pain.

She tried to rise from the place where she had fallen against a cypress. Tried to run. But the Indian was screaming again, reaching for her. Her arm was caught, and she was thrown back to the ground. The brave's knife, already deep, dark red with the life's blood of so many of the men who had fallen around her, was rising above her breast.

Then that powerful voice of command that had stilled the action of the massacre before rang out again. Even as she blinked and gasped for air, Teela saw that the muscled warrior was wrenched from atop her. She didn't dare wonder why. She rolled over, struggled to her knees and to her feet, and started to run again. She wouldn't die without fighting, without trying.

Fingers tangled into the length of her hair. She cried out in agony as she was determinedly dragged back. She struggled fiercely, catching hold of her hair yet not managing to free it from the firm grasp of that large bronzed hand. Even as she tried to kick and flail again, she found herself spun around, plucked up by the waist, and tossed back to the ground. She thought, fighting hysteria, that she was back where she started.

No. This was worse. Much worse.

For this man now straddled her, capturing her wrists, pinning them to the ground high above her head with the use of just one of his wickedly long-fingered hands. She was blinded by the blanket of sun-torched auburn hair that fell in a tangled sheath over her face. Twisting brought the merciless pressure of his thighs closer about her hips. Each gasp for breath, every effort to scream, all but caused her to choke and strangle upon her own hair.

Then it was swept from her face. She felt those fingers stroking her cheeks, sweeping away the wild and tangled strands. She opened her mouth to scream, and yet the sound never left her throat, and for shattering moments, still moments, moments in which she could feel or hear nothing but the pounding of her own heart, she stared into the eyes that seemed to pierce into her and through her, pinning her to the ground with every bit as much strength as the arms and legs that held her so fiercely. . . .

They were blue eyes. Shockingly, vibrantly blue. A blue that could burn cobalt with anger, lighten like a summer's sky with laughter. A blue that had haunted, compelled, fascinated, and drawn her before, perhaps for the very bronze of the face they shone from within.

Running Bear.

They had a name for him here in the dark green shadows and dangerous rivers of grass in the swamplands. They had a name for him among his people.

One that fitted him, one that had become his on the day he had left childhood behind within his tribe and taken the black drink. It was a fitting name for one who would be both fleet and graceful and powerful as well. She knew about him because she had made a point of knowing about him; her fascination had been complete. Today he was half naked, clad in doeskin breeches, silver necklaces, hide boots, and nothing more. The fantastic, ripple-muscled strength of his chest and shoulders was plainly visible. He wasn't heavy; she was certain that he would have shared his portion of food with any man, woman, or child of his people in need, but despite that, the raw force used in his expeditions through the land had apparently kept him honed like a razor, and enemy or not, white man, red man, he was an extraordinary example of the male physique. His hair was ebony but rich, and with a wave that betrayed his white heritage, the same as the majestic blue of his eyes. His face combined his races; it was an exceptionally strong face with high, broad cheekbones, a stubbornly squared chin, long, narrow nose, wide, full, sensual lips, high forehead, arched ebony brows, and those eyes.

She closed her own against them, her heart racing. She knew those eyes, knew them too well, had felt their blue fire before.

He was Running Bear now.

But he had been James McKenzie that first night she met him. So savage here with his bared flesh and simple silver adornment. She'd seen him first in a white frilled shirt, black breeches, crimson waistcoat, and black boots.

She'd seen him in the white man's world, seen the elegance of his movement across the dance floor, heard the eloquence of his arguments when he'd spoken. Feminine hearts had fluttered excitedly, for that aspect of danger had somehow remained about him. There was a vitality, a tension, a heat, that seemed barely contained within him. Yet his appearance had been that of a civilized gentleman. Indeed, she had met him as one.

No. He had been neither civil nor a gentleman that night, either. He had taken on the guise, and he had played the white men's games, and that had been all. And the blue fires had blazed in his eyes because he had raged with bitterness already, for though white guns had not taken his family, a fever caught within the swamps where they had ventured to escape the white settlers had done so with equal precision.

He had hated her that night. Hated her for her father. Yet even then, to his own great horror she was certain, he had . . .

Wanted her. And no matter how he had infuriated her, she had felt that wretched fascination. Almost beyond her own power, something that compelled her to walk to him when she should have been running away. He wasn't of her world. Even as she longed to cry out that she wasn't part of the things her father did, she wanted to hate him for the very way he assumed that she was, despise him for the very contempt he seemed to feel, and cast so ruthlessly her way. But even then—

"Look at me," he commanded her, and laughter seemed to bubble up within her again, for she was surrounded by savages, some of them half dressed and glistening bronze in the sun, others clad in doeskin breeches and colorful cotton shirts, feathers and ornaments. All of them armed with knives and axes and guns.

And still, his English was so perfect, his voice so cultured. *Look at me.* He might as well have commanded that she pass the tea.

Her eyes flew open and she met his again, and she

wondered if his coming would mean that she should live, or just die more slowly.

Even he couldn't change the fact of whose stepchild she was, or all that her father had done.

She gritted her teeth hard, fighting the trembling that had seized her. She wouldn't cower before him! His bitterness had always been great; he had never loved, perhaps he had not even liked, her. He had even hated her, and perhaps himself sometimes, because she had been white. And still, a strange wild fire had burned between them, and she knew that he had been entangled in it as well, and at times even, perhaps, she had drawn his admiration. She had never cowered before him, not yet. She had never betrayed her fear, and she suddenly vowed to herself that she would not do so now.

"So you are a part of a war party. Kill me, then, and have done with it!" she challenged him. "Slaughter me, slice me to ribbons, as your people have done with these men."

"It was a fair fight," he warned her, eyes narrowing.

"It was an ambush."

"The captain leading your party ordered the direct annihilation of two entire tribes, Miss Warren, men, women, and children. Babes still within their mothers' wombs. Yet to you these soldiers should have been shown mercy?"

"I know there is none within you!" she cried. She hesitated. She knew that he spoke the truth about their captain. She knew it; she had seen him in action. What good did it do now to admit that white men and red were merciless, brutal, and cruel? "There is no mercy to be found in this wretched hell, I am well aware, so do whatever you will! End it!"

He arched a brow, then leaned down closer to her. "End it? But we savages do so enjoy torturing a fiesty victim!"

Her blood seemed very cold. Ice within her. Yet where his body touched hers, it seemed she was still afire. She closed her eyes again, listening as the warriors rummaged through the soldiers' belongings. They sought food, she knew, above all else. It had been a military tactic to attempt starving the Indians into submission.

"What were you doing with these men?" he demanded.

Her eyes opened again upon that set of blue ones that so determinedly pinned her to the ground as the pillage went on around them. It didn't matter. She didn't want to look. He had power among his people. Enough to stop another from carrying out her murder. But no chief could stop hungry men from seeking food or whatever other spoils of war they might now seize.

Thank God the darkness was coming to cast its cover over the men who had perished. Over the Indians who searched the corpses so desperately for any small morsel of sustenance.

She couldn't even blame them. She'd been ill when she'd first heard her stepfather describe with relish his exploits against the Indians. The Americans who complained of brutal tactics didn't realize that they dealt with "subhuman" people he believed. The Indian question really needed to be settled permanently. Wretched little Indians grew to be wretched big ones, and they were much more easily dispatched when they were small.

Not all the soldiers were monsters. She'd met many good ones. Fine men, courageous men, kind men. Men who longed to leave the Indians in peace, to learn to live together.

But under the circumstances they would all pay for Colonel Warren's military prowess, as he described his maneuvers.

"What were you doing with the men?" James repeated angrily.

Her eyes went directly to his. "Leaving," she told him.

"For where?"

"Charleston."

He arched a brow again, and she thought that she sensed anger within him. Yes, she'd been running away. She'd had no choice. She'd never be able to make anyone realize that she despised Warren as deeply as any enemy might.

But damn it, since she'd met James, he'd been telling her to go away!

He was suddenly up, on his feet, having pounced there with the speed and agility of a graceful great cat. Again she thought to run, to escape them all, to hide somehow, to make it into the swamp and to St. Augustine. She twisted with her swift speed to rise, but she didn't even manage to turn. His hands were on hers, drawing her up, suddenly slamming her close to his own body. Once again his eyes knifed into her, impaling her, and had he held her or not, she could not have moved at that moment.

"Fool!" he charged. "You will not be going any-where now!"

"You're the one who has always told me to leave," she reminded him fiercely. "You'd have thrown me off your precious land were it possible. You told me to go—"

"And you didn't listen."

"I was trying—"

"Apparently, you didn't listen in time," he snapped, and she became very aware again that she was flush against the heat and force of his body. "Leave my side now and you are dead, Miss Warren, don't you see that?"

A dizzying sensation overcame her. Dead men lay around her, and she didn't dare look at them. She didn't want to recognize them. She was afraid that she would pass out. Tears suddenly sprang to her eyes as she thought of the men. She had hated some of them. But others . . .

He had a strange perception. Or perhaps he had lost a few white friends here tonight as well. She wondered at the emotional tugs he must feel in his own heart. His only blood brother was white. His nephew was white, his father had been white. And he had tried very hard to stay out of the fighting, but events had made that impossible.

She heard the anguished cry of a man. Her face must have gone very pale, and her enemy must have had some shred of mercy, though he would deny it. He shouted out a command in his Muskogee language, then started dragging her away by the upper arm. "Don't look down and don't look back!" he ordered brusquely.

She tried not to. Tried very hard not to see the carnage. A Seminole brave, a feathered band around his head, his chest bare and painted blue, a breech clout all that covered him, lay in death over an army corporal. They all but embraced. A terrible cold seemed to seep into her. Her teeth chattered. In a moment she would burst into tears. Never, never in front of this man.

He had a horse, a beautiful animal. A bay mare, with her ribs showing only slightly. Teela found herself thrown up on the animal, and he swiftly mounted behind her. In a few minutes' time, they had left the scene of the ambush behind. She didn't know where they were going. His people were so much on the run now that such a thing as a village scarcely existed, except very deep and hidden in the swamp. The women could be far more vicious than the men when they chose, so she prayed that he wasn't taking her to where many of her own gender awaited. Seminole punishment included scratchings with needles, often doled out by the women. Or she could endure ear and nose clippings and other maimings . . .

She felt ill as they rode and rode, the sights and sounds and memories of the savage assault all weighing down upon her. Had any of the men lived? Did they lie in torment? Did they have a chance of survival?

James was silent, anxious only to ride hard, so it seemed. Lush foliage was thrashed around them. Darkness had fallen, and she couldn't have begun to tell in the pine-carpeted green darkness in which direction they traveled.

At first she thought that he had merely brought her

to a river to drink. Then she saw that a *hootie,* or shelter, had been thrown up hastily in the copse near the water. Cabbage palms created the roof, and warm blankets carpeted the floor space.

He had come here alone, she thought, and she was grateful. Even when he roughly set her upon the ground, she was grateful. She didn't want to face any other members of his tribe. She didn't want to face him. How strange. She had lived long days and nights in fear, longing for just the sight of him.

As Michael Warren's stepdaughter, she had always been in danger of much more than a swift and certain death.

Set upon the ground, she stiffened her spine. She walked to the water, fighting a new wave of hysteria and a flood of tears.

"So you were leaving Florida," he said suddenly from behind her. "Going back to graceful drawing rooms, fine company, and the elegance belonging to the life of such a well-bred young lady."

She gritted her teeth, stiffening her spine still further.

"I wasn't trying to go back to anything."

"You were just trying to leave—this wretched wilderness?"

She spun around. Her lips trembled, her eyes were liquid and wild. "I was trying to leave the wretched battles and the horror and the—death!" she whispered. She gained some control. "Your friend meant to slit my throat."

His arms were crossed over his naked chest. Ink black hair streamed over his shoulders, a single band with no adornment wound around his forehead. "I'd have killed him very slowly had he done so," he said in a low, smooth voice.

"How reassuring," she murmured. "I could have cheered on your efforts from heaven."

"Or hell," he commented dryly. Then he asked furiously, "Why did you leave my brother's house?"

"I had no choice."

"Jarrett would never have cast you out."

"I had no choice," she repeated stubbornly. Perhaps he understood.

Perhaps he never would.

He strode to her then, and she longed to back away. But there was nowhere to go except the river. And she wasn't prepared. He was moving with his fluid grace and a startling swiftness. He was on her before she could have gone anywhere at all, even if she had determined to cast her fate into the water.

His hands were on her arms, and she was against him again, against all the fire and vibrance and fierce, furious life of the man. And before she could struggle, he had her hand palm down upon his naked chest. "You left Cimarron," he said huskily, "but not for home then, when you could have sailed right out of Tampa Bay. You forged across the territory! What then? Did sense come to you at last? Did you run from the war?" he demanded harshly. "Or did you run from *this*? Bronze flesh, copper flesh, *red* flesh?"

She wrenched her hand away from him with all her strength. Dear God, but she was so emotionally entangled, and his passions and his hatred for her were all that seemed to rule him. "I'm not afraid of you!" she cried out furiously, fingers knotting into fists at her sides. "I'm not afraid of you, you—"

"You should have been afraid," he told her. "You should have been afraid a long time ago. You should have run back to the chaste gentility of your *civilized* Charleston drawing room the second you set foot in this territory. Damn you, you should have gone away then!"

"Go to hell!" she cried to him.

"I think I shall get there soon enough," he assured her.

She'd scarcely been aware that he'd moved, but he was close in front of her once more. His hands were on her shoulders once again. He was still moving, backing her along the riverbank, until she was forced against an old, gnarled cypress, and as he spoke, the hot whisper of his words came from lips just inches away from her own. "Weren't you sufficiently warned that there was a war on here? Didn't you hear that we pillaged, robbed, raped, ravished, and murdered? That red men ran free in a savage land?" His voice didn't rise. The depth and emotion within it deepened. "Didn't you hear? Or didn't it matter? Was it tantalizing to play with an Indian boy? Touch, and back away, before you got burned?"

"Anyone who touches you is burned!" she cried out. "Burned by your hatred, your passion, your bitterness. Anyone is burned—" She broke off with a gasp, for he suddenly jerked her shoulders and jerked them hard. The fierce blue of his eyes sizzled into her heart and mind. And the words he spoke then were but a whisper, vehement in their warning—or promise.

"Then, my love, *feel the fire!*"

His hands then were upon her bodice. She fell back against the tree as she heard the rending of fabric, and felt the fire indeed, the sweeping liquid inferno of his lips upon hers, ravaging, demanding. Her lips were parted by the force. His tongue filled her mouth. She wanted to hate him, rake his eyes out. She wanted to scream and shout and cry and never surrender, for he never would, he would die before he accepted any terms of surrender. And she tried. Tried to twist from his onslaught, tried so very hard not to feel the fire that ignited within her, scalding the blood that surged throughout her like a river, seizing sweet, mercurial hold of her limbs and being. She fought like a tigress, in fact, bringing her arms up between them, pelting him with her fists. But she found herself plucked up and slammed hard to the ground, where her fall was barely cushioned by layers of pine and moss, and where the rich, verdant scents of the earth arose to encompass her with new sensation.

He straddled her, caught her wrists. And she ceased to struggle, but stared with hot fury into his eyes, her fight and accusation now eloquently silent. And her hands were suddenly free, yet still she didn't move.

"What in God's name am I going to do with you?"

he demanded very softly, and she lay still as she felt the stroke of his fingers upon her throat, the caress of his hand pushing away torn fabric to close over her breast, the palm rotating over the hardened peak of her nipple.

She knew. She knew exactly what he was going to do with her. Knew that his lips would be tender now when they touched hers, coercing them to part, demanding still, but so seductive. Indeed, she felt the fire. It burned her heart and mind, seared her flesh, ignited her soul. His lips descended upon hers once again.

"Bastard!" she charged breathlessly.

"Perhaps. But tell me to leave you be. Say it with your eloquent words, and mean it with your soul!"

The earth could cave in, and she would not want him to leave her now.

"Bastard!" she repeated softly.

"I know, I know," he moaned, his lips finding hers once again, his fingers threading into her hair. Once again the sheer force and hunger of his kiss seduced her. Then she felt his lips upon her throat, his hands upon her torn clothing. His mouth closed over her breast, his tongue played over and savored the nipple, and once again a scalding seized her, liquid fire coursing from that intimate spot he touched, filling her limbs and core. She cried out incoherent words, her fingers tearing into the ebony length of his hair. His hands and mouth continued a wild ravishment upon her. She heard again the rent of fabric as he sought her in his haste.

She felt again the fever of his lips, his hands. Upon her belly, the smooth flesh of her hips, the length of her thighs. She felt the searing wet heat of his tongue laving her belly, touching her inner thighs, his fingers, touching, finding, his tongue again . . .

She cried out in the wilderness and fought him anew. Fought the passion, and the hunger, and all the raw, explosive things he awoke within her. It was a battle lost, for the fire she had touched was one that burned indeed, a conflagration that was caught by the wild winds of the wilderness and sent flying to the heavens. Sweet waves of ecstasy burst into the soaring golds and crimsons of that fire, and she shrieked out in the night, closing her eyes, opening them again only to find that his blue gaze was now pinning her to the moss-strewn ground, and that he had leaned to one side to loosen his breeches. Before she could speak or stir, he was with her, enveloping her in his arms when she gasped and shuddered, her body accepting the swift, knifing invasion of his. He seemed to fill her, and fill her anew. Sink into her until she thought that she would scream and split and die, then withdraw, and fill her again, and with each touch, bring her closer to that magic once again. Yet the swift seduction of his first thrusts gave way quickly to something much more reckless, ruthless even. Savage.

A hunger so deep, it swept her away once again. Brought the earth against her back, the breath ripping from her body. Slick, rippled bronze muscle slammed against her breasts; rock-hard hips commanded the rhythm of her own. The fire of his sex burned within her, steel, hot, touching her, filling her, burning within her . . .

Exploding within her . . .

A liquid fire. Encompassing her body, seeming to seep throughout it, touching all of her with all of him. She trembled as ripple after ripple brought her back down to the bed of moss, down into the moonlit darkness, once again into the slick, powerful arms of the man who held her.

His weight moved from her. An arm cast over his forehead, he stared up at the stars now covering the night sky. After a moment Teela pulled the tangle of her hair from beneath him and tried to gather the remnants of her clothing. She felt him watching her. Her bodice lay in pieces; nothing was salvagable. She ignored his piercing blue gaze and stood naked, walking to the water's edge. She knelt down and bathed her face in the coolness of the river. She felt him by her side, and looked ahead. "Feel the fire!" she whispered softly, bitterly.

"You should have known better than to play with an Indian boy from the very beginning," he said, his voice husky.

She stared at him hard. "I never played," she said with dignity, and rose again. Looking around the ground at the ruined fabric, she murmured, "It will be a cold night."

He stood, walking back to her. "I will warm you through it. In the morning we'll worry about something for you to wear."

She lifted her chin. "I don't intend to stay the night."

"You wanted to play the game. It is well under way. You didn't run to your drawing room soon enough. Now, Miss Warren, you will be my guest."

"Prisoner, so it seems."

"Whatever. You will stay."

He plucked her up from the ground, his eyes upon her as he walked to the shelter he had created in the woods. One easily made, easily destroyed, as his few belongings were easily carried through the wilderness he knew so well. His land, a savage land. And land he had vowed he would keep. There would be no surrender; his people would be the undefeated, the unconquered.

Now he set her down upon the furs within the shelter, giving her one to cover her shoulders as she shivered. He offered her water from a leather gourd, and she drank, then returned it.

"You'll never keep me if I choose to take my chances and leave," she promised him. "I came from a drawing room, but I've learned your jungle of cypress and palms."

He arched a brow. "A challenge? Then let me assure you, if it is my choice, you'll never escape me."

"Damn you—"

"Teela, would you escape me to meet another brave anxious for the beauty of your hair—ripped away along with your scalp?"

"I'd escape you to find freedom from this travesty. Not all Seminoles are barbarians—"

"What a kind observation, Miss Warren!"

"Nor are you any more a Seminole than you are a white man yourself! Don't tell me about the bronze of your flesh—even your mother carries white blood in her veins. Indeed, you are actually more white than Indian—"

"Teela, one drop of Indian blood suddenly turns the color of a man's flesh, and you are worldly enough to know that it is so. Look at my face, and you know that I am Indian."

"I look at your face and know that you are a creation of two worlds!"

"Then know this—life has made me Indian in my heart, and you must not forget it."

"Life is making you cruel—"

"Enough, Teela. Enough for tonight."

She gritted her teeth and swallowed hard and lay down upon the furs and skins. A moment later, she felt him beside her, felt his arms come around her and pull her close. His nakedness sheltered her. The smoothness of the wall of his chest created warmth against her back.

Enough . . .

Enough for tonight. She had started the day assuming she would be on a ship, bound for a new life, or the old life, a life she had once known very well. One she had once left behind easily enough, but which could now shelter her from the pain that had come to exist within her heart.

Then she had nearly lost her life, and now . . .

She closed her eyes tightly. So she had played with an Indian boy!

No, she hadn't played. She had fallen in love. She was the white girl. Yet he was the one with the past, with a hatred for all that she represented, with the bitterness for a love now long lost.

And nothing more than a fiery passion for her, one he could not deny, yet loathed within himself.

But he held her now, held her through the night. He had saved her life. She knew it, no matter that she threatened to leave him. She knew that she could not wander through the swamp and hope to explain to a band of Seminoles in a chance meeting that she had never wished them any harm. She was alive now because James had either happened upon the army party taking her northward, or because he had come—for her. Either way it didn't matter.

He was her enemy still.

His choice.

Dear God, what would the future hold, what *could* the future hold?

Yet as she wondered that, she felt a stinging threat of tears press against her closed lids. To ponder the future, she had to remember the past.

And the first day she had come here, to this savage land.

And to the first night she had seen him, in all his glory, the strikingly handsome, civilized man in his elegant suit with his impeccable manners, yet the savage danger beneath the smooth veneer all the while.

The first night . . . when he had touched her.

And she had first felt the fire.

It had not been so very long ago.

Chapter 1

The *Marjorie Anne* cut cleanly through turquoise waters on one of the most beautiful days Teela Warren could remember seeing in all her life. Gentle white puffs of clouds appeared like dream creatures in a sky a glorious shade of powder blue. The sea breezes were easy, soft, so gentle beneath the benign heavens. They felt delicious, cool, and promising against her cheeks as she stood near the ship's bow, her heart beginning a slow thunder against her chest.

They were nearly there. Tampa, the rough, tough city grown up around the military post at Fort Brooke. Gateway to a savage wilderness.

Well, she would take the wilderness, if only she could.

Sometimes, on the ship, the sweet promise of adventure had been strong. The weather had not always been so sweet; storms had come, and an angry sea had tossed and buffeted the ship. And she had loved it all, standing at the bow as she did now, feeling the wind. There was something about it that promised freedom, something that let her forget . . .

It had helped that her apelike guardian-escorts were not good sailors. Trenton Wharton was a good six feet two inches tall, and well over two hundred pounds; Buddy MacDonald was a bit taller and even heavier. Either one of them could easily pick up a half dozen grown men at the same time—and certainly stop a wayward young woman right in her tracks—but neither seemed to have a decent sea stomach whatsoever.

But, alas! What difference did it make? There was

nowhere to escape on the open Atlantic, in the Florida Straits, or the azure Gulf of Mexico. All that she could possibly do was face the wind, feel it with her flesh, and with her soul, and dream. Of freedom.

Her fingers tightened and tensed over the rail as she watched the sea before her, the land seeming to come closer and closer.

She wasn't quite sure when she and Michael Warren had grown to despise one another so completely. If she could only go back, she could perhaps change things. She'd been young when he'd married her mother, but her real father had been dead scarcely a year, and she had loved him with all her heart. Michael Warren had entered her world and taken her into his own, treating her just as he might a green private in one of his army companies. Discipline! It was his life. He made it hers. More than once he had seen fit to break pine branches over her shoulders and back. He had legally adopted her, and with his *discipline* and determination—sympathy had no place in a well-ordered life—he had buried her own dear father deeper and deeper with each passing year. Her mother had tried to reason with her. Point out that Michael Warren was a good man, just an army man. Strict and determined to keep his household in the same good order as he kept his men.

But he wasn't a good man. He might have convinced her mother that he was good beneath his hard exterior, and he no doubt believed it himself. He prayed often enough. Turned to the good Lord daily, and attended church with an extraordinary vigor and regularity. But to Teela, no amount of churchgoing could atone for deeds done or the manner of a man, and though, for her mother's sake, she had tried to find that goodness in him, she could not. He reveled in cruelty; he enjoyed inflicting pain. She could hear the pleasure in his voice when he spoke with his friends and fellow officers into the wee hours of the night in *her real father's* plantation hall. He liked war; he liked killing. Most of all, he liked killing Indians. They were all firebrands of hell. It didn't matter the age. He'd fought in a number of the Creek wars; he'd fought at times with Andy Jackson when Jackson had been a military power in the field before he had become the president of the United States, only recently replaced by his friend Martin Van Buren.

Van Buren might be the president now, and Jackson might have retired to his plantation to live out his days as a gentleman farmer, but Jacksonian politics were still being played. Jackson's determination that the Indians must move west had not ended with the Creek wars, or the sad migration of the Cherokees. The government remained intent on moving the red men out of Florida. And the Florida Indians remained intent on remaining right where they were. It left a field of war, and a great deal of work that Michael Warren relished completely.

Michael Warren had earned medals for his heroics in the War of 1812 against the British, but those medals meant little to him. He hadn't really enjoyed fighting the British; he loved fighting the Indians.

Military life had often taken Michael Warren away. And while Teela's mother had lived, life had been bearable, even enjoyable for Teela—since the army had so frequently kept her stepfather far from home. But last summer, when Michael had first been temporarily assigned as a regular army commander in the "hellhole" of Florida, as he called it, Lilly Warren had died. Gentle, sweet, and delicate as a rose, she had simply seemed to fade. In death she had been as beautiful as she had been in life, her radiant auburn hair spread out in a fan over the white satin bedding of the coffin, her lovely features at peace. Teela had watched her fade, had sworn to herself that she would stay as long as her mother needed her, and then turned her back on the graceful plantation that should have been her inheritance. Warren's name was now on the property deed, even if Teela's real father had built the place brick by brick. It didn't matter, and she was certain her father would have understood why she had to abandon it. Teela wasn't staying with Warren. The pity of it was, she soon discovered, she was underage. She certainly couldn't leave until her mother was properly buried, laid gently and lovingly to her eternal rest. Michael Warren naturally returned for his wife's funeral. But even as Teela mourned Lilly, kneeling at the coffin, Michael paced behind her, describing the future he had in mind for her.

Letting him know in no uncertain terms that she didn't intend to stay and accept any of his dictates had proved to be a tremendous mistake. She'd found herself locked in her room. Nor was Warren a fool. He never left any of the gentle household slaves to guard her. No. She could not coerce or trick or charm anyone into easing his guard—military men were set to watch her. The one time she managed to leave the house, she was dragged back.

Only to discover that she was to marry the very wretch who had forcefully dragged her back.

But no matter what Michael Warren did to her, there was only so much he could force.

She had walked down the church aisle with Warren, taken the hand of her "betrothed"—and point-blank flatly refused to wed in the very midst of the ceremony.

Warren, of course, had been humiliated. And admittedly, she had been terrified of him that night, and with good reason. The lashings he had dealt her with his belt were barely healed. But though he had drawn her tears that night, he had not drawn submission.

She had hated him all the more, and her resolve against him had grown stronger.

The good thing—it had seemed—was that he had been permanently assigned to Florida almost immediately following the near wedding. At least Teela had thought it good at the time. Michael Warren lived by his own strange code of honor. He was her stepfather, allowed by God's own law to dictate to her and attempt to beat her into submission. He was a good churchgoer, a God-fearing man, even though Teela was a little amazed by his concept of Christian charity, and of good and evil. But in his absences, though she was watched, though she had scant chance for escape, she also had a certain freedom. She was delighted when he left.

Delighted, in a way, with the terrible news that came forth from the Florida territory. There was fierce war raging down there. The government had imagined that it would be an easy thing to force the Seminole Indians out to new lands in the West.

They'd underestimated their adversaries. The Indians had dug in, hard. Into a savage land where they could strike and hide, disappear, and return out of darkness and swamp to strike again. Many soldiers had been massacred.

Michael Warren might not come back.

It was wrong to pray for a man's death. She tried not to do so. She didn't pray that he'd die. She simply prayed that he'd disappear. Be swallowed into the swamp.

But Michael hadn't been swallowed.

He had sent for Teela, and so she was now approaching the coast of a savage land where warfare was being waged on a brutal and desperate scale.

She sighed, watching the water. It was a land where many before her had come seeking freedom. Long before her stepfather had been sent to the frontier Florida territory, she had been intrigued by newspaper and magazine stories. Slaves escaped their masters to run south, to join with the Indian bands there. For decades now Creeks and other Indians had found themselves pushed southward by the encroachment of the white man. They had joined with tribes all but extinct. Newly immigrated Creeks, Muskogee-speaking Seminoles, Hitichi-speaking Mikasukis, were all grouped together by the white man as Seminoles, Cimmarons, renegades, runaways.

Treaty after treaty had been signed with them. Wars had raged. Treaties had been broken. And finally absolute violence had erupted with a December slaughter now known as the Dade Massacre, and since then the situation had only worsened. Teela read, and she listened to the army men, and she had no choice but to know her stepfather's opinions. The Seminoles, once quite loosely banded, had a hero now, a war chief or *mico*, a leader of extraordinary capabilities, a man called Osceola. Under his leadership the Indians had learned to fight and run, to create death and havoc and damage, and disappear into the wildness of their swamps. Amazingly—since the general white consensus had been that a few companies of good regular army men should be able to quell the disturbances of a handful of savages— the Seminoles had pitched the country into a dreadful war. Americans were expansionists. They wanted land, and they didn't care if the Indians were on it or not. Reservations in the western section of the country would do for the native people, so the Seminoles were ordered to emigrate.

Some had indeed been transported west.

Many more had dug in, moving more swiftly than the wind, more silently than the whisper of a coming twilight. White settlers—men, women, and children—had been horribly slain and mutilated.

Entire Indian villages had been decimated.

But still they fought on. With an uncanny ability. And the trained and civilized army sent by the United States government was all but helpless against the tactics of the natives.

Only Michael Warren would insist that a stepdaughter be brought into such wickedly dangerous circumstances, Teela thought. But then, Michael Warren assuredly believed that she should either learn to follow his dictates, or else deserve to die a wretched death at the hands of savages. Besides, according to Warren, they were close to a truce at the moment. March had brought another treaty.

The problem was, like all other agreements between the whites and the Indians, this one seemed to be failing.

Soldiers were starting to raid villages again.

Seminoles were attacking white farms and plantations. The war continued even as Teela traveled toward the wild frontier of the peninsula. The long way, all around the length of the east coast down the Atlantic and up the west coast within the Gulf of Mexico, because Warren would most probably be assigned to Fort Brooke, although it seemed that the sporadic fighting was now taking place just about everywhere.

Teela didn't care. She despised Michael Warren, but she was anxious to see the frontier territory of Florida, the exotic birds she'd read so very much about, the sunsets ... she wasn't even afraid of the mosquitoes, or the hardships of a military fort.

While Lilly had lived, Teela had strived to be everything her mother had expected her daughter to be. She had entertained her mother's friends—and even Michael's associates—with all the grace and hospitality taught her by Lilly's gentle hand. She had played the spinet and sung ballads for their guests, gone to teas and balls and dances, flirted and charmed to the exact expectations of her society. She had never missed church; she had followed Lilly constantly to bring aid to the needy and ill. She resented none of these things—in fact, she had enjoyed nursing, and would have loved to have studied medicine.

But Lilly was gone now. And there was no pretense between her and Michael. She loved Charleston, but not beneath her stepfather's dictates.

She lifted her chin to the wind, smiling slightly, and wondering to herself just why she was so excited to be coming here. The things she had read had fascinated her. She wanted to see the swamps and the hammocks, the spectacular sunsets, the exotic birds. Even feeling the wind aboard the ship, she felt a sense of excitement. It seemed that life, no matter how deadly or dangerous, would be vivid here. Splashed with color. She was eager for the very wildness that was promised and threatened, for the beauty, however savage it might be.

And however much she might see, she reminded herself ruefully, for assuredly, if Michael Warren had summoned her here, he'd had a reason for doing so. She would probably find herself betrothed again. And this time Michael would have surely chosen someone old and grizzled—but rich, of course. And strong. Strong enough to force the issue with a reluctant bride, since Michael would be wary of her now himself.

Never, she promised herself silently. He could do many things to her. He could not force her to wed, and he never would. This frontier land would not be like Charleston. And Michael would frequently be engaged in battle. There would have to be a greater chance here for her. . . .

A chance of what? she wondered.

Freedom, something whispered in her heart.

A ship's whistle suddenly sounded, and Teela became aware of a flurry of activity as orders were shouted, orders to trim the sails and bring the ship about.

They were approaching land.

Teela forgot her own reflections as she looked toward the shore, both fascinated and, admittedly, a little dismayed by the view that stretched before her.

The stockade itself was crude and wooden with high walls and towers, something that almost seemed to grow out of the earth itself. The small community surrounding the fort was little better, just a conclave of poor wooden houses, fences, domestic animals, and dirt roads. But she realized that the poor fledgling city was surrounded by a frame of startling beauty. The river, shimmering green, stretched through the growth of trees and foliage that forged inland, while the bay itself seemed touched by the light of a thousand diamonds, creating a dance of blue and aquamarine upon the horizon. There were beaches, too, encircling the city, white sand beaches that looked as if they were soft silk thrown out to buffer whatever thorns and brambles might lie within the land beyond.

"Miss Warren, we're nigh to docking," Teela heard, and turned quickly, first to her left, then right. Her stepfather's watchdogs were with her, both a little green. Indeed, Trenton, who had spoken, *was* green, his flesh nearly matching the color of his eyes. Poor Buddy was almost as white as the sand of the beaches. But despite their distress, both men were back in full uniform.

"It don't look like much, I know," Buddy told her apologetically. He was a freckle-faced farm boy out of Tennessee, born and bred to a military tradition, with the call of duty above even that of honor. But he was a nice young man with a good heart, and she was glad that he tried to cheer her now.

"It looks wonderful," she said. It was only partially a lie. The beaches and sea and sky were extraordinary. Only the fort and houses were wretched.

They'd come into the harbor. Shouts were loud; half naked men leapt about the rigging as the ship was steered and then pulled into her berth. Ropes were thrown to the dock and the ship was secured. The gangway was set down. Before anyone had disembarked, soldiers came quickly aboard, meeting with the captain.

"News is always the first thing needed," Trenton said, his voice somber.

"It's good news just to see the city standing, and not in ashes," Buddy agreed.

The group of soldiers who had come aboard with their messages and information disbanded, and the kindly old naval captain of the ship came hurrying toward Teela. "Fuzz-bucket!" Trenton murmured of the captain.

"He's a navy boy," Buddy said sorrowfully.

"Some of them have use, and some of them don't," Trenton observed. "Though I admit, I myself am happier at the fort when we've the extra bodies of the marines assigned to duty there. It's just that this particular navy man—"

"Miss Warren!" Captain Fitzhugh bellowed. She tried not to smile. Her watchdogs were right. He was a strangely mincing little man with a big belly, small, skinny legs and little feet, and a face full of white fur. He was continually worried, a fussy little man.

"I'm in great distress! Your stepfather was to have been here to greet you, but he had been detained farther

north, battling the heathens!" He made the sign of the
cross dramatically over his chest.

"Ah, dear! What a shame," Teela lied, her tone re-
morseful, her eyes sparkling.

"Not to worry. Some good friends of us all, Josh and
Nancy Reynolds, who run a fine shop here, will greet
you ashore, see to your provisions, and escort you inland
to Cimarron, where a regular army escort will soon arrive to bring you to your father."

"Thank you," Teela told him. Sweet, blessed *Jesu*! She
was to be on her own to first taste this wondrous new
place! She would have fallen to her knees with gratitude
were not so many men watching her. She smiled, and
on the captain's arm she descended the plank to set foot
on Florida soil.

Perhaps the houses were little more than log shanties.
Perhaps the fort was rough—and half the soldiers and
civilians more heathen-looking than she imagined the
savages were. It didn't matter. She felt a thrill of exhilaration as she came ashore, and as they came down the
dock to the dirt city street, she was greeted with a warm
cry. "Miss Warren, Miss Warren!" A second later, she
saw a pretty, plump woman with brown hair beneath a
wide-brimmed hat approaching her, a huge, muscular
man just beyond her. The woman flashed a smile to Captain Fitzhugh and offered her hand warmly to Teela.
"Welcome, we're delighted to have you here. We've
heard so very much about you—"

She broke off with a little gasp as her husband elbowed her in the ribs. "Josh Reynolds, Miss Warren,
and we do welcome you, and don't you worry none, we
don't go judging people by Charleston standards."

"Josh!" Nancy in turn elbowed him.

Teela was a bit startled to realize that gossip was
strong enough to precede her to this wilderness, but she
couldn't help but smile since it had served to make her
more interesting to this warm and giving pair.

"I'm very glad to be here," she told them.

"Are you, then?" Josh queried, seeming surprised to

look at her and determine that it was the truth. "Many such a lady as yourself would scorn our poor city."

"Ah, but then you've heard the gossip about me already, right?" Teela teased lightly in return.

"Oh, we don't go listening to gossip!" Nancy began, but she broke off and started laughing. "Miss Warren, you may just do fine here in our wilderness."

"Pure paradise!" Josh corrected her.

Twenty minutes later, Teela wasn't quite sure how Josh had managed to find his life a paradise, here or elsewhere. He and Nancy ran a store that offered just about everything in the world. They supplied a number of the traders and sutlers who tramped into the interior of the state, though, as Josh told her, there was darned little left of any white civilization in the interior. Too many times the army had been forced to desert its various posts. If the Indians weren't bad enough, there was always the fever, and the fever took away more men, women, and children than did war.

Despite the troubles, though, Josh and Nancy were thriving. The whole front section of their log dwelling was store. They sold food, medicines, tools, clothing, boots, liquor, and even farm animals. They sold coconuts and exotic wild bird feathers, mostly brought in by the Indians. If an object could be acquired at all, it would be sold at their general store.

In the back there was a kitchen and parlor combination, one big, drafty room, but with a fire burning cheerfully in the hugh hearth. Though they were moving into spring, the days were still just a little chilly. Beautiful, Teela thought, with the sun coming through the windows, but inside the cabin it was wonderful to feel the touch of the flames. Wonderful and wild. Josh and Nancy had a full house, with toddlers seeming to be everywhere and the oldest of their children only seven.

A very different kind of paradise, Teela thought, but sitting in the parlor, playing hide-and-seek games with the little, enormous-eyed children, she realized that she was happier than she had been in a long time. Josh was attending to customers, and Nancy was determinedly finding Teela the proper size of good boots for the south Florida terrain.

If only Michael Warren were never to come . . .

She was down upon her knees playing ball with the three-year-old when she sensed that someone was with her. She spun around toward the door that led to the shop and was startled to see a very tall man with ebony hair standing there, watching her with the child.

"My apologies, I didn't mean to startle you."

He was an exceptionally good-looking man, somehow both rugged and elegant, his appearance entirely commanding. The little girl she was playing with let out a shriek of happiness and went to him, crying out, "Uncle Jarrett, Uncle Jarrett!"

He caught the little girl, sweeping her up, giving her a sound kiss on the cheek, and setting her down upon the ground once again. By then Teela was standing, watching, waiting. "Jarrett McKenzie, Miss Warren. My wife and I have a home down the river, and if you're in agreement, you'll be our guest until Captain Argosy returns to bring you to your father."

"How do you do," Teela murmured, "and yes, of course, thank you very much."

He watched her for a moment. "You must be disappointed to have missed your father."

"Stepfather."

"Ah . . . This must be a strange and frightening land without him here to greet you."

"I'm not frightened easily, Mr. McKenzie."

He smiled suddenly. "Good. My ship is at the dock. I'll see to it that your things are brought aboard, and I'd like to leave within the hour while the sun is still high."

"Thank you."

He turned to start back through the doorway into the shop. "Mr. McKenzie!" Teela said softly, calling him back. He paused, arching a brow at her.

"You don't seem to care for Michael Warren very much. Why are you doing this for him?"

He seemed startled, either by her question or intuition. He smiled slowly. "I wouldn't send you into the wilderness alone, Miss Warren. My wife would never allow it."

"But you don't like my father."

He hesitated, then shrugged. "Miss Warren, I did not say that."

"Mr. McKenzie, I don't like him, either."

The man laughed suddenly. "Well, then, maybe we can keep you at Cimarron as long as possible, eh?"

Then he disappeared.

Teela didn't see him again until she was on his ship, with Nancy and Josh at her side, giving all kinds of last-minute advice. She needed to be careful of all swampland, it bred fever. She needed to watch out for insect bites, for snakes, and for 'gators. 'Gators were mean—she wasn't ever to let anyone fool her on that fact!

"Ain't too many deadly snakes, just four to be exact. Rattler, pygmy rattler, coral snake, and cottonmouth. They'll leave you alone if you leave them alone."

She was just up the gangplank on the deck. The ship was much smaller than that which she had sailed in on, with a crew of only five. She could see one sailor rolling his eyes as Nancy continued her advice. Teela smiled.

She heard the deep, rich voice of her host behind her then. "She does seem like an intelligent young lady, Nancy," Jarrett commented.

"Forewarned is forearmed!" Nancy said with a sniff. "You be careful yourself," she chastised firmly, then gave Jarrett a huge, warm hug. "There's a blanket for the baby in that satchel for Tara, Jarrett McKenzie. You give the wee one a mighty hug for me. And Tara as well. Tell her I'll come out soon."

Josh was shaking his head. "Nancy's afraid to come."

"Afraid?"

"Ah, well, the settlers here are just getting over their fear that the Seminoles might attack Tampa at any time," Jarrett said.

"It's a dangerous river," Nancy said.

"Not with me," Jarrett said softly, offering Nancy an encouraging smile. He shook Josh's hand and gave Nancy a kiss on the cheek. "Get off my ship, now! I've a good twenty-four hours to home, and I'm anxious to see my wife and child."

"Remember, we're here if we can ever help you," Nancy called to Teela as her husband escorted her firmly from the ship. She waved in return.

Before long, they had cast off from the dock. Teela kept waving to the couple.

When they were just leaving the city behind them, Teela gasped suddenly, seeing two men in army issue uniforms come tearing down the dock where the small ship had been berthed.

McKenzie stood behind her, she realized. "Friends of yours?" he asked.

"Not exactly," she murmured uncomfortably. "They're my—escort."

"Watchdogs?"

"But really not bad fellows, considering."

"Do we go back for them?" he asked politely.

"Oh, no. Please, no!" she exclaimed.

"They can find Cimarron themselves, you know."

She sighed, looking down into the water. "Perhaps. Maybe we should go back. Michael would be furious if he knew they were left behind purposely."

"Would he really?" McKenzie queried.

She spun around. His eyes were dark. Almost as dark as his hair. There was definitely a devilish light to them now. He leaned toward her, his voice a conspiratorial whisper. "Then we definitely leave them." He raised his voice suddenly. "Men! Full sails. Let's catch what breeze there is. Let's move from this place!"

Then he turned and left her, and she couldn't help but smile as she left her first taste of this strange new territory behind her and moved ever inland.

Chapter 2

Cimarron

As James rode through the trail of trees that broke onto the lawn, he stared at his brother's house, and felt a welcome lightening within his heart. He'd helped build the house, he'd lived the dream of its creation with his brother, and to this day he loved it.

They'd planned to build another together. One that would be his home. Though they'd both grown up for the most part among the peoples who had traveled into Florida and become *Seminoles* to the whites, they'd both grown up with their good Scots father as well, and they'd been tutored in white ways as well as Indian custom. James knew how to plan and build such a home, and he also knew how to manage fields, cattle, and laborers. He was also familiar with the works of Defoe, Bacon, Shakespeare, among others, just as he had been taught the fine music of Mozart and Beethoven.

But he'd fallen in love when he was very young with an Indian girl. Deeply in love. And he'd joined her clan, because he'd been needed there. And through his mother's bloodlines he had found himself in line to be a *mico* for a band who had pleaded for his leadership, and so he had lived with his people in a sprawling, beautiful hammock. . . .

Until war had come.

But no matter how bitter the war that raged, no matter how deep the pain and anger that too often guided him still, he loved his brother, just as he had loved their father, the most enlightened man he had ever known of any race. Since his birth, his life had always been entertwined with his brother's—no war could change that.

"James!"

He heard his name called from the porch, and he dismounted from his horse, seeing his sister-in-law, Tara, emerge from the house and start down the steps, running to greet him. He stood by his horse, waiting. When she reached him, he spun her around and hugged her, then set her upon the ground again. She was a stunning woman, golden blond, blue-eyed, as delicate as porcelain, yet absurdly strong and determined. She had made his brother the perfect wife.

She touched his cheeks, as if assuring herself of his health, then stepped back, frowning. He was clad in denim pants and a rawhide vest, with a band about his hair and moccasins on his feet. She shook her head. "It's still cold!" she chastised him.

"Tara, it's never really cold."

"It can be cold enough."

"It's spring."

"The air is cool."

"How's my daughter?"

Tara's eyes went alight and she smiled. "Growing like a weed. She is an incredibly beautiful little lady, James. She is so smart. And so good with the baby!"

"Ah, yes! And how is that little rascal nephew of mine?"

"James, he remains an angel," Tara said indignantly. "He isn't much more than six months old. All children are angels at that stage."

"Well, since he is my brother's child, don't count on it for long," he warned sternly. "But Jennifer is well?" he asked again, a certain note of strain coming into his voice.

He couldn't help it, couldn't quite help keeping the fear at bay. At times, no matter how he hated it, he could almost be grateful for the war. It kept him from thinking. From remembering. From spending hours beneath the sun wishing that he could die himself. From the anguish that could never be healed.

From hating everyone and everything white . . .

"Jennifer is very well, I promise," Tara said. "Come, you'll see her." She caught his hand, leading him toward the house.

"What news?" she asked tensely as they walked.

He was quiet a moment. "There wouldn't be much new if it wasn't for Major Warren," he said.

"I heard," Tara whispered.

Warren, gaining more power constantly within the military of the territory, was a bloodthirsty bastard. In the midst of mayhem and battle, James had usually found that most white men—even those who thought Seminole emigration westward the only solution to the "Indian problem"—were capable of reason. No man knew better than he that there were whites in the U.S. Army who would refuse to kill a child, any child. Life had taught him to be colorblind himself in judging men. Just as there were men who were innately good among the whites and the red men, there were men of both races who were innately evil.

Warren, he judged, was one of the latter, and he should have been shot long ago.

James had taken up arms against his father's people, the whites, often enough since the war had begun—he'd been left with little choice. When his family and friends had been fired upon, he had fired in return. But he had never raided into the white world, burned a plantation— killed a white woman or child. When he had been able to do so, he had played the part of mediator. He had pleaded for his people on occasion, seeking reason. He had brought in those determined to obey white dictates and go west, and he had fought for those who were determined to stay. He had straddled a fence danger- ously at times, but he had maintained his standing among the Seminoles and remained close with those whites who had always been his friends. It was a wretched existence, one he loathed. One he fought hard to maintain now, because since Naomi and his child had died, he had felt rages so strong he feared he would rip apart anything he touched—a white man's property, a white man himself . . .

They hadn't been slain. They hadn't been shot down and stabbed through with bayonets, like the women and children and old folks in the village Warren had raided so recently. They had died of disease.

God, but he could remember it all too well. Remember it with a clarity that robbed him of his breath, staggered him with the pain. They had contracted the fever because they had been running. Running deeper and deeper into the swamp because the soldiers were after them. Soldiers who would slay any Indians they came upon, young ones, old ones, men, women, maidens, little children. James had been gone when they had taken ill. He had been traveling in the area of Fort Brooke, engaged in negotiations for friends who were weary, admitting defeat, ready to travel to the dry, barren lands in the far west where the whites had decreed the Indians could live free. Friends had warned him that his wife had stopped her flight because she had been uanble to go farther. Then he had run himself, run hard and fast, a desperation in his soul.

He had run and run and run. But he had come too late. He had almost rejoiced to see that his brother had heard, too, and come in his stead, but his brother had come too late as well. James had come to find Jarrett kneeling on the ground, his black head bent low.

All too clearly he could relive those last few footsteps he had taken then!

When he had approached Jarrett, he had discovered that his brother held the body of his wife, and that Jarrett's tear fell upon her soft golden flesh. *I'm sorry, oh, God, so, so sorry, I loved her, too . . .*

Running, falling. He'd taken her body himself, cradled it there in the earth, sobs like howls shaking from his body, until there was sound no more, until silent tears streamed down his face.

Then he'd discovered that he'd lost his child as well. He'd wanted to die. He'd grieved without thought of water or sustenance, grieved the night, the day, the night, and still, with him, at his side, his brother had remained.

No, he could never hate his brother. But searing, awful fury and the need to strike in revenge had been with him ever since.

His father had taught him all the white ways; he knew the white world. He was no fool, and he knew the whites' strength, and knew as well that he fought a desperate battle he most probably could not win. But neither could the whites beat the swamp, and therefore they could not beat the Indians. No one seemed to see that as yet.

"How many were killed in Warren's raid?" Tara asked him, bringing him back to the present.

"Almost a hundred. He had sent out word that food and clothing and extra provisions would be given to any of those Indians who chose to move west within the month. He promised payments in gold. So many women, weary of running, of watching their children starve, were willing to believe him. I could have stopped them if I had reached them in time, but I was near Micanopy while they were south of St. Augustine. They went in ready to surrender, and Warren raided them at night. He claimed he thought it was warriors camping out, preparing to attack white farms, when an outcry was voiced by even those Floridians most hardened against the Indians."

He decided not to tell Tara the rest. Speaking it out loud made it all the more horrible.

White soldiers had seen to the disposal of the bodies. But news leaked out. Infants had frequently died with their head bashed in—why waste a bullet? Women had been slit from throat to groin; old men had been mutilated as well as murdered.

James scowled. "So much for the cease-fire of March."

"James, I am so sorry!" Tara said. "I beg you to re-member that not all whites—"

"Are like Warren," he agreed. "It's just that too damned many are."

They had come to the porch. Tara led him to the cradle that rocked gently in the breeze. His nephew, Ian, six months old now, lay within it sleeping peacefully. James smiled. The boy was a McKenzie, all right. De-spite his mother's glorious blond hair, his small head was capped with a surplus of shiny black hair. "Watch out for this angel!" he reminded Tara.

She wrinkled her nose to him. "And now—"

She didn't get to finish. Another little dark-haired creature suddenly came flying out of the house from the back breezeway doors. His surviving daughter, Jennifer, now going on five years old, came hurtling into his arms. "Daddy!" she shrieked happily.

He lifted her up into his arms, held her tenderly against him. Her little heart beat quickly; she was warm and vital and alive. She smelled sweetly of Tara's per-fume. Nothing was as precious to him in all the world now as his daughter. She was all he had left. She had lived with Tara and Jarrett since her mother and sister had died, and she did so with the full understanding that he couldn't always be with her. She was so very grown up for her age.

He held her still, but at arm's length, studying her. She had a beautiful face, slim, golden. Her eyes weren't his blue but her mother's beautiful hazel, a shade of green and brown that sometimes seemed to haze to-gether into a magnificent amber. She had pitch black hair that waved and curled to her waist, and she was dressed today like the most elegant of little white chil-dren. Tara made beautiful clothing for her, and show-ered love and attention on her. *Poor thing*! he thought suddenly, *what have I done to her*? For she was now a part of both worlds just as he was, torn between them, aching for them both, as he had always done.

"Jennifer, you are ravishing!" He hugged her close to

him again, looking at his sister-in-law over his daughter's shoulder. *Thank you,* he mouthed.

"Daddy, you are ravishing, too," Jennifer told him solemnly, taking his face between her chubby hands. "So handsome and form—iddable. Wickedly dangerous. Absolutely de-*lect*-able!"

Startled that such words should come out of a mouth so young, he looked at Tara, who was blushing furiously. "Well," she murmured uncomfortably, "you do create quite a stir. Chloe, the Smithsons' daughter, was here to tea the other day with her cousin, Jemma Sarne."

"And?" he demanded, baffled.

"Well, they're young. Impressionable. They think of you as a noble ..."

"Savage?" he supplied.

"James—"

"It's all right. So, my daughter is parroting their words."

She was silent a moment. "You are ... an appealing man, James. I've told you that often enough."

"And you are the one and only pale creature I find appealing, Tara. Alas, you're married to my brother. Spare me from your friends who are entranced with the idea of a wickedly noble savage, will you?"

"That's not really it at all—"

"Oh, Tara, I have been at enough of your parties. I have had numerous offers from supposedly innocent women, young and old, for comfort in my time of grief. It's amazing how those offers come when I am decked out in European finery. If these same women were to come across an Indian village and find me fighting in the heat along with others dressed in breech clouts, I doubt they'd be so eager."

"You might be surprised," Tara mused softly.

"Ah, yes! Then bring on the fathers of these illustrious maidens. See what they would have to say about their daughters forming liaisons with a half-breed."

"You are not so prejudiced as you pretend. I have heard rumors regarding a few of your liaisons."

He shook his head, setting Jennifer down and telling her, "See Othello there?" He indicated his tall bay horse. "Catch his reins and walk him to the greener grass, sweetheart." Jennifer smiled broadly, thrilled with the adult task. James watched his daughter hurry on, then turned to his sister-in-law. "Tara, I am a bruised and bitter man. There is nothing I have done with anyone since Naomi that might be considered a liaison, and I am very careful where I take solace at all, for I've nothing to give of myself. Your giggling young friends both amuse and annoy, for they are so bold to come forward, so eager to whisper and sigh. But watch their fathers come into the room, and see how fast they run. I am too hardened to be entertainment for any woman, white, red, or black—or as you once told me—zebra-striped."

"Well, I am having a party tomorrow night, good friends, old friends, no army men, not even Tyler Argosy, though I have received a strange letter from him, telling me that he is on his way to fetch a child for some military commander. Jarrett comes home tonight or tomorrow. It's a simple get-together for his birthday, and those here will all be people you know, friends. You will stay?"

"Tara—"

"It's your brother's birthday."

He sighed. "Ah, yes. Dress me up, put me on display. Let them all see just how civilized a savage can be."

"James!"

"Tara, I'm sorry. My bitterness is not toward you. Fine, I will stay. I have matters to discuss with my brother anyway, and I am anxious to see him."

Tara gave him a kiss on the cheek. "I'll tell Jeeves you're staying for dinner and the night. Your room is always ready for you, and always awaits you."

"A soft bed and good meal will sit well with me tonight, I think," he told her gently.

She smiled and hurried on into the house.

*   *   *

Moments later, Tara McKenzie returned to the rear breezeway doors to the wraparound porch.

James still stood there, looking westward, into the interior of the territory, to the property line where the wild tangle of brush and trees began.

He stood in the sunset, the golds and mauves of the sky casting a true copper glow over his skin. She could see the taut, rippled muscles of his abdomen and chest beneath the open vest, the bronze strength within his shoulders and arms. The life he led had honed him to something as sleek and powerful as a great cat. In his close-fitting breeches and simple doeskin vest, he seemed an extraordinary figure, the noble savage indeed. But she knew him well, knew his anguish, his heartache— and his anger. And even as she watched him she shivered fiercely.

Heaven help the fool who teased the beast! she thought, then turned swiftly again, leaving him to the sunset and his own reflections upon it.

Chapter 3

Jarrett McKenzie made record time coming down the river, arriving at his home dock when the sun had scarcely risen in the sky.

His guest, however, had been awake for some time. Even as they neared the shore, she stood at the bow, clearly fascinated by all that she saw.

He smiled, watching her.

Warren's daughter! Who could have imagined!

Stepdaughter, he reminded himself, as she had been so determined to point out. But even so, she had grown up with the man as her guardian, and she had somehow escaped the evil that seemed to cling like a miasma about the man. She was eager, bright, and honest.

And stunning.

He was glad his marriage was completely sound, or else it might be difficult explaining such a lush creature on his ship, unchaperoned. Teela Warren was like one of the indescribably beautiful wild birds of the area. Her coloring was vivid, her hair a rich, deep, sun-touched shade of red, her eyes as green as an endless field in the early summer. She was moderately tall for a woman, slim and lithe and yet exotic as well—even her volumes of clothing hinted at a ripe and beguiling figure. Her nose was small and pert, chin just a shade pointed, face a cross between an oval and a heart, brows a shade darker than her hair with a provocative, flyaway arch. There was a restlessness about her that seemed as enticing as her more obvious charms. He was enchanted by her, as he was sure Tara would be.

And he was heartily glad to do anything that might irritate Warren.

Last night, when he hadn't been involved in sailing the ship, he'd spent some time with her. She'd spoken lovingly of her mother, and admitted that the gossip about her was true. She had walked out of her own wedding, but she'd had no choice. He couldn't help but be amused. She was a fighter, striking back in the only way she knew how. If she had worried that she might be judged here, then she didn't really understand this land of runaways yet. She would.

Ah, well, Jarrett would delightedly host her in his household as long as she wished, but there was little he could do when Warren sent for her. Warren hadn't even asked him for the hospitality—Jarrett's old friend, the army lieutenant Tyler Argosy, had asked him the favor. Jarrett had found the letter from his friend upon his arrival in Tampa for supplies. Tyler—or a very fine young soldier by the name of John Harrington—would probably be chosen to act as the girl's escort, since both those men were the most knowledgeable—other than Jarrett himself—regarding the Indians in the area as well as the terrain. He'd heard rumors that Warren was interested now in a match between his daughter—stepdaughter—and Harrington. Young Harrington's family was quite wealthy, and very influential in political circles.

Harrington, Jarrett thought with amusement, must be worrying right now about his senior officer's determination that he wed the man's daughter—after all, Harrington hadn't even met the young lady. He was probably imagining the girl as a female version of Michael Warren.

Jarrett shuddered, then smiled. Harrington was going to be pleasantly surprised when he met Teela Warren.

Jarrett called out the order to bring his ship in, then came down the starboard side to where she stood, staring at the land, excitement bringing a shimmer to her eyes. "What do you think of Cimarron, Miss Warren?" he inquired.

What did she think? Teela shook her head in amazement. "It's ... extraordinary." She'd seldom seen such a beautiful house, even in Charleston, where wealthy men prided themselves on the grace of their homes. The house was huge, whitewashed, elegant. Massive columns stood across the front, along with a veranda that encirled the whole of the first floor. Breezeway doors stood open to catch the air, cool though it still was. And even as men jumped from the ship to the dock, a woman appeared upon the porch, a tall, lovely woman with sun blond hair and a supple build, waving even as she started to run toward the ship.

Tara McKenzie, Teela thought. The wife the captain so adored. She'd heard little from him last night that didn't circle back to his wife and his infant son.

Jarrett McKenzie was, in fact, off the ship with a smooth leap over the bow rail. His wife had made it to the dock by then, so he didn't have far to go before reaching her, sweeping her up high, and clasping her in his arms. They met in a searing kiss, one so filled with both tenderness and passion that Teela found herself seeking somewhere else to look. It wasn't difficult. The dock, though belonging to the one home, seemed a busy place. The crew greeted other men who had come from the fields or the house, clasping hands, tossing up bales and barrels. Everyone smiled at Teela even as they studied her with both frank curiosity and welcome.

"Miss Warren!"

McKenzie had remembered her. Teela turned quickly, and saw that both Mr. and Mrs. McKenzie stood at the gangway, awaiting her. Startled that she should suddenly feel so shy, Teela hurried ashore.

Tara McKenzie slipped from her husband's arms to greet Tara with a little hug. "Welcome, welcome to Cimarron." She stepped back, smiling ruefully. "I admit, you're not quite what I expected. I received a message from Tyler warning me that he presumed Jarrett would be bringing me a child."

"Not a child," Teela said. "But still beneath the wing of a guardian."

Tara nodded, keeping her opinion on that silent. "We're absolutely delighted to have you. In fact, you have arrived at a perfect time, for we're having a small party this evening, a dance for my husband's birthday. I assure you, our little community will be delighted to meet you. We do just love fuel for gossip here!" she warned teasingly.

"You'll scare her!" Jarrett said.

Tara smiled, shaking her head. "Who could have been discussed more than me, eh, my love? Come now, Teela, you must see the house."

With Tara's arm linked through hers, Teela walked across the beautifully manicured lawn. Tara pointed out how the river ran, and the general directions in which their closest neighbors lived.

"Don't you fear Indian attacks here?" Teela asked her.

"No," Tara said simply as they came to the porch. A tall black woman was standing there with a baby on her shoulder. Tara reached for the child with a smile, but Jarrett reached past her.

"May I, Jeanne?" he asked politely, though it was his own child he plucked from her arms. The woman smiled, giving up the boy, and Jarrett held him high in the air while the baby gave out a delighted squeal.

"Ian McKenzie," Tara announced. She glanced at her husband.

Teela smiled, watching the baby. "Congratulations," she said softly. "He's a beautiful child."

"Thank you," Tara said. She started to take the boy from her husband and hesitated. "Would you like to take him?"

"May I?" Teela inquired. She lifted the baby and laughed, delighted by the one-toothed smile he gave her. He reached for a strand of her hair. She caught his little fingers instead, laughing again. She hadn't had a chance to really play with a baby in a long time, not since she had done some nursing with her mother before Lilly took ill.

"He is just beautiful!" she said again, cuddling him against her. He smelled clean, a newly washed baby, wonderfully warm and sweet.

"Well, I'm very glad yo approve. We'd have had to throw him right out if she didn't, right, Jarrett?" Tara teased.

Teela was surprised at how quickly the bantering made her feel welcome. They entered the house, and she was further entranced. The wooden floors were polished to an exquisite shine. Draperies hung from the window, and the wall coverings were certainly the latest fashion from Europe.

"I simply cannot believe that this house can be here," Teela said, spinning around. The nurse came to take the baby back, and she reluctantly let him go.

"Thank you," Jarrett said. "I do take that as a compliment."

"It was meant as one, I assure you."

"And you have a home here for eternity if you choose," Tara said with a laugh. "You have complimented the two things nearest and dearest to my husband's heart—his house and his son."

"I protest! She's yet to compliment you," Jarrett told Tara.

"Your wife is gorgeous," Teela told him solemnly.

"All right, she can stay. Forever," Jarrett agreed.

"You definitely get to stay," Tara said. "You can see the house later. For now, let me give you a room so that you can freshen up."

"She might like to lie down for a while. I heard her up all night."

"I'm sorry!" Teela gasped. "I didn't mean to disturb anyone. It was just so very dark, I couldn't resist looking toward the shore. I have never seen anything like the darkness that surrounded us on the river, not even at sea."

"It can be a frightening land," Tara said lightly. "But

if you're tired now, perhaps you should rest awhile. I'll have water sent later for you to bathe. Our guests are due at sunset, and you'll want to meet them all, I'm certain."

"I wouldn't mind sleeping," Teela admitted.

"Everyone seems to need to catch up on his and her sleep here!" Tara said with a good-natured sigh.

"Not me," Jarrett said blandly, staring at his wife. "I've no desire whatsoever for sleep."

Tara flushed, smiling slowly. Teela turned quickly away as Jarrett took his wife into his arms, kissing her tenderly. Something in the touch seemed to burn into her heart. She felt tears sting her eyes, and she was glad that two such charming, giving people should be so happy together.

She had never felt so keen a sense of loneliness herself.

It was strange. When Michael had been so determined to arrange her marriage, she hadn't really hated the man of her stepfather's choice. She simply hadn't loved him. She knew now, watching these two—or trying not to watch them—just what her objection had been. This was what she wanted. This fierce kind of love. Nothing less. And if she could not find it, then she wanted independence.

And nothing less.

Easy to want, hard to achieve . . .

Tara eased herself from her husband's embrace and led them up a sweeping staircase. "This room, Teela," she said, indicating a doorway, "is yours. I hope you'll find everything you need. If not, there's a bell pull by the bed. Jeeves will be happy to bring you anything you require."

"I'm fine, thank you very much," Teela said.

"Rest well," Jarrett told her.

Before she had quite closed her door, Jarrett had set his hands upon his wife's waist and was leading her down the hall.

A second later, she heard a door close with a soft

click. The master was home. The mistress was in his arms.

Teela *was* exhausted. She walked across the room with a giddy sense of excitement, so glad to be there.

Warren was sending someone for her, of course.

And when that time came, she would suffer again. But she wouldn't ruin the excitement and wonder of now for what was threatened to come.

She stretched out on the bed, glad of its softness, glad to sleep on a bed that wasn't on a moving vessel. She closed her eyes. Miraculously, and very quickly, she slept.

She awoke much later to a tap at her door. "Teela, guests will be arriving soon. Please come down whenever you're ready!" Jarrett McKenzie called to her.

"Thank you!" she returned.

Sometime, even as she had slept, a servant had brought water, left a kettle to boil over the fire, and seen to it that her trunks had been brought up. Teela rose, washed and dressed swiftly, and left her room behind, anxious to see more of the house—and the guests who would soon fill it.

Cimarron had been prepared that evening for entertaining. It was obvious from the moment Teela stepped from her upstairs guest room.

The breezeway doors, leading to the lawn and river in front and down into stables and lawn and foliage in the rear, had been thrown open wide. Lanterns had been hung along the porches, adding soft light to that which burned from within the home. To either side of the main hall, the doors to parlors and sitting rooms had been cast open as well, making virtually one huge hall of all the downstairs rooms. Even as she came down the stairway, she could see clearly into the main parlor to her right.

When she first saw the tall figure standing before the fire, she thought that she had come upon her host. The man stood with his legs slightly apart, feet firmly planted

upon the hardwood floor, hands folded idly behind his
back, head slightly bowed as he stared into the flames.
His shoulders were broad, his waist was narrow, and his
height and physique were emphasized by the cut of the
elegant black frock coat he wore, ruffled, snow white
shirt beneath, the collar and sleeves visible from her distance. His jet black hair waved just below the collar of
his coat. With the fine cut of his clothing, the dignity of
his stance, he gave every appearance of an elegant, cultured man, a ruggedly handsome but civilized man . . .
her host.

Then he turned.

Teela started, for though the resemblence to Jarrett
McKenzie remained, this was not her host at all. Something was familiar in the face and yet not familiar. It
was perhaps one of the most arresting faces she had
ever seen, the skin bronze, eyes a startling, burning blue,
cheekbones high and broad. He was white; he was Indian. He was a man definitely created by both races, and
created extraordinarily well. From this first sight of him,
she felt something, as if his very life and vitality were a
physical portent, lightning in the space that separated
them, something that snapped and sizzled like a whisper
of smoldering fire. Her breath quickened as he returned
her stare, as he studied her in turn. Then he smiled
slowly, bitterly—mockingly. He knew her thoughts exactly. Knew that she felt a draw. Knew perhaps his own
sensuality or appeal, and knew that something screamed
within her as well that he was forbidden, that he was
Seminole.

Quite suddenly he bowed to her. When his eyes rose
to meet hers once again, the blue glitter within them was
sheerly wicked, taunting. Even touched with a flicker of
contempt. And maybe even just a shade of self-mock-
ery . . .

"Good evening."

His voice was rich, cultured, with a deep timbre to it.
Absurdly, she felt as if she trembled somewhere very
deep inside her just at the sound of it. Her fingers

gripped more tightly the stair rail she held, and it seemed as if the very blood within her quickened, heated, came to life. He had a strange appeal, one that seemed to reach beneath all civilized veneer and touch raw instinct and emotion.

Teela instantly gave herself a mental shake, reminding herself that she had actually seen very few Indians, actually met or talked to even fewer. Nor had she ever imagined feeling such an intense and perhaps amused scrutiny by such a man, or that such a man could even exist.

"You do speak English?" he said, an ebony brow arched. She imagined it was a question he had heard directed to himself on occasion, though his white blood was every bit as apparent in his features as his Indian blood.

"Yes, I speak English," Teela said, glad to hear a note of irritation slipping into her own tone.

"Do you plan to cling to the stair rail all night? You needn't be afraid. I've yet to seize a white scalp in my brother's house, miss . . . ?"

Her heart slammed suddenly against her chest. He didn't know who she was. She hadn't known who he was, and it was a bit difficult to equate Jarrett McKenzie with this man, except that the two did resemble one another physically. It was just that one was Indian, one was not.

She couldn't begin to imagine admitting to any Indian that she was Michael Warren's daughter, or even stepdaughter.

She forced her hand to go light on the rail, and to descend the steps in the most dignified and serene manner ever attributed to southern womanhood. She came to the landing in the foyer and faced him through the thrown-open doors to the parlor. She hesitated, appalled to think that she was almost afraid to go farther, afraid to come closer to the man, the impossibly elegant half-breed. But in all of her life, she had refused to show fear—Michael Warren had somehow given her that, at the least. She stepped forward again, sweeping into the room, coming to the fire that burned in the hearth and stretching out her fingers to be warmed as she continued to study him as unabashedly as he watched her.

"I have no fear of losing my scalp, sir," she informed him.

A dark brow arched even higher. "Then you are a fool, ma'am. All scalps are in danger in this territory as we speak."

"You did just assure me that you had yet to take a scalp in your brother's house. And since it seems you are well versed in civilized manners, it would seem to me that you would consider it incredibly rude to begin taking scalps here tonight from a newcomer to *your* territory."

She was startled when he reached out, touching the lock of hair that she had left free from the twist of braids at her neck to wave over her shoulder. She was tempted to draw back, too fascinated to manage to do so. His hands were large, powerful, yet as lean and hard as his build. His fingers were very long and deeply bronze.

His eyes, with their startling shade of blue, touched upon hers even as he idly fingered her hair. "Ah, but what a prize such a dazzling swatch of hair would make. You should be warned to take the gravest care, ma'am, for such irresistible flames in the night are seductive and dangerous."

She drew back slightly, amazed that she should be so breathless at the nearness of any man, so unnerved. She had shocked society herself by steadfastly refusing to wed at the altar, by determining that somehow she would live by her dreams rather than her stepfather's dictates, and still, she did feel a curious fear by even speaking so as she did with a stranger, not even speaking, but simply listening to the things he said. . . .

"Ah, and there leaps the light of fear into her eyes. There is no color on a man—red, black, or white—that will rub off upon your person. Though I can scarcely imagine that my flesh could be more radiant than your hair."

"You really do presume too damn much!" she heard herself hiss softly.

A slight smile curled his lip once again as he looked into the blaze that burned in the hearth.

"Ah! She swears!" he exclaimed, a teasing tone in his voice. He did not seem shocked, nor did he seem to mind.

"I'm not afraid of you in the least, sir," she said. "Of your color, of your words, of anything, Mr. McKenzie."

He looked to her again, arching a brow. "How do you know my name—since I remain ingnorant of yours."

It was her turn to smile. "You are most obviously a McKenzie, and you have mentioned that this is your brother's house."

"What makes you think I am a McKenzie? I might be related to Jarrett by my mother."

"Your pardon. Are you a McKenzie?"

He hesitated. "Yes," he said softly. "At least, to some, I am a McKenzie. . . . Why are you here?"

She opened her mouth, then hesitated with a sinking feeling. She could be glib. *I am here because my stepfather is busily slaughtering all the Florida Indians he can find.*

Ah, but not now, not with this man.

"I have come to join my stepfather in Florida, and as it seems he's been occupied with business since my arrival, I was most kindly brought here until I could be brought to him." She extended her hand, looking to shake his. "My name is Teela," she told him, carefully omitting her last name.

He took her hand. He didn't shake it. He turned it within his own, studying the back and then the palm. His eyes remaining upon hers, he bowed over her hand, his lips brushing it. The palm, not the back. Somehow the touch seemed incredibly intimate. And sensual. She should have never allowed it.

But then her hand was free, and he had stepped back,

and she felt as if he studied her again from some vast distance, and with both amusement and disdain.

"Teela. Have you a last name?"

"Have you a first name?" she cross-queried.

His smile deepened. He was about to respond when they were suddenly interrupted by another arrival. "James, my good fellow!" came a sudden bellow.

Teela started, stepping back from the half-breed. She looked toward the open doors, where a man was entering, a young, handsome fellow with light eyes and a quick smile, as elegantly dressed on this frontier as he might have been in the finest of drawing rooms from Boston to Savannah. "Ah!" he stopped, seeing Teela. Then his smile deepened and he bowed to her, extremely correctly.

"What new flower is this to grace our wilderness?" he inquired. "James, a friend of yours? Introduce us, I do beg you!"

"Alas, Robert, I am afraid this fiery rose is a new acquaintance of mine as well. Teela, Mr. Robert Trent. Robert, Miss Teela . . . ?"

She still refused to supply her last name. She extended her hand again. "Mr. Trent, how do you do?"

"Suddenly, quite well," he responded. He kissed her hand. The top of it. He was utterly charming. His features were pleasant, his smile contagious. He was tall, but the man she now knew to be James McKenzie was taller. Robert charmed. James somehow captivated. He seemed created of fire and energy and leashed passions, all giving off a heat that intrigued and mesmerized her.

"Well," McKenzie said suddenly, "I see our hostess, and must share a word with her. I will leave you lovely children to become acquainted with one another."

He bowed, and strode toward the parlor doorway. Tara McKenzie was indeed there, having come down the stairway. Two older gentlemen with their wives at their sides had come into the house, and there seemed to be a growing commotion at the entryway as more and more guests arrived.

"I am frequently a visitor here," Robert Trent was saying, "yet I had no idea that we might expect a newcomer this evening."

"I just arrived this afternoon on Jarrett's ship," she told him.

"Are you staying with us long?"

"I . . . I'm not sure." He waited patiently with a pleasant smile for her to continue. "My father—my stepfather—is with the army. He summoned me to join him, but apparently he became embroiled in some action when he was to have come for me. I am to receive an army escort from here to join him."

"Who is he? For the vast distances you will find here, it can be a curiously small world."

She hesitated. "Michael Warren."

"Warren!" Robert gasped. Then, very quickly, he tried to compose himself. "I'm sorry—"

"So am I!" she admitted softly. Even as she spoke, she heard musicians from the center hallway tuning their instruments. Guests had wandered into the parlor. A waltz was struck, and Robert bowed very deeply to her again.

"Shall we?"

"Indeed, thank you."

He swept her out to the floor. Just moments ago she had been alone in the parlor with the strangely intriguing James McKenzie; now the dance floor was filled with swirling couples.

"Warren!" Robert repeated softly.

"A monster, I know."

"Well, thank God! I'd feared to hurt your feelings by betraying what ill will I bear the man. Yet I must say, I cannot imagine him as the father of any creature so exquisite and refined!"

Teela smiled. His compliments were bold, but sweetly spoken, apparently sincere. "Thank you," she told him. "He's my stepfather."

"Still, a crime."

She was smiling again, enjoying the exhilaration of

being swept around the floor. It had been a long time
since she had been at anything remotely resembling a
party, a very long time since she had had her ego stroked
by such kind words. Robert Trent was charming. And
handsome. And she was enjoying his company very
much.

Yet suddenly she was no longer spinning. Robert had
stopped at a tap upon his shoulder.

James McKenzie was there again, eyes burning their
blue fire as he spoke politely to Robert. "May I cut
in, sir?"

"Indeed," Robert said with a sigh. "Alas, such is life!
I cannot sweep you away for the evening!"

He released his hold on her. Teela found herself swirling across the floor once again, guided by the commanding touch of the striking half-breed.

He was an excellent dancer. Lithe, graceful, skillful.
She might have floated on air. She was painfully aware
of his touch, of his gaze upon her. Curious, intrigued,
and still, after all, seemingly touched with a hint of contempt. Because she was white? Because she had suffered
his improprieties without slapping his face?

"Is it just me? Or all white women?" she found herself asking.

She was startled by his rueful smile. He hadn't expected the question.

"All white women," he assured her.

"I'm so glad."

"But then ... you especially."

"Then why are you dancing with me?"

"I'm still after your hair."

"But you wouldn't take a scalp in your brother's
house."

"Perhaps I've no interest in removing it from your
head."

"Just what is your interest?"

"I'm not quite sure..." he murmured, his voice
strange. "Indeed, I'm not just exactly sure myself."

The music stopped suddenly. They remained before each other, staring at one another.

Then Teela heard her name called. "Miss Warren! Ah, there you are!"

It was her host. Jarrett McKenzie, moving through the now crowded dance floor, coming nearer and nearer.

"James! Ah, well, I see you've met our guest."

James stared at his brother. "The, er, child to whom Tara referred?" he asked, his question for his brother, his eyes still on Teela.

"She was a bit older than we expected."

"You just called her Miss Warren."

There was a deadly chill to his voice.

"She's his stepdaughter, James," Jarrett said.

But suddenly James wasn't listening or talking to his brother any more. He had lowered his head to her, his lips very nearly against her ear as he spoke. "Your name is *Warren*?" he demanded of Teela, his tone so low and husky it sounded like a growl.

Teela moistened her lips. "Yes, Teela Warren," she stated, chin high as she clenched down hard on her jaw.

To her amazement, he suddenly started laughing. His laughter had a bitter sound to it. Taunting, rough against her ear.

"Warren!" he spat out. Softly. So softly. "Ah, well, now I understand my interest in you, and it's not one that would please or entertain you in any way, Miss Warren. I would simply like to see the whole of your wretched family burn in the most blinding fires of hell for all eternity."

He spun around, exiting the room with long, hard strides. A chill swept through Teela, and it was long moments before she realized that he had spoken so very quietly that only she, and not even his brother, had heard the full bitter impact of his words.

Music filled the room again.

Chapter 4

James sat on the porch rail, staring out into the night. The breeze was balmy and he closed his eyes, listening. He could hear laughter and music from within the house, and he could hear the sounds of the night from without. The slow lap and fall of the river, the whisper of the breeze through oak and cypress. Crickets letting out their night call. The mosquitoes didn't seem to be biting tonight, the gentle wind moving a little too quickly for them. It was a perfect night, the air a gentle caress, and, with the sounds of revelry within muted slightly, it seemed as peaceful as could be. Of course, quiet brought out the true beauty of the place. Sliding downriver silently in a canoe, seeing the wild orchids growing, the glitter of the water where sun broke through the tree branches ... yes, there was the beauty. And there were still places to go where that peace was unbroken. Where the modern world had not intruded, where the sounds of gunfire didn't shatter the balmy green tranquility.

It was a pity he could so seldom see those places, so seldom touch them.

He could feel the ruffles of his frilled shirt against his wrists and throat. Once again he could clearly hear the music from within. He leaned his head back against the column that braced the rail. Most of the people inside the house were his friends. People he had known for years. He had lived their life; he had received white schooling, he had been welcomed in his brother's grandfather's house in Charleston, and because he was his

father's son, many whites had ignored his Indian blood.
He could feel his heart ache for many of the white people who had been caught in the war. For the young
plantation wife who had watched her husband killed, her
farm burned. Who had felt a bullet pierce her side, a
Seminole knife lift her scalp from her head ... and then
lived to tell of it by playing dead while bitter Seminoles
shrieked their triumph and danced before the fires.

It was a horrible picture.

But he had been in battles himself.

Just last year Andy Jackson, still President Jackson
then, had given the command of the army to Florida's
governor, Richard Keith Call. Call had plodded along,
determined on a course of action, bogging down in
swamp, losing men to fever and sickness, finding that
supply depots he had ordered built had never risen out
of the muck. But a major offensive had still taken place
on the Withlacoochee River. The men under Call had
assumed the black water was very deep; it hadn't been
much more than three feet. Major David Moniac had
attempted the crossing, but a Seminole bullet had sent
him facedown into the river. No one else had tried the
crossing. Hundreds of men, women, and children behind
the fighting forces had been saved by that failure of action. The strangest thing was that Major David Moniac
had been a full-blooded Creek Indian, a graduate of the
United States Military Academy. The whites were trying
to convince the Seminoles to move west and rejoin their
now distant kin, the Creek nation, but meanwhile they
were using Creek troops against the Seminoles. There
were so many ironies.

James had fought that day. Caught up in the running,
in the skirmishing, in the drive to survive. Desperate as
any man to protect the innocents behind the battle line.
He had fired his gun, used sword and knife savagely. He
shook now to think of it. He had feared that at any
moment he would come upon a soldier he knew, a man
with whom he had shared whiskey or wine, a debate, an
argument, a drawing room poker game.

Caught between two worlds, he had created his own ethics, his own standards and rules. When troops attacked, he would fight back. He had no choice. But he would never take part in a raid, and come hell or high water, he would never make war on women or children. His white blood didn't necessarily dictate that decision. He knew many braves who refused to take part in the slaughters on the plantations. Even Osceola despised the idea of war on women and children, though as war *mico* Osceola had turned his gaze from depraved acts of war often enough. But for as many "red men" who would slaughter whole families, there were equally as many who would not murder innocents, even in the name of war.

James knew there were as many good men in the white military—despite the things that happened under such men as Michael Warren.

Just thinking of the man again seemed to seize mercilessly upon his temper, cause his blood to writhe and boil within him. He looked down and saw that his fingers were shaking slightly. He'd learned about the Supreme Spirit from his Indian kin, about the Christian God from his father. They were one and the same, and no matter what the Great Father was called, James was grateful to him suddenly that Naomi had died of fever and not at the hands of a white man.

He clenched his teeth together tightly against an onslaught of pain that was like a physical blow. He would never, ever forget coming home, back to the place deep in the swampland where he had secreted his people, and seeing the fire, the back of the man, Naomi draped in his arms. The man, his brother, turning slowly, tears stinging his dark eyes. Naomi, beautiful in death, striking, so lovely that she seemed to sleep. James had taken her from Jarrett, held her in silence, and his brother had remained beside him, not speaking a word, knowing, sharing what he could. But it had been worse. His younger daughter, Sara, had been dead three days. His mother had been very ill, but well enough for the People to take her more deeply into the swamp to keep her from the danger of the encroaching white troops. Such men as Warren would not care that she had been tender and good, that she had raised and adored another woman's white child as she had Jarrett. Robert Trent had taken Jennifer back to Cimarron and Tara, and Jarrett alone had waited with the bodies for James to come, a brother to share a brother's grief, a brother who knew more thoroughly than most full-blooded Indians how a burial for such loved ones should take place.

But she hadn't died by white hands. By a bullet from a soldier's gun, or the steel of an enemy's blade. If she had died so, at the hands of such a man as Warren . . .

His eyes opened. He stared out at the night again. From within he heard the soft sound of a woman's laughter.

That she could be the man's daughter!

He'd had to walk away. Walk away or do something terrible there, in his brother's house. Do what? he mocked himself. When he had first seen her on the stairway, it had seemed as if the entire world, except for the woman, had been swept away. Receded to nothingness. She was startling with her vivid beauty. Her hair was red, not an orange red, but a burning, deep red, as mesmerizing as the dancing flames of a wild blaze. Framed by the startling shade of auburn, her face seemed like ivory, perfect in every way, flesh soft as silk and pale. Then again, her coloring dominated in eyes so green they dazzled like a gem, so deep they rivaled the shades of the forest after summer rains. Her lips were poetically rose, her features arranged with classical perfection. She stood tall, and slim and lithe, and still, against the taut velvet green bodice of her evening dress. The full rise of her breasts was unbearably evocative, and he found himself instantly thinking, *I want that woman.* Not a woman. *That* woman. And he hadn't thought of Naomi or the war, or even of the world, as long moments ticked by, fading into history. He simply wanted her. She was beyond beauty. Passion and pride seemed to shimmer like an aura of heat around her. He wanted to reach out and touch the fire of her hair, and see if it burned. He wanted to stroke the perfect alabastar of her cheek, and discover if it was as soft as silk. Most of all, he wanted to wrench her from the stairway, strip her of velvet and satin and lace, and find out if the passion and heat were real, and if they could obliterate the pain and the anger and the hatred and chaos that his world had become. . . .

Moments of anguish, moments of hunger!

Until at last sanity returned. She was intrigued by him; she returned his stare as boldly. Another pretty little white girl fascinated by a red man. Yet there was a strange honesty about this one. She didn't flinch, she didn't flirt. She was swift to retort, she seemed to possess both intelligence and courage.

He had buried Naomi and with her, he thought, set to rest his youth, his soul, his ability to love. He could not completely forget the hungers of the flesh—that could only come, he surmised, with his own death, and he had not pretended to himself that he didn't want a woman upon occasion. But in all worlds, red, white, and black, there were women to fulfill those hungers, and he had met a number of them. But he didn't want another Indian wife, and the last thing he could have possibly wanted was a white temptress playing with fire for her own amusement. She was an exotic beauty. She tempted beyond human strength. Yet like so many such vivid creations, she could probably be quite deadly—to him.

Yet when he'd tried to walk away, he'd come back. He'd seen her in another man's arms, and an entirely irrational fury had arisen within him. And though it disturbed him now, he realized that he had been determined to show her that a red man could dance with every bit as much skill and grace as a white man. He could play the role, *when* he chose.

Then he had heard her name . . .

And his hands shook; his fingers trembled. Rage, like a living evil, had been awakened within him. He had seen her vivid but delicate beauty, and he had thought of the children killed with their heads bashed in to save bullets. He'd wanted to shake her, hurt her, and tell her that she was the child of a monster.

It was his brother's house. And "savage" was not a race, it was a state of mind, a way of action. And still, he had to get away. To the night breeze. To the soft sound of the river. The whisper of the trees. The song of the night birds, and the call of the cricket.

"James!"

He heard his name called with enthusiasm and turned to see a man in a handsome dress-regulation army uniform coming toward him. The fellow was tall, with sandy hair, a slim build, and amber eyes. He was a soldier—the kind James had shot at during battle.

So much for "no military," as Tara had promised him. Still, he felt no dismay. He was friends with a number of the soldiers, and this one was a good man. His name was John Harrington, and he had often served as a liaison when James had done the same for some of the war chiefs, and for some Seminoles weary of starving and fighting who had chosen to go west. He was a lieutenant who had served now nearly two years, a man who had not succumbed to the heat or the mosquitoes, or to any of the fevers they brought. He loved the swampy land, and sometimes seemed like a child when he observed it. Like James, he loved the river, and was a good companion on a journey along it.

"John, I hadn't known you were due in," James told him, rising, accepting his outstretched hand to shake it firmly. "Tara told me she and Jarrett weren't expecting guests from the military."

"I wasn't expecting to be here myself; I've just arrived on a mission."

"Ah?"

"A routine service assignment I hadn't been expecting, but am finding quite intriguing," John said, smiling. He slammed a fist against James's shoulder. "Damn, man, but you are one fine figure, sir, in that suit! And it's good to see you here. One of my greatest fears is that I'll charge into battle and face you with a rifle or bayonet."

"It's always a fear," James agreed softly.

"I heard from Jarrett you have a few families interested in moving west."

James nodded. "What's left of a tribe. Four women, three very old men, ten children. The warriors are dead. The rest of the clan are dead. They cannot run anymore. They will starve, and those fighting cannot protect them."

Harrington sniffed. "Well, since your great Osceola once masterminded the murder of one of his own for agreeing to go west, such a pathetic group seems brave for coming forward. They have my pity, James, for they are caught between the fire of their people and the might of the United States. In fact, you are lucky as well that Osceola has not pierced your heart with a bullet or blade for the friendship you have shown the whites."

"John, you have met with Osceola, you know that he is no raving lunatic—"

"How would I know? He is an actor as much as anything else. He refuses to speak English, yet I could swear he knows the language. He is a handsome enough fellow, soft-spoken, for all the death and mayhem he has caused."

"Death and mayhem have followed him all his life. He has little choice. And he has white blood himself and does not hate all things white. He is a man at war, but he is a man who understands blood and kin and friendship, and far more than any of your foolish generals out there, he is a man capable of judging other men for what they are."

"He has killed mercilessly."

"He is at war. To save his people, his nation, a way of life."

"He is lucky to have such a fierce defender. I hope he never turns on you, as he did on Charlie Emathla."

"John, you needn't fear on my account. He understands my life. He respects Jarrett and admires Tara. I have told you; he judges men and situations individually. I am not afraid of his wrath for what honorable arrangements I might make with you. He is not angry about desperate women giving in to hunger and terror and doing what they feel they must to survive. He is not against negotiation. You are an intelligent and honest man, John. You have admitted yourself often enough that the treaties made here have been willfully broken again and again, that military power and might were used unfairly—and that men such as Osceola have a right to their grievances."

John sighed, leaning against the rail beside James. "And you are an intelligent man, my friend. Far more so than I. You must see that more and more soldiers will come. That the government will only become more determined to win this war."

"Ah, but the army men weary of this war! Men who signed up for short enlistments will run home as soon as they can. Some of your army commanders have committed suicide," James reminded him softly. "I heard tell of a fine young fellow who came to an abandoned fort in the interior, ordered to halt there. His men instantly fell ill to the fever; he suffered from the heat himself and perished not at Seminole hands but by swallowing his own sword. John, my people are fighters. They are desperate. They will not finish their time with the regular army or militia and go back to homes in Tennessee, Kentucky, or Georgia."

John shook his head sadly. "I fear for us all!" he admitted. "The United States will not let go. And for all that you say, Osceola, no matter what his manners and intellect, can be as fierce and ruthless as a wild creature. Think back! When did this current war begin? With the massacre on Major Dade and his men. And where was the great war chief Osceola on that day, my friend? Murdering the Indian agent Wiley Thompson!"

"There are some men, white as well as red, who suggest Thompson deserved to be murdered."

"You are purposely missing my point. Osceola did not

put the good of his people first that day. He should have been with the warriors attacking Major Dade."

"It seems to me," James suggested softly, "that Major Dade and his men died quite pathetically enough without Osceola's help."

"The point is that Osceola was being selfish—he was determined on his revenge above all else."

"Wiley Thompson had Osceola chained. It was a tremendous humiliation to such a man. He was like an animal before his own people. Thompson signed his own death warrant that day."

"Osceola has attacked plantations. Men, women, and children. Don't fool yourself, James, that he is a good man."

"But aren't we all good men, and monsters too, depending on the point of view?"

"That I will not argue with you," John said slowly, smiling again. He shook his head sadly. "It's just that I so fear the future. You are my friend, many full-blooded red men are my friends. We talk, we part. And the day will come when we must seek to slit one another's throats. Dear God, I'm being morbid. I just wish that you would remain in the suit you wear tonight, reside in your brother's house—"

"Become white?"

"You are white."

James shrugged. "The whites will accept me because they cannot throw me off property when I have the same legal title to it a white man might have."

"Admit that you are white!"

"I have never denied it; my father was one of the greatest men I have ever known. My brother Jarrett is his image. But I cannot be blind to the things being done to my people. I would be half a man indeed if I could do so."

"I will pray for you, always," John said somberly.

James smiled. "And I will pray for you as well."

"Maybe we will both survive this to spend lazy days fishing down cypress-shaded rivers."

"Maybe. So what 'routine' assignment has brought you here now?" James asked him, suddenly curious.

"Ah! A most delightful one!" John said happily, amber eyes alight with pleasure. "Escort service brings me." The light in his eyes suddenly faded, and he grimaced. "I'm afraid to go further, I know how you feel about the colonel who has sent me here. But have you seen *her*? I don't give a damn what a man's color, he'd have to find her exquisite. She's the most beautiful woman I've ever seen, and I was so damned afraid. Like him or not, Warren is my superior officer, and when he suggested most strongly that a marriage should be arranged, I was deeply worried, as well you can understand! He is such a harsh, unyielding, bastard. . . ." He shuddered fiercely. "I mean, could you imagine Michael Warren a woman? She would be hideous—I had, indeed, imagined a most unfeminine creature—with a dark, coarse mustache perhaps. Even sideburns, mutton chops! I thought she'd be a monster, with a monster's manner to match! I mean to tell you, I came here all but trembling in my boots, and your wretched brother was no help. He rolled his eyes and taunted me most cruelly upon my arrival, I will tell you. Then I was brought to her, and I was so overwhelmed I couldn't even find voice to speak when we were introduced. I think your brother is still laughing at me."

Something within James had been winding tighter and tighter as his friend spoke. He clenched down very hard on his teeth, willing his features to remain expressionless.

"You're referring to Miss Warren?" he inquired.

John Harrington sighed deeply, like a man already in love. Infatuated beyond redemption, at the very least.

"Yes, indeed!" John said. "Have you met?"

"Oh, yes, we've met," James said grimly.

"There's such a magnificent spark of fire to her! So many other young women would be distressed to find themselves consigned to the wilds of Florida, but she isn't afraid. She's already asked me dozens of questions. She is curious, intelligent—"

"And quite remarkably well put together," James observed lightly.

"Well, yes, there is that—" John admitted innocently, then slapped James hard on the back, laughing. "Yes, there is that. But, James, of all men, you realize that there is more!" he continued earnestly. "A wife is a companion, and one who can understand a man's love for a land so raw and savage as this . . ."

John Harrington had found a mate for his paradise, or so it seemed.

"Perhaps you should go join her. When do you escort her to her father, and where? The last I heard, he was murdering men, women, and children in an area south of Ocala that would now, obviously, be very dangerous ground for anyone even remotely associated with the man."

"Oh, we'll not be leaving too quickly. I've got to take some dispatches to Tampa and return for her from there with a much larger escort. Warren has purchased a home in Tallahassee, but I still haven't received word if that is where I am to take her. I believe Warren intends to go into politics when the war is over. Indian fighters seem to do very well in politics. Well, there was Andy Jackson," he said, his voice bordering on the apologetic.

"Jackson survived all his wars. We'll have to see . . . if Michael Warren survives his," James murmured.

"Warren is tough."

"So are a number of our war chiefs. Hell, I'd just as soon shoot the man as look at him," he admitted.

But John Harrington wasn't giving him his full attention anymore. He was staring straight forward, a smile curving his lips. "She just isn't anything like him. Not anything at all."

"How can you be so certain so quickly?"

John's smile remained in place, and he shook his head. "I've spoken with her."

"Well, there you have it!" James agreed with obvious sarcasm. But it was lost on John.

"She's so interested in everything. You included."

"What?"

"Oh, she's very curious about you."

"In what way?"

"Oh, the past, your upbringing . . . you know. That's my whole point. She's not one of those silly women who think that Indians are barely a step better than wild animals. Begging your pardon, James, but some people do feel that way—"

"As I am well aware. Go on."

"She's intrigued. With the languages, the life."

"Hmm," James muttered. "If she's lucky, she'll not find out too much about it."

"You are a somber man this evening, James McKenzie."

"I lead a somber life."

"My friend, you need to learn to enjoy peace during the fragile moments when we share it."

A moment's guilt touched James. He was too somber. It was part annoyance, part envy, and both were threaded through with the fury he felt toward Michael Warren, exasperated by the appearance of the man's stepdaughter. He told himself that the girl and Harrington would be perfect for each other. He should be happy for his friend.

But all he could think about was the swift burn of excitement she had made him feel. A sensation that would not leave him, that simmered and grew inside.

She wasn't what he wanted or needed—or could have, he reminded himself firmly. He tried to see reason, to remember that Harrington was a fine man, a good friend. An enthusiastic friend at the moment.

James slowly grinned, nodded in rueful agreement to John. "Perhaps you're right, and I do need to learn to enjoy peace and quiet while I can."

Even as he spoke, he saw his sister-in-law at the breezeway doors, looking for them, he realized.

"There you are, you two. What are you doing out here?"

"Solving the war," James replied, "at least between the two of us," he amended.

"If it were between the two of you, there would be no war. But in truth, tonight there is no war in my house. Come inside, both of you. I've Jarrett's cake positively bristling with candles, and I intend to force him to get them all with one breath."

The two shrugged to each other and followed Tara back into the house.

James didn't intend to look for Warren's daughter; he did so anyway. He remained in the background as the cake was brought into the foyer and a table was drawn up for it. Jarrett was teased by his wife, congratulated by a group of nearly fifty guests now. Challenged by Tara, he managed to blow out the candles with a single breath. He was told he belonged in Tallahassee with the big-winded politicians, and laughter rose along with the music that began again.

Jeeves, the dapper, ebony-skinned butler—true ruler of Cimarron, as James affectionately called him—came to James with a silver tray loaded with champagne glasses. "James McKenzie, there's too grave a look upon your face, my good young man."

James accepted a glass of champagne. "I seem to be hearing that frequently enough tonight."

"Enjoy the night, for tomorrow will come!"

"Now *you* are sounding grim and grave, my good man," James said, saluting him.

Jeeves smiled, his teeth flashing remarkably white against his dark features. "I am merely admitting to the fact that our days are hard, and therefore, sir, I am suggesting that you seize the moment, the night, the magic, whatever there is to be seized, sir."

James laughed softly, finished his champagne, and set the glass back. "If it will make you happy, then, my friend, I shall grin from ear to ear for the rest of the night."

Jeeves held the tray with one hand, offering James a second flute of champagne with his free one. "This will help, sir. In a roundabout way, it's come straight from France."

"Well, then, it must be good and French, eh?"

"Get on with enjoying the night, sir," Jeeves said, chin a bit indignantly high as he moved away.

James moved on into the parlor, where the guests were swirling about the room to the cheerful tune of a fiddle.

He wasn't looking for her, but he found her right away. John Harrington, straight and handsome and just a bit stiff in his regulation uniform, was whirling at a dizzying pace with the Warren girl. His eyes were rapt upon her. She seemed not to notice. She was talking, speaking with the man all the while.

The music stopped. They were far across the room, but James watched as John politely spoke to her, then walked away from her, certainly on his way to fetch punch or champagne.

She stood alone on the dance floor. The music began again, a much slower ballad, the strains slow and heart-wrenching.

James strode across the room before he knew quite what he was doing. He had her in his arms, and swept her across the floor without giving her the first chance to acquiesce or protest.

But she didn't attempt to object. She arched a brow high, staring straight into his eyes as he guided them through the dancers in the parlor, those in the broad hallway, and out onto the porch, beneath the moon. There were no other dancers out there, but they could still hear the music plainly and continued to dance.

"So you've come to Cimarron, and met your fiancé, all in one day, Miss Warren."

She shook her head, frowning slightly. "What do you mean?"

"My good friend Major Harrington."

"But Major Harrington is not . . ." Her voice trailed away.

"He's one of the finest white men I've ever met," James told her. After a moment he added, "One of the finest men."

"He is charming. But he is not my fiancé."

"He is. It seems Colonel Warren has been remiss."

"Colonel Warren does not dictate my life."

"He is your guardian. He gives orders."

"I am not in his army. And I do not take orders."

"No?"

"From any man," she informed him coolly.

"Perhaps you'll be in for a bit of surprise in our wilderness, Miss Warren. Sometimes it's best to take orders. Sometimes it is safest. I assure you of this—it would be far better among the rivers and hammocks and swamps if you were known as Harrington's wife rather than Warren's daughter."

"I shall try to keep that in mind, Mr. McKenzie. But I am curious. What has my stepfather done to you?"

"Directly?"

"Indeed, directly! Has he injured you, hunted you, insulted you?"

The hair at his nape seemed to rise, and his hand tightened upon her so that he actually saw her wince. "No, Miss Warren, bad Indian that I am. He has never touched me—were he to do so, I promise you, he would be a dead man. But he has offended me as few other men have ever managed to do. He has offended me with his brutality—"

"Brutality has been used against whites, too."

"Not by me, Miss Warren. Not by me."

"You are hurting me," she told him levelly. "You are holding me too tightly."

"Then you should not be held at all."

"You came to me; I did not ask you to dance."

"Indeed." He stopped short. So quickly that she collided with him, slamming hard against his chest. She was so startled that she did not move away.

And he did not release her. He felt the thunder of his heart mingling with hers. Breathed in the sweet feminine scent of her. Felt those eyes of hers, emerald as they burned into his.

"There you are! The two of you!" they heard someone call.

James knew John Harrington's voice. He stepped back, releasing Teela Warren.

"Champagne!" John said cheerfully. "Teela, James . . . ?"

"Thank you, I've had quite enough," James said, then bowed to Miss Warren. "If you'll excuse me."

He turned, leaving them. He slipped through the crowd in the hallway, greeting old friends, being waylaid by a few. It was painful; it grew more painful as the war went on. The whites were afraid. They grew more hostile with their fear. They didn't understand that the Indians were also afraid. That the war was a bitter burden on them as well. Their young men died. Their villages and homes were decimated. Their children starved.

He tried to say reassuring things. He tried to defend his people. How could any man defend war?

He escaped up the stairs at last. He looked in on his brother's infant son, assuring himself that the boy slept peacefully in his cradle by his mother's bed. He walked on down the hallway and peeked into his daughter's room, assuring himself that Jennifer slept comfortably as well. She did. She even slept with a smile, her dark hair tumbling around her angelic little face.

She was a beautiful child. Her white blood was evident, but she looked like her mother. Her eyes were so amber, her hair so black with such a wonderful, rich, cascading, telltale wave. James kissed her forehead, and felt his heart twist once again for the wife and child he had lost.

In his own room, the guest room kept waiting for him always, he stripped off his dress frock coat and frilled shirt. Once again he was drawn to the night. In his breeches and boots he pressed open the doors that led to the balcony which overlooked the lawn and the rear of the house, back to the end of Jarrett's property where the wilderness began, cypress forests, exotic hammocks, dense acres of colorful foliage, ancient trees, winding rivers. There was fertile land to the east, but land that was now being charred and decimated as the Indians were raided, battled, and attacked—forced ever farther south.

He heard a noise suddenly and glanced down the balcony.

She had come out to stand beneath the moon as well. She hadn't seen him as yet. She had tentatively opened her bedroom doors and slipped outside. She walked to the rail, held it. Looked up at the moon and the sky, and shivered deliciously at the feel of the night breeze.

Her hair was free, newly brushed. The moon touched the radiant streaks of red that flowed down her back. Her nightdress was simple white cotton, all but entirely sheer in the moonlight. Her breasts were high and full, her waist tapering and tiny, her hips round and enticing.

Her effect on him was entirely maddening. There was nothing subtle or slow about it. His damned breeches barely contained the swift, violent rise of his sex.

"Damn her!"

He muttered the words out loud.

She spun around, startled, frightened.

He was in shadow, against the wall. He stepped forward and she nearly screamed, catching the sound with a hand quickly brought up to cover her mouth.

"What are you doing here?" she demanded, frowning.

He stepped forward, pointed at his room, then folded his arms across his chest and strode closer to her. He leaned against the balcony rail at her side.

"I have a room here. It is my brother's house."

He thought that she would move away from him. She did not. She looked him up and down, studying him in the moonlight. "You claim your brother frequently enough when it is convenient to do so."

"I always claim my brother."

"But it is all right to be rude to his guests."

"I am not frequently so."

"How comforting to realize that I am special."

"Miss Warren, quite frankly, you should be glad that the first Indian you've encountered was rude to you and no more."

"If that's your room, perhaps you'll return to it."

"Ah, but I was here first. You've disturbed my evening."

She didn't reply. She had turned slightly and looked straight at him. The breeze picked up her hair, lifted it to waft and dance beneath the soft glow of the night. Her eyes were so steady, so deep, so lustrous in their color. Her flesh again appeared as perfect as marble. Her nightdress was so thin, the rise and fall of her breasts so evident . . .

He touched her, goaded by sheer temptation and desire, by the heat that had been simmering inside him from the first moment he saw her. His knuckles rose to her cheek, brushed it. His hand fell to her shoulder. He drew her against him and lowered his head, driven by the desire to taste the fullness of her lips.

Her mouth was sweet, tasting of mint. Warm, evocative. His lips molded on hers, his tongue pressed them open. The rise of his manhood that seemed to all but cripple him stirred again. His fingers wound into the wealth of hair at her nape as his tongue plunged deeper. Not enough. He held her with his left hand, brought up his right. Caressed her breast, palm lifting the fullness of it, rubbing over the nipple.

She tensed. Palms fell against his shoulders. A strangled sound seemed to catch within the kiss.

He shuddered with a sudden rise of desire so violent that it convulsed the length of his body.

What in God's name was he doing? He went rigid from head to toe, heedless of the anguish within him. *He could not do this. Could not, would not.*

He set her firmly from him. She was trembling, shaking furiously in the wind, as she stared at him, stunned. Because he had touched her? Because he had let her go?

"Get back to your room!" he told her angrily.

She spun, heading toward her door as if to obey him. But she stopped dead and spun around again. Her eyes were a green blaze as she strode determinedly back to him. "You, sir, white or red or spotted with purple, have an incredible chip upon your shoulder, the manners of a monkey, and the crude audacity of a boar!" She lifted a hand and slapped him as hard as she could.

He should have seen it coming. He didn't. He retaliated instinctively, catching her wrist, slamming her hard against him. He stared down into her eyes, wild eyes that still offered no apology or even fear.

His grip around her wrist must have hurt; she didn't wince, nor did she fight his hold. She stared at him furiously, and she waited for him to release her.

"This once," he warned her, "you'll get away with that. But remember, we're at war. Strike a red man, he strikes back."

She didn't reply. She continued to wait, seething, staring at him.

"Go back to your room!" he snapped at her, releasing his hold on her.

She rubbed her wrist, still staring at him. Then she spun around, heading toward her open doors.

But she paused there, head high, looking back. "This once I'll do as you so courteously request. But we *are* at war. And this part of the balcony leads from my room, and it's damned free territory, neutral ground. While I'm in residence, it is my place, and you'll not order me away from it, sir."

She finished the last with a passionate hiss, then spun around again and disappeared into her room, closing the doors sharply behind her.

He went into his own.

And to a long, fitful night that seemed to plague him with all the tortures of hell.

Chapter 5

The dream began sweetly.

They were deep in the lands that had been good. The old Indians, native to the area, had all but died out when the Creek had first seen the vacant lands and come south to claim them. Land rich and abundant with deer and otter, wild fowl and fish. The soil was rich—corn and numerous other crops could be easily cultivated. There were acres to hunt, to run, to play ... to fall in love.

They'd been from different clans, of course, for a man was expected to marry outside his own. But he had known her for many years, loved her since they were both children. He had come of age, educated by his father's family and taught the way of the world by his mother's brothers and kin. He had taken the black drink and shed his boy's name for his man's name. At the Green Corn Dance he would officially make her his wife. While adultery might be sternly punished—ears and noses were sometimes clipped for the crime—sex before marriage was not considered evil, and the time had simply come for them to be together. They were both in love.

The sun dappled through the trees. The day was hot beneath the sun but cooled by the shade. They had ridden into the forest, dismounted, sipped cool water from the stream, collected berries to eat. He had all but dozed beneath the tree when he heard her laughter, and caught her eyes upon him. She laughed again and ran toward the river when he threatened to make her pay for her laughter.

She was fleet; he was faster. He caught her mid-river, but even in his dream he could remember the moment just before he did. She turned back to him, laughing. Her hair, darker than ink, falling thick and rich and arrow straight to her thighs, spun like a black shawl around her as she turned. She laughed still, breathlessly. She'd never had a chance and she knew it. She did not want to escape him.

He touched her and they fell together into the cool waters. White-tipped, it rushed on by them. He rose then, and she came to her knees, looking up at him. He reached down for her, and she came into his arms. She wore white that day, a bleached-white doeskin dress with leggings to match. He could still remember pulling the dress over her shoulders, dropping it into the river.

They made love there, in the water, the sun casting shadow and light upon them. They lay again beneath the low branches of a pine, and they spun their dreams just as any other young couple in love might do, with the whole of their lives before them.

They'd laughed again when they had to travel far down stream to find her embroidered white doeskin dress.

He tossed in his sleep. She was running again in his dream. He was trying to catch her. He couldn't keep up. When she looked back, she wasn't laughing. . . .

She was gone. He stood in blackness. He saw the back of a man. A white man, kneeling down, his shoulders shaking with his tears.

James saw his brother's face. Took his wife from his brother's arms.

She lay in her coffin. Jarrett and he had built it from the thick trunk of a cypress, just as they had built a much smaller one for Sara. So small. A child's coffin.

He had dressed Naomi in the embroidered white doeskin. She had kept it since the day they became man and wife. She was beautiful in it, beautiful even in death. No ravages of the fever remained. The dress was so white, her flesh smooth and copper. Her hair ebony against it.

Suddenly, he seemed to be standing in darkness. The coffin was so far away. He had left it in a burial cove, above the ground, shadowed by trees, her belongings with her, her pots and pans, her clothing, her beads and necklaces. He could see the cove, but something was wrong. He tried to see into the coffin ...

Naomi wasn't within it. *She* lay within it instead. He could see the blazing red cascade of her hair spilling over the cypress. She was dressed in white, an embroidered gown in cotton and lace. Her face was so pale; her hands were folded before her.

Her eyes opened, met his. And she was suddenly screaming, aware that she was in a coffin. It was filling with blood. She was reaching out, calling his name ...

James woke with a start, bathed in sweat.

He sat up, exhaling and gritting his teeth to ease himself from the tension of the dream. He stared outside. Darkness was just being lifted by the first pale streaks of dawn.

He groaned aloud and lay back down. Oddly enough, after his wretched dream James at long last fell into a deep and restful sleep. He thought that he was dreaming again when he first heard the tapping on the door. "Mastuh James, Mastuh James, coffee, sir!"

It had to be Dolly, a plump free woman of Bahamian and Indian descent who served in the kitchen. "Bring it in, then!" he called back, rolling over, his back toward the door. It had been one hell of an awful night. But now he was awake, and he wouldn't sleep again. His brother's house could make him too soft if he wasn't careful.

Still, he closed his eyes anyway.

"Black, or cream, Mastuh James?" he heard. Right at his back. The damned woman just wasn't leaving him in peace.

"I'll take care of it myself, thank you," he all but growled.

"On your head or in your face?" the voice inquired sweetly.

He swung around, shooting to a sitting position. Miss Teela Warren, fresh as a spring flower, dressed in a yellow muslin that somehow seemed to emphasize the rise of her breasts, stood by his side, coffee cup in hand. He had the unnerving feeling that he was about the wear coffee somewhere uncomfortably low on his body.

"If you're considering dropping that cup, may I suggest that you don't?" he inquired.

"Why, Mr. McKenzie, since I am living in your brother's house, I am trying to come up with some kind of peace terms for the duration."

"Mmm," he muttered doubtfully, pulling the white bedsheet up against him. He was completely naked beneath it. Surely, she must know it. But she didn't seem discomfited; she waited politely, coolly, for an answer on the coffee.

"Black!" he snapped, taking the coffee from her before she could do any damage with it.

A small smile played on her lips. "I intended no harm."

"But you might have had an accident."

"I'm quite careful."

"You're quite the southern belle. I'm sure all your accidents are well planned ... Are you accustomed to bringing men coffee in their beds?"

She considered that and shrugged. "Actually, no. I've not had the opportunity before."

"And I doubt that it could be considered proper behavior for a young woman of your breeding."

"Probably not."

"Alas, Miss Warren, it seems you will rot in hell."

"Well, my sins are many, so perhaps I will. Though not, I think, for bringing you coffee."

He sipped the coffee, staring at her. She had remained by his bedside. She had left her long hair free once again, and it was brushed to an extraordinary shine. It curled and waved and cascaded over her shoulders. Her dress was a perfectly decent day dress, he realized. It was just that the woman within it was exceptionally lush.

Damn it. Things were rising again. He drew up his knees to create a concealing tent of the bedding.

She sat down at the foot of his bed.

"Miss Warren, what are you doing?"

"Trying to make peace."

"This is not the place—"

"Mr. McKenzie—"

He set his coffee on the cherrywood nightstand by the bed and reached forward suddenly, almost losing the sheet. He wound his fingers around her wrists and drew her forward, almost against him.

"My, my, Miss Warren, let's get to the truth here. I'm your first Indian. I speak English. I've got white blood. You're curious. Intrigued. Maybe even a bit tempted. Well, then. Touch while you've got the chance." He drew her palm against his chest, held it there while she gritted her teeth and struggled against him. "Ah, look at that! The color did not rub off. And guess what, Miss Warren? There's no other difference. Two arms, two legs, one . . ." His gaze dipped down to his lap. "Or did you want to check that out, too?"

She went dead still. Her eyes narrowed sharply, but she gave no other sign of her fury. "I don't need to. I'd damned well bet it was pronged! You are atrocious."

"You came into my bedroom! What would your fiancé say?"

"I haven't got a fiancé—"

"I've told you I think he's a damned good man, Miss Warren. Don't be cruel to him; you'll have the devil to pay."

"He's a gentleman; he'd never hurt me." She tugged her arm, but he held it fast. "Why do you insist on behaving like such a wretched bastard?"

"Because you're playing games, Miss Warren!" he suddenly roared and released her wrist.

She drew her hand back, tried to slap him. He was ready and caught her wrist again. "I told you, not again."

"Let me—"

"No, let me. You're playing with fire. You want your truces, you want to pick and poke and query. Well, you're a fool, Miss Warren. And I guarantee you, you're going to get hurt."

"Mr. McKenzie, please quit worrying about me!"

Just who was he worrying about? he wondered. He was the one in agony, sitting with the woman almost on top of him, the sheet tented up in protection of his "pronged" desire.

He released her, twisting to throw his legs to the floor and sit up at her side, dragging his sheet along with him. He pressed his temples between his palms, then stared at her again. "Miss Warren . . ."

His voice trailed away. She was staring at his shoulders. She looked forward, then down to her now folded hands. Miles of red hair seemed to fall around her, shadowing her features.

"I did come to make peace," she murmured.

"Don't make peace. Don't try to make peace. Don't stay in Florida. Go home. Go back to Charleston. It's a beautiful city."

She shook her head. "It wasn't exactly my choice to come here." She was still for a moment and then shrugged. "I was ordered to come here. Army boys and I, Mr. McKenzie, have much in common. We are all supposed to jump on command."

"If he doesn't send you out of here, he is a fool. He will lose you. He is hated, and you are in danger."

"Well, he considers himself above any threat, Mr. Mc-Kenzie. And I am not unhappy to be here. In fact, I'd be quite happy if it weren't for the fact that . . . never mind. I love what I have seen so far. I've been reading about the Florida territory all my life. I am anxious to see St. Augustine, Jacksonville, Tallahassee. More. I want to sail by the Keys sometime at a leisurely pace; I want to swim in the rivers. I want to see and feel and taste it all."

"You'll feel a knife at your scalp, Teela."

"Perhaps not."

"Marry Huntington if you want to stay here. He's absolutely infatuated with you. He'll jump when you snap your fingers."

She stood up. "I don't want anyone to jump when I

snap my fingers, McKenzie. And John is very nice. But I'm not going to marry him."

"Oh? You've decided already."

"I'm not in love with him."

James laughed, which definitely seemed to offend her. She barely managed to lift a hand when he caught both her wrists and dragged her back down beside him. "You're not in love with him? My dear Miss Warren! I am familiar with your world, and you and I both know that love doesn't always enter into marriage agreements. Your stepfather has conceived what he considers a very proper arrangement for you. What right have you to object?"

"It's not my choice, Mr. McKenzie."

"You'd refuse John just because your father chose him?"

"Stepfather."

"All right, you've refused John just because your *stepfather* chose him?"

"No one will make me marry."

"No," he said softly. "John would never make you marry. But perhaps you should get to know him better."

She stared at him. Her eyes seemed like emeralds, liquid, shimmering. Strands of her hair curled over his fingers. He suddenly lifted his hand, bringing hers with it, placing her palm and fingers over his cheek this time. She didn't wrench away. Soft as silk, her fingertips moved over the contours of his face. He caught her wrist again. He meant to set her hand away. Instead he turned it within his own and lowered his head, kissing her palm, the tip of his tongue teasing its center. He heard the ragged intake of her breath. When he looked into her eyes, she was staring at him still. He leaned toward her. She moistened her lips. Her eyes half closed, her lips parted.

He should have left her just sitting so. Ignored the seduction. Let her know that she couldn't ignite the least bit of hunger within him ...

But she could. And did. A hunger that was almost

physically painful. It twisted inside him. Grew with each encounter.

He leaned closer. Touched her lips with his own. Closer still. He enveloped her in his arms and kissed her deeply. Stroked her face. Her throat. Again, she tasted like mint, and the fires of hell roared through his body, making his erection painfully hard. His arms guided her downward until she was half flat upon his bed. Her hair was entangled around him. Her palm fell against his cheek, his shoulder. Warnings shouted within his mind but went unheeded. He caught the hand that touched his burning flesh and brought it low over the sheet against him. He brought her fingers down over his body, down, over the heat of his erection.

She twisted from him then. He thought he heard a desperate "No!"

He released her instantly, then shoved away from her. She didn't move; she seemed to lie there stunned.

"Damn it, Miss Warren, get the hell out of my room. Don't play games with me; I am not a swamp toy. I cannot be touched and played with, and set back upon a shelf."

She leapt up and spun, clearly eager to strike. But he was up himself, heedless of the sheet and his very obvious physical condition. Firmly, he guided her to the door. "Out!" he commanded, and set her into the hallway, closing the door in her wake.

The door opened immediately again.

"The damned thing *is* pronged!" she swore, then slammed the door.

He heard her footsteps hurrying away. He paused, shook his head, and then laughed.

But his laughter faded, and he felt a grip of pain. Cold fingers closed slowly around his heart. She really was playing with fire, a moth to a flame, but now he wondered which one of them would get burned.

Maybe she wanted to flirt with him, a Seminole, just to irk Warren. Maybe that was her game.

He swore softly aloud.

He had best leave his brother's house before tonight.

He spent the afternoon with Jarrett, giving him the names of those Indians who were ready to accept the government's determination that they go west.

John Harrington, he discovered, had already traveled to Tampa, and would spend a few days there before returning. A contingent of marines, recently assigned to the base, would join John to bring Teela inland and north. It would be a long and hazardous journey for her. "Warren is insane," Jarrett told his brother. "There are skirmishes almost daily. Hostiles raid a farm, so the whites go in and decimate a village. And he wants his daughter traveling through it!"

"Harrington will protect her." He shrugged. "John is popular, even among my people."

"Yeah," Jarrett agreed unhappily. "The brave who scalps him will regret it, but then he will cherish that scalp for the rest of his days!"

James felt a cold chill. It was true.

"If Harrington moves with a large enough force, he won't be bothered. We have had tremendous losses lately, Jarrett, but there will be warriors to fight until the end of time. Unless the whites do manage to kill every last one of them."

"James, you have to take care—"

"Yes, even you have to take care, brother. The time is coming quickly when we are no guarantee for each other."

Jarrett sighed, standing in front of a window to the rear lawn. "The war will not come here. I will not let it." He smiled suddenly, and James was aware then of the sound of laughter coming in from the lawn. He rose and joined his brother.

The women were out there. Tara, Teela, and his own little Jennifer. The back lawn to the trees sloped slightly, and Tara and Teela were teaching Jennifer how to roll down the thick green grass.

"It's a nice sight," Jarrett murmured.

It was. Tara with her golden hair, Teela with her fiery

red, Jennifer with her ebony black. All were dressed in soft pastels. The scene was peaceful, natural.

"I may head back inland tonight," James murmured. "I think I'll go see my daughter a few minutes now, if you'll excuse me?"

"Be my guest," Jarrett said.

James exited the house and came out onto the porch, still watching the trio. Little Ian McKenzie slept in his cradle, oblivious to all the shrieking going on around him.

Jennifer suddenly saw him. "Daddy!" she yelled happily. A second later, she was a little ball of fire, running for him, vaulting up into his arms. He hugged her close to his body. Tara and Teela, both panting slightly, came up behind her.

"We rolled!" Jennifer told him.

"So I saw."

"I can't believe Teela had me rolling out there!" Tara exclaimed, laughing.

Jennifer placed both her palms on James's face, drawing his attention to her. "Teela is fun."

"I think I shall ask Jeeves for some lemonade," Tara said. "Of course, I've something stronger if you wish, James?"

"I don't care for anything, thank you, Tara," he said.

Jennifer was squirming down from his arms. "I'll help Aunt Tara get lemonade," she announced.

She disappeared, hand in hand with Tara. For a fleeting moment it was painful to see his daughter disappear so. Then he was simply grateful that she had a wonderful, loving home when he spent so many of his days without food or lodging, traveling through swamp and bog, sometimes fighting, sometimes trying desperately to stop the fighting.

"You are lucky," Teela told him. "You have a beautiful child."

"Do I?"

"You question that?"

"I don't. I just wonder if you do."

"Ah, that damned chip gets bigger and bigger, McKenzie."

He shook his head. "You're stubborn and naive, Miss Warren. I have some influence with Harrington. He'll get you out of here safely."

"You have influence with him?" she queried, somewhat amused. Well, maybe she had the right to be amused. No one's influence would be needed for John Harrington to want to marry Teela Warren.

"Influence to get you married quickly," he clarified coolly.

"McKenzie, I've told you. You needn't worry about me."

"Can't help it. It's a concern for the scalps of others."

She flushed but lifted her chin. "McKenzie, if I choose to, I will marry Harrington, but I shall never do so on another man's say-so. And Mr. McKenzie, I don't run easily."

"You should."

"I love it here."

"You haven't seen the bloodshed yet."

She shook her head, looking at him. "But I have seen a sunset. I've seen the most extraordinary birds. I've seen wild orchids and cabbage palms. Cypress hammocks, moss dipping from the trees to touch the water ..." Her voice trailed away. She looked at him again, as if she could feel the intensity of his stare.

"You should get out of here while you still can."

"Thank you for the words of warning. They are duly noted," she said, and started to walk by him.

He caught her arm, drawing her back, amazed by both the passion and the fury that seemed to seize him.

"Damn you, but you should learn to take care. I'm not giving warnings, I'm giving promises. Play with a savage wilderness, and you may not leave it alive."

She tried to wrench free from his hold. He couldn't quite manage to let her go. She lifted her chin.

"Your brother's skin is darker then yours, McKenzie," she said.

He tightened his grip on her. "The next touch is for real," he said very softly.

She fought his grip to free herself again. This time he forced himself to let her go.

She turned her back on him with tremendous dignity, and nearly bolted for the house.

At dinner that night, Teela sat across from James. Jennifer had come down to eat with the adults, and they kept the conversation casual. The little girl was gravely aware of the war and the consequences of it; she had lived with it long enough herself. No one felt she needed to hear too much about it, and so the conversation ran from theater and literature to plants and beasts, with nothing said about guns, knifes, battles, or danger.

James McKenzie could be charming to his daughter, Teela realized. And to his sister-in-law as well. Teela herself seemed to be the only one cursed with drawing his venom. But then, she had tried to cross some inner sanctum, she realized.

She had watched him last night. Watched him when she had danced with John Harrington, watched him when he had paused to talk to people in the foyer before he ran up the stairs. He had been polite but distant.

She had watched the women who waylaid him. Watched their eyes. Watched the way they liked to touch him when they talked. She had felt the most absurd pangs of jealousy.

Then last night she had lain awake, staring at the ceiling, remembering the feel of his lips. And she should have been ashamed and horrified by her behavior. She'd always been confident, stubborn, and determined, but she had never even considered behaving so recklessly with any man.

This was something entirely different. This was something that had taken hold of her. She wanted so badly to touch him again. And again. Feel his skin. The ripple of muscle. She liked the feel of his eyes on her, no matter that they mocked her. She wanted to know him, un-

derstand his thoughts, crawl beneath his skin. She
burned with her thoughts, amazed by them, alarmed by
them. But they remained.

And now, in the midst of a statement about architecture in Charleston, she suddenly remembered how his
hand had taken hers. Brought it down. She remembered
the feel of him, the intimate feel of him, the heat, the
life, the almost violent promise within the pulse ...

He meant to scare her away.

She was scared.

But she still wanted to touch. She felt flushed. She set
her fork down, her appetite lost.

He was staring at her. As if he remembered as well.
He was strikingly handsome. His shirt so white, his hair
so dark. Eyes so grave.

"I must leave after dinner," he announced, drawing
his eyes from hers to look at his brother as he spoke.
"If you'll excuse me, I've a few things to pack. Jennifer,
come help your father. Then I'll tell you a story and
tuck you into bed."

"James," Tara said, frowning, "surely you can stay
awhile longer."

Jarrett set a hand upon hers. "Tara, perhaps he cannot."

"I'll say good-bye," James told her.

She nodded, tried to smile, and looked down at the
table.

"Miss Warren," he said.

Teela looked up.

"It has been a pleasure to meet you. I will pray for
your safety."

"I will pray for yours," she responded politely.

He turned and left the room, Jennifer at his heels.
Teela stared quickly down at her plate. He was leaving.
She needed to be thankful. She might do something im-
possibly embarrassing. She might ...

What?

She didn't know. But it didn't matter. He was leaving.
She'd never felt this way before; she would never do
so again.

She felt like crying.

"It seems a rather glum night," Jarrett said softly. "Miss Warren, are you all right?"

"Yes, yes, of course . . . tired, I suppose," she said.

"We'll understand if you wish to retire for the evening," Tara told her.

Teela nodded, making no pretense. Her host and hostess were probably just as eager for their own privacy this night. "Thank you both so much for your hospitality. It is wonderful here."

"We're glad you're happy," Tara said.

Teela smiled, then fled from the dining room. Upstairs, she shed her clothing and dressed for bed.

She paced her room.

She heard footsteps in the hall, conversation in the room next to hers. Male voices. The brothers saying their farewells.

How could Jarrett let him leave? she thought angrily.

How could Jarrett stop him? she answered herself wearily.

She lay down. She tried to close her eyes. Tears stung them.

She heard Jarrett bidding his brother good-bye.

She raced out to the balcony, beneath the moon glow. She stepped into the bedroom she knew was his.

But it was empty. He had gone.

With a soft sob she turned and ran back to her own room. She leapt into the bed, shivering. She closed her eyes, damning herself for the full bath of tears that threatened to come sliding down her cheeks.

She opened her eyes to blink furiously. She gasped then, sitting up.

The moon was full that night. And the detailed length of his height was silhouetted there in the balcony doorway. Broad-shouldered, half-naked, he stood there, staring in at her. She swallowed back a scream, staring at him. She was in the darkness. He was in the light. Yet she was certain he could see the wide-eyed amazement on her face, while she could make out nothing of his features.

It seemed that he stood there for an eternity, shoulders impossibly broad, stance straight and incredibly still. She might have imagined him there as the fine white muslin curtains whispered around the darkness of his body.

Then he moved. Striding toward her, where she lay.

She found motion herself at last, leaping up, standing defensively by the bed. But it made no difference. He reached out for her, caught her wrist, wrenched her into his arms. His chest was bare, and she felt the fevered heat of it burning through the thin white fabric of her nightdress.

"You've no right," she began brokenly. "You can't come here like this—"

But he had. And he didn't speak a word, just captured her face between his two palms, found her lips with his own. Forceful, passionate.

Savage . . .

His lips parted a breath from hers. "You were just in my room," he told her huskily. "What did you come for?"

"To say good-bye," she whispered.

"No."

"To say good-bye!"

"You're a liar, Teela. You came for more. Much more. And I promised you, a touch again would be for real."

"No . . ."

"What did you come for?"

"To say—"

"What did you come for?"

"I told you—"

"The truth."

"I came . . ."

"For me. For this . . ."

His mouth covered hers again. Forceful, heated, undeniable.

She raised her hands to beat against him. They fell upon

his tautly muscled arms, fisted. She tried to strike him again. Her fingers opened upon his flesh instead. She couldn't breathe. She'd felt the sensation before. Everything within her seeming to tremble, her blood to run swift and hot. His tongue had found entry to her mouth. Liquid and searing. Sweeping her mouth, driving deeply into it, stealing breath and strength. She was kissing him back. Dear God. Maybe not. She wasn't fighting, she wasn't protesting, she was afire within his arms, tasting . . .

She twisted from his onslaught. She opened her mouth to whisper a no once again. But it would have no meaning. She didn't quite understand his ferocity; she was a little frightened by it. But any denial would be a lie. She didn't care that he half hated her; she didn't care that he had come like a windstorm in the night. She knew merely that she was entangled with him in some inexplicable way, and all meaning in life seemed to have come down to this moment.

"I had thought to keep away from my brother's house," he told her, his whisper a hoarse caress against her cheek. "But then, you belong within my brother's house. You belong with soft cotton sheets and down pillows, in the sheltering comfort of a white man's bed."

His lips touched her throat. Teased. Moved on. She might have told him that she didn't need anything, that a bed of earth and grass would be sufficient, when she was held by him. Ah, what she needed was sanity, but it was not forthcoming. What she needed was strength to fight him, the sense to remember that he mocked her, disdained her . . .

She was suddenly standing free. She heard the violent ripple in the air as he wrenched the covers from the bed. The moonlight fell over them both. The swivel mirror reflected them. She could see herself, the fabric of her nightdress all but sheer, the lines of her body clean beneath it, her breasts all but bare beneath the lace of the bodice, color and shadow all too visible. The gown was white; she was white, pale except for the fiery flare of her hair cascading down her back.

He stood just a foot away as sheets and comforters settled, staring at her, pitch black hair unqueued, falling with
a slight wave to the tip of his shoulder, that shoulder a
deep copper, bunched with muscle, broad and naked. His
feet were bare, his chest was bare. He wore doeskin
breeches, nothing more. For a moment it seemed that the
differences between them were enhanced by the reflection
in the mirror, everything enhanced, the strength and size
of him, the delicacy of her own figure and flesh. Then he
took a step toward her, blue eyes intense against his handsome features, and she felt a trembling seize her with the
strength of a north wind.

Another step, this time his hands upon her shoulders,
his heat, his scent, hot and alluring in the shadows of
the night.

"Wait!" she gasped.

"You would have me wait?" he demanded imperiously.

"You said—"

"You played, Miss Warren, teased and tormented, and
I walked away. Now I've walked back. Will you stop
me?"

She tried to swallow, tried to turn from the fire in his
eyes, tried not to feel the all-consuming fire that swept
her. She gasped when she felt his fingers upon the lace
of her bodice, felt it tear to his determined touch, sweep
softly over her flesh as it drifted to the floor. She realized
almost dimly that she was naked, that he had made her
so in a matter of seconds. She was up in his arms,
weightless, then falling down hard upon the bed, his
hard-muscled form atop her, hands catching her wrists,
pinning her.

And again he was staring at her.

"I will not have you mock me!" she cried. "I'll not,
I'll not!"

"It's myself I mock," he whispered. "For I will not
leave Cimmaron tonight. I'll not leave you tonight. The
moth has flown too close to the candle."

Chapter 6

The night seemed to have a touch of the unreal upon it. From the moment he had seen her come floating into his room like a wayward angel with her fiery hair and snow white gown, he had ceased to think.

A raw, simmering instinct, something that had filtered into his blood, body, and being, had caused him to follow her from one room to the next. Something even more basic had brought him to stand before her, touch her, strip away the virginal white, and bear her down with him to the softness of the bed.

And now he spoke the truth. And he didn't speak the truth. She had teased, indeed. He shouldn't have come. He didn't want to think. He wanted to touch.

And taste.

Fill himself with her. Still the obsession. Free himself from the invisible silken ties she seemed to have cast over him. Know her. *Solve* her.

Yet he knew already, inside, that by touching he would not be free. He refused to admit that he might be ever more tightly bound.

Moonlight spilled softly into the room. It seemed to carry a strange whisper of fog with it, something that softened and made him want to cry out with each subtle nuance, each twist or shift of her body. His arm stretched with hers above her head, his dark against the moon-bathed whiteness of hers.

She was the silk he had imagined . . .

The fire of her hair was silk, the brush of her flesh. His left fingers curled around her wrist while his right

knuckles rode a gentle trail down her inner arm, the side
of her breast. He watched her eyes in the ivory glow, the
green darkened as her pupils dilated, her stare steady on
him. She swallowed hard, no sound escaped her. He
leaned low, finding her lips again, savoring their sweet
taste, hungering for more. The length of her flush against
him. All silk. Breasts teasing his chest, slim legs entwined with his. His sex rested against her abdomen,
touching silk there, too.

He found himself mesmerized by her features. By
those eyes, huge, defying fear, shadowed just the same.
Her fine, high cheekbones, small, straight nose, delicately cut chin. Radiant waves of her hair framed her
face, the color nearly matching that of her lips, slightly
parted, damp in the moonlight. The breath seemed to
rush in and out of her.

He shifted down against her. Against the whiteness of
her flesh, enhanced by the moon glow, her nipples as
wildly red as her hair. He nuzzled one with his lips and
caught it within his mouth, caressed it with his tongue.
She shifted against him, and a choked sound fell from
her lips.

He shifted farther. His lips pressed against her abdomen. Lower. He no longer held her wrists; his hands
were upon her hips, his head against her belly. Her fingers curled within his hair, tense. The length of her trembled violently. But she didn't speak. She didn't seek to
stop him in any way.

He leaned up on an elbow and sought out her eyes.
They were closed, dusky lashes brushing her cheeks, face
pale, lips still damp and parted, so sensual. His gaze
swept her body, savoring every detail. She was elegantly
slim, yet generously curved. Her flesh was as perfect as
ivory from head to toe. The soft V of hair at the juncture
of her thighs was vividly red. He set his palm upon it,
brushed his fingers over it, then within it.

Her eyes flew open. He swiftly leaned forward, capturing her lips. His mouth ravaged and consumed as his
fingers pressed farther, stroking, exploring. He wanted

her so much. Wanted to touch her inside and out. Taste, feel, breathe her in. He'd never known such urgency, such intense hunger, such a need to have everything, all at once. But touching her seemed to exacerbate the anguished heat that had coiled within him since he had first laid eyes upon her. He could feel himself, rigid, swollen against her, and he could wait no longer. He arched his weight and pressed his length between the silken softness of her thighs, caressed the fire red thatch of hair at their apex, and thrust himself into her.

She didn't cry out; she didn't let the smallest wimper escape her. He went still himself, wondering vaguely why he had been so certain that she would have known a lover before. He shuddered fiercely, unable to withdraw, unable not to feel the wave of emotions that engulfed him. He was angry, he realized. With her for coming so near him, like that moth to the flame. With himself for having been so desperately captivated.

But the emotions meant little against the strength of the raw need that shrieked within him. He forced himself to lie still, to allow her body to adjust to his. Braced on his hands, he looked down into her face, but her eyes remained closed. She was so pale, so motionless, she might have been dead except for the pulse that leapt at her throat, the fine sheen of perspiration that bathed her, the now rampant rise and fall of her breasts. He opened his mouth to speak, but the right words would not come. He closed his mouth, gritting his teeth. Some hoarse sound of defeat escaped him, and he allowed himself to move more deeply within her.

She seemed to envelop him like a glove, a touch of hot liquid silk once again. He meant to move slowly, to seduce . . . yet the sensation of her seduced him instead, and a wild surge seized him in the moonlight. He caressed her buttocks, holding her close and firm, thrusting with a driving momentum that soared higher and higher. A last he filled her with the fullness of his body and a cry escaped him. The war was gone, white was gone, red was gone. The world seemed to split with an explosion of light as the violence of his climax ripped from his body and into hers. He held her still, thrusting again, and again . . .

Then he fell to her side, his heart thundering like wildfire, his flesh drenched with a copper sheen, his breathing just barely slowing. He turned quicky, determined now to see her face. She'd still not whispered a single word.

Nor did she offer her eyes to his. She'd curled away, her back to him now, head lowered, a spray of red hair hiding her features and her emotions.

With his desire sated, he could curse himself once again. What a fool. No. He rose on an elbow again, staring at the sleek curves and perfection of her body, at the rich blanket of hair that tangled around them both in lustrous waves. He would want her again. And again. She had touched something deep within him. She was like a drug a man should not taste, addictive, beguiling.

What the hell was the matter with him? He groaned inwardly. In the midst of the war he had taken an innocent white woman. Michael Warren's daughter. No good could come of it.

"Teela—"

"Please, don't," she murmured determinedly, her back remaining to him.

"Don't what?"

"Apologize."

"Apologize!" he exclaimed. He clenched his jaw as he threaded his fingers into the hair at her nape, forcing her to turn his way. "I wasn't about to apologize," he assured her flatly, staring into the depths of her eyes. She had never cried out, never even whimpered. Maybe he *had* intended to apologize. Not now, of course. "I want to know just what the hell you were doing in my room."

She shook her head, trying to look away, but she could not.

"You are pulling my hair."

"Then don't tug against it."

"You have gotten what you wanted—"

"Oh, have I? Or have you? Was this done to torment your father? Perhaps you want to have him swearing to kill me. Perhaps he'll just have another damned good reason to say that we're all heathens and animals and deserve to die!"

"What has Michael Warren to do with this!" she hissed, tugging her hair to free it from his hold. Tears were beginning to show in her eyes. She slammed her fists against him suddenly, determined to force him to free her.

He had no intention of letting her go.

"You tell me," he insisted, his grip in her hair every bit as strong.

"Do you plan on scalping me by ripping it out strand by strand?" she demanded rigidly.

"If I have to."

"Let go of me or I will scream."

"If you think my brother is going to hang me, you're wrong."

"All I want is for you to leave me alone!"

"But it's too late for that, Miss Warren. Far too late."

"You're mistaken. It's easy. Get up and walk out the door."

He shook his head slowly. "I told you, I am staying the night."

"You've your own room. It's your brother's house, remember?"

"But I am comfortable where I am."

"You are not welcome where you are."

"Seminoles hear that constantly. We have learned to ignore it. And dig in." He eased his grip on her hair, but his fingers remained entangled. She lay facing him. If she tried to turn, she would be held back. For the moment he had her where he wanted her. He reached out, touched her cheek lightly with his knuckles.

"Why, then?" he whispered.

"Why what?"

"Why didn't you fight me, stop me?"

"Why did you come?" she asked, sidestepping his question.

"Well, that's obvious, isn't it? The savage after the white man's daughter?"

"You are sarcastic and bitter."

"Am I?"

"Offensively so."

"Well, then, excuse me, I will try to remember not to be so offensive the next time I see a village being razed by your people or children on a trail barefoot and in rags."

"You have slain white women and children."

"I have never."

"Your people have."

There was no denying that. The silence stretched out. "Why?" he repeated to her at last. The word was soft. He was suddenly glad of where he was, she was. Raw hunger sated, the woman beside him still. He was glad of the moonlight as it fell upon her naked flesh, glad to study her. He wanted to hold her again. Just hold her. Breathe in the clean, feminine scent of her hair. Feel the warmth of her. As they lay now, he wasn't even touching her. But he was stirred afresh by the sight of her generously afforded him now, the fullness of her breasts, the silken smoothness of her flesh, the graceful line of her throat and shoulder, the rise of her hip and length of her legs.

She shook her head, lashes sweeping her cheeks. "I—I don't know," she whispered at last. "I wanted . . ."

"Wanted what?"

"You."

"An Indian?"

She sighed with exasperation, green eyes suddenly riveting upon his with a blaze of anger.

"I wanted you. That simply, McKenzie. That simply. Put more into it, if you will. Cast the whole cause and effect of the Indian wars upon it. I can tell you no more. Now, if you would be so good—"

"Ah, but I will not be so good, Miss Warren. Not at all."

"But—" she began, trembling.

"But! The moment of obsession has come and gone, and you have learned it a painful thing and wish to be alone to nurse your wounded body and soul."

"Something like that, perhaps."

"But I will not leave."

"You must—"

He shook his head. "Not yet."

He leaned close to her again. Touched her lips with barely a breath. Moved his caress to her throat, pausing where her heartbeat quickened. He straddled her, lifted strands of her hair gently, let them fall back upon the whiteness of her flesh, half covering her breasts. She stared up at him, eyes closing when he set his hands upon her, fingers softly stroking around the sides of her breasts, palms coming light atop them. He bent low to capture one nipple within its tangle of hair. Her hands fell upon his shoulders, fingers raking his shoulders, nails digging. He ignored the pain, caressed and teased, and willed the heat within him to come slowly now.

His body rubbed against her as he came down upon it. His fingers stroked, his lips followed each touch. His kiss moved in a liquid trail over her stomach and hip, along her outer thigh. Her inner thigh. She tensed, writhed, but could not stop him, for his movement had left her limbs parted, his body between them. The moonlight was almost magic—he was able to see, to savor, touch, tease, torment.

Seduce.

That was important. He'd offer no apology, his pride was too great, their searing connection too strange. But he meant one. Meant to offer something for the swift, staggering pain she had so stoically endured. Meant to have it forgotten by the red-gold streaks of dawn.

"Please . . ."

She whispered the word. Once, again. Her head tossed, red hair floating in the ivory moonlight, spraying out in its endless curls upon the white pillow. Her fingers dug into his hair now and tugged hard.

He'd wind up scalped himself . . .

Ah, but it would be well worth it.

She did not open her eyes. He paused briefly, watching her before his last sweet, sensual assault. She seemed so cool, yet felt like fire. The trembling in her limbs was hot. He lowered his head against her. Nuzzled the nest of red curls. Parted her with a stroke of his thumbs. Caressed her with his tongue.

White-hot fire cascaded into him with the wild bolt of her body, the twist of it, the soft cry she barely captured as it gasped from her lips. She tried to ease up the bed; he caught her hands, entwined his fingers with hers. She writhed. He allowed no mercy. Fervent, whispered pleas fell upon deaf ears. She would never bow or bend with words, never give in to his demands. She would answer what she chose to answer, meet him defiantly in this as with all things. Yet he would have a certain surrender, even if seeking that surrender now seemed to stir and torment him beyond endurance, tie him in corded knots, awaken the gnawing hunger again as if it had never been appeased. Ah, but he would wait. Taste and tease and savor while exquisite torture ravaged him in turn. Touch, caress. Sweet torment . . .

A sudden cry ripped through her. He held dead still, feeling the violent shudder of her body, the sweetness of her release. He rose above her instantly, sinking into the liquid warmth of her. Amazingly, her eyes were open. Dazed. She closed them quickly at his gaze, gasping slightly again as she twisted her head. He caught her cheek with his thumb and forefinger, drew her back to face him. He didn't care that her eyes were closed. He leaned to kiss her as he began to move with her. Taking her lips as he took her body. Hungrily. Savagely.

His climax was swift and violent. Ripping from his body. This time he was certain that he caused no pain, that he swept her with him. She trembled within his arms, and he held her close against him even as he eased himself from her, locked his arms around her, her back flush to his chest and groin, the red spill of her hair now between them, entangling them both.

She didn't speak. She didn't protest his being there. She didn't even protest his hold on her.

She seemed to breathe raggedly for a long time. He wondered if she was crying, if she had been hurt. If she had gotten much more than she had ever imagined—or really wanted.

He could wonder forever, he thought. If she was crying, she would never let him see the tears.

He closed his own eyes, wondering at the surge of pain that suddenly seized him. He'd slept with women, Seminole and white, since Naomi's death. But none of them innocent, and certainly none like Teela. He had slept with them because they had been available; he had slept with them casually. He barely remembered a name or a face, and he had not been expected to.

And he had never held any of them through the night. It was painful to do so now, but he could not let go. He tried to reason out his feelings for her, but there was no reasoning. It remained that he was obsessed. Foolishly so. There was nowhere to go from here.

He stared up at the ceiling and realized that something about her had changed. She hadn't actually moved; she had softened, the tension slipping from her body.

Ah, yes. She slept, he thought ruefully. He eased from her, studying her in the moonlight.

"You have cast us both into the flames of hell!" he charged her softly. She didn't stir. He touched her cheek and felt dampness there. He damned her, then damned himself.

But then he stretched close down beside her again. Slipped his arms around her. The future could not go gently for them.

It seemed imperative that he have the night to hold her.

*   *   *

Teela awoke to the soft sounds of knocking on her door.

She opened her eyes. James remained beside her, propped on an elbow, watching her. He had been awake for some time, she thought. And now, as the knocking continued, he remained dead still. Waiting. An ebony brow arched as he continued waiting, watching, a small smile just curving his lips.

"Oh!" Teela cried. She sat up, trying to draw the covers along with her. His body rested upon the sheet, and he smiled rather than free it. She thought for a moment that she had bedded down with a blue-eyed devil, and in that same moment her heart seemed to quicken. Being so suddenly awakened to the brilliant light of day was disturbing. She needed more darkness, more time. She might have dreamed her own behavior, it was so unbelievable. But of course she hadn't dreamed—hadn't dreamed him, his words, his touch. The thought of it made her tremble violently. Crimson flooded into her cheeks. She was deeply embarrassed because she knew very well that although he was by nature and design a demanding man who offered no quarter, she had wanted what had happened. Not consciously, perhaps. She could never have put all that happened last night into her conscious desires. But the temptation to touch had been there from the beginning. And seeing him now, handsome copper body whipcord lean and heavily muscled as he stretched upon the sheets, she could feel a certain shame but no remorse. She had wanted him. She hadn't begun to imagine what might be found in his arms; nothing so intimate had ever played within her mind.

The knocking sounded again.

"Please?" she whispered desperately.

Something flashed into his eyes. An understanding that caused her heart further dismay. She was not so horrified herself at what had happened, but she didn't want to be caught. Warren's unmarried daughter with a man. Not just a man. A half-breed. It was one thing to play. Another to be caught.

"'T's Jeeves with tea, Miss Warren," came a soft, clear voice. "Mrs. McKenzie is going riding this morning and thought you might like to join her, and so I apologize for waking you."

She leapt out of the bed, reaching for her gown, discovering it torn and ragged. She spun again to stare at James. He was still smiling, but he had risen. With a fluid motion he pulled on his breeches. He moved silently across the room and quietly opened one of the wardrobes in the room where her things had been hung by one of his brother's upstairs maids, and he found a cotton robe to toss to her and stepped just outside on the balcony.

She was tempted to lock the doors behind him, but Jeeves knocked softly again. "Miss Warren?"

"Yes, yes . . ."

She flew across the room and opened the door. The tea tray looked heavy. She flushed with a bit of guilt. "The table there, by the window, will be fine. Thank you very much. And tell Mrs. McKenzie that of course I would love to ride with her."

"I will indeed, Miss Warren." He started to leave the room but hesitated at the doorway.

"Mr. McKenzie," he said softly, his back still toward her so that Teela stared around him, wondering if Jarrett was outside in the hallway.

But Jarrett wasn't outside, and Jeeves wasn't addressing him but the younger McKenzie, who stood just outside the balcony doors. "I've taken the liberty of bringing two cups. And I've informed your brother and sister-in-law that you did not leave Cimmaron last night, but decided late to stay another night. Since you weren't in your room this morning, I thought perhaps you'd decided to join Miss Warren for a bit of breakfast, and again, I apologize for the intrusion, but the household is up and moving."

Jeeves stepped out of the room. Teela continued to stare at the door after it closed, astounded. She heard a soft noise behind her. Before Teela had spun around,

James had stepped back in from the balcony. Feeling pale and breathless, she kept her distance from him, staring at him from the opposite side of the table.

"My God!" she whispered.

He helped himself to a piece of toast, straddling one of the slim upholstered chairs at the table. "Jeeves is the very soul of discretion, Miss Warren. You need have no fears that he will tarnish your reputation."

"I don't—I don't care about my reputation."

"No?" he inquired tauntingly. The blue eyes on her now were cold, his voice sounded hard.

"You've no right to keep judging me!"

"Why the horror that you should be discovered?"

"Because it just—isn't done."

"I beg to differ. It's done frequently."

She moaned softly, then jumped when he seemed to rise with the swift, graceful leap of a panther to come around to her. She tried to back away; he caught her wrist. "Will you just sit, please?" he demanded. He pulled her forward, drew out the second chair. Both hands on her shoulders, he pressed her down into it. "Shall I pour you tea?"

"I can manage."

"Good. I'll have mine with cream and sugar. A luxury, of course. In my customary savage life I make do with black chicory coffee."

"Will you stop that?" she hissed, sitting forward, fingers trembling only slightly as she strained their tea. She poured out cream and sugar mechanically, and started to hand him his cup. She went dead still, more blood draining from her face.

James turned to see what had so dismayed her. She had seen the snow white bed sheet, dotted with lost innocence.

To Teela's surprise, he rose and stripped off the offending sheet, knotting it into a small bundle. He left it on his chair and walked to the door, opening it cautiously, then disappeared into the hallway. She stared after him, thinking they had both lost their minds.

But a moment later he was back, a clean folded sheet in his hands, which he cast upon the bed before taking his chair again and picking up his cup. He took a sip of his tea. "No bitterness intended, but I do most often make my bed beneath the pines. You will surely be more adept at remaking that bed than I."

She stared at him, amazed at the hot sting of tears that threatened to flood her eyes. She looked down at the table and nodded. He was such a strange man. Cold one minute, mocking her again, maybe even hating her still in his way. She seemed all the more the pampered southern belle this morning who longed for the excitement of the game with none of the repercussions. The dangerous thrill to be had ... without the payment.

"I'm sorry," he said huskily after a moment, startling her again. She stared up at him. His eyes were still very hard. "I shouldn't have followed you back in here. No, that's not what I mean. I shouldn't have ... taken you."

She was sure that a more graphic word had been on the tip of his tongue; he had pulled it back. She shook her head.

"If I could go back—"

She lifted her chin. "If I could go back, Mr. McKenzie, there is nothing I would have done differently," she said, her words cool and smooth. But her eyes fell at the last, and she found herself picking up her teacup for something to do with herself.

But he was up again, and surprisingly on one knee by the side of her chair, reaching for her hands. "Ah, Teela!" he said, smiling, but it seemed that his smile was rueful now, and that he didn't mean to taunt her in the least. "What would your young fiancé have to say to that?"

"I am not engaged."

"Major Warren intends that you should be."

"Major Warren has intended many things."

"John Harrington is a good man, a friend," James said, and he felt a pang of anguish harden his voice. Yes, Harrington was a good man, a friend. And he was white from his light hair to his pale toe, a military man, Warren's chosen for his daughter.

He felt uncomfortably as if he'd betrayed a friend.

"I liked Mr. Harrington," Teela said evenly, her eyes narrowing with smoldering anger. "He does indeed seem to be a fine man. We have both agreed on that point, I believe."

"You laughed easily enough when you danced with him," James said. Of course, she hadn't looked at Harrington the way that Harrington had looked at her.

"What has this to do with anything?" she demanded.

"Damn it, Teela!" he swore. He stood, pacing to the open balcony windows. "What do you think can happen, where do we go from here? I'm not Harrington. It's not as if you carried on a small indiscretion with a proper young man, a proper young white man. The damage cannot be easily reversed with a proper white wedding."

She stood up, staring at him. "I've not asked you for anything, and I don't want anything—other than that you let this alone!" she told him angrily.

"Mmm. In an evening your curiosity is satisfied, and it's quite fine that I run back into my swamp?"

"I don't give a damn where you go, but I really wish you'd vacate my room now since you are so intent on being so damned offensive!"

He left the window, coming her way with his panther strides. She started to back away. Too little, too late. His hands were on her shoulders. "Damn you, stop this game. Passions run too deep, blood runs too deep ..."

But then his voice trailed away. His fingers threaded into her hair, he pulled her close. She brought her hands against his chest to shove away, but she felt the copper fire of his naked chest, the thunder of his heart.

His lips crushed down upon hers, passionately, bruisingly. She wanted to hate him, to be furious. She wanted to fight him. She felt instead the simmering spiral of longing rising within her, hot fire that defied all other emotion. She felt the tempest of his lips and his touch, the heat of his mouth, his tongue, his steel-muscled frame.

She should have fought him. But she didn't. And he released her quite suddenly, his fingers still threaded in her hair as he mocked her.

"Oh, excuse me, you did want me out of your room, didn't you, Miss Warren? Well, then, I must behave like a civilized being, and remember that I am half white."

His hands fell from her. He bent low in a mocking, graceful bow.

Then he spun on bare feet and strode firmly toward the balcony doors. He paused briefly to snatch up the discarded sheet from the chair.

Then he disappeared into the bright glare of the morning sunlight.

Chapter 7

"I could swear I said good-bye to you last night," Jarrett told James, joining him in the library.

James, in a white shirt and dark breeches, sat behind his brother's desk, only the doeskin boots he wore a departure from the latest European fashion. His legs were extended atop the desk, ankles crossed. He leaned back, a brandy snifter in his hand, amber liquid swirling within it, a somber expression on his face.

Before he could reply, Jarrett told him hastily, "Not that I am not glad to see you here. Every time you ride out these days, my heart seems to jam in my throat again for fear I'll never see you again."

James smiled, lifting his glass to his brother. "Thank you for that sentiment, Jarrett. You are a damned good brother."

Jarrett took a seat on the edge of the desk. "Why the brooding?"

James shook his head, paused, seeking an answer in his own mind. "There are times when I feel that I can function, that I can play my part in all this, follow my conscience, and come out perhaps not only alive but sane. But I was just thinking now how easy my life is at this moment. I come here and eat good food. My revenue from the lands we share keeps me well clothed. But I have run with warrior bands when they have been forced to move their villages, their old, their women, and their children. I have watched children grow skeletal for lack of food, and I haven't the power to feed them all. Now I sit in your fine leather chair, and there is no threat to my back when I look out at the beauty of your lawn and the river. I have had the luxury of giving you my daughter. But then again, I cannot simply stay here. I cannot forget Mary, the ways I was taught as a boy."

"There is not a minute that I do not worry about Mary in all this," Jarrett said tensely.

"I know that you worry, that you are every bit as good a son to her as I am. But you can't change the fact that you are all white. I can't change the fact that I am not. I can't forget my friends, my people. When the white soldiers threaten the villages, I find myself in the fight. I've tried so damned hard never to deny anything that I am ... and as I have said, sometimes I function. I can carry on a conversation with any of your dinner guests, I can be the intriguing oddity at your socials. I can join the parleys with the American generals and agents, and I can, better than most, translate the truth of all the words and the falsehoods of the promises to both the whites and the Seminoles. But there are days when I feel that it will soon cost me my soul."

Jarrett stared at him a moment. "I think I need a brandy, too," he told his brother, and walked to the small table where the crystal decanter and snifters were kept. He poured himself a small portion, paused, doubled it. He leaned against his desk again, facing James. "It's got to end soon."

James shook his head. "No. Think on it, Jarrett, before it all began. You tried to warn the white brass what was coming. Hell, all the Indians were trading their otter pelts for gunpowder. Lots of warriors were planning this. You yourself said that the treaty of Moultrie Creek was an abomination, but it was supposed to have stood for another nine years. It wasn't to be. Too many Indian lands just looked too damn good. Wiley Thompson chained Osceola, Osceola murdered Thompson, and Dade and his men were massacred. Now we have General Thomas Sydney Jesup. He scares me the most. Jesup has come in with the determination to remove all red men from Tampa Bay to the Withlacoochee. He has realized what kind of a fight he has on his hand—that he must find the manpower to hold his forts and depots and still have enough soldiers left to pursue his enemy into the swampland. He's doing one hell of a job of it. He keeps his men in the field. I know his problems with the volunteers and militia who have poured in from the southern states. I've heard how some of them came with such bold courage and raw nerve and lost it when the owls hooted in the night and the wolves bayed at the moon. But Jesup is damned good at moving himself. He is a sharp, intelligent man. I understand he and Winfield Scott are now all but bitter enemies over his movement in the Creek War, but from the viewpoint of an enemy, Jesup's speed and preparedness far surpass Scott's!" He lifted his hands. "Many of the warriors signed the truce this spring—believing that they did so in Micanopy's name. It was then that *your* newspapers so viciously attacked the man because he stipulated that the Indians *and their allies* would be free in the west, the *allies* being the Negros who are free men here or who have become slaves of the Indians here. Too many white men were too damned determined to have their blacks returned to them."

"There are black bands among the Seminoles," Jarrett reminded him. "Many people were afraid that their former slaves would be attacking them in their towns and cities."

"I know," James said softly. "But can you blame the former slaves who have found freedom? What man will willingly give it up after he has tasted it?"

"No man," Jarrett said. "I have said these things to friends in politics and in the military. Jesup has told me, though, that the orders regarding escaped slaves come straight from Washington."

"Ah, yes. Secretary of War Poinsett! Under President Martin Van Buren. Protege of past president Andy Jackson. Well, now, he has never hidden any of his feelings for the red man, has he?"

"No one in Washington seems to have much choice

with the current mood of the country. There is a growing voice among the abolitionists, but I don't think it will grow loud enough to help matters down here anytime soon. It is a volatile issue on Capitol Hill."

"It has always been. Thomas Jefferson knew it was going to be a viper's nest when he drafted the Declaration of Independence."

Jarrett grimaced. "You did study your American history."

"I always did intend to survive. Know your enemy and all that."

"Well, I'm American, and I'm not your enemy. I'm your brother."

James lifted his glass again. "And a damned good one, as we've both agreed!"

"Here, here!" Jarrett said, lifting his snifter as well. "Are you going to stay awhile then? I'd be delighted."

"No, I can't stay. Perhaps just a little longer ... but I've got to get to those who've agreed to come into Fort Brooke and make sure they understand the provisions. I need to find Osceola—"

"Who surely will keep this war going on forever and ever," Jarrett interrupted.

James hesitated. He stared into his snifter and then looked at his brother. "I don't know. He's not well."

"Sick?"

James shrugged. "He has suffered from fever. He has not looked strong since." He hesitated again. "I even wonder if some of his power is not fading."

"Trust me, his name is spoken with dread among the white soldiers."

"Osceola is a strange man. Fascinating, charismatic— and as much feared by some of the Seminole chiefs as he is by the whites. Some honor him, some wish to honor more traditional leaders. I do admit that I admire him greatly, yet I feel that I know him better than others. I also feel he has been wrong at times. But I have to return to him, ride with him. And when he is anxious to parley, I am anxious to do the talking for him. I pray daily, to Mary's Supreme Spirit and our father's God, that this will end. But, Jarrett, it will not. No matter how far south or how deep into the swamp we are pushed, warriors will fight. Fight and run. Oh, many will agree to go west. Anything at all will look better than the life they are forced to lead here. Even barren desert out in no man's land with the Creeks! And hundreds will die. The blood that streams from us all is red, and will cover the landscape like rivers. I can see it, and I hate it, but I cannot stop it. I can only let it take me where it will."

"James, no man can do more than you have done, try harder than you have tried. You have been true to your heritage—to all of your heritage. We can only do the best we can in the windstorm that sweeps us. I hate to say this because I fear for you, because I wish I could make you safe from army guns, but you must do as you said before—follow the dictates of your conscience. Then, my brother, no matter what else happens, you will save your soul."

James rolled his glass in his hand, then looked at Jarrett, smiled and shrugged. "You're not just a damned good brother, Jarrett. You are a wise and damned good man."

"Thank you. I strive for perfection."

"Is Tara aware of that?" James teased.

"I'm trying to convince her."

"To Tara!" James lifted his glass. He shook his head again. "Damned fine brandy. The comfort of being here, though, does cause me shades of guilt. To feel so filled, so warmed, to sleep in such ... comfort," he said, strangling out the last a little.

Jarrett frowned at him.

"I'm growing too fond of the brandy." He set his snifter down and rose. He strode to the window. "Jesup is supposed to clear good land of all the red men. But there are a lot of bands out there in that region. Osceola is near, Philip, Alligator. Jesup will have to march his men hard through the jungle and swamp. But I believe

Jesup will do it. I hate it, Jarrett!" he said suddenly, passionately. "I hate knowing that it will go on and on and that I am tangled within it, straddling a precarious fence, having to fight when I don't want to fight, speaking out desperately and knowing half the time my words are barely heard. I hate repeating lies. I hate praying that it might end . . . I pray for a future. For Jennifer. For myself. For a different time, a different life."

"I know," Jarrett said quietly. "Dear God, I know."

"I wish . . ." James began again, but then he paused, the slightest smile curving his lip as he stared out the glass pane to the sweep of lawn beyond. "There's Tara, riding. Your wife is really quite exceptional, you know."

"Yes, I think so," Jarrett agreed.

James frowned to his brother. "She is careful how far she rides these days?" He had first met his sister-in-law when his own band had still lived close, and Tara had ridden a little too far and recklessly into the interior. Jarrett had determined that she'd learned her lesson that way, but James worried that she didn't realize thing had only grown worse since the beginning of the war.

"She is very careful. She never leaves the property," Jarrett assured him.

"She is riding with Warren's daughter," James murmured.

"Mmm," Jarrett said with some annoyance.

James sighed. "I have apologized to you for my rudeness to her at your party."

"But have you apologized to her?"

"I believe I have explained myself to her," James said, his voice just a little tense.

"If you're staying at all, perhaps we could join them. And you could be polite—just on my account."

"I will be polite," James said flatly.

"Promise?"

"Yes."

"Cross your heart?"

"Jarrett, we're grown men!"

"Cross your heart. Even Mary used to make you do that, remember?"

"I resent your doubting my word."

"Your word will always be good with me," Jarrett assured him. "Especially when you cross your heart," he added.

James sighed loudly to show his brother his impatience. "Cross my heart." He made the motion with a vast show of exaggeration. "Now, did you want to join your wife before she's old and gray?"

"Ready when you are," Jarrett said, sweeping an arm toward the door and bowing politely.

"Too much white blood in you," James said, shaking his head. But he grinned as he walked past his brother.

The McKenzie property was vast and beautiful, Teela quickly realized. She loved it. She loved the oaks that dripped with moss over the creeks, and she loved the manicured lawn and the slope to the river. Tara had shown her numerous trees and plants, otters scurrying into the water, colorful birds soaring from the surface of it into the incredible blue sky. They had ridden through grazing fields and farmlands. She had pointed the way to Robert Trent's, their nearest neighbor's home, and she had pointed out to Teela the trail that had led to her brother-in-law's village. "Of course, there is little there anymore. Some of the cabins still stand, but James has moved his people, those who did not die with the fever or in the conflict."

"He was close?"

"Very close."

"His wife . . . ?" Teela inquired, then gasped softly. "She wasn't killed by soldiers, was she, Tara?"

Tara shook her head, eyes narrowing at Teela. "The yellow fever took her. He has grieved for her terribly. Sometimes I think that is why he is able to ride so recklessly, going from the war chiefs to the white officers, heedless of bullets or arrows that might stop him. He loved her very deeply, and I don't think he has accepted her death. He had another daughter, a little older than Jennifer, as sweet and adorable and innocent as you could possibly imagine. She died with her mother. If Jennifer had not survived, I might wonder whether James would care about his own life at all. Of course, he and Jarrett are closer than most full brothers. Their bond is tight; life has made it so."

Teela stared down the overgrown trail, feeling her heart pound painfully again. James had deeply loved his wife; he mourned her still. Perhaps the whites had not killed her, but she had died in the midst of this awful war. She felt slightly faint, remembering both his touch and his angry words. What had she expected? He had come into her room because she had come into his. She had teased; he had taken. There was nowhere for them to go. He was sorry only that he had defiled a woman he considered to be a friend's fiancée. There was nothing there. No emotion other than passion, no force other than basic human need.

What *had* she expected, what had she wanted? He was a half-breed living most of his days in a savage swamp, inviting bullets. He was contemptuous of her, wanted nothing more from her than what he had taken.

Yes, all that was true, but . . .

Her cheeks burned and she turned quickly from Tara.

All that was true, but still the memories of the night were so vivid and so intimate. She knew somehow that she would never taste anything so sweet again, know anything quite so wild, reckless, and passionate again, ever. She would never touch any man with so great a fascination, so strong a longing.

Her obsession had not dimmed, she realized painfully. There was nowhere to go.

And yet she wanted something more.

He needed another good slap, she thought. No, a shower of them, aimed right at his arrogance and presumptions!

He would ride away today, she thought.

And her heart felt heavy again. He would ride away, and she would not forget.

"Speak of the devil," Tara murmured.

Teela brought her chestnut gelding around and looked across the field toward the outbuildings and stables of Cimarron. Jarrett and James McKenzie were racing toward them. James rode a spotted gray; Jarrett was atop a handsome bay. Both men rode bareback, their horses running neck and neck.

"They're racing," Tara said, shaking her head. "Boys will be boys."

Teela smiled. They might be racing, but neither brother seemed able to get the advantage. Nor did they seem to want to admit—to themselves or others—that they were racing.

They both slowed their horses as they approached the women.

"Well, Miss Warren!" Jarrett called cheerfully. "What do you think of Cimarron?"

"It's beautiful," she told him, trying to ignore James. Damn, if she just didn't feel the heat of that blue stare upon her. "Possibly the most beautiful plantation I have ever seen."

"Anywhere?"

"Anywhere. Although, of course, Blue Forest, my family home in Charleston, does rival it in some ways."

"Charleston is a beautiful place. We've family there," Jarrett said. "But since you find Cimarron so charming, we hope that you will truly consider it your home away from home, right, my love?" he added to Tara.

"Always," she said earnestly. "This can be a frightening land."

"Filled with savages, wild creatures!" James warned, and she turned to meet his challenging gaze, her chin high.

"I believe I have already encountered such creatures," she said smoothly. "But then," she added, smiling to Tara and Jarrett, "Blue Forest is near swamp and woodlands—not so wild as this, perhaps, but close. And I have discovered that most creatures become savage when they are threatened or afraid. When they discover that there is nothing to fear, they are much more pleasant."

"Some creatures," James informed her, "are never tamed."

Tara, completely innocent of the subtext of the conversation, warned her, "There is no such thing as a tame rattler, so don't be fooled if you hear one in the woods!"

"I will learn to take the gravest care," Teela promised her, casting a grim smile toward James.

"You've shown her the whole of the property?" Jarrett asked his wife.

"Well, all that is safe to travel," Tara told him.

"You two must be thirsty and famished. Perhaps we should return to the house and see what Jeeves can arrange."

"Well," Tara said, moving her mare closer to her husband's mount, "since I had hoped you might finish with business and join us, I asked Jeeves if he couldn't arrange a picnic out on the porch. The day is beautiful. It's still cool, but the sun is so warm against the breeze."

"A picnic sounds wonderful," Jarrett told her.

They smiled at each other. They were an exceedingly handsome couple, Teela thought, feeling a slight pang again, and then yearning to withdraw somehow. She felt as if she was intruding on something very intimate, though the two were not even touching.

She looked away.

And caught another McKenzie's eyes upon her. They still seemed to search for something. As if he judged her. Looked her up and down, sought some secret within her. She felt herself growing warm. She couldn't keep the thoughts of last night at bay. She wondered if a decent woman would have come so close and intimate with a husband of a decade. But it didn't matter. She remained a little lost, confused, and breathless every time she thought of it. She feared she had shared things with him she might never share again.

But he had been married. Deeply in love. He probably wouldn't even understand the way she felt.

She didn't exactly know herself.

"Let's head back for the house, shall we?" said Tara.

Tara rode ahead with Jarrett. Teela fell naturally behind with James. A short distance slowly lengthened between the pairs of riders.

"You're still here," Teela murmured after a few moments. "At Cimarron."

"Yes."

"Are you staying?"

"Not long. I must see to some things."

"Oh."

They rode in silence another moment, then James asked politely, "Are you all right?"

"Of course. Why would I not be?"

He stared at her, arching a brow. "Perhaps you hadn't realized, you'll never . . . be quite the same again."

She stared straight ahead. "I am quite fine. I am not completely naive, and I do not need your concern. And you needn't be so abrasive and rude—"

"I was not being rude—"

"Cruel, then."

"What?"

"Perhaps it's your attitude. Perhaps it's the way you phrase things, perhaps the way you mean them—"

"Oh, do excuse me! You don't want my concern? What do you want, my undying gratitude for allowing me to defile your tender, innocent white flesh?"

She stared at him furiously, then started to nudge her horse forward. He reached over from his own mount and caught her arm. "I'm sorry. Perhaps I am being rude. And in truth, I am sorry that I gave so little thought to my actions."

She still stared at him. He smiled ruefully and continued. "I'm afraid, though, that I am not sorry for my actions themselves."

She looked quickly down and flicked a strand of her horse's mane from one side of its neck to the other.

"I don't want you to be sorry for your actions," she said softly.

"It is never pleasant to hurt someone," he said.

"You didn't hurt me."

"You're lying."

"Only a little."

"You were hurt a little, or you're lying a little?"

"Both."

He laughed softly. She loved the sound of it. It was as alluring as his smooth copper flesh, his striking and handsome features, the hot feel of his taut-muscled body and the searing sweep of his blue gaze.

Don't love it so much! she warned herself. But he had been right when he had whispered in the darkness that the moth had come too close to the flame. Her wings were scorched. She would never just fly away.

Even if he rode out of her life.

"James—"

"Take care!" he warned softly. "We've come to the house."

Before them Tara and Jarrett had reined in their horses just before the rear porch of Cimarron. Two young boys, almost identical and of mixed blood, came to take the horses, waiting for Teela and James to dismount as well.

"Lemonade is already on the table," Tara said cheerfully. "Jeeves has determined to create an oasis of peace here, James, no matter what lies around us!"

"Jeeves is a marvelous person, dear sister, and you must never forget that," James told her, his voice overly grave, his lips twitching. He shrugged toward Teela. She tried not to blush, but cast her lashes downward anyway, despite all her best efforts.

"I'll run in and tell him we're ready for lunch," Tara said.

"Come, have a seat, Miss Warren," Jarrett said.

She was startled as she felt James's hand at the small of her back, escorting her up the steps to a small table that had been laid out with silver, linen napkins, glasses, and a frosty pitcher.

Jarrett pulled out her chair for her, eyeing his brother.

"It seems that you have graciously forgiven James his outrageous behavior at the party last night?" he said.

Teela started to reply, then paused, staring at James. Her turn to play the game.

"I have forgiven his absolutely outrageous behavior of last night, yes, Mr. McKenzie."

James slid into the chair beside her. "She has a most forgiving nature," he said politely. Then his eyes narrowed. "But I fear I cannot beg anyone's forgiveness for my feelings toward Warren."

Teela stiffened.

She could not beg anyone's forgiveness for her own feelings regarding the man.

But James McKenzie had no right to look at her so.

"James—" Jarrett began.

But Teela pretended not to hear him. She set her napkin on her lap as she softly interrupted with, "Are you guilty of all your father's sins, Mr. McKenzie?"

"My father had none," he replied simply.

"Every man has some."

"Not my father," James said softly. She realized that he revered the man, and she felt a sudden sympathy for him. If he had so adored his white father, as deeply as he cared for Jarrett now, this Indian war must truly be hell for him.

His fleeting moments of tenderness were addicting. But he was equally and coldly determined to keep a good distance from her, and she would not lose pride and soul along with all else.

She hadn't caused this wretched bloodshed. And she wouldn't be made to pay for it.

"What a coincidence!" she murmured. "My real father, my birth father, had no sins, either. Not a single one. He was a perfect man in every way."

Jarrett laughed softly. Even James allowed the flicker of a rueful grin to touch his lips.

"Lemonade?" he inquired.

"Please," she murmured.

"Are you staying another night?" Jarrett asked him.

He looked at Teela. "It's a tempting proposition. The comfort within this house is always seductive."

She reached for her glass. Her fingers were trembling so that it nearly slipped through them. Jarrett looked at her oddly. He started to speak.

But just then Tara hurried through the breezeway doors, smiling as she came toward them.

"Jeeves will be right out," she told them cheerfully. "James, after we eat, you must come see! Jennifer was playing with her baby cousin Ian while we rode, and they fell asleep together on the big bearskin rug in my room. They look like a pair of cherubs."

"Jen is really that good with the baby?" James asked his sister-in-law, smiling as he leaned back, looking up at her.

"She's wonderful. I told you that. I wasn't making it up." Tara reached across the table, squeezing his hand. Teela felt another little lurch in her heart. They were all so close. Some bond surrounded not only the brothers, not only man and wife, but all of them, the children as well. It was a family, she thought, and nothing got in the way of the love that was shared.

James McKenzie, white-Seminole that he was, would never understand her envy of that. She'd had her mother. She'd loved her, cared for her. That love had been returned. But with Lilly's illness and death, Teela had been on her own. She'd fought alone, she'd dreamed on her own. Other than Lilly's love, the rest had been bitterness, all of her life.

"Jennifer is truly a beautiful little girl," Teela heard herself saying aloud without thought. James stared at her instantly. She wondered if he doubted her words. If he was waiting for her to add, *a beautiful little girl for an Indian.*

"Is she like your wife?" she blundered on.

Thankfully, he decided not to take offense. "Yes,

quite a bit like Naomi," he said. His voice was low, not angry.

"But your daughter has your hair," Teela said.

"Our father's hair," Jarrett said.

"Our sinless father's hair," James added, and Teela was glad to see his rueful smile.

She grinned herself, then became aware that Tara was rising, staring out toward the river.

"Jarrett, someone is coming," she said.

Jarrett stood as well, frowning. A small sloop was indeed coming down the river. "It's a military ship," he murmured, looking at his brother.

James shrugged, and they all sat tensely, watching as the ship came into dockage.

"Were you expecting someone?" Tara asked her husband.

"Harrington . . . but not for a few days. And this ship appears to have come in from the west."

A gangplank was lowered from the vessel, and a man in full army-regulation uniform came striding immediately down it.

Teela gasped, jumping to her feet as well. She couldn't believe it. Dismay filled her in great, cold, rushing waves.

"Warren!" James grated out, rising beside her, all of his feelings of hatred and contempt naked in his voice.

Warren. Indeed.

Teela gritted her teeth, barely breathing, watching as her stepfather reached the dock, spoke to the men there, then came quickly across the lawn and to the porch of Cimarron.

James might be a savage, but he was right on one point.

There was no greater demon than her stepfather.

And here he was, destroying the beauty of the day. Destroying the small taste of intimate magic that was just beginning to be hers within this close-knit family.

She blinked, then closed her eyes tightly. Let it not be true! Let it be a horrid daydream. A nightmare in the light of day.

She opened her eyes. Of course, it was not a dream of any kind. Warren was real, a demon in the flesh.

Ready to drag her back down to his hell.

Chapter 8

In appearance Major Michael Warren was one of the most correct military officers James had ever seen. His uniform blue was precise, his collar perfect, his trousers impeccably creased. Only his slouch hat gave credence to the merciless sun in Florida, while the plume that flew from it was surely a minor concession to vanity. He was a man perhaps in his late forties, curly brown hair winged with gray, very serious dark eyes, nose dead straight, features well arranged and very hard. His lips were narrow, often all but disappearing into the sun bronze of his face. He might have been a handsome man; it was almost as if he had willed himself not to be.

"Mr. McKenzie!" Warren greeted them, his eyes upon Jarrett. He had met James on occasion. Bitter occasion for the most part, for though they'd not met in battle, they had come close several times. They had met once on opposite sides of an envoy's desk, and once in the midst of Alligator's camp when the Seminoles had kept their promise of truce with a far greater honor than Warren had ever offered himself. Warren was well aware that James was a McKenzie and Jarrett's half brother; he had frequently shaken his head at James's failure to use his heritage to become as white as he possibly could. That James's blood was tainted was a fact beyond a doubt; that James didn't use his father's name to save his skin was false and foolish pride and sheer stupidity on the half-breed's part.

Warren came up the steps, drawing off a leather glove, offering his hand. Jarrett hesitated just briefly before taking it. Warren nodded to Tara, murmuring, "Mrs. McKenzie, it's a delight to see you."

Tara murmured something. Jarrett said, "Major Warren, it was my understanding that John Harrington was coming to bring your daughter to you."

"I had not thought to be in the vicinity. As it is, I am pleased to thank you in person for your hospitality on her behalf."

"We're delighted to have her," Jarrett said.

Warren's eyes flicked over to his stepdaughter. James was startled by the simmering hatred that seemed to burn in the man's eyes.

Quite obviously it was returned. In fact, it was a most unnatural greeting. Neither father nor daughter had yet to speak to each other; they certainly did not rush forward to greet one another with a warm hug. They didn't even seem inclined to be polite for the sake of propriety.

"Running Bear," Warren addressed James at last. James felt Teela's eyes dart swiftly to him. He smiled. She hadn't heard his Seminole name as yet; perhaps it was a shock to her. Perhaps it was good for her to realize that he had a Seminole name, and that it was the one by which her stepfather chose to address him, as did many of the soldiers.

"Major," he said evenly, inclining his head just slightly.

"It's good to see you in such civilized surroundings," Warren said.

"It's good to be at my brother's house." James would not be baited.

"It would most probably be very good for your health, sir, were you to spend more time within it."

"Alas, Major, we all have our duty, and strive to do it," he replied.

Warren shrugged. "I trust your journey was safe enough," he said at last to Teela.

"I have come in one piece," she replied.

"Without your guards."

"You mustn't fault your daughter, sir, if we have misplaced a few army fellows. I hadn't known they were expected to accompany her," Jarrett interjected smoothly. "I am afraid I am guilty of having left the young men behind in Tampa."

"The danger of the Florida Territory is everywhere and unpredictable," Warren said. "Which makes a constant guard necessary."

"Not at my house," Jarrett replied. "Though, Major, you do speak the truth of the danger. In fact, it is curious that a man so busy with warfare himself, sir, should think to bring his daughter here." Jarrett said the words with a gentlemanly smile that somehow seemed to make the reproach still sound courteous and proper. But Warren did not give a damn what reproach other men might offer him.

"We are a military family, sir, and wives and daughters of military men have long awaited husbands and fathers right behind the front lines. And, Mr. McKenzie, as you and your fair wife may one day discover, daughters can be as dangerous as the swamp, often as treacherous. This one is safest near me, wherever that may be. I admit, though, at the time I commanded her here, I had thought to be based at Tampa. But General Jesup drives a hard campaign, and I am most frequently in the thick of the wilderness now. I have, however, bought property in Tallahassee. I've wretchedly little time to see it, though, since so many of the hostiles have reneged on the agreements made in March."

James was not going to be dragged into the argument the man seemed to want to take up with him.

"Tallahassee is a long way from here," he said politely.

"In times of trouble, certainly," Warren agreed. "It doesn't matter. It will be some time now before I manage to reach my property and provide a home there for Teela. But she is a strong lass, don't be fooled. Stronghearted and strong-willed. She'll do well enough with me wherever it is I need to travel."

"There are formidable warriors out there," James reminded him.

"I am a formidable man," Warren said determinedly.
"And a careful one."

Jeeves came out of the main house before anyone
could reply. He carried a large silver tray and walked
with a small black girl at his heels with a second serving
platter, hers piled with silver flatware rolled in linen napkins. "Major Warren," Tara said as Jeeves and the girl
prepared the table. "You must join us for a light
supper."

"I shall be delighted. In fact, Mr. McKenzie, as I am
expecting Harrington to return by tomorrow, I hope you
will allow my ship to remain at your dock until he
comes."

"You are welcome, sir, as long as you remember that
I will have no battles fought on my property, sir," Jarrett said.

"I don't imagine I've anyone here to battle, have I,
sir?" Warren asked James.

James extended an arm to indicate the forest that
stretched inland from his brother's property. "Sir, you
know there are bands this side of the Withlacoochee.
But no Seminole will come here to seek battle, of this I
am certain."

"So they do remain close!"

"My home is neutral ground," Jarrett said. "General
Jesup is aware of that."

"Is Osceola?"

"Indeed," James supplied firmly.

"Shall we all sit?" Tara suggested.

The five of them sat in the wrought iron chairs around
the porch table. James found himself between Teela and
Warren, while his brother was between Teela and Tara.
Tara was the perfect hostess, quickly pouring Warren
lemonade, determined to stop explosive conversation before it continued any further.

There was, of course, little to be said to Warren that
did not become explosive.

"It's a pity, sir, that you weren't just a day earlier," Tara said. "We could have shown you what delightful parties we manage to have here."

"Yes, it's a pity, I would have liked to have introduced Teela to young Harrington myself. I hope she realizes how fine a man he is."

"He is a very nice man," Teela said coolly.

There were baskets of fresh-baked rolls on the table, sliced ham in raisin gravy, early greens. Teela mechanically passed dishes as they came her way.

She took very small servings herself and barely touched her plate. She sat stiffly and pretended to move her food about. Warren had cost her her appetite, James thought, and he was started to find himself wishing he could do battle with the man not just because he was a murdering bastard who had decimated many of his people, but because he could not bear the man having such power over his stepdaughter.

"Well! I am glad to see that you've some sense in your head, daughter. I'd not have another disaster upon my hands as occurred in Charleston."

No one asked, but Warren was determined to continue.

"Imagine this, Mrs. McKenzie. A father does his best for his child, not even his own blood, as it happens. I arrange a brilliant marriage for the girl, and in the middle of the ceremony, she simply says no, she will not honor, cherish, or obey, and she turns and walks back down the aisle! I cannot tell you the cost and the embarrassment of that day!"

Teela didn't flinch but kept her eyes steadily upon him. "I had said from the beginning that I would not marry Jeremy Lantreau. No one listened, except the good Episcopal minister there at the end of the aisle. I'd no wish to cause anyone pain or humiliation."

Warren forgot himself for a moment to wag a fork at her threateningly. "Girls wed where they are told by those older and wiser, missy. They obey their fathers, and that is that. Still, what happened is in the past.

Young Harrington will make a better husband for you. He is not quite as financially stable on a personal level, but he comes from an excellent family and is an exceptional young officer, and will rise swiftly within the ranks. If there is anything remiss about the boy, it is his penchant for kindness, but it is a weakness he will overcome, fighting here in this swamp."

James lifted his lemonade glass and took a sip of the sweet-tart liquid. "If I'm not mistaken, Major, Harrington has served in Florida since the beginning of the present hostilities. Somewhat longer than you, sir."

"He is a fine young man!" Tara put in swiftly, offering James a frown and a pleading glance.

"Tell me, Major," Teela said, pointedly addressing the man by rank, "what does Mr. Harrington know of this?"

"We have discussed the marriage. I believe he is willing."

Teela was silent for a moment, staring at her plate. It was obvious she hoped to avoid trouble with Warren, but it was clearly impossible for her to do so.

"Sir!" she exploded suddenly. "I am not willing to marry a man I have met but once."

"You have just informed me that you find him a fine young fellow!" Warren said, irritated.

"Sir, perhaps it would be advantageous to us all if you were to allow me to meet your prospects before bartering me at the marriage market."

"My girl, perhaps it would be far better if we were to discuss your future when we are alone."

"Indeed," she replied coolly, her eyes lowering once again as she fought for control.

Warren stabbed his ham. "When you really get to know young Harrington, you will realize what all here see—that there is no finer choice to be had! McKenzie, tell the girl. You know Harrington well."

"Sir," Jarrett said, "we all agree that Harrington is exceptional."

"And you, sir," Warren continued, looking at James. "Harrington deals fairly with you on all occasions. You have brought men and women to him. You have seen his excellent handling of your brutal and pathetic situation!"

James paused, seething. Tara was still staring at him, hard, pleadingly.

"As my brother has said, we all agree young John Harrington is an exceptional man."

He felt Teela's eyes on him then, like green fire.

"You see, Teela. He is a great man, which only demonstrates your pigheaded obstinancy."

"Major, I will choose my own husband."

"Girl, that is nonsense."

"It was your suggestion, sir, that we not discuss this here and now."

But Warren didn't seem willing to quit, no matter how hostile their audience.

"Think on it, Teela. If you were to wed Harrington, you'd be awaiting *his* return from each battle rather than mine. Perhaps he would even be willing to have you wait out the war here at Cimarron, if Tara does not object, of course. He will be close enough." Warren turned to James again. "Because the Seminoles are out there. The very men who signed papers in March, who agreed to go west. They are out there, attacking whites, stealing cattle, creating havoc!"

James nearly bent his silver fork in half. He set it down, staring at Warren. "Major, there are points which have eluded you, so it seems. Perhaps you have been so busily engaged in the killing that you are not aware of certain sentiments. The truce was ridiculed by whites furious over the Negro situation. Therefore, on *your* side, it could not be kept. Now as there is no one single ruler among my people—"

"There was a fair election. Micanopy—"

"Aye, Micanopy is a solid hereditary chief, and he is respected by many. But you can hold all the fair elections you choose, and it will not negate the fact that each band is separate. Many times the chiefs or *micos* group together for a common good and defense, but you will never sign a truce with every band. Never. And there are many you will be fighting for a very long time."

"Treacherous liars, all."

"Michael Warren!" Teela gasped.

He wagged a finger at her. "You will obey me and speak when you are spoken to, young lady, or pay the price!" he threatened before turning back to James, his mouth open to speak again.

"Sir! We all seek not to have war at this table where you and I are guests," Teela said, stiffly polite.

Warren did not get a chance to respond as James cut in.

"If my people have learned treachery," James informed him with a low, level tone, "they have learned it from the whites who have stolen their land and way of life in every way imaginable. If they learn to commit atrocities, sir, they learn from damned good teachers. And, no man has behaved more heinously in warfare, Major, than you have yourself."

Warren stood up furiously, nearly taking the table-cloth with him.

"We should settle this here and now, Running Bear."

"Major Warren, not here!" Teela cried, leaping up. "Have you completely lost your senses?"

Warren nearly leapt at her, but Jarrett was on his feet as well, Tara soaring up beside him.

"Major Warren, we do not fight the war here!" Jarrett exclaimed angrily. "Hear me, heed me. *We do not fight the war on my property.* You are welcome here only so long as you remember that!"

"Then I'll have to take my daughter and leave this place with all haste, since you are determined to allow this man to hurl insults upon me."

"Don't be a fool, sir!" James hissed furiously, standing straight as a blade. He bowed with the grace of a diplomat. "I will vacate the premises, Major Warren, and pray that you'll not risk your daughter's life because of your disavowal of the simple truth."

James swung around and stalked into the house.

There was stunned silence for a moment as he departed. Not even Michael Warren seemed to have a quick response to James McKenzie's departure.

Then Jarrett broke the stillness. He threw his napkin down. "You will excuse me," he said coldly to Warren, leaving the table to follow his brother.

"Mr. McKenzie!" Warren roared after him. "There is a war on! You cannot straddle a fence here, don't you see it? You're a white man! White men, *and their wives,* fall prey to savages day in and day out. You will have to take a stance."

Jarrett paused, shoulders straight, his back to them all. He turned slowly and replied quietly, "Don't ask that of me, Major Warren. The savage Indian who has just left his place here is my brother, my blood, and if I am forced to make a choice ..." His voice trailed away. "He is my brother. My blood." He turned once again to follow James.

Teela started after Jarrett. A hand fell upon her shoulder, and she was wrenched back. "Where do you think you're going?"

"To apologize for your bad manners!" she told Warren furiously.

He slapped her across the face.

Tara still stood at the table, watching. She gasped with horror. "Major! I am appalled!"

"Madam, you've not spent your life raising an unruly and willful child. Sometimes a man has nothing but the power of his fist to put the fear of God back into such a wicked body."

Teela gritted her teeth against the tears that had rushed to her eyes at the stinging slap. She was less in pain from the blow than she was from the humiliation that Tara had witnessed her distress. Perhaps that was what suddenly gave her renewed fury and strength, and all-out recklessness.

She returned his blow, hard.

Warren caught her wrist, dragging her close. Tara was still close, ready to cry out for Teela's defense. Teela feared she had taken things too far. She didn't want Tara calling for the men to return and bring the war to this haven where peace had managed to reign so long.

She didn't protest his hold. She bowed her head and listened as he whispered to her, his voice hateful but so low only Teela could hear his softly enunciated threat. "Think, daughter! Remember the beating you took when you walked out of the church? Tonight I will make you realize that was a small slap, girl. Tonight, your screams can blend with the wretched cries of the birds and the howls of the wolves. You will learn to listen to me, obey me, and honor my opinions! Or else this war will come here. And the McKenzie brothers will go down, both of them, so help me, God, I swear it! And you, you—precious creature!—will be the cause of it."

"Let me go!" she cried, then hesitated. She had to control her fury and her hatred for the moment. "Please, sir, let me go." Not enough. But she knew him well. "Major, I will pray tonight for guidance from God that I may become obedient to your will."

"You will come with me now!"

"I need my things, sir."

She wrenched free from him, then made haste to enter the house before anything further could happen.

But she could hear Warren speaking stiffly to Tara as she made her escape. "Mrs. McKenzie, you will be so good as to make sure that my daughter knows I demand her presence on my ship. I'll allow her an hour to pack her belongings. Then she will come to me, or I will come for her. And I beg of you, Mrs. McKenzie, I don't know what kind of sweet spell she seems to have put upon you and your husband, but she is my stepdaughter, I am her legal guardian. The law is on my side, and even your hotheaded husband knows that he must turn her over to me. I thank you for your hospitality, truly. I thank you for the care of the girl."

Just inside the breezeway doors, Teela leaned against the wooden frame, listening to him, her heart thundering.

She pushed away, running into the parlor and then into the library. The downstairs seemed to be empty.

She rushed upstairs, running from room to room.

As Tara had said earlier, the children slept sweetly together. Jennifer lay curled protectively around her baby cousin, Ian. Teela turned and ran from the room, tearing into her own again, running to the balcony and into the room that was always kept ready at Cimarron for James.

She burst into the hallway, almost colliding with Tara. "Teela, if you're looking for James, he is gone," Tara said softly.

"So quickly—"

"So angrily. He couldn't have stayed. He would have strangled your father—"

"He's *not* my father!" Teela cried out, almost sobbing.

"I'm sorry, I'm sorry!" Tara said swiftly. "But James had to leave, you understand. Jarrett can order Michael Warren off his own property, but if James was to kill him here, there would be all hell to pay, you know."

"I hate him!" Teela cried vehemently.

"James?" Tara murmured, stunned.

"My stepfather!"

"Poor girl!" Tara said softly, and somehow, quite naturally, slipped her arms around Teela and they held tightly for a moment. "I am so very sorry. We can't refuse when he demands that you come to him, he is your legal guardian. Dear God! I am horrified by the way he treats you. I long to strangle him myself! But it is not illegal, and he is unfortunately within his rights . . ."

Teela was silent. She gritted her teeth hard, fighting the urge to burst into desperate sobs. She couldn't abide Warren anymore; she couldn't bear to go with him and watch his vicious warfare.

"You'll have to get your things together. And don't worry about James. He's fought this war and men like your father a very long time."

"I caused what happened, I'm afraid," Teela said miserably. "That he's gone is all my fault—"

"Nothing that happened here today was your fault. Nothing. Remember that," Tara said firmly, setting her away. "And we'll always be here for you if we can help you. I'll speak with Jarrett when he has had a chance to calm down—we all play a diplomat's game here as well—and see if he can convince Warren that you should remain with us. I know that it's terribly hard for you, but a show of humility often does help. Jarrett knows General Jesup well and has strong influence with him. I'm certain Jesup will have influence with Michael Warren. We will help you, honestly. We'll do everything that we can, but until then it would be best if you went to him obediently. Somehow we'll get you back."

"He's a monster!" Teela said miserably.

"So I've witnessed," Tara agreed. She lifted her hands helplessly, her beautiful blue eyes wide and sympathetic. "But we'll have to play his game. And best him at it. Just don't give up. We will find a way if you can be strong and endure."

Teela drew away from her. "I'll get some things together," she said quietly. "I don't want to cause your family distress, and God help me, I don't want battle coming here. I don't want your family involved, or paying the price for me in any way."

"Don't worry about us; we're all quite strong," Tara assured her. "Go ahead, then, ready your belongings. I'll find Jarrett and speak with him," Tara promised.

Teela returned to her room, closing the door behind her. She rushed across the room and found the small velvet purse she had travelled with, dumping it upon the bed to pluck up the money she had left and drop the paper and the coins into her skirt pocket. She wasn't sure what United States money might do for her here, but there was no sense in leaving it.

Tara would try to help her. She believed it with all her heart, and she loved Tara for it.

But no one could help her now. She had to help herself. She could not go with Michael Warren tonight. And she would not throw herself upon the mercy of the Mc-

Kenzies. She would make sure that they could not be involved; she would disappear.

She threw open the wardrobe and found her heavy cloak.

All the while she told herself that she was thinking like an insane woman.

She couldn't run away. Not here.

There was nowhere to go.

Unless ... Into the wilds beyond the house and lawn and fields of Cimarron, there was a deserted village. Tara had told her about it; it wasn't an endless ride. It existed down a long, overgrown trail, and she would find it.

Then what? she mocked herself.

Despite her hatred for Warren, he had kept her and Lilly in pampered, civilized comfort. She had grown up with a personal maid, but she had run the household and all the servants. She had worked hard to keep things in order. She knew how to make soap and candles, how to dye fabric, how to smoke meat and can vegetables. She could embroider beautifully, play the spinet, sing with a passable voice, and mend almost anything.

She was not equipped to kill her own food and cook it in a wilderness.

There were alligators out there.

Snakes. Rattlers in the hammocks, moccasins in the rivers.

And worst of all, there were Indians out there. Even Indians with names like Alligator and ...

Running Bear.

She closed her eyes for a moment, praying for courage. She had to get away from Warren. She could not go with him as she had been ordered. She thought that she would rather die.

She didn't dare dwell on this any longer. She couldn't stay with the McKenzies; she couldn't risk Warren's anger against them. She had to leave Cimarron and escape, and she didn't dare spend too much time dwelling on it. She would lose her nerve. And she really wasn't sure if a snakebite or even losing her scalp could be worse than what her stepfather intended for her.

She opened the hallway door cautiously as she threw her cape over her shoulders, grateful that though it might get fairly cool at night, she would not face the bitter cold of a frosty South Carolina spring night.

If the night air did turn chill, it would be the very least of her problems.

She hurried along the hall and to the stairs. She tiptoed silently down them, then paused in the breezeway hall, listening. Tara and Jarrett were in the library, talking in tones that rose higher and higher.

"He should be shot! I should have done it myself."

"Jarrett, Jarrett! You can't even think such things. I could not bear it if you were taken from me, no matter how much he might deserve it. We've got to try to talk to him. Jarrett, he slapped her. As if he hated her. Really hated her. She slapped him back and he nearly broke her wrist. She barely flinched when he threatened her with something then, but Jarrett, it's awful! We've got to get her from him somehow."

"How, Tara, how?"

"You've got to swallow your pride and your hatred for the poor girl's sake!"

"She should just marry Harrington and be safe with the man!" Jarrett said impatiently.

"Perhaps that would be best, and perhaps we can talk her into it. God knows, John was entirely infatuated with her. And if John wasn't so entirely infatuated, Robert Trent would gladly marry her and rescue her. But we can't accomplish any such solution tonight. We've got to find a way to reason with him and keep her somehow. Jarrett, he's vicious. He thinks God has given him the right to parent her in any way he sees fit. He'll beat her, I'm certain of it."

Teela heard a long, painful sigh come from Jarrett. "He's her guardian, I'm afraid he does have the right."

"There is no right!" Tara protested. "Jarrett, there is no right in such behavior, you know that—"

"For the love of God, Tara! Yes, I know that. All right. We've an hour. I can try to convince him, but we may well have half the army swarming into the house to wrest her away."

"Perhaps not all the men will obey him."

"Then the men will suffer for it."

"We will have to reason with him."

"Tara, my love, I swear to you, I will do my absolute best to reason. I will humble my pride, since you ask it. I will find a way to reason."

Teela felt tears sting her eyes; she was so grateful to them both. She didn't wait to hear any more. She didn't dare. The last thing she wanted to do was cause trouble for the two people who had been kinder to her than anyone in her life since Lilly had died. And what neither of them knew was that there was no way to reason with Michael Warren.

She fled past the library, slipping out the rear breeze-way doors and running to the stables. She found the beautiful little roan mare she had ridden that morning in the fourth stall. As quietly as she could, she found the mare's bridle and slipped it on her. She worked quickly, securing a blanket and saddle next. She was just tight-ening the girth when she had the uneasy sensation that she was being watched. She turned to the low wooden gate of the stall.

She was being watched. Jennifer had awakened, and stood there now watching her with her wide amber eyes.

"You're running away," Jennifer said sadly.

Teela brought a finger to her lips. "Please!" she whispered. "I am running away, I have no choice. My—my father is not a good man like yours. He will not let me stay here, and I am afraid to go with him. I don't know how to make you understand, but I must go." She smiled suddenly. "I will miss you very much. I loved being able to play with you and the baby."

"I will miss you, too. My father will miss you as well."

"Your father—your father is gone."

She nodded once again, too painfully aware for her young age. "Yes. Sometimes he must leave very quickly."

"This time it was my fault," Teela admitted to the little girl. "I'm sorry. Very sorry."

"It's all right. I love my father. And he will come back," Jennifer said with a child's complete confidence. She raised her hands suddenly, and Teela was surprised to see that she carried a fair-sized wooden canteen. "This is water. Follow the trail to your left all the time, and you will come to the old abandoned cabins. They are strong against the night wind, and the wolves don't like the human scent that still lingers there."

She opened the gate to the stall and offered up the canteen. Teela took it from her, and the little girl slipped her arms around her, hugging her. Teela hugged her tightly in return. "Thank you for the water. I wasn't even smart enough to realize how much I might need it. I'm very grateful to you."

"Well," Jennifer admitted with a smile, "there is water along the way. But there are snakes as well, and some creeks with alligators. The alligators will not bother you if you leave them be, but you mustn't disturb the snakes."

Teela nodded. "Thank you. I will be very careful, I promise."

She drew the mare from her stall and hugged Jennifer one last time. "I will come back, too, you know. To see you. When I can."

"I know you will," Jennifer agreed solemnly. "My father left because of you," she said. "Are you leaving because of my father?" she asked.

"I'm leaving because ... I'm leaving because I can't stay here, and because I can't go back. Do you understand that?"

Jennifer nodded after a moment. She drew away from Teela's hug, as if urging her to hurry. "I will tell them you went the other way. Toward Uncle Robert's," Jennifer said gravely.

"Thank you!" Teela said. She leapt up on the roan mare.

"Remember, always keep to the left. It is many hours' ride," Jennifer said.

"Thank you, and take care of yourself," Teela told her. She smiled. The little girl smiled bravely in return. Her eyes were troubled. She had seen too much, and nothing surprised her anymore, and she wasn't even six years old.

Teela flicked the reins and started out of the stables. She paused just a second, looking back at the house and praying that she wasn't being observed from there or from the military ship berthed at Jarrett McKenzie's dock.

She nudged her heels against the mare's flanks. The mare took flight.

Within minutes, Teela was leaving the house and stables, and then the lawn behind her.

She had reached the dense growth of trees and foliage where Jarrett's property ended.

And where the raw wilderness began.

She hesitated just briefly. Even the blue of the afternoon sky was darkened by the growth of pines. Her horse's hoofbeats were muffled by the soft needles that lay so heavily strewn beneath them. The green darkness seemed all but overwhelming.

Keep to the left, Jennifer had told her.

Keep to the left . . .

She closed her eyes, afraid of all that awaited her. A bird cried out in a sudden lonely screech, and Teela was nearly startled from her horse.

Snakes . . .

Alligators . . .

Indians . . .

She heard someone shouting from behind her, from somewhere on the McKenzie property.

She didn't dare wait to find out who was calling out, or why.

She squeezed her knees into the mare's sides. "Hie!" she cried softly to the animal.

The mare leapt forward, plunging them deeper along the trail.

And into the heart of the savage land.

Chapter 9

Tara burst back in on her husband, who sat at his desk, brooding over the situation. He looked up at her, startled by her wild appearance.

"She's gone!"

"What do you mean, she's gone?"

"Gone, not in her room, not with the baby, not upstairs, not downstairs!"

"She wouldn't have gone to the ship alone, I don't think," Jarrett said slowly. He shook his head. "No, she wouldn't hurry to his command, of that I am certain." He rose. "I'll search outside."

Tara nodded. "I'll try the outbuildings, the kitchen, smokehouse, stables . . ."

"Stables!" Jarrett said.

They both ran from the house, down the porch steps, along the trail that led to the outbuildings, and burst into the stables. Indeed, Heidi, the roan mare, was gone.

"She has taken her—" Tara said anxiously. Then she gasped, realizing that Jennifer was standing in the stall, her little back against the wood wall of it. "Jennifer, come here!"

Jennifer obediently came to her aunt, stretching out her small arms with a smile when Tara reached for her. Tara looked worriedly at Jarrett.

"Do you know where Teela has gone?" Tara asked.

"On Heidi," Jennifer offered.

Tara nodded, "Yes, yes, Heidi is gone. But what about Miss Warren? Sweetheart, it can be very dangerous for her here. She grew up in a big house in a big city, and

she has never really spent any time outside alone
before."

"Maybe she went to Uncle Robert's," Jennifer
offered.

"Did you point out the way to Robert's property?"
Jarrett asked Tara anxiously.

"Yes, yes, but I didn't think she'd try to ride that way
by herself!"

Jarrett knelt down by his niece. "Jennifer, is that the
way Miss Warren went? I need to know, because she
could be in danger."

Jennifer shook her head, looking down. "I don't
know. I stayed in the stable."

Jarrett groaned. "I should ride into the bush."

"You can't!" Tara said with alarm. "Teela's hour is
up. Warren will be here any second. Jarrett, he'll follow
you, and you might lead him to her."

"And if I don't go after her, the fool girl could wind
up dead!"

Tara stared stubbornly at her husband. "What is the
choice exactly? Let him catch her and half kill her, or
take a chance with a few hours? Once it's dark, you can
start searching."

Jarrett sighed deeply again. "Uncle Jarrett!" Jennifer
said softly.

He came to his feet, spinning around. The hour was
up, all right. Warren was back, standing at the broad
doors to the stables with two of his officers. Both big,
brawny men. Jarrett squared his shoulders, fighting the
fury that smoldered within him. If Warren thought to
threaten him, he had another damned thought coming!

"Where's my daughter, Mr. McKenzie?" Warren
demanded.

"Major Warren, with my whole heart I wish I knew.
It seems that she has borrowed one of our horses."

"You let her escape!" Warren exclaimed angrily.

"I had not known that she was my prisoner, sir!" Jarrett informed him indignantly.

"And, sir, I tell you, we are on the fringe of a veritable jungle! She risks an agonizing death!"

She had run from an agonizing life, Jarrett thought, but bit back the words before he could say them. Tara was right. He would have to fight his pride for the girl's sake. "It is our belief, Major Warren, that she has ridden toward a neighbor's property. We—"

"You will show my men the way, Mr. McKenzie, and I beg you, make haste. I will return to my ship and inform our minister that she is lost, and have him pray God to protect her person and her soul! You will inform me immediately if she is found. You will not need to mince words with me, I will know instantly of her fate!"

Jarrett longed to snap out a reply.

Tara squeezed his arm, and he swallowed his words again. "Major Warren, I will saddle my horse and arrange for mounts for your men. I understand your fear for your daughter, sir, and how painful this must be for you, and of course, I know that you tremble for her safety."

Shaking, he turned around, striding down the length of the stable to reach his horse's stall. Tara was calling for the young grooms to come saddle horses for Warren's men.

She had squeezed his arm, Jarrett thought, and managed to keep him at least halfway civil, but she couldn't seem to manage a single word for Warren herself.

But then as she slipped by the men to make her way indignantly back to the house, she sniffed and muttered, but loudly enough for all to hear, "It is a wretched thing indeed when a young woman must fear her father more than scalping!"

At the rear of the stables, Jarrett smiled.

And he took his damned time saddling his horse. He was only taking the men so far anyway. And he was only going to vaguely point out the way to Robert Trent's plantation and hope they were green enough to get lost.

Then he would wait for darkness to fall.

*   *   *

She was not afraid. The green darkness seemed all around her; she couldn't tell most of the time what was trail and what wasn't. Stay to the left! She could go in complete circles without even realizing it. Oh, it was so frustrating!

No, she was not afraid . . .

She was terrified.

There was silence in the forest. A silence so great it seemed that all the world had stopped. Then the hoot of an owl would shatter the stillness and scare her out of her wits.

She rode by a stream, and the silence seemed to bear down upon her again. Then she heard a splashing noise and turned swiftly and nearly cried out herself, seeing the beady black eyes of a 'gator just protruding above the water as the creature seemed to glide sleekly through it. She nudged her horse forward, terrified that the thing meant to swim after her.

She panicked the roan.

They went flying helter-skelter down the trail, Teela just keeping her seat and praying that she was still bearing to her left.

She had been riding for hours.

Darkness was coming.

It came beautifully. First with radiant colors, crimsons that splashed through the trees and over the water. Shimmering gold, striking orange. The colors seemed to fall upon the long-legged, elegant birds that stalked through the streams and swamp. Egrets were shaded in pink and yellow, cranes seemed to glisten in gold. The vivid colors faded to pastels, and the pastels then ebbed away and shadows deepened.

She had stopped to watch the sun fall upon the water. Now she shivered fiercely, silently calling herself a fool. This was madness. She hadn't the least idea of what she was doing.

A wolf howled. The sound seemed to shoot straight along her spine. She shivered again and forced herself to continue onward.

Soon she was thanking God for the moonlight that rose above her. If not for that moonlight, she would be blind. Each time the moon slipped behind a cloud, the darkness was all but complete. She had to draw in on her reins then, sit tight and shiver, and wait for the light.

It grew worse. Oh, so much worse! When she sat, she could hear rustling. Tree branches moving. There were creatures near her, creatures of the night. Wolves, bats, perhaps.

Indians.

It grew to where she could not stand the sound of the slightest rustle. She talked to herself aloud. She sang. But she had to listen.

She welcomed the baying of the wolf.

She knew what it was.

But the rustling . . .

She didn't know what time it was. She had been riding for endless hours. Her stomach growled: she was half asleep and still terrified as she rode when she heard a rustle again.

Right behind her.

She reined in. Wide awake now, listening with such an intense effort that it was painful.

Nothing.

She nudged the roan. Moved onward.

And again . . .

There came a rustling.

She drew in on the reins. The roan pranced, letting out a whicker of unease. But once again Teela could hear nothing from behind her. "Come on, girl, now, come on," Teela said encouragingly to the horse—and to herself. "Those cabins must be up ahead somewhere very close. We've got to reach them."

She gave the roan a little kick. They started off at a trot, but Teela slowed to a walk. She could scarcely distinguish the trail before her.

She ducked beneath a branch. A scream rose in her throat as the branch moved.

The branch was a snake.

She didn't know what kind of snake, perhaps a harmless one. She hadn't heard a rattle, and she was on dry ground now, riding away from the river, so it shouldn't be a cottonmouth.

It didn't matter! If the creature had landed on her, she would have screamed and screamed. She would have become hysterical. She would have galloped into the darkness, galloped even into death ...

Thank God the snake hadn't fallen on her, but the rustling was sounding behind her again. Her heart leapt to her throat. She wasn't imagining it; it was real. She was being followed. Stalked.

"Hurry, girl, oh, hurry!"

She nudged the mare again, this time heedless of the darkness ahead or any threat that might await her there. She was being followed. What she had done had been insane. There were wild bands of Indians out here, Indians who hated Warren, Indians who would gladly take the scalp of a young white woman with long red hair.

The thrashing behind her grew louder. Boldly louder. There was a horse behind her!

She turned back.

In the darkness she could see only a bare-chested horseman. Dark-haired, intently riding down hard upon her. She screamed out loud; it didn't seem to matter. She slammed her heels against the mare's sides, ready to plummet into whatever hell awaited her rather than lose her scalp.

The hoofbeats caught up with her. She leaned low against the roan's neck, but it did her no good. Strong copper arms reached for her, wrenching her from the roan's back. She tumbled to the ground, the powerful body of a man atop her. She inhaled to scream, but gasped instead as her name was snapped out: "Teela!"

She blinked against the sudden spill of moonlight that dispelled the shadows on the face above hers.

"James!" she cried.

"What the hell are you doing out here alone?"

"Why were you stalking me?" she asked instead of replying.

"Are you alone?"

"Of course I'm alone. And you nearly scared me to death. My God . . ." She slammed both her fists furiously against his bare chest again and again. Until he caught her arms, wrenched them down. "Stop it!"

"You bastard! You could have let me know it was you—"

"I had to know that you were alone," he insisted angrily.

"But—"

"Even now," he snapped, "Warren could be following you. What are you doing out here, fool woman? Do you know the dangers of this place?"

"Yes!" she snapped.

"Then?"

"Will you please get up?" she asked coldly.

He did so, offering her a hand but dragging rather than helping her up. He still seemed exceptionally angry and tense. He caught her arm and propelled her forward.

"What—"

"The cabins are ahead."

"We can ride—"

"We could have ridden, yes. But the horses have gone on ahead of us," he informed her dryly.

She walked stiffly before him, aware of his heat so close behind her. It seemed to Teela that they came upon foliage so heavy that there couldn't possibly be anything ahead of them but brush. Then James went before her, shoving branches, leading the way.

She cringed, slipping through the leaves and branches, wondering what crawled upon them. She was glad of the darkness so he couldn't see how frightened she was.

At last the foliage cleared, and they came into a copse where there were several strongly built cabins hewn out of logs. Teela paused, and James went before her. She followed. He entered one of the structures, and she hesitated, but a moment later, light came from the cabin, and she followed him inside.

In a hearth against the far wall he had built a small fire. It cast a fine glow of warming light against the darkness. She walked toward it slowly, searching the cabin.

There were still signs of life here, though the village itself seemed a ghost town. There were rolled bundles of cloth, an area by the fire where there were a number of utensils, wooden spoons and bowls, a cast iron skillet, a coffee pot, and steel tongs. The cabin seemed sparse, only a few blankets covering the plain floors, but tonight it seemed the most welcoming place on earth.

Much more welcoming than the man before her.

He stood straight, shirtless, wearing only boots and breeches, his arms crossed over his chest. He glistened copper in the fire's glow, muscles rippling with each breath, chin set and hard, eyes like blue steel.

"What are you doing out here?"

"Well, I promise you, I didn't come to find you!" she assured him.

"So what are you doing here?"

She sighed. "What difference does it make?"

"An incredible difference. If you've led your father out here—"

"Stepfather!" she snapped. "Stepfather, stepfather, stepfather!"

He stiffened harder, staring at her. "If you have led him out here—"

"Led him out here? I am trying to escape him!" she cried.

Her voice seemed to linger on the air. He didn't move, nor did she.

Then slowly he exhaled. "You just came riding here by yourself in the dead of night?"

"It wasn't the dead of night when I left."

"You rode on a trail, having no idea of where it would lead?"

"I had some idea," she said uneasily. He stared at her and she shrugged. "When we were riding this morning,

Tara told me that there were cabins out here, that you had lived here. Once. Before . . ." Her voice trailed away. She swallowed miserably. She started over. "I didn't know that I'd find you out here. I just hoped for a place to . . . wait awhile."

He still stared at her, then shook his head wearily. "No one knows you came?"

She shook her head fiercely. "No! Except—"

"Except?" he demanded.

"Your . . . daughter," Teela said. "Jennifer brought me water."

"My six-year-old has more sense than you do. And she would certainly have more chance of survival alone."

"I was doing fine until you attacked me."

"I didn't attack you."

"Well, I was on my horse. And then I wasn't. My greatest danger then was dying from fear. I was on the ground; you were on top of me. Close enough to an attack, I'd say."

"I had to know that you were alone."

She was silent a moment, her own anger suddenly beginning to boil. "How dare you! How dare you behave as if I would willingly bring him after you!"

He shrugged. "I don't give a damn if he comes after me. I think I would like him to!" he added in a strange whisper. "But I don't want him out here. My people— survivors and mediators—come here to use these cabins, seeking shelter from the wilderness, from the night. From the cold that sometimes comes. I don't want them burned down. I don't want the white army finding this place."

"But your people have fled."

"I don't want the village burned," he repeated.

"I came to escape, I swear it. I did not come to cause any trouble, to you or this place."

"You *are* trouble," he said irritably.

She fell silent, then swung around, heading for the cabin door. "Fine. Then I will leave."

"Get back here!"

She kept going. A foolishly defiant gesture because in seconds he'd taken a firm, biting hold of her arm and swung her back around. "Now what are you doing?"

"Trying not to be trouble, to leave you in peace," she said angrily.

"It's too late for that," he said. He prodded her toward the fire. "Sit down, warm your hands. They are freezing."

She hadn't much choice. She didn't even really get to sit; his little push sent her down to her knees, but the fire was warm, and she did stretch out her hands, shivering. The warmth was wonderful.

He came down beside her, pressing a silver flask into her hands. She stared at him. "Brandy. I imagine you need it."

She did. She swallowed some down, winced, and swallowed another sip before handing the flask back to him. He stared at her a long moment, then shook his head. "Why? Why would you risk your life, riding into hammock and swampland you know nothing about?"

She stared into the crackling flames.

"I didn't lie to your fa—to Warren today. There are bands of warriors out here. Off Jarrett's property you could be in very serious danger. It's probably well known by now that Warren has a daughter. I cannot tell you how fiercely he is hated."

"And I cannot tell you how fiercely I hate him myself!" she cried softly.

It seemed an eternity that he still stared at her; then he suddenly reached out for her. She stiffened, then slowly eased back into his arms when she saw that the anger had died out of his eyes. She rested against his chest, and they both stared into the flames.

"Did you really walk out of your own wedding right at the altar?" he asked with a trace of amusement.

"I didn't do it to hurt anyone."

"You are a defiant little creature," he mused. "But that casts you into even greater danger here."

"Why?"

"Because there is a war on, a horrible war. You should go home, go back to Charleston."

"I didn't ask to come here; I was *brought* here."

James shook his head, his chin brushing her hair so that she felt the motion rather than seeing it. "Jarrett will have friends with influence over Warren; you've got to go home, get out of here. You don't belong here; you're not a part of this."

He caught her shoulders, setting her from him so that he could meet her eyes. His own blue had narrowed and all but darkened to black as he stared at her intently. "Marry Harrington," he told her. "Let him send you home."

She jerked from his hold. "You are beginning to sound just like Michael Warren!" she accused him. She stood up and paced away from the fire.

She looked around the walls. A deerskin lined one of them, with drawings of a hunt upon it. There were other small touches: calico curtains decorated a small window.

She turned again to watch him and realized they were thinking the same thing. This had been his family home. He had lived here with his wife. She was invading a sanctuary.

He looked away from her, throwing a stick upon the fire. "Jarrett will be here for you by morning," he said.

"But—"

"There are only two directions in which you might have ridden. One would take you to Robert's house. The other would bring you into the woods and swamp. My brother will send the soldiers to Robert's. Then he will slip out by night and come here himself."

"Then," she said resignedly, "I will either ride back with him. Or—ride deeper into the swamp."

He stood up, angry and impatient again. "You are not going to risk losing your scalp—not to mention your life, you little fool!" He strode across the room, picking up one of the bundles and releasing the tie. It was a sleeping pallet, and he spread it out by the blaze, then brought another near it along with two red plaid blankets. "Not exactly my brother's fine house, Miss Warren, but I suppose it'll do for the evening."

She hesitated, but she was exhausted. And she didn't have much choice.

She walked to one of the pallets and sat stiffly, amazed at how comfortable it was. She stretched out, staring belligerently up at him.

He stood over her, looking down at her. Suddenly, savagely, he spat out two words:

"Damn you!"

And a second later, he was down beside her, on his knees, his hands upon her shoulders, drawing her up to him. She felt his mouth, searing, invading, harsh, so demanding. And then, so suddenly, so seductive. Tongue teasing, lips molding to hers ... She brought her fingers tentatively to his hair, stroked them through it, drew him closer and closer. Upon her knees she pressed to the length of him, feeling the naked fire of his chest through the cotton of her riding habit. One hand cradled her head, the other moved up and down along her spine, holding her closer, crushing her against him, then slipped lower to her buttocks, lifted and rocked her against him.

He lowered her to the floor. One by one he eased open the buttons of her jacket and then her blouse, parting them both. He found the string of her corset and pulled it, and her naked breasts sprang forth. He lay his face against the valley of her breasts, feeling the warmth of her with his cheek, listening to the pummeling of her heart and the catch of her breath.

He came to his knees again, determinedly pulling her clothing from her, piece by piece.

And when it was shed, corset here, boots there, stockings dangerously near the fire, he paused suddenly, staring at her almost harshly in the fire's glow. He fell on her, capturing her mouth, spreading her legs, loosening his breeches to sweep and thrust into her with a raw passion that nearly brought her to a precipice instantly. She closed her eyes against the golden glow of the reaching flames, and felt the man, the fire, and the earth be-

neath her. It was all poignantly real, all bathed in orange
and gold. It all shimmered together and became part of
the drive, part of the desire. She was lifted above herself
in the orange mist, striving for sweet surcease. It burst
upon her, shimmering in color and warmth. She shuddered with it, trembled, fell . . . and became aware again
of the earth, the flames, the cool night air. The still hot,
slick flesh of the copper man who spoke perfect English,
his searing blue eyes and rock-hard body. She turned
from him, curling away, angry and heartsick, and wondering why she fell so easily each time to his seduction
when he would but mock them both later.

But his arm came around her. He ignored the fact
that she stiffened. He pulled her close, secure against
him once again. He stared at the flames over the length
of her body.

"Damn you!" he said softly to her. Tenderly.

She shook her head, fighting tears. "Damn you!" she
told him.

"Don't you see, you've got to go back. I'm telling you
now, this war will grow worse. Ever more violent. I'm
telling you to run, Teela, while you can." His voice hardened. "Go back, go to Harrington. Don't you see?" he
said harshly. "There's no way I can protect you. I cannot
take you from Warren. I am constantly on the run, I
shift from place to place. I have no world for you. This
is not your life!"

"Life is anything away from him!" Teela whispered.

His lips touched her back, so achingly tender. Teela
felt the threat of tears again, his touch was so gentle.

"Jarrett can do something. He can go to the governor,
he can go to Jesup. Hell, Jarrett even served with Jackson once, and Jackson and Van Buren are still close. A
military man like Warren would not defy the president!
I want you out of here."

She rolled within his arms.

"I want to be free from him, but—"

"You've got to leave!"

"I'm not afraid—"

"Then you're a fool."

"James—"

"Running Bear, remember?"

"Will a different name make you a different man?"

"Sometimes, yes," he said very softly. But he smiled suddenly, looking into her eyes. "I am putting you firmly out of my life, and out of danger, Miss Warren, I swear it. But I am glad that you came into it."

His mouth touched hers. Once again, passion slaked, his touch was almost unbearably light, teasing. Still, Teela determinedly twisted her lips from his and forced her palms between them.

"You don't want me as any part of your life. You want me away and out of it!" she cried.

"Tomorrow, as soon as I can make it so," he agreed. "But that leaves you mine tonight, and when you have run back to your elegant bed in Charleston, I want you to remember, upon occasion, what sweet southern comfort could be found upon the dirt floor of a savage's cabin in the woods. In that savage's arms . . ."

"Damn you!" Teela protested again, trying to escape his hold.

But the savage's arms were very strong indeed, and the tenderness in his lips upon her flesh was even more powerful. The tension eased from her as the fire burned and blazed high again, casting a spectacular glow upon his nakedness, and her own.

She could damn him all she wanted.

But she could not refuse him.

Chapter 10

Tara waited with an outward show of complete calm as she watched Michael Warren stride toward her porch in the midnight darkness. She stood serenely at the rail, reminding herself that Robert Trent had followed the soldiers back to her home, and that she was not alone. Of course, Warren wouldn't dare cause trouble for her; no matter what his sympathies, Jarrett was one of the most respected men in the territory. But still, it was good to know that their very good friend stood behind her along with Rutger, the tall, husky German fellow who managed their farmland, and Jeeves, who, despite his elegant deportment and distinguished accent, was as tall and brawny and threatening as any of his ebony Zulu warrior cousins. With the knowledge that the three men hovered just behind her in the house, she need have no fear of Michael Warren.

"All right, Mrs. McKenzie," Warren said simply, not coming up the porch steps. "Where is my daughter?"

"Sir, I am sorry to say that I do not know."

"Do you want to know what I think?"

"Do share your thoughts with me!" she murmured, her tone laced with a sarcasm that seemed lost on Warren.

"I think that renegade red brother-in-law of yours has kidnapped my girl."

"Don't be absurd, Major. James would never kidnap anyone."

"This is a war, Mrs. McKenzie. And James McKenzie is a red man. A Seminole. Runaway, renegade."

Tara gripped the porch rail firmly, praying for patience. "Perhaps your daughter was a bit distressed, Major, and so ran rather recklessly into the forest. Jarrett has gone to find her, and he will do so, I assure you."

"Before or after the savages have gotten their hands on her, Mrs. McKenzie? Before or after she's been bitten by a rattler, drowned, mauled, ripped and consumed by a 'gator?"

"Major McKenzie, as I'm sure you're aware, alligators prefer smaller prey than a full-grown woman. Teela is an intelligent—"

Warren interrupted her with a loud sniff. For a moment Tara was startled into staring at him as he shook his head with weary impatience. "Mrs. McKenzie, the Good Book says that a daughter is to honor her father. It is God's decree! From the moment I married her mother, I was a father to that girl, and from that first moment, she needed discipline. I used my position to see that she was to be wed to an affluent man who could provide for her and keep a firm hand upon her lawless, reckless, godless soul, and for my pains she humiliated me. Now she has evaded my righteous wrath, and I do not know if she has done so on her own, or with the help of that half-breed."

"Major," Tara said softly, her eyes narrowed on Warren, "may I suggest that you do not refer to James McKenzie as 'that half-breed' while you stand on my husband's property?"

Warren leveled an arm at her, his finger wagging. "If he has taken her, there'll be the devil to pay!"

"You are sadly mistaken if you think that James would abduct anyone. That he would *want* to abduct anyone. Half the women in this territory, married or otherwise, would be delighted to enjoy his company, and they wouldn't care, sir, if it were here, or in the very depths of the swamp. So I beg you, take your suspicions elsewhere before you create a battle within this war that turns upon you more viciously than any band of Indians ever would!"

"I want my daughter by the morning, Mrs. McKenzie," Warren said firmly. "And that's final."

He spun around, striding away toward his ship.

Despite herself, Tara was shaking.

Why in God's name had Teela run so recklessly into the interior? Tara paused, angry for a moment that Teela's behavior was going to hurt James. He had a tremendous inner strength; it allowed him to walk with his head high and steady between two warring peoples. He still managed to do so, even with the hostility increasing daily. But since his wife and daughter had died, he'd had his share of anguish. He didn't need it increased with a man like Warren on his heels.

She let out a shaky breath, her anger replaced with a twinge of guilt. Teela couldn't have known that her stepfather would instantly cry abduction if she ran away. She had just fled his tyranny, pure and simple. And James could be very far away by now.

Tara turned to walk back in the house and paused again, smiling. She was ringed there by her three protectors; Rutger, Robert, and Jeeves.

"You handled him with good McKenzie courage!" Robert applauded her.

"I was quite proud, ma'am," Jeeves agreed.

Rutger swept off his cap to give her a bow.

"I wish I felt I'd done something!" Tara said, shaking her head. "What if something horrible does befall Teela? What if Jarrett doesn't find her? Warren will be lobbing cannon fire on this house by tomorrow night!"

"Jarrett knows the land out there like the rooms in this fine home, Mrs. McKenzie," Rutger assured her. "He'll find the girl."

"Oh, I think that Master James will have found her long ago, Mrs. McKenzie," Jeeves said knowingly. "In fact, were I a gambling man, I'd bet on it."

Tara frowned at him, wondering at his certainty.

"Tara, we're not without political pull here," Robert

Trent reminded her, a handsome smile curving his lips. "If Warren becomes too difficult, we can do more than fight him. We can put some military pressure on him from above that will curl his toes. And speaking of which ..." Something caught his eye and he stepped past her. "Rider coming, from the direction of my house!" he said with surprise.

"Oh, God, now who?" Tara murmured.

"More military," Jeeves murmured.

They all stared at the rider coming closer in the night.

"Ah, the military!" Robert said, and laughed. "The *good* military. What a fine scenario, eh, Tara? We've got good military and evil military, good Indians and savage killers. Oh, God, but what a wretched war! And still, Mrs. McKenzie, this fine fellow riding so hard upon us may just be the trick to save us all from a very nasty situation, eh?"

He grinned at her, stepped past her, and hurried from the porch to greet the man who raced so hard to reach them.

Michael Warren strode aboard his ship, saluting to naval captain Julian Weatherby. Weatherby saluted sharply in return.

There were forty-two men aboard the sloop *U.S.S. Lysandra,* not counting Warren and Weatherby: twenty-five of them the remnants of two companies of regular infantry while the remaining seventeen were navy. Most of the navy ships on patrol around the territory of Florida were stripped down to skeletal crews in order to provide General Jesup with the manpower needed to solve the Indian problem. Michael Warren and these men were to meet up with several other companies of regulars and Florida militia to join in the pincer campaign Jesup was determined must come about before the year's end. Warren knew, however, that he had time on his side. As usual, coordinating movement in the territory was frustratingly difficult. Government policies seemed to change daily, from the official attitude toward the Seminoles to the pay and rations for the soldiers.

They'd made a serious mistake in Washington when they'd tried to exchange the soldiers' whiskey ration for sugar and wheat. Enlistments had dropped off sharply, and complaints within the ranks rose bitterly.

Nothing would happen too quickly toward the grand movement Jesup was planning. Skirmishes would continue, especially since Osceola and Alligator and Wildcat were in the near vicinity. But Jesup's grand scheme would take time. And Michael Warren could take some time with it.

Captain Weatherby eyed Warren suspiciously after his proper salute. Weatherby didn't like Warren, and Warren knew it. Weatherby was a Southern salt, not Floridian but right out of the Louisiana bayou. He fit into the swamp waters as if he were a 'gator himself. And he'd had too much time to meet up with the Indians. He liked a few of them. He was too quick to sympathize with their plight.

Warren didn't have that problem himself. He'd seen the face of his enemy, and his enemy was a heathen, an enemy of God.

"Did they find your daughter, Major Warren?" Weatherby asked politely. He knew the answer. Warren wanted to smack that phony worried expression off his face.

"They're not going to find her too quickly," he growled. "It's as clear as day that half-savage red man has taken off with her."

Weatherby arched a brow. He shook his head. "I've known James McKenzie a good while, Major. Doesn't seem likely to me he'd be forcing anyone anywhere. The man's still grieving for his wife, for one."

"He can kidnap and grieve at the same time, can't he?"

Warren was the superior officer here. But Weatherby was a stubborn man.

"Can't see it, Major."

"Don't you go feeling sorry for the redskins, Captain. You'll find a knife in your throat for your efforts."

"I just know James McKenzie. He's an honorable man."

"Honorable man or no, Captain, if I don't have my daughter back by morning, he'll be one dead Indian."

"Half Indian," Weatherby corrected.

"You will follow orders, Captain!" Warren reminded him.

"Yes, sir, I'll follow orders, Major," Weatherby said.

He watched Warren head for his cabin. He spat on the deck. "In a pig's eye!" he retorted after him. He wasn't going to get himself and the navy boys killed because Warren wanted to take after James McKenzie into the swamp. McKenzie didn't want to kill anybody. But if he was pursued, he damned well might join up with old Philip's son, Wildcat, or Alligator, or worse. He might just join up with Osceola, and then there'd be hell to pay, all right.

Weatherby was a military man. He didn't mind going to war, even when he'd parleyed with his enemies and made a friend or two among them. But he'd be damned if he'd outright commit suicide just because Michael Warren was one of God's great asses!

He started to head off for a good night's sleep himself, but he paused, listening to Warren talking to his men on deck.

"When you see a little cockroach, boys, you don't pause. You don't think, 'why, that's just a *baby* cockroach.' No, boys, no, you don't! You take a look at the ugly little thing, and you know it's going to grow up to be a big hideous old cockroach—just bigger, faster, and harder to kill.

"Or think on a young rattler! Not much venom when it's small. But it'll grow up to be deadly. Well, Indians, especially Seminoles, are just the same. We chase them into swamps, and they just get tougher. Little ones still have that rattle on their tails. They will grow up to be big and deadly. So when you see a little rattler, you can't think that it's just small and insignificant. Remember that it will be one big monster to sink its fangs into you later down the road. You've got to squash it. God's own justice, you've just got to squash it out when you see it, and boys, you can't listen to that claptrap you hear about good Indians. The only good Indian is a dead Indian. The so-called 'Spanish' Indians ain't good, and the Negro Indians ain't good, and not even any of those half-breed Indians who talk as good as you or me is any good. If I don't have my daughter back when the sun comes up tomorrow, for the love of decent white women everywhere, we're going in, men. We're going in to battle that savage!"

A cry went up on deck. A battle cry.

Weatherby winced. Warren's men on board must still be a little green if they could let out a holler like that. Give them time. Let them hear a few Seminole war whoops in the midst of battle. Those injun cries were enough to make a man's hair stand on end.

Weatherby was a fairly religious man himself. He looked up to heaven. "Lord, I don't mind dying when I must. But if you're going to lead me into death, don't let it be with a man who seems to keep his brains where he sits . . . in his pants, if you know what I mean, Lord!"

He turned around to head for his cabin. It looked like tomorrow was going to be one damned bad day.

The dawn was barely a promise against the darkness when James awoke.

When he first opened his eyes, he lay very still, feeling her against him. Soft and feminine, so warm. He closed his eyes again. Once this had been life. Waking every morning while holding a woman in his arms, breathing in her scent, savoring the softness of her. There was a comfort, and a strength in that comfort. He missed Naomi. It had been gut-wrenching anguish for a long, long time. Then a dull ache that just never seemed to go away. He had thrown himself passionately into the plight that had assailed his people. The Seminoles and their allies. The Negros who had run for freedom, the "good" Spanish Indians, the Hitichi- and Muskogee-speaking peoples who were all just grouped together as *Seminoles*. The full-breeds, the half-breeds, the little children who were already appearing in rags, thin and ill.

The absolute last thing he had imagined in his life was a night with a delicate white southern society belle. And now, quite impossibly, it had gone beyond that. Except that it couldn't. It couldn't because there was a war on. Because he was not a southern planter like Jarrett, he was the half-breed brother. He was not penniless; he would never be. But he might well become a hunted man at any time, and he slept in the woods more often than in a bed.

There was no life he could offer her, was he of a mind to do so. There was no life she could accept. Naomi had been born in the Florida territory, and she had lived on the land all of her life. She had been as natural as the earth itself, aware of the rattler, content not with silk and satin, but with the beauty of the wild orchid and the white wings of the crane. She had belonged with him here.

While Teela ...

He stroked her back, admitting that he was mesmerized by the beautiful curves of her, the feel of her flesh, the fire of her hair. The emerald of her eyes, even the feel of her voice against his senses. He had never closed his eyes and imagined that he held Naomi again; he had needed no pretense. There had simply been an undeniable attraction from the beginning, and circumstances had only deepened what wild emotion ignited between them. Perhaps he had imagined that first night that he could touch her and still remain unscathed, uninvolved. He could not. She had wrenched him from his self-pity and grief. Only to cast him into a form of hell again, for she could not come with him into the swamps. She could not fight his battle. He invited her death to keep her anywhere near him at all.

A filtering of dawn's color leaked into the cabin, and

the fire he had built burned very low. Between them they created a hazy pink light. It set the color of her hair afire, and enhanced the ivory color of her flesh. He moved his forefinger very lightly down her spine, then frowned, noting a small spot that seemed just a shade different from the smooth perfection of the rest of her skin. He stilled his finger as a shard of ice seemed to shoot through his body. Warren beat her. A trembling sensation seized him, hot, causing his vision to blacken. He prayed to the one supreme being, the Christian god, the Great Spirit, that in this hell on earth he might meet with Warren in battle and be victorious. He had never felt such a hatred in his life as he felt for Warren. Knowing Teela had merely deepened his passion. He wanted to protect her so desperately from the man. But while Warren might be vicious with her, he wouldn't kill her. And she could easily die at any time in his company.

Still . . .

He moved his finger along her spine once again, touched the flesh of her shoulder. She didn't waken, but she moaned slightly, rolling against him. She lay upon her back, her hair like a fan of fire beneath her and around her, curling over her breasts, down along her ribs, over her hips. After a moment, her lashes flickered. Her eyes opened, the lashes fell, rose again. She looked at him, still half asleep. There was something incredibly vulnerable in her eyes. Trusting . . . sensual. They closed once again. She sighed, still not fully awake.

He leaned over and kissed her lips. He rose and shifted his weight, coming between her thighs. He pressed his lips against her throat. Her breasts.

He never made love to her tenderly. Arousing as he awakened, seducing as he touched. She moved with him, writhed, awoke more fully. The hunger seized him, the hunger she created in him, a passion that could be slaked but never sated. Tenderness erupted into raw fever, swept them both into a maelstrom. In the end she was very much awake, shuddering violently in his arms, a soft cry tearing from her lips as the sweet, erotic surcease of climax burst upon them. Shuddering, swallowing, she searched his face. Her eyes were on his again, very large, emerald.

She was definitely wide awake.

But even as he opened his mouth to speak to her, he heard a noise from outside. Hoofbeats against the dry earth.

He sprang from her, sleek and naked, going for his rifle where it had lain through the night just above his head, within easy arm's reach.

"James!"

He eased, hearing his brother's voice. But he had barely laid down his gun and pulled on his breeches before Jarrett was pounding on the door, then pushing it open.

Teela was not able to dress with such speed; in fact, all that she was able to manage before Jarrett had the door open was to pull the blanket to her chin and inch back into the shadows.

Her face was very pale, her hair pure fire against it. Her eyes were wide against her face, creating a fierce anguish in James as he longed to protect her. His brother, however, offered no danger. Yet he forced his heart to harden, wondering if she wasn't just embarrassed to be discovered here with him—naked.

But it was too late to worry about their situation. Frankly, he had to be grateful that it was his brother who had come upon them. He was accustomed to being very careful through the night, to sleeping with an eye half open ... damn, he was accustomed to being alert and weary. But this morning ...

His alertness had all been for her.

Jarrett, simply dressed in cotton shirt, high boots, and breeches, was already in the doorway.

"James, we've serious trouble. I have been riding half the night, searching all the while, praying the rest. Miss Warren has run from her father, and it seems that the major—"

Jarrett broke off cleanly in mid-sentence.

He had been staring at his brother.

Now he was looking at Teela.

Jarrett was not easily taken by surprise, and he was quick to recover form it, but not until his pure amazement at the situation had registered upon his features.

"Sweet *Jesu!*" he whispered, stepping into the cabin and closing the door behind him.

"She is aware that she has to go back," James said rather harshly. "As a half-breed and intimate of Osceola, I rather doubt her father will entrust her into my care, and I cannot lead him into the very Indian hideouts he would most like to destroy."

"Well, I'm damned aware that she has to go back—" Jarrett began.

"Will you please cease discussing me as if I were a vegetable, gentlemen?" Teela interrupted.

Jarrett arched a brow to James.

James shrugged. "She's a reckless little firebrand. No wonder Warren has such problems with her. She has to go back with you, but there has to be a way to keep her from being dragged about Florida with him. She'll die along with him if some of the warriors whose families he has murdered get to him. And ... he beats her."

Teela turned to stare at him with startled eyes. Miserable eyes. They fell as her cheeks took on a pink hue. He had embarrassed her. She was very proud, and very unhappy, that he knew, but still, Jarrett had to know the truth as well, and there was little time to be subtle about anything now.

She spoke with her eyes downcast. "I am a remarkably strong person, gentlemen, and I am not afraid of my stepfather." She hesitated. "I hate him, but I am not afraid of him."

"You haven't the good sense to be afraid when you should," James said impatiently.

"If you will both listen, we believe we have the solution. John Harrington is here. He came the back way to Robert's plantation while his troops went on by river to meet up with Warren. He'd not even been aware that

Warren was on the river, able to get here so quickly. He has orders that they are to take the river as deeply inland as they can, then start marching eastward to join up with another command. Warren will have precious little time to take his daughter anywhere, and John is determined that he can convince the major he must leave his daughter at Cimarron."

"How does John intend to do that?" James asked.

Jarrett hesitated. "Perhaps he should explain . . ."

James shook his head. "He intends that they should announce Teela's agreement to an engagement with him?"

"Yes," Jarrett said flatly.

"I cannot do it," Teela gasped.

James spun around and strode to her, pulling her to her feet with a strength and passion that left her no recourse but to struggle to claim her blanket rather than fight with him. His fingers remained like a vise around her arms as he spoke to her, as harshly and coldly as he could manage.

"You must do it. You've no choice."

"It isn't fair to—"

"It must be done, you must go back. Dammit, Teela, you can't just run away in a swamp!" He kept his eyes furiously hot on hers, not relaxing the brutality of his hold on her in the least, and spoke to his brother. "You've got to get her out of here completely, Jarrett. When they have all gone to battle, see that she is sent home, back to Charleston."

"I'll do my best," Jarrett said quietly.

"I don't wish—" Teela began.

"It doesn't matter. You must tell your father that you will marry John. Perhaps you should give it some real thought," he added, wincing at the hardness, the bitterness, of his own voice. "John is a damned decent fellow, and will make a delicate little white girl a fine husband if he just survives this all with his scalp."

"Let go of me!" Teela whispered furiously. He

thought that there were tears in her eyes. He couldn't really tell, they were so filled with anger.

Jarrett cleared his throat. "I think I'll step outside while you, er, dress, Miss Warren. We must get back. If we don't, your stepfather will have his crew halfway here, and this is a safe haven for many of the orphans who are moved throughout this nightmare. We don't want the copse found."

The door closed. Teela jerked her arms to free herself from James's hold.

He was tempted not to release her. He felt the most agonizing urge to force her down to the ground again, forget the world outside, hold her, make love to her again, fast, furious . . .

It was insanity.

It didn't matter. He wanted to damn Warren to every hell on earth and beyond. He wanted not to care if the man rode a thousand men inland searching for them both. He didn't want to give a damn about the war, about the women or the children, the whites or the reds. There were a hundred places in the swamp where he could take her. Hammocks where she couldn't be found . . .

Maybe. The white soldiers pushed ever deeper, the Indians ran ever harder. She would be at risk no matter what he did. If he held her, others would be tortured for information they would not have. He would be a complete outcast.

He would never be able to see his daughter. Teela would never get to feel the simple touch of a soft bed. Dine off delicate porcelain, sip fine English tea.

"James—"

He released Teela instantly. Turned his back on her. "Get dressed," he said sharply.

"I know that I have to go back. I wouldn't have Michael Warren following me here, hurting you—"

"He'd die if he tried," James assured her, softly but passionately.

"Hurting others. I know that I must go back, but it

was the truth you heard at the table, I will not marry a man I have not chosen myself—"

"Harrington is in love with you," James grated out, fingers clenching into fists at his side.

"I am not in love with him."

"You haven't given him half a chance."

She was silent a moment. He felt her eyes piercing into his back.

"You needn't fear," she informed him, her voice very proud and tinged with ice. "I will do nothing that will betray you."

He spun around. "I have already told you; I am not afraid of Michael Warren. I would welcome the chance to kill him."

"Or die in trying!"

"I will not die until he is dead."

"You are flesh and blood!" she cried out.

"I will not die until he is dead," James repeated. His heart seemed to pause, skip a beat, then pummel with a slam against his chest. She was halfway dressed, but still her bodice was loose, and her breasts were nearly bared. Her wild red hair was tumbling everywhere, and her chin was very high; she was quite determined. He took a step toward her and caught her arms, drawing her close to him. "Go back with my brother and John. Don't take pride to a point of stupidity. John is a good man—"

"Yes! And I cannot use him or lie to him—"

"Then don't lie. But give him a chance." He released her again, turning her around to deftly do up the ties at the back of her dress. He lifted her hair from her nape and fought the temptation to press his lips against the smooth soft flesh there one last time.

He let her hair fall.

She stood very stiffly and whispered, "What chance would I give him when—"

"A fair chance!" he snapped. "For there can be nothing for you here except games you would play with a red man!"

Before she could speak again, he turned swiftly and exited the cabin with all speed, not daring to look back.

Outside, he found Harrington along with his brother. John and Jarrett were both dismounted, standing by their horses, talking quietly as they waited.

"James!" As always John Harrington offered him a warm smile and a firm handshake. James felt his stomach lurch. From the moment Harrington had first seen Teela, he had been in love with her. Or in love with being in love. It didn't matter which. How could he define or judge anything John might have felt for her when he couldn't describe or understand his own passion and obsession?

And pain.

"Thank you for coming, John. I understand we're in the midst of quite a situation with Warren."

"Warren is a bastard!" John said softly, looking over James's shoulder. Teela would be coming out of the cabin. "Thank God you found her, James, before some evil befell her."

"There are seldom any warriors in this immediate area now," James said.

"I meant evil within the terrain itself, James. What manner of man could be so hideous that his own child could welcome a rattler?" He lowered his voice still further. "I swear I will do everything in my power to keep her safe from him."

Their hands were still clutched together in a firm handshake. James felt his hold upon John tighten. "Keep her from her father, and from the battlefield, John. That is all I ask you."

"I swear it."

"I am in your debt."

"I have been in yours many times."

"Marry her quickly, if that is what it takes."

"James, sweet *Jesu!*" John said uncomfortably. "I haven't the right—"

"No. I am the one without rights."

"We must go," Jarrett interrupted quietly. "She is waiting, and we should make all haste back."

James turned at last to see that Teela had come out of the cabin and that she had remained a good thirty feet from them, standing quietly, waiting.

She had subdued the wild mane of her fiery red hair, winding it into a regal knot at her nape. Her hands were folded before her, and she stood very straight and very still, very dignified.

Only the liquid turmoil in her remarkable green eyes seemed to give away the tumult within her.

They had left their horses in the copse behind the cabin. James walked around for hers and brought the mare back to the front. Jarrett and John had mounted their horses already. James brought the mare right up beside them, then lifted Teela when she would have mounted on her own. She stared down at him once she sat atop the horse.

"Take care," he told her. She continued to stare stonily down at him, and he turned to his brother.

"Keep her safe. She will not have the sense to remain so herself."

"We'll manage," Jarrett promised him.

He nodded again to John, took Jarrett's hand. "God go with you, brother," Jarrett told him.

James nodded with a smile. "You, too, brother."

"Take care when you come back in. Warren is trying to claim that you abducted his daughter."

James glanced at Teela, allowing his eyes to slide over the length of her again.

"James," John said, "it's a serious matter—"

"I will be with the people who have asked for their government settlement and agreed to go west. I will meet Warren on the field, or in any court of law." His eyes remained on Teela. He bowed suddenly, very deeply, with every bit of courtly manner he had ever learned. "Good-bye, Miss Warren."

"Good-bye, Mr. McKenzie."

James stepped back. The horses started forward. He

watched them as they moved onto the trail. She did not turn back.

But then . . .

She did.

She stared at him as he stood just outside the cabin, still barefoot, bare-chested, loose black hair just touching his shoulders, skin bronze beneath the heat of the sun. Barely dressed.

Hardly civilized.

She had to go . . .

Yet he felt like doubling over with the pain of it. He lifted a hand to her. She couldn't possibly have heard him, but he spoke out loud softly anyway.

"Until we meet again, Miss Warren. Until we meet again."

They shouldn't meet again, he told himself firmly.

But something inside him knew.

They would.

Indeed, they would meet again.

Chapter 11

weaker, the drinking weakness of humanity were tell-

I have ended. I tell you I have been on behalf

a grave at Fort Brooke

there are now

could. The widows are weary. The children are starving.

The old are in pain.

Osceola stared at the warrior, a wild form minutes be-

into reptiles. He stared at James once

stretched round in a few strong

"So, you have come to join us in battle again, Running Bear. You have spent your time with your brother, and learned again that one drop of Seminole blood makes a man's skin red."

James shook his head, dropping before the fire to sit cross-legged and study Osceola. He had spent nearly ten days traveling and looking for the war chief, a fact that was wearying in itself. The ground was hard, harder for those who did not know it. The Seminoles could run in any direction and slip into the earth itself, or so it seemed.

He had found Osceola traveling uncomfortably near Fort Brooke with a large contingent of warriors. But, James thought, Osceola did not look well, was not well, and it was obvious that Osceola knew it himself. The war *mico* was a proud man, an intelligent man, and still a fierce one. He was handsome with his fine eyes, broad cheekbones, and penetrating stare, and James liked him even when they disagreed. Perhaps James was lucky he had never felt Osceola's wrath; the agent Wiley Thompson had caused Osceola humiliation, and he had paid with his life. Charlie Emathla had wearily turned himself in, and in so doing turned against his people in the eyes of Osceola, and he, too, had died. Osceola had begun this war as a firebrand, and he did not regret the blaze a bit. But he was human. He had run and fought in the cold of winter, in the cruel heat of summer. He had run through the rains and lightning. The war, the fight, the weather, the damning weaknesses of humanity, were telling on him.

"I have come to tell you that I am planning on leading a group of survivors from the otter clan to Fort Brooke. There are no warriors among them. The warriors are all dead. The widows are weary. The children are starving. The old are in pain."

Osceola stared at the fire for several long minutes before replying. He stared at James again.

"General Jesup is a strong enemy."

James shrugged, lifting his hands. "He is a strong enemy, but he has faltered under the pressure of politics and swampland, just as the many tough men who came before him."

"Some men will fight forever," Osceola murmured. He stared at James. "And some they will never catch. Some will fall because they will be pushed so hard that they must do so or die. And some will die." He inhaled and exhaled on a long sigh. "They think that they can do battle, catch me, Alligator, Wildcat, and others, and so end the war. They just don't see that they fight a hundred enemies." He looked hard at James. "I have heard that General Jesup is planning a pincer movement against us, much like General Winfield Scott attempted."

"It would make sense."

"You heard nothing from your brother?"

"The military is careful with my brother these days."

Osceola tilted his head, a slight smile hovering on his lips. "Your brother still has not joined them."

"My brother will not make war on his stepmother's people. If he was ever attacked, he would defend his wife and child and home. I know of no *mico* who will attack Jarrett. I know of no *mico* Jarrett will attack."

"I think that I have some information that you do not this time, friend," Osceola told him, smiling. "When did you last see your brother?"

James frowned, instantly alarmed by the words. It had been nearly two weeks since he had seen Jarrett.

He had followed his brother, Harrington, and Teela

back to Cimarron that day at a careful distance. He had
waited, watching as they had met with Warren on the
lawn. Crept closer, even more carefully, when they had
gone into the house.

With a bit of help from Jeeves, he had even managed
to watch much of what had gone on in the dining room.

There had been some argument. Teela had turned to
Warren in a fury once, but Jarrett McKenzie, man of
manners that he was, had nearly crushed her toes, and
she had fallen silent.

Young Harrington had played his role to perfection—
the delighted young man determined to secure the life
and safety of his future wife. He was unbelievably con-
vincing, but then, he probably told no lies. Jarrett held
his temper. Tara was charming, and Teela was silent.

Miraculously, in the upshot Teela was for the time to
remain at Cimarron.

James had never announced his presence that night.
He had found his brother alone in the library later to
let him know that he was aware of the way things had
gone. He said good-bye again, slipped into Jennifer's
room and said good-bye to his daughter, then slid back
into the woods.

It had been late by then. By the soft glow of candlelight from the house, he had seen Teela come to the
balcony of her room, dressed in white.

The temptation to run back burned within him, an
agony that surely surpassed all the fires of hell.

But he had already said good-bye to her. He told her
that she should consider John Harrington as a husband.
There were still a number of soldiers near and on the
property. He wasn't afraid of meeting one; he was afraid
of bringing the war to his brother's house.

Most of all, he didn't think that he could hold her and
walk away again. There was no choice for him but to
leave. So he watched her in the soft glow of light.
Watched it touch the red of her hair, so deep at night.
Watched the beauty of her face and form, hidden yet
enhanced by the flowing white gown. For a moment he

thought that he would die right there. Everything within his being tightened and constricted, breath seemed to stop, heart failed to beat. But he was painfully alive, and he had turned at last and ridden away.

"What has happened to my brother?" he demanded of Osceola hoarsely.

"Nothing has happened to Jarrett McKenzie, his wife, or child. You are just behind in some of your information. Your fine General Jesup wrote to the war chief, a man named Poinsett, for the new white president. Jesup asked that we be left alone in the swamplands to the south."

"Yes, I was aware of that," James murmured.

"He got his answer," Osceola said. "We must be forced west. If they were to leave us be, the Cherokees on their sad journey west might protest. Others might take up arms again. That is what the white man Poinsett thinks. The war will go on."

"Had you ever really thought otherwise?"

Osceola arched a dark brow to him. "We live with hope, we fight with hope. What white man seeks to make his home in the wretched, infested swampland where they force us to run and fight, eh, my friend?"

James shrugged wearily. The war would go on.

"There has been action not so very far from your brother's house, and many of our men are now in the detention center at Tampa. The whites have taken our Wildcat, Coacoochee, son of Philip. Alligator is now a prisoner. They seek to take others."

"They are learning," James said. "They are beginning to realize that no one man may speak for all among the Seminole Indians. They are trying very hard to round up the chiefs."

"They threaten to hang Seminoles when they are captured if they will not lead the military to the strongholds of others. They use any treachery."

James tried to phrase his words carefully. "You must understand that they sometimes feel the Seminoles have been treacherous as well. In March, many signed the peace agreement—"

"The whites did not keep that treaty, either."

"But they feel that the chiefs came in and accepted food, then reneged on their word."

"They have stolen our food, our land, our cattle. We have managed to have a few meals at their expense."

James wasn't sure how to explain that such actions would only allow the whites to be treacherous in return. "It is just that in the future, Osceola, you must take care that the whites do not feel they are not obliged to be truthful."

"They have never felt so obliged."

There was little argument James could give him.

"Are you with me, Running Bear?"

"With you?" James said, frowning.

"No, you cannot be with me," Osceola said softly. He shook his head, smiling. "My heart often bleeds for you, my young friend. You are so split. You are in horror often of the things I have done, or the things done in my name. Yes, Seminoles have raided white plantations. Women have died, sometimes children die. In days past we took captives. We brought children and women to live among us, to join us. The small sons of our white enemies sometimes grew to be fine warriors. The daughters grew with us to become good wives and mothers. Now . . . we live nowhere. Now we are furious and bitter. We have never fought such a battle for survival. So women and children die. Just like our children die. I have never seen anything more evil than a soldier intent upon the death of a child and the saving of a bullet all in one! The soldiers crack our infants' heads against trees as if they were coconuts."

James stared downward at his hands. They were clenched together tightly, the knuckles white. Yes, such things happened. Jesup, who fought the Indians with a vengeance, often grew weary of his own fight, of the slaughter. James was aware that Jesup had really wanted it to end; he had earnestly hoped Poinsett would allow him to leave the Indians in the south of the peninsula.

But then there were men like Michael Warren. Perhaps none quite as savage as he. No man was more guilty of outrage and cruelty than Michael Warren.

Osceola leaned forward over the fire. His now lean but still striking features were highlighted in the orange of the blaze.

"Think of your daughter, Running Bear. Think of her youth, her beauty, her innocence, shattered."

"My daughter is safe with my brother."

Osceola nodded. He had never desired war with Jarrett McKenzie. Jarrett understood the Indians more than most white men could; he had grown up among them. He had been given an Indian child's name, and he had taken the black drink and received his adult name, White Tiger, as well.

"Your brother would die for your child, which is the most any man can do. Jennifer will survive the white man, that much is certain, perhaps when we are all dead, my friend. But as for my children, for the other children . . ."

"I know what is suffered!" James assured him tensely.

Osceola stood. "Wait before bringing in your women, children, and orphans, Running Bear. I am going to release some of our people who should not be confined. I know that you cannot come with me and attack the detention center at Tampa Bay. I know, too, that you cannot, will not, betray my cause. When I have released the warriors, then you may bring in the children. Wait a few more weeks."

"Teela!"

She sat on the slight hill that crested the lawn of Cimarron where it sloped between the river and the woods. Jennifer was before her, the baby, Ian, at her side, as she brushed out the thick, luxurious skeins of Jennifer's hair. She looked up at the sound of her name, somewhat dismayed to see that it was John Harrington, his broad smile in place, who hurried toward her from a ship berthed at the Cimarron river dock.

She did like him. She liked him very much. In all her life probably no one had ever been kinder to her. That was why it was so hard to feel that she was hurting him. She knew that he cared about her, and she knew that she could not give back the intensity of affection he offered. He was a good friend; she wanted to be a good friend in return. He was also a pleasure to be with, intelligent, fun, quick to laugh, slow to judge. If only she didn't feel quite so guilty . . .

John had announced their engagement to Michael Warren when they reached Cimarron that night, which seemed like a million years ago now. He had been so boisterous and filled with enthusiasm and plans—and determination—that Michael had been drawn right along.

John also carried their military orders, and any mention of Teela leaving the safety of Cimarron caused him to visibly cringe and insist that he must feel that his future bride would be far from the danger they fought.

Tara, whom Teela had learned had come from a theatrical background, assured Teela that she had seldom seen such an excellent performance on any stage.

Tara, of course, watched her strangely now at times, and Teela was certain that Jarrett had explained to his wife just exactly in what disarray he had found Teela and James. She hadn't asked Teela any questions, a fact for which Teela was glad. She didn't really have any answers—she didn't know quite what to say—and she still hadn't unscrambled her own very complicated feelings regarding the whole matter. She knew she couldn't honor any engagement she and John pretended to make; she didn't love John.

She didn't know quite what she felt for James. She mocked herself constantly, demanding to know in her heart if she was willing to cast aside all comfort, her known world, and follow him into the bush.

If he would allow her to do so, which he certainly would not.

And if she was to do so, Warren would surely have a massive bounty on his head.

There was nowhere to go ... and she tried to tell herself that it did not matter. James had felt an attraction to her, nothing more. He was dedicated to his own way of life and his fight, and he didn't want her as any part of either. He was gone; he was not there for her to see, to want, to long to be close to, to touch. But it didn't matter. He filled her mind, in her dreams when she slept, in her thoughts with every haunting, waking moment. She realized that she was living to wait, and that all she waited for was a chance to see him again. She was afraid to define her feelings. She knew only that she ached for him, and that any other man would pale in comparison to him, the sight of him, feel of him, scent of him. His passion was fire, and she could never accept anything less.

Maybe that was love ...

Whatever, it made her feel guilty to see John Harrington again, no matter how much she enjoyed his company.

"It's John," she said cheerfully to Jennifer, rising and reaching for the baby's basket. But John swept up the basket as he greeted her with a pristine kiss to the cheek. "And you, Miss Jennifer McKenzie!" he said, greeting the child. "How do you do?"

Jennifer smiled, her charming little dimples deepening. She executed a perfect little curtsy in return. "I do well, Lieutenant Harrington. Very well, thank you."

"Ah, that I am glad to hear!" he said. "Would you be so good as to run along and find your aunt Tara and beg her to allow a weary soldier to join you for supper?"

Jennifer blushed happily, then nodded, and ran off to do as she was bidden.

Teela stared at John, certain that he had purposely sent the child rushing on ahead so that they could talk alone.

"What's wrong?" she asked him worriedly.

"Nothing that terrible," John assured her quickly, carrying the basket with Ian as they started toward the house. "I just wanted you to be forewarned."

Her heart quickened. "About what?"

"There were a number of Seminoles being held at a detention camp in Tampa. And among them many of the war chiefs. Osceola and some of the other braves came and rescued their fellows. Perhaps some seven hundred Indians in all escaped."

"So the war goes on and on!" Teela murmured. She stopped walking because John was staring at her. "There's more?"

He shrugged unhappily. "There's a rumor that James McKenzie was among the warriors who caused the escape."

"I don't believe it," Teela said stiffly. "He would not put himself or his brother into such jeopardy—"

"I don't believe it, either. James has tried very hard never to attack the whites; he has fought but only when attacked. His value among his people and the whites has always been in his ability to reason when all else has failed, to mediate when the lives of hostages were at stake. He has always been trusted by both sides." He hesitated. "Teela, there's another rumor out there as well. There's talk that he abducted you, and that you and I both deny it because we are a pair of pathetic sympathizers who refuse to see the complete Indian menace."

"Oh, God!" Teela whispered miserably. "Had I but imagined that I might give Michael Warren such a fine excuse to do his wretched evil that day, I'd have never run!"

"Don't take it upon yourself!" he warned her kindly. "James would not want you to do so; he would gladly risk himself to save you from harm."

"My harm would not have been so great. And John, I am heartily sorry for what I am doing to you as well—"

"It is no hardship to say that I am engaged to the most beautiful woman in all the territory."

"But—"

"Hush, please," he said, and paused in their walk. "I know that your feelings for me do not include the desire to become my wife. Be content in knowing I am pleased with any service I might offer you." He hesitated. "Or James."

She stared at him in awkward silence, and he continued conversationally. "He saved my life once."

"How?"

"At the Second Battle of the Withlacoochee. He fought; he had no choice. We were close to closing on a large encampment of women, children, and the Seminole aged. He had family behind him, and the soldiers might have crossed the river. A Creek commander was killed; no one ventured out into the water after that. But there were skirmishes up and down that day. I'd lost my musket, my knife, my powder. A big fellow had me by the hair, and James intervened, half killed the Indian. I don't know what he told him at the end; I have tried, but I have not gained a good usage of either Muskogee or Hitichi. The brave returned to the battle, and James dragged me to safety." He shrugged. "We have been friends since we first met, here in this house. Perhaps my most fervent prayer in all this is that I don't meet him when we are both caught without a choice once again."

"I'm glad that he saved your life," Teela said quietly. "It was a life well worth saving."

He started to speak, but they were both startled by a popping sound that seemed to come from down river. Far on the horizon, Teela could see as a dozen birds in their snow whites and beautiful array of colors burst from the trees and into the air.

"Gunfire!" John murmured. He started to move toward his ship.

"Wait!" Teela gasped, taking the basket with the baby from him. "Where are you going, what are you doing?"

"We've got to go down river!" John said distractedly.

"Wait! I'm coming!" Teela told him.

"What?" he demanded.

She was already running wildly for the house. Jeeves had come out to the porch. With a hand above his eyes, he was staring toward the area from which the shots had come.

Teela thrust little Ian—blissfully sleeping through it all—into Jeeves's hands. "Don't jar him too much now, Jeeves," she said hastily.

She turned to run.

"Now, you wait a minute there, Miss Warren—" Jeeves began sternly.

But she had already spun around and was racing after John. An order had been called out; soldiers were unknotting the ties that held the ship to the dock.

It was a small craft, Teela quickly discovered, but manned with two cannons on each side, complete with three tall sails as well as numerous oarlocks. She couldn't tell how many men were aboard when she raced along the dock, just reaching the gangplank as it was being drawn in.

"Wait!" she shrieked again.

John, conferring with an officer, looked to see her racing aboard. He couldn't stop her; she would have plummeted into the sea.

"Teela!" She had jumped onto the main deck of his sloop even as he spoke. "This is madness; you mustn't come—"

"I have to come, I have to see—"

"But, surely, it is just a skirmish."

A number of officers stood around them, some watching Teela with a certain amusement, others with curiosity. John pulled her close to him. "My fiancée, gentlemen, Teela Warren."

"War zone is no place for a lady," said a young, slim man with a Tennessean accent.

"Perhaps it is," suggested another man. He was in a fringed buckskin hunting jacket, a clean-shaven man with slightly graying auburn curls queued neatly at his nape and a slouch hat pulled low over his forehead. He stepped forward, offering Teela his hand. "Warren's daughter, engaged to a commissioned lieutenant. Like it or not, boys, she might as well learn a few of the calamities of a soldier's life. I am Joshua Brandeis, company field surgeon. If our boys are out there, a few of them may need patching up. If you've a stomach to give me a hand, then I say that you are welcome aboard!"

Teela took his hand with her eyes steady on his.

"Have you taken the Hippocratic oath, Doctor?"

"Indeed, young lady."

"So what happens when a red man falls into your care?"

Joshua Brandeis paused for a moment, watching her. He shrugged. "Well, now, miss, it's for sure that I don't share your stepfather's vision of this war. Whatever man comes before me, I am sworn to pluck a bullet from his flesh, tie a severed artery, splint a broken limb, pour sulfer on his wounds. Are you with me?"

"I don't want her in a battle zone—" John began sternly, but Teela ignored him, her eyes still hard on those of Joshua Brandeis.

"I'm with you, Dr. Brandeis," she announced firmly.

"Teela!" John said softly, spinning her around to face him. "If I can't manage my own fiancée, how will I ever manage to have my men listen to me?" he asked.

She replied very quietly. "You don't let your men hear what you are telling me, and that way they will not know when I disagree."

"Disobey."

"John, for the love of God, I do not obey anyone. You have surely realized that by now. And I have to come with you now!" she said fervently, very close to him now. They were already moving swiftly down river, coming to the point where the shots had been fired.

"I promised to keep you safe."

"What if James is out here?"

"There are hundreds of Seminoles—"

"What if he is among them?"

"What if he is? Will you watch him die?"

She exhaled softly. "John, please, I beg of you—"

"We are already there!" he said. He turned from her, calling out an order to disembark to his men. There was no dock, and the ship had to be kept in the deep-water center of the river. Dinghies were dropped swiftly into the water, and the men boarded them in disciplined military order.

John was among the first to go. Dr. Joshua Brandeis was at the rear with his surgeon's leather bag slung over his shoulder. He looked back to her, reaching out a hand. "Coming?"

She didn't hesitate. She ran to him, accepted his hand and then his help as he lifted her easily and set her into one of the dinghies, already being lowered down the starboard side. A quick leap and he had joined her along with the other eight men in the dinghy.

"Miss, keep your head low!" one of the men warned.

"Ah, now, you needn't fear while you're with us, miss. We're a volunteer regiment, the remnants of a few different companies come together to serve good old John. We'll let no danger befall you!"

"Thank you," Teela told them. Then she cringed at another burst of gunfire. They were close now. The explosions that erupted with each fired bullet were deafening. She heard screams. Screams of pain, war whoops.

The dinghy scraped the bottom of the river. The men began to leap out, dragging the small boat high upon the grassy shore. Teela was left with Joshua Brandeis, who sloshed ashore just a bit more slowly, surveying the near landscape with a narrowed eye.

"Hurry along, now!" he told her.

Teela obeyed, leaping from the boat, sinking knee high in mud, struggling from it to reach more solid ground.

Bodies lay scattered about, nearly hidden by the tall grass. She gasped at the first one she came upon.

An Indian body. This warrior had dressed in his finery for battle. His shirt was a bright print; silver medallions in crescent shapes hung from his neck. He wore thigh-high crimson leggings, and a fine, bright turban now trailed away from his head.

Dark brown eyes were open, glazed in death. He had not been caught by a bullet. He had been skewered through with a bayonet.

She stared at him in horror, fighting great waves of nausea. She suddenly heard a moaning and spun about nervously.

The warrior's opponent lay just feet from him. He was young, skinny as a reed with wheat-blond hair. He was militia, wearing worn trousers and a plain cotton shirt and simple low black leather boots. Blood stained his shoulder. He clutched it and moaned again. His eyes, blue like the sky, opened on Teela.

"Help me!" he whispered. "Oh, Lord, I'm dying. There's an angel in this hellhole!"

She knelt down beside him, startled as Dr. Brandeis pushed by her, kneeling in the tall grass as well.

"Bullet, son?" he asked, opening his leather bag.

"Yes, sir."

"Musket fire?"

"A clean ball, sir, wedged right in, I'm certain."

Brandeis ripped away the soldier's shirt. "Bullet forceps!" he said to Teela.

She swallowed hard and delved into the bag. She hadn't ever been present even at a childbirth, but when she looked among the instruments, the bullet forceps seemed obvious enough. She snatched it up quickly. Brandeis then asked her for a scalpel.

His orders came fast and furious. She held back the soldier's flesh while Brandeis extracted the ball. She threaded a needle with silk sutures and sopped up blood as the doctor sewed a ripped artery. She washed the wound with whiskey, winced as the soldier screamed, treated the wound with sulfer, and sat back at last as Brandeis bandaged it with startling speed.

"They'll be by for you in a minute, soldier. Miss Warren, come along!"

She was bathed in blood, she realized.

And she was numb.

But she followed. Brandeis was quick and thorough as they walked the shoreline. He could spot the fallen bodies—Seminole and white—very quickly where they lay. Teela paused over a brave once.

"That one's dead," Brandeis said bluntly. She sought a pulse anyway. Brandeis was right. They moved on.

Two soldiers had been hit in the limbs. One of the bullets had gone clean through the man's flesh; one had lodged. One man was hit in the gut. Brandeis treated him with whiskey.

"He'll not make the trip back to Fort Brooke," he told Teela quietly as they moved away. She drew in a deep, shaky breath. He clutched her arm tightly. "Many of them will live! We keep looking. Do you understand?"

She nodded and followed him onward.

He was true to his word. He paused to help the wounded Indians as well.

Teela had heard sporadic gunfire several times when they first arrived, but she suddenly realized that she heard no more. The skirmish had come to an end. The dead and wounded lay within the tall grass, into the trees that stood twenty yards inland.

Teela stood after assisting with a tourniquet on a young private who would surely lose his foot. The young man tossed his head, his eyes opened upon her, and he tried to smile. He winced and looked at Brandeis. "We were just out on patrol, hoping to surprise a few Indians. We surprised them, all right. And they surprised the hell out of us. Oh, pardon me, ma'am. I ain't dead, am I, Doc?" He smiled again. "No, I guess not. Your hair's too red for an angel, right?"

"You're not dead," Teela assured him. She knelt down again, taking his hand. "You're going to be just fine. Dr. Brandeis has set you up for the time being; they'll take better care of you once they get you off the field."

He nodded. "I'll be fine." His eyes closed.

"Whiskey is still the best cure I know," Dr. Brandeis said, rising, already looking through the grass for his next patient.

Teela stood again. Her heart seemed to ache terribly within her chest. She still felt stunned, exhausted, overwhelmed. Her fingers were numb, her mind as well.

She arched her back, trying to ease the soreness there. Her eyes fell upon a patch of color in the trees directly ahead of her. Frowning, she started forward, hurrying more quickly with each step. There was a man there, a Seminole, down. His back was to her. He was clad in dark breeches and high doeskin boots. His cotton shirt was patterned. His black hair was thick and wavy.

A blood stain spattered his back.

She choked back a sob, running hard until she was almost upon him. She circled the body, falling to her knees before it, reaching down to move the hair from his face.

A breath exhaled raggedly from her. It wasn't James. This warrior was of mixed blood as well; his features were very fine, his hair almost curly. He was sadly injured through the left shoulder, but he was breathing. A pulse ticked at his throat.

She turned, starting to rise, ready to call Dr. Brandeis.

She froze instead, the words dying on her lips.

James was there, moving to her from his stance beside the trees. He had been there all the while, watching her, his brown breeches and green patterned shirt blending cleanly with the earth and trees.

The breeze moved the trees as she stared at him. They seemed to chant and whisper. He was very tall there, straight, strong, silent. She ached to touch him. He seemed unbelievably powerful, as if he could defy the entire white army and stand against every Seminole warrior as well. Even his features seemed exceptionally strong, implacable, indomitable.

He came to where she stood, staring at her hard all the while. She couldn't seem to move. She could only return his stare.

He didn't touch her. He squatted down by the wounded warrior.

She moistened her lips. "Dr. Brandeis is very good. He tends the Seminoles as well as the whites—"

"Shush, and get down here." He stared past her, a wary eye on the soldiers that still hovered on the shoreline. He carefully examined the warrior. The man awoke as James probed his wound. James quickly brought a finger to his lips. He said something to him in his language; the warrior nodded.

Teela threw her hand over her mouth, smothering a gasp as James reached into the warrior's shoulder with his bare fingers, digging out the ball. She turned away, afraid she was going to be ill.

"You've got sulfer. Give it to me."

She turned back, startled. She was still carrying the little glass sulfer bottle. She handed it to James, who liberally spattered it over the bullet wound.

The warrior hadn't let out a single sound. She knew why he was quiet now. He had lost consciousness.

"Brandeis would have taken care of him!" Teela whispered. "He is a good man. They make good men even in the military!"

"I don't deny that," James said, ripping his shirt from his chest and fashioning a bandage from the torn strips. He still kept a careful eye on the soldiers near the shore. He expertly tied the cotton around the man's shoulder and arm.

"You've got to leave him—"

"I cannot leave him. He is Yohola, Thomas Artaine to the whites, and he has sworn that he would rather die than leave his homeland."

"But—"

"Your good military doctor will patch him up and ship him west against his wishes. Leave it be. Now, what the hell are you doing out here?" The question was so sudden and furious that she was taken aback.

"I—"

"I told you to leave here, leave Florida!"

"It's not so simple—"

"It's damned simple!" he hissed. "What game are you playing? This skirmish occurred by sheer accident; the soldiers did not seek it, nor did the braves. What do you think would happen to you in a major engagement? Especially if the Indians were to massacre the soldiers around you?"

"I came to help—"

"Damn you! You cannot help! You are not a part of this. Go home!"

"You wish to stay," she said stubbornly. "Perhaps it is my determination as well."

"You will go home!" he insisted.

She shook her head, then realized that their voices were rising.

"You've got to go!" she told him.

His mouth moved into a bitter curl. "Yes, I understand I helped some seven hundred Indians escape after abducting a white girl and doing God-alone-knows-what with her."

She gritted her teeth, fighting the rise of her temper. "No one believes it—"

"Someone does."

She couldn't argue with him now. "You've got to go!" she pleaded, knowing full well that he was right.

But he didn't move. He leveled a finger at her. "*You've* got to go. And damn you, I will see to it."

"Shut up! James, don't be a fool. Don't be caught in the midst of this action!" she cried softly.

"But I am in the midst of it," he said smoothly. "And we are on opposite sides here, so it seems."

"James—"

"Brandeis!" he called out suddenly, loudly.

"Sh!" Teela gasped. "What is the matter with you? Someone *will* come!" She leapt up and spun around to see how many soldiers were ready to come running at the sound of his voice. None of them had heard, so it seemed.

She spun back. He had hefted the fallen warrior over

his shoulder. He was purposely goading her, trying to show her the very narrow and deadly fence they walked between two worlds.

"Your friend needs help!" Teela insisted angrily.

"I will tend to him," James said.

Then she nearly screamed aloud as he took a step toward her, his free hand falling hard upon her upper arm, fingers a vise. He held her against him. She lowered her eyes quickly, not wanting him to know that she felt a glad weakness surge through her just to feel his heat, his warmth, his strength. To know he was alive and well. She lifted her eyes.

He was very angry. His grip was a brutal one. It definitely seemed as if he despised her.

"Let go of me. Go tend your warrior!" she cried out.

His grip tightened unbearably.

"Indeed, I'll tend to him. And I will tend to you as well, Miss Warren. Damn you. You keep your lovely little white behind at Cimarron, or you get it the hell out of the territory altogether, or I will tend to you. I promise you. Don't be caught at a battle site again."

"Damn you, James—"

"I'm warning you! The whites don't always win the battles, and I won't always be around. The right—or the wrong—Indians get a hold of you in a battle or skirmish, and they'll kill you, you little idiot!"

His fingers fell from her arm. His eyes seemed to blaze the threat of his words into her own.

Then he turned, silently striding through the shelter of the trees.

And then she was alone. It was as if he had never been there at all.

Chapter 12

Teela realized even as the sloop pulled in at the dock at Cimarron that she had behaved rashly once again. Tara was at the dock, nearly hysterical. Jarrett held his wife, who all but engulfed Teela when she stepped off the sloop—blood and all.

Jarrett McKenzie was not quite so quick to forgive. "Teela Warren, what, shall we keep you under lock and key?" he demanded angrily. "We've sworn to keep you safe, and you risk yourself so recklessly that my word of honor becomes nothing more than a mockery. You frightened us until we were half mad with worry."

"Oh, God, I am sorry!" Teela said remorsefully, railing against herself inwardly for being such a coward, since she was glad to keep Tara between herself and Jarrett. She pulled away from Tara at last. "I am sorry, I was just so frightened myself—"

"So frightened that you ran straight into a battle?" Jarrett demanded.

"I—I had to see ..." she mumbled.

Apparently, Jarrett realized that she had been terrified she would find James in the midst of the battle.

Or find him dead.

"What's done cannot be undone," he said wearily. But then John Harrington came down the gangplank, Dr. Brandeis at his side. "John!" Jarrett said with stern reproach.

John Harrington instantly flushed to a fine rose. "Jarrett, I didn't mean to bring her, truly I didn't."

"I was damned glad that we did have her aboard!"

Brandeis said with a sniff, smiling as he shook Jarrett's hand. "Miss Warren proved herself to be invaluable. I believe one or two of the poor wounded fellows we have aboard the sloop will survive to tell the tale of this day because her instinctive efficiency allowed me to move so swiftly in the field."

Jarrett McKenzie's eyes fell upon Teela, still stern. "If only simple competency could keep one alive here!"

"But it's over now," Tara said softly. "Teela has literally been baptized in blood; it covers her still. Come to the house. You can linger in a very hot bath and sip strongly laced tea. John, are you staying?"

He shook his head. "Thank you, Tara. We'll remain docked till near dawn, securing our wounded as best we can, but then we'll be making haste toward Tampa Bay, since many of these men need to be taken to the hospital at Fort Brooke."

"Field surgery is a survival tactic and little more," Dr. Brandeis said. "Miss Warren, may I say that I find you far more useful in the field than your father?"

John Harrington stamped upon his toe, and the good doctor winced. "You may say it," John told him softly. "If you are seeking a court-martial or a bullet in your back while we're within the scrub."

Brandeis had his own kind of confidence. He shrugged, stepped forward, took Teela's hand, and kissed it. "Adieu, fair maiden. If you're ever inclined to aid in the tending of our poor, wounded patients, I shall be most anxious to have you at my side once again."

"Thank you," Teela said, very grateful to him, for she hadn't thought anything about the day would cause her to smile.

"Good-bye, my dear, take care," John told her, stepping forward. Teela closed her eyes while he set a chaste kiss upon her forehead.

"You're welcome to come to the house, gentlemen, should you find the time," Jarrett told them.

"Thank you." John stepped back and, with Joshua Brandeis, boarded his ship once again.

"Come," Tara said to Teela.

She allowed Tara to lead her toward Cimarron while Jarrett remained by the dock, staring reflectively at the ship and the river.

Teela was startled to realize that she was trembling now that it was all over, and she didn't know if it was because of all the horror of death and injury she had witnessed, or because she had come so close to James again before he had disappeared. Perhaps she even trembled because his status had worsened since she had come, maybe *because* she had come. Most whites would not believe him a traitor to any cause. The army men who knew him, the Floridians he had befriended.

But there were always men like Michael Warren's troops. And they had made an outlaw of James.

They came to the porch, and Tara sat her upon one of the wooden rocking chairs there. "I'll have the bath brought up," she told Teela. "Your dress is ruined; nothing will take out that much blood."

"It doesn't matter," Teela said.

"No, it doesn't," Tara agreed. "No matter what its cost, clothing is cheap. Life is dear and precious."

She went on into the house. Teela still sat on the porch, watching the sun fall and create glorious colors over the quiet horizon. Jarrett McKenzie returned to his house, stared at her hard, then walked in. She leapt up, deeply disturbed by the look he had given her, wanting both to apologize and defend herself at the same time.

Not finding him in the breezeway or the parlor, she tapped upon the library door and opened it without waiting for a reply.

He was there, hands folded behind his back as he stared into the cold ashes in the fireplace. He stood very much as his brother had stood the first time she had seen James. He didn't turn around as she entered. He knew it was she who had come.

"Close the door, Miss Warren," he told her.

She did so.

He turned around. His gaze swept over her. She felt

a patch of some poor soldier's blood sticky against her cheek. She lifted a hand to wipe it away, realized it would not go so simply, and let her hand fall.

"Just what are your intentions regarding my brother, Miss Warren?" he demanded.

"Your pardon?" she whispered.

"Are you playing a game? Is that it?"

"Excuse me, sir, but shouldn't this line of questioning be direct at your brother rather than me?"

He shook his head, unrelenting. "Perhaps under normal circumstances. But these aren't normal at all, are they? My brother is a half-breed, caught in bitter times. He could quite easily be dead before it's over, slain by either side. At best, for the foreseeable future he will abide in the forest, the hammock, and the swamp. He needs to give his full attention to surviving with his body and soul intact. He cannot afford to be distracted by a young woman entranced with some romantic notion of carrying out a minor indiscretion with an intriguing red man. So again, I ask you, what are your intentions regarding my brother?"

She felt herself trembling uneasily, longing to strike out at him, wondering what he wanted from her. Her eyes narrowed, she stood very straight, her chin high. "There has been nothing 'minor,' sir, in anything that I have done."

"Why did you run like a little idiot into the gunfire today?" he demanded angrily.

"Because the shots were so close to Cimarron. Close to where Ja—I had to ... know!" she cried back.

"Was it worth it? Worth the fear you caused us, the possible repercussions should your father hear of this. Tell me, did you get your answers?"

"Yes!" she snapped. "Yes, yes! I saw him. I saw him whole and well, and I know that he is alive."

Jarrett exhaled slowly, watching her. "You saw him today?"

She nodded and spoke very softly. "The others did not see him. He collected the wounded body of an unconscious friend and disappeared. But he was alive and well, uninjured himself."

Jarrett nodded after a moment. He continued to stare at her. "I don't mean to hurt you," he said after a long moment. "But he is my brother. I have no choice."

"He is your brother but a grown man," she said, groping for the right words. "I have not . . ."

He smiled. "You have not had this affair on your own. I know. I am just frightened. For you both. I don't see where it can lead."

"Perhaps your brother is not interested in leading me anywhere."

"Perhaps he feels that there is nowhere to lead. And, indeed, have you given such things any thought? Would you be a happy young bride, quite possibly carrying a child, ducking through the foliage and running for your life while soldiers chased you down?" He paused, and Teela felt a sweep of color rush to her cheeks. It wouldn't matter if James was descended from four grandparents as white as snow if she was still carrying on an illicit affair.

There could be no pretending that she was not deeply involved with James when she talked to his brother; he had found her with James. He had never appeared to judge her; neither had Tara. But it seemed he wanted to be as blunt and brutal as he could at the moment. "Now, if they were chasing you, soldiers might see the red of your hair and hesitate, but I tell you, I have watched this wretched war a long time now, and I have seen how indiscriminately men can kill. For the Seminoles, I tell you, it's a very hard life. Sometimes the heat in the hammocks and swamps is over a hundred degrees. Sometimes, in the north, it falls below thirty. Sometimes they run through dangerous water up to their throats to escape the soldiers."

He fell silent, watching her.

Teela willed herself to speak quietly and to try to remain calm and dignified. "I have told you, Jarrett, that

I don't believe your brother is interested in leading me anywhere."

"I repeat, my brother feels that he has nowhere to lead anyone at this moment other than down a path to destruction. You need to consider going home," he told her.

"I will consider it. Am I no longer welcome here?"

He sighed, shaking his head. "You are always welcome here. I'm just trying to make you understand the situation. Again, I fear for you both."

"I am full-grown as well," she told him.

He smiled at last. "Full-grown and full of fire, but woefully innocent of the dangers to be found here!" he assured her. "And that danger includes James."

"Wherever it goes," she said slowly after a moment, "I seem to have no choice but to follow."

"You little fool," he said, but the chastising words were said gently now. "You are in love with him."

"Am I?"

"So it seems."

"What of your brother?" she heard herself whisper.

"I don't know," Jarrett answered honestly. "He still grieves for a wife and a child. And a nation. And this war comes first with him now. It has to. Until he comes to terms with himself, he can have no life."

She continued to stare at him, stubbornly proud.

"Go upstairs," he commanded softly. "Your bath will be ready. The blood of others is not comfortable to wear."

He turned back to the fire. Teela bit her lower lip, turned, and left the library behind to hurry up the stairs.

Tara was in her room along with two of the household servants, a lean, slim black boy called Jake and another, slightly older young Irishman named Sean. They hauled huge kettles of steaming water to the metal-rimmed wooden hip tub, pouring it in.

"I think we're all set here, thank you, boys," Tara said. When they had gone, she said, "There's some hot brandy-laced tea right on the small table, Teela. Towels and soap there by the tub." Just before she left the room, she paused in the doorframe. "I thought you might like a little privacy for a while, some moments alone. Take your time, and come down this evening whenever you feel like you'd enjoy company again."

"Thanks," Teela told her. She walked forward, almost overwhelmed with the kindness and understanding she always seemed to feel from Tara. She hesitated, realizing again that she was covered in blood. "Thank you," she said again.

Tara nodded and closed the door behind her.

Teela moved to stand before the full-length swivel mirror near the bed, by the washstand. She looked like the murder victim in a theatrical production. But it was no play, and there had been real victims, and their death had been a very violent form of murder indeed. She touched her cheeks again, shivered, and began ripping the blood-spattered clothing from her body. She tossed it all by the fire and gratefully sank into the hot water in the hip tub. She threw the pins from her hair and sank beneath the water. For a few minutes, she couldn't seem to scrub herself strenuously enough, from her scalp to her feet. Finally, convinced she was free from the crimson stains of death, she laid her head back against the rim of the tub, her fingers resting idly atop it as the steam rose above her.

Fear shrieked within her as a hand suddenly clamped firmly over her mouth. Her fingers dug into the tub as her body stiffened, then tore at the hand upon her mouth as she strained to twist and see her assailant.

She went dead still. James lifted his hand from her mouth, drawing a finger to his lips.

He had come straight in from the bush where she had last seen him, bare-chested, hair still queued back, a knife thrust into a sheath at his hip. He held a rifle in his free hand. His doeskin boots were damp, as if he had waded through water in his trek to return to Cimarron.

"What are you doing?" she demanded, furious that

he had frightened her so. She hugged her knees within the tub, inching back against it as far as she could.

"John's ship remains at the dock. Are there any soldiers in the house?"

She shook her head. "No," she told him. "Even John has remained aboard the ship."

"Why?"

"They are going to bring the wounded to the hospital at Fort Brooke as soon as possible."

He walked away from her, going to the table where Tara had left her the tea tray. Along with the liquor-imbued brew, there was a plate of small meat pastries and tea cakes. James set down his rifle, selected a pastry with each hand, wolfed them down, and then poured a cup of tea. He drank it swiftly, shuddering with the warmth of the brandy. Then his eyes were back on her again, and he returned to the tub, staring at her. He arched a brow, then knelt down beside her. "I was very hungry," he said softly. "Hazard of the job."

"Why were you in that battle today?" she asked him.

"Scarcely a battle. A skirmish, nothing more."

"What does it matter what you call it? Men died."

"Do you refer to red men or the white ones?"

"All of them."

He shook his head slowly after a moment. "I just don't think you realize sometimes that I am as much a part of them as I am a part of . . . of this. Jarrett's life. The men out there today who let out their awful war cries. The ones in breech clouts, turbans, and feathers. Who speak a different language, who paint their faces. Scalp white soldiers. And their wives."

"Why were you in the skirmish?" she asked stubbornly.

"Because I was with those men. They were part of the group Osceola and friends liberated from the detention center at Fort Brooke the second day of June."

"Liberated?" she queried softly. "Some men are saying that Osceola forced some of them to escape whether they wanted to or not. Even here, at your brother's house, I hear all the rumors and news."

"I don't know exactly what occurred," James said evasively. He swore softly with impatience. "I am one with them and not one with them. They seldom let me in on their plans if they involve bloodshed; they are well aware of how divided my life has become. I come into council meetings to give opinions, as spokesperson for what remains of my own tribe, and to advise on what the white soldiers may or may not do."

"One day," she warned softly, "Osceola might kill you."

He shook his head. "You do not know him, you do not understand him. He will not kill me. He knows that I was with many of the men, guiding them southwestwardly. Once they've reached their families, I'll know who still wishes to come in and accept the government's compensation for moving west. Today was not meant to be a battle on anyone's part. The soldiers weren't really looking for Indians; the Seminoles definitely weren't looking for the soldiers."

The water was growing chill. She lifted her hands together and looked at them.

"There was so much blood!" she whispered miserably.

"And so much more will be spilled," he said. "And you need to be out of it!"

"I have become a part of it."

"You are no part of it! Do you think that a day trailing after the soldiers will make it so? You belong in your silks and lace, behind a spinet. On the ballroom dance floor."

"I was good on the field today."

"Patching up Seminoles as well as good white soldiers?"

"Yes!"

"I might have lain out there, injured, bleeding."

"Stop it!"

"You shouldn't have been where you were."

"I was *afraid* you might have lain out there, injured, bleeding."

"You cannot be afraid for me."

"You cannot fight!"

"That's what you refuse to see! Sometimes I have to fight. Realize it, accept it. I was born to this. You were not. Go home, go away!"

"You had to be with the warriors; I had to be with the soldiers."

"Don't you see, it is not your place!"

"It was where I had to be!"

"Damn you! You are risking your life!"

"You risk yours constantly."

"It is my battle, my very existence. It is not your war to wage!"

"I've every right—"

"No, damn you, you have not!"

He was suddenly up on his feet, reaching for her, catching her hands, pulling her to her feet. She shivered violently with the chill of night air against her as the water sluiced from her body. He seemed heedless of it. Nothing seemed to matter at all, no words were important. He caught her about the waist and lifted her from the tub. Instinctively she clung to him, arms about his neck as he strode across the room, water dripping from her damp body and soaking hair across the fine rug and highly polished hardwood floors. She closed her eyes for a moment, nearly dizzy with the sweet pleasure of having him near again. She didn't care what he was saying to her. His chest was hot and sleek, rippling with hard muscles, alive with the thundering beat of his heart. She was so very glad he was here, and yet afraid in a way she had never been before.

She had lived without him now, after knowing him. She had come to feel the loneliness. The cold of having touched the fire, then knowing privation from it. She hadn't known how to describe what she felt for him, and now she knew that Jarrett was right. She was in love with him. All of the reasons that she should not love him added to the fact that she did. That he would not take an easy path, that he demanded he be recognized for all that he was, that he could not help but fight the injustices against the Seminoles, all these things were a part of what had so entrapped her. Perhaps. Yet she had known as well the first time she had seen him that he would enter into her heart and soul, into her dreams, her longings. It did not help to realize how deeply she cared, how much anguish she would feel when he slipped away again, a wraith in the night. An outlaw, a renegade.

Her eyes opened and met his. "You cannot so simply do this," she informed him.

"No?"

"You slip into a room without knocking, after throwing threats at me over the fallen body of a friend. Your manners are those of—"

"Of a savage?" he suggested.

"Don't play games with me!"

They had come to the bed. He held her tightly for a moment, then eased her down, coming atop her.

"But I feel very savage," he said softly.

The scent of him was sensually musky and masculine. His flesh seemed to generate a heat that eclipsed everything around it. His body against hers stirred desire and haunting memories and sweet promises of magic.

"Then perhaps you should run back into the woods," she told him.

"Perhaps not. Perhaps I am right where I belong for this moment."

"Where you will not stay when the moment has passed!" she challenged him.

He inhaled sharply, staring down at her. "You," he said sharply, "need to go home. To remember that my manners are wretched. That I belong in the woods. Do you understand me? You need to remember all that!"

"You needn't keep warning me!" she cried.

She was startled by the sudden violence of his movement as he leapt from the bed. She shivered, her naked flesh left cold by his departure. But he was as restless as a panther stalking the woods, as swift, as fluid, casting aside doeskin boots and trousers, covering her once again with the warmth of his body.

A savage warmth, as he had warned ...

He had never taken her so swiftly, with so little thought to the art of seduction, with such a stark purpose. She wanted to feel anger, to protest his invasion, thunder against his very touch. She swore softly, damning him. She did allow her fist to pummel his back. But then a ragged sob escaped her, and she held tight to him. The encroaching darkness of the night seemed to sweep over her, and into her, and under its cover she dared to let the intensity of her longings rise and soar. In time she was dimly aware of a staggering constriction within him, of a thrust that seemed to tear into her heart. Warmth like a flow of molten lava filled her, and she shuddered violently, finding sweet release in a moment of all but blinding pleasure.

He didn't let her go. He stayed with her, holding her.

Then, to her amazement, he was suddenly swearing. His weight shifted from hers; he was up, slipping into his breeches and boots.

As she lay dumbfounded, he exited the room into the hallway.

Shaking, Teela sat up. Furious with him, with herself, she rose and hurried to the tub, where the water was now startlingly cool. She scooped handfuls to her face, allowed it run down the length of her, cooled herself again. She found her towel, rubbed furiously, and wrapped it about herself, talking aloud in a hushed and miserable whisper.

"Damn him. Damn him. Damn him! It has nothing to do with being savage, he is just rude and cruel. I hate him. I'll have nothing else to do with him, I won't, I won't!"

She drew a chemise and pantalettes from a drawer within the wardrobe, wrenched the first over her head and stumbled into the second, then tried to tighten the ties. She stood in front of the swivel mirror, drying her hair with her towel, brushing it through with her fingers.

Time slipped away; her hair began to dry. She grabbed up her brush and gave it a furious hundred strokes, then a hundred more. Her emotions continued to plummet and spiral. She felt numb one moment, ready to cry the next. She was not going to do so. She was going to dress and walk downstairs, and the next time he appeared anywhere near her ...

The door opened and closed softly. She spun around at the sound.

He was back. He appeared almost ridiculously civilized now, wearing a clean white shirt along with his brown breeches and boots. His black hair was unqueued, brushed and sleek. Standing there, he was tall and striking, dignified, somber and handsome, and she was alarmed by the anguish that raced through her at the sight of him.

"I don't care how 'savage' you're feeling. If you enter my room again, you had best knock first!"

He didn't respond for a moment. Then he told her quietly, "I told my brother that you will not be down."

"Well, you have no right to speak for me. I will be going down."

"No, I think not," he said, striding toward her. He smiled, and she realized that she was holding her brush in a threatening manner.

He reached for it, taking it from her hand. "When you are here, near me, involved in this wretched war, I am determined that I must speak for you."

"I will be going down."

"Not tonight."

"You will not tell me what to do. You walk in here like the king of the forest. You simply take what you wish—"

"I was very, very *hungry*," he said softly.

Tears stung her eyes. "You simply take what you wish," she continued, "then walk away. You—"

"I came here," he interrupted, "and barely remembered the one who is the most important person in my life, my daughter. I barely remembered her because of you."

"You might have said—something."

"Damn you, I came to you first."

"You came to me to find out who was in the house."

"I came to you first," he repeated tensely.

Teela fell silent, watching him. He stood so close to her. Every breath she took seemed filled with him. The air seemed charged as if with lightning.

"I will be gone when you awaken. But until then I will tell you again to go home, to turn away from all of this, to run away from me. That's exactly what I want you to do. I just want you to do it tomorrow. After tonight."

"Go away now!" she whispered vehemently.

But again he shook his head. And she gasped a desperate little sound, throwing her arms around him. He caught her, held her very tight. He kissed her hungrily, slowly, sensually. He ran his fingers through her hair, down her back, over her buttocks, holding her tighter and tighter against him. At last he lifted her and carried her until she felt that she was falling down into clouds. Her chemise and pantalettes were luxuriously stripped away; his own clothing was more quickly shed. His every touch was erotic, unbearably so, tenderly so. A stoke here against her flesh, the intimate brush of his lips there, the caress of his palm, and again the feel of his lips, the hot, liquid fire of the tip of his tongue . . .

Toward dawn he held her. She savored the feel of being where she was. She didn't want to sleep; she wanted to grasp tightly to every last moment. But exhaustion seemed to overwhelm her.

She dozed, then heard his voice, fierce and determined. "I will not love you, Teela, will not, cannot! Damn you, you will go home, away from here. You must."

Her eyes opened, drowsy, upon his. His eyes were burning a furious blue. "Get out of this life!" he insisted angrily. But his lips ground down upon hers.

"Go to hell!" she mumbled against his kiss.

He made love to her again.

But in the morning, as he had warned her, he was gone.

Chapter 13

The days and weeks passed by.

At first Teela feared that any moment Michael Warren would appear, demanding she follow him somewhere. But it seemed that he had now determined, through the help and kindness of John Harrington, that she intended to be a dutiful daughter in the matter of marriage. Teela felt terribly guilty about John. She wondered frequently what might have happened had she met him under different circumstances, away from here.

Before she had met James.

She heard nothing from her stepfather, and gradually she began to relax. There was no hardship to living at Cimarron, and she was grateful to be living with Tara and Jarrett, for summer was a tense time in Florida. As the heat increased, so did the fear. It was multiplied by the fact that so many soldiers fell prey to disease in the summer. The bugs were so numerous; bites became infected. Men were down. Teela knew this because the young captain, Tyler Argosy, remained assigned to the Tampa area, and when he could, he took the river down to Cimarron. At first Jarrett had tried to keep her from hearing any of the military discussions. He and Tyler had retired to his library each time the captain arrived. But Jarrett McKenzie was accustomed to having his wife with him on most occasions, and when Teela confronted him, begging to be allowed to know what was going on as well, Tara took her side, quietly asserting that if Teela had survived life with Michael Warren, she was strong enough to deal with the brutality of any situation. Jarrett

McKenzie had stared at her a long while, and she had felt a strange stirring in her heart—in a way, he was so like his younger brother. Sometimes she still thought that he harbored an angry disapproval of her; then at others she thought that he understood. His attitude toward her was often that of a stern parent, but his actions and words were always softened by those of his wife. Upon occasion, late at night, if they sat together on the porch and watched the beauty of the moon rising over the river, his words would be gentle, and she would realize that the silken ties of affection linking her to Cimarron, Tara, the children, and Jarrett himself were just as equally returned. He didn't dislike her; he feared for her, and for James. But he believed that his brother saw the realities of life while she did not. For his brother's sake and perhaps for her own, he would protect her as he would his own family.

Thanks to Tara, though, she was welcomed into the library for sherry and brandy—and the truth of the situation. The soldiers were often in very sad shape. For the Seminoles life was even harder. But summer, which brought so much sickness to the whites, was a time of gathering for the Indians. They would be desperately storing food supplies from now through the fall before the cold came. Winters could be hard. The soldiers destroyed whatever crops they could find. The Indians raided white farms, plantations, and settlements whenever they could. It was a tug-of-war. A time of tension, like the hot, brooding time that seemed to press down before a storm. And General Jesup wanted a storm. He plotted and planned and strategized as the soldiers, and the Indians, waited through the long, hot days of summer.

On the days when Tyler came to dinner, Teela came to the library and listened.

During too many nights she waited.

But James did not reappear in her balcony doorway, and she heard nothing about his movements.

Like everyone else, Teela grew weary of the constant heat, and the wondering, the waiting, and the fear.

Of course, most other whites lived with the fear of Indian attack. Teela lived with fear for James.

Occasionally, she rode with Tara or Jarrett to Robert Trent's plantation, not far from Cimarron. She liked Robert very much, and on one particularly still and sullen day, she entreated Jeeves to escort her over on her own. She spent the day with the pleasant, handsome young man, who entertained her lavishly with stories about pirates and funny tales about explorers. On a more serious note, he dragged down books and maps and told her about the earliest tribes that had lived in the territory, about their demise. He showed her where the Upper and Lower Creeks have lived, how they had journeyed south. He told her where the different bands had originally settled, the Alachuas, the Tallahassees, the Mikasukees, and more. She stayed very late and found herself Robert's guest for the night.

Robert's house, though much smaller than Cimarron, boasted beautiful balconies as well. She was startled in the morning to slip out onto her own and witness a strange sight. Robert, in breeches only, stood by the rail outside his own room. He didn't see Teela, for his gaze was fixed on the edge of trees that bordered his property before disappearing into the brush.

Teela quickly followed his gaze.

The Indian girl stood so still that Teela nearly missed her. She wore beige doeskin and no jewelry. Her pitch black hair hung freely down her back. Her face was soft copper in color, her eyes as coal as her hair. Her features were slim and stunning. She brought her fingers to her lips, touched them briefly, and turned. Amazed, Teela stared at Robert again. For a moment he looked toward the brush into which the girl had disappeared. Then he seemed to start, aware that Teela was watching him. He stiffened.

"Miss Warren. How did you sleep?"

"Fine, thank you. Robert, who was that?"

"No one."

"Robert, the girl—"

"I tell you, no one."

She fell silent. "As you well know," she said very softly, "I would certainly understand—"

"Teela!" he insisted, "you saw no one." Then he amended his words, a bleak touch of misery in his words. "This is different," he said very quickly. "James McKenzie is a man who can make his own rules. Your stepfather is a butcher, but he will not slit your throat, or kill you for your actions, whether he knows or only suspects exactly what you have done. The Seminole women have not fallen prey to either the white settlers or the white soldiers. They do not betray their men. If it was even suspected that Tamara came here, she might well be murdered by her own kin, and I and my house would be burned to the ground. Do you understand?"

"I saw no one," Teela said quietly, and she returned to her room, leaving him the privacy of his balcony. She didn't speak of what she had witnessed again.

She thought about it often, though.

Jeeves returned for her that afternoon. Early that evening, with Jennifer helping her, Teela bathed the baby while Tara was supervising in the smokehouse. She had the baby smiling and cooing and Jennifer giggling when Tara returned to the room, and she then realized that Tara was staring at her. Once Ian was put down for a nap and Jennifer had gone to her own room, Teela excused herself to change for dinner, but Tara stopped her.

"Did you enjoy Robert's house?"

"Of course. He is a fascinating man."

Tara smiled. "Yes, he is. He knows so very much. He is interested in everything around him. He is a very good man."

Teela nodded, wondering where this was leading.

Tara hesitated. "You stayed very late. We were almost hoping . . ."

"Hoping what?" Teela inquired.

Tara blushed slightly. "That you . . . that you two were

simply enjoying each other so much that . . . that that is
why you stayed," Tara finished a little lamely.

Teela lightly bit her lower lip, looking down. She
shook her head, and her voice was husky when she
spoke. "Tara, is it not bad enough that I am supposedly
engaged to one man, while I . . ."

"Am sleeping with another?" Tara inquired.

"Well," Teela said, her voice with a slight edge, "I
am not exactly sleeping with anyone." It had been so
long now since she had seen James. It was painful. More
painful because she felt abandoned, no matter that there
was a war on.

And that he as often as not considered her the enemy.

Tara came over to her and set her arms around her
shoulders. "You are misunderstanding me. I have no intention of judging you. Indeed, you have come here full
of courage, and I was all but dragged, and came only
because I ran away from a greater horror."

Teela arched a brow to her. Tara smiled. "It is a very
long story, but I was hiding in New Orleans and came
upon Jarrett and Robert. Jarrett actually married me just
because it was necessary to get me out of New Orleans."

"I don't believe it! He adores you!"

"I have been exceptionally lucky and blessed in that,"
Tara agreed with a wry smile, "yet it did not start out
so. Anyway, I'm telling you this because Robert was a
very good friend to me at the time—so good, in fact,
that for a while Jarrett was irritated, and so, since I know
Robert, and his kindnesses, I have to admit that I was
hoping that something might come to pass between the
two of you."

Staring at her, Teela shook her head. "No," she said
very softly. "As he is to you, he is a friend to me."

"And you remain in love with my brother-in-law,"
Tara said sadly. She walked across the room to stare out
the window.

"I don't—I don't know that I'm in love with him,"
Teela lied, feeling the need for a little pride at the mo-

ment. "I am involved. I cannot change what . . . what I do feel," she added a bit stiffly.

"I love James, and I understand your feelings," Tara said softly. "But he cannot change what he is. You cannot understand the depths of his grief for Naomi and his child. You aren't a part of his world. You are a ward of Michael Warren. Dear God, Teela, I cannot see a happy ending in this for you, do you understand?"

"I am not asking anything of James McKenzie."

"You are waiting for him," Tara said. "And none of us knows if or when he will come."

Teela felt her hands trembling and folded them together to hide the fact. She lowered her head, not meeting Tara's eyes.

"Perhaps I should leave."

"Oh, dear Lord! I didn't mean that!" Tara said, horrified. "We want you here, truly. It's been wonderful to have you. Jennifer loves you, the baby loves you—I love you!"

Teela looked up, really frightened because tears were stinging her eyes. She didn't want to shed them; she could wind up in a pool of them.

"I love you all, too. Very much. And I'm so very grateful."

Tara walked back across the room and hugged her. "I didn't speak to hurt you, I hope you understand that. And I know that James is fiercely attracted to you. It's just that—oh, God, you must see, it's such an awful situation!"

Teela nodded, pulling away from Tara, looking at the other woman.

"We'd best get dressed for dinner," Tara said.

Teela started out of the room. She was at the door when Tara called her back.

"Teela?"

"Yes?"

"Obsessively attracted," she repeated. "I think, in fact, he'd be ready to douse me in the river if he'd any idea I was encouraging you to look elsewhere."

"He's suggested that I marry another man," Teela said.

"In a way, he probably means it. He wants you to live, to be safe. To be out of this. Then again, he is fiercely possessive. It surely caused him great pain to walk away, yet he knew he must. I wonder if he could do so again."

"I wonder, too," Teela said softly, and she left Tara, hurrying to her room to dress for dinner.

Later, she and Tara sat with Jarrett for supper downstairs at the big, polished table in the dining room. Conversation was casual, and they all kept it away from the subject of the war. Jarrett asked her about her stay with Robert, his dark eyes enigmatic. She told him that Robert was very well, and that she'd enjoyed her stay.

It was then that the messenger arrived.

Jeeves came into the dining room and spoke softly and politely with Jarrett. Jarrett excused himself, leaving his wife and Teela to stare at each other. Then Tara leapt up and Teela followed her, racing out to the open breezeway doors to see that a Seminole of indeterminate age with wizened dark features and gray-streaked long black hair sat atop a thin horse, waiting as Jarrett read a letter.

"What is it?" Tara asked tensely.

Jarrett shook his head. "It is nothing. Everything is well." He switched to the Indian's language then. When the man replied, his voice deep and quiet, Teela felt his dark eyes on her. He didn't seem to judge, but he did appraise, as if he was going to give an accounting of her to someone at a later time.

She didn't understand a word of the conversation, but she was certain that Jarrett was offering the Indian some kind of hospitality. The man accepted leather saddlebags brought out by Jeeves. He seemed to thank Jarrett for the goods in the bags, but refuse to accept anything more. He could not stay. He raised a hand to Jarrett, then turned his scrawny nag about to head back into the wilderness.

"Who was that?" Teela asked anxiously.

"Shall we go back to the dinner table?"

"But—"

Jarrett was already walking back in. The women followed him, taking their seats. Jarrett sipped from his wineglass.

"Please!" Teela exploded.

He gazed at her as with surprise, then smiled. "Teela, nothing has happened. That was Jim Johnson, a man of mixed blood who has always lived with my brother's people."

"Then—"

"He brought word from my stepmother that she is well and fine, and far from the fighting and danger."

"Stepmother!" Teela gasped.

"Mary McKenzie," Tara told Teela.

"My brother's mother," Jarrett said, watching her as he swirled his wine. "She raised us both."

"And she's living out there—somewhere"—Teela gasped with horror—"while soldiers like my father track Indians down and slaughter women and children as well?"

"Your stepfather," Tara reminded her with a trace of amusement.

But Teela felt a constricting fear seize her. "Jarrett, how can you let her stay in the swampland and the bush with so much danger?"

"How can I stop her?" he asked politely in return.

"But you must—"

"Teela," Tara interrupted, "Mary does not wish to come and live with us; I have entreated her to do so, as has Jarrett, and for that matter, James. Her way is a difficult one. Filled with many hardships. But she loves her life, and finds it every bit as civilized and rich as any we might lead."

"But—" Teela began again.

"Enough! I haven't the right to force my way of life on her," Jarrett exploded.

Teela shook her head, unaware of just how hard she

was pushing. "What if the soldiers do win? What if the warriors are killed to the last, and the women and the children are shipped west? What will you do then? What if the warriors are all killed and men like Michael Warren move in to exterminate all the Indians who remain? Will you let her be slaughtered to maintain her way of life?"

"Teela, to some people a way of life *is* life," Tara said quickly, trying to make peace. Teela saw the warning in her eyes and bit her lip, determined to fall silent.

But it was too late. Jarrett stood up suddenly, casting his napkin down upon the table. He started from the room, pausing by her chair. "You may rest assured, Miss Warren, no member of my family will suffer extermination or execution while I draw breath. But neither will I force my stepmother or my brother to my opinion or viewpoint; nor can I fight any battle for James. Each man wages his own war."

He left the room.

Teela looked miserably at Tara. "I'm sorry. I had no right. It was just that I was so surprised to learn that his stepmother was alive, that she is in the wilderness . . ."

Tara shook her head, smiling slightly. "It will be all right. It's just that he does suffer terribly, worrying about his stepmother. Jarrett adores Mary. As I do. James and Jarrett both pleaded with Mary to come to Cimarron after Naomi died, but she pleaded right back that she would rather stay with her people and run farther south."

"What's she like?" Teela found herself asking. It was foolish. There was no future for her with James; she needed to stay out of his life. He had certainly managed to stay away from her. But she couldn't seem to help herself.

"Mary?" Tara said, thinking. "She's very sweet. Generous, giving. Strong, intelligent." Tara smiled. "You can tell by the sons she has raised."

"And what was Naomi like?" Teela heard herself inquire.

Tara hesitated.

"She would have been beautiful by any man's standards," Tara said softly. "She would have been a part of James, of his way of life. She would have understood his people and his language. He would have loved her very much instead of just wanting her."

"Teela—"

Teela stood, smiling at Tara. "Don't, please don't. You don't need to say anything to me. I don't mean to sound morose. I am full-grown and quite able to take responsibility for my own actions. You're very kind, and you ache easily for those around you. Don't suffer for me."

"Teela—"

Teela pretended not to hear. She hurried out of the room and ran to the porch, anxious to breathe in the fresh air that drifted off the river. She clung to a column, feeling that she had been cast into hell. These were wonderful people. It hurt to be with them. She loved the territory, loved the sunsets, the heat, the soaring flights of the exotic birds ... loved it, but had no place within it. She would leave it, but unless she ran very hard and very fast, she would simply find more soldiers on her doorstep to bring her back. Unless she could find a way around them.

"Oh, God!" she whispered aloud, and pressed her temple with her palms. It was then that she heard the creak of a rocker behind her. She spun around to see that Jarrett had come outside, too. She blushed a shade of crimson, miserably lowering her head. He rose and walked to her, lifting her chin with his thumb and forefinger.

"If I am cruel or impatient," he told her gently, "I do not mean to be so."

She drew back, trying very hard to stiffen her spine. "You are not cruel. And as I told Tara, you mustn't worry on my account. I am not as fragile as I appear. My actions here have been of my free will, and I accept all the consequences."

She was startled to see that he was smiling with a certain amount of amusement. He sat upon the porch rail, leaning back against one of the massive columns.

"You don't appear at all fragile," he told her.

She arched a brow, and his smile deepened.

"And there, my dear Miss Warren, is the dilemma I face. For my brother, I would keep you safe. My brother who covets you on the one hand, and yet would be faster than Michael Warren to push you down the aisle to marry young Mr. Harrington, if that would take you from the territory, and from danger. But as to the *fragile* part, no, you are not that! You have a will as wild and flaming as that hair of yours, a determination of steel. That, as much as the *delicacy* of your beauty, is the attraction that obsesses my brother."

"So you would push me down the aisle with John as well?" she asked somewhat bitterly.

"Maybe."

"If you're angry—"

"I'm not angry. If anything, I feel a sense of guilt. I brought you here. I had no idea of what it might mean to the two of you. I wish that you had come here and somehow found happiness."

Teela smiled slowly. "You *were* angry with me because I didn't understand that Mary had to live her own life. You were right to be angry because I should have seen it myself, perhaps more than anyone else. We all have to lead the lives we choose. I wouldn't change anything that has happened. Perhaps the future is bleak, but I'd not have changed anything. I'm not sorry."

He studied her for a minute. Then he said, "Jim Johnson did come with a message from Mary, but he had also seen James."

Her heart seemed to catch in her throat. "Yes?"

"He is at a council with Osceola, Philip, Jumper, Micanopy, and others. He is well."

"But he is in the path of the soldiers."

"He is well, Teela. And well able to care for himself."

She nodded. "Thank you," she told him.

"You should get some sleep."

She nodded, thanked him again, and went into the house. She lay awake, certain that James had known that Jim Johnson was coming to Cimarron. And James had sent no message to her. In his mind, there was nothing for him to say. He had said it all already.

She slept very late and very badly. She awoke to hear a pounding on her door. Tara was calling to her tensely. "Teela, wake up! Quickly."

Alarmed, Teela ran to the bedroom door and threw it open. Tara was pale.

"James . . . ?" Teela whispered in horror.

"No, no!" Tara said quickly. "It's—it's Michael Warren. He's come for you."

James was all right. That was the only thought that spun in her head. The world suddenly seemed to spin black, and she pitched forward in a dead faint.

Teela awoke to discover that she was lying on her bed with Tara anxiously hovering over her. "Just breathe easily. I shall do something if Jarrett doesn't. I'll—I'll shoot him! You won't have to go with him—"

"Tara!"

Teela sat up, pushing back her hair, fighting the last few waves of dizziness that assailed her. "Please! I'm not afraid of Michael Warren. I was just so relieved because when I first saw you, I was so frightened. About James."

"Warren has come for you, Teela. He's been assigned across the territory to a newly built depot that is heavily fortified and manned. Tyler Argosy is with him, and Dr. Brandeis, and they're traveling with him as well, so I'm certain that you'd be safe, but you don't have to go, there must be a way out of it—"

"Tara, you can't shoot Michael Warren for me," Teela said, managing a slight smile.

"Still—"

"It's all right. I'm not afraid of him, really. And remember, I'm engaged to marry John Harrington. Michael will have to take care."

"I doubt if anything makes such a man take care," Tara said.

Teela mentally steadied herself, then rose. "I'll just dress and be down," she told Tara.

"I will be at your side," Tara said.

Tara left her to dress, which Teela did quickly. She tried not to think, but she had to think, and amazingly, she realized that she was ready to go with her stepfather. She still loved Cimarron—and the people who had shown her such kindness here.

But she did know Michael Warren. She had been on borrowed time all of the days that she had been here. And she could not stand another day of pining away for James.

When she hurried downstairs, a still and ashen Jeeves directed her to the library. She paused to kiss his cheek. "I am going to be all right, Jeeves!" she assured him, and hurried on in.

Jarrett McKenzie stood behind his desk, tall, straight, imposing. Joshua and Tyler were seated in the upholstered chairs that faced the desk, while Michael Warren stood before a globe of the world, whirling it slowly. Tara stood very stiffly some distance from him, and though the room had fallen silent when Teela entered, she was certain that the conversation had been heated before.

Joshua and Tyler both stood as she entered. "Miss Warren!" Joshua said enthusiastically, coming forward to take her hands. "Tyler here has had the sweet opportunity of seeing you often, alas, having met you, I have missed you."

"Thank you, Dr. Brandeis, it is good to see you again," Teela told him. Her stepfather was staring at her then with his hard, cold eyes.

"You'll have ample opportunity to enjoy the good doctor's company, Teela. I have been assigned to bring men and supplies across to Fort Deliverance. Even Mr. McKenzie will agree that you may abide in safety there, for over two hundred men are to travel with me, and even more are stationed at Deliverance. I know that you will be anxious to accompany us, since John Harrington will also be assigned to the fort on occasion."

"Major Warren, you are talking about traveling nearly a hundred miles through harrowing territory—" Jarrett began sternly.

"But—" Teela jumped in, interrupting him with an apologetic smile, "I am deeply interested in the terrain. I will be safe with so many soldiers, surely. And if Dr. Brandeis has found himself in need of my services . . ."

"Most definitely," Joshua said, and he too looked at Jarrett. "She is extremely efficient and helpful. A natural."

Jarrett stared at Teela. "You are welcome to remain here. Indeed, we would most certainly prefer it if you were to remain here."

"We?" Michael Warren inquired politely, staring hard at Jarrett.

"My wife and I, sir," Jarrett said.

"And I thank you both with all my heart and hope that I might return," Teela said. She couldn't look at either of them as she added, "John might come to Fort Deliverance. I should be there."

"John has always and frequently come here," Jarrett said.

"Harrington is assigned as I myself am, sir," Michael Warren said, "to the area south of St. Augustine, where it seems many of the spitfire chiefs have gathered to discuss their war and their business. It is a place from which we will smoke them out in the months to come. We've great strength there, Mr. McKenzie, I do assure you. Though I need not do so. Teela is my daughter."

"Stepdaughter," Jarrett, Tara, Teela, and even Tyler Argosy said in unison.

A slight smile played on Teela's lip. Michael was not amused. "Teela is my ward, my responsibility," he said firmly.

"And I will be fine," Teela said earnestly, looking at Jarrett.

He stared at her a long while, then threw up his hands. "If you are willing to go . . ."

"Yes," she said simply.

"I will help you with your things," Tara said.

"Perhaps Teela should not leave my sight this time," Michael said, his eyes narrowed on Teela.

"I will be right back down," Teela assured him. He seemed to know that she meant it.

He shrugged. "Then take your time, daughter."

Teela fled the library with Tara close on her heels. Upstairs, once they had both reached Teela's room, Tara closed the door quickly and told her, "You don't have to go. You're agreeing because you don't want to cause trouble for Jarrett and me. But you needn't be afraid."

"Tara, really, it will be all right. Joshua and Tyler are both with Michael. He will have to behave decently among such men."

"But—"

"Tara, I can't stay any longer. I love the house, I love the children, I love visiting Robert and poring over his library. But I feel that I need to go. I can make a difference when I'm with Joshua. I can help save lives."

Tara was silent for a moment. "All right. I'll help you. James will not be pleased."

"All I hear is that James must fight his own war and live his own life. Well, I must do the same—or go mad!" Teela told her.

Tara didn't reply to that.

But later, when Teela was ready to go, they hugged each other fiercely, and it was hard to part. It was hard to kiss the baby, harder still to part with Jennifer. Then there was Jarrett, still disapproving and stern as he stared at her, then more gentle as he held her and kissed her forehead. "Guard that red head carefully, Miss Warren," he told her.

"I promise."

"I wonder if my brother is aware of just how much you do love him."

"I hope not, since he does not feel the same."

"He would die for you. What more could you ask?"

"He would die for many; it is a trait in certain men that you two seem to share."

Jarrett shook his head. "It is his war in a way that it cannot be for you. Try to understand that. And rest assured, he would die for you. For *you,* Teela. Not for the sake of a cause. As I told you, he is a realist—"

"And I am not?" she asked with a slow smile. She kissed his cheek. "Don't worry. I will not let him die for me. If I ever see him again," she added with a pained whisper.

"I almost wish that you would not. But quite strangely, I am quite certain that we will meet again. So again I tell you, protect that beautiful head of red hair, keep well and safe."

"You do the same."

Her throat was choked; tears threatened. She turned quickly and headed along the dock to reach the sloop where her father waited.

Joshua leapt forward to help her. He lifted her to the deck, steadying her as she landed.

She turned back. The McKenzies were together. Jarrett, tall, dark, so imposing, had his arm around his wife. The baby was cradled in her arms. Jennifer stood before them, and Jarrett's free arm rested on her shoulders. She lifted a hand to wave to them, and tears did blur her eyes.

The ship moved away from the McKenzie docks, along the river, inland.

She heard a voice from behind her. "We've a day on the river, girl, then we march inland. And I've little to say to you now that should be heard by this company, but I promise you, Teela, I'll have plenty to say once we've taken up our march on land."

He left her. The men on the deck rushed about with the business of sailing the ship.

The McKenzie dock slowly faded and disappeared around the bend of the river.

Chapter 14

The army moved quickly.

On their second day of travel, the last transport vessel—a fishing boat "borrowed" from a Tampa fisherman—reached the landing whence they were to start on their eastward march. There were two hundred soldiers in the movement, with Michael Warren in command. Fifty-five mounted men, one hundred and forty soldiers on foot, some militia, some regular army, some marines and navy men, loaned by their own commanding officers for land duty.

They made a sweep through what had once been thriving Indian lands, clearing the way, carrying supplies that had arrived at Fort Brooke. They brought with them rifles, haversacks, and tents—wall tents, common tents, hospital tents. Huge sheets of rubber cloth, sheepskins for many uses, saddle blankets, halters, harnesses. Horseshoes, kettles, tools, food. Bags of rice and corn meal, astringent wines, foods that would survive the wretched heat that assailed the party day after day.

Jarrett had often described the life of the Indians to her. She could have told him now that it was almost as bad for the soldiers who had been sent out to track them down. But Jarrett would have known that as well.

The soldiers themselves were a strange lot. Many were immigrants who barely spoke English. Many were, strangely enough, men who had trained for other walks of life, such as the ministry or law. But the whole of the country had been suffering from hard financial times, and some men had joined the army just to feed themselves and their families. Teela had found some friends among them.

She also accrued a few enemies, specifically regular army men who were her stepfather's elite core.

On the third day of their march across the peninsula, they discovered a small band of Yuchis, and one company of Warren's men was sent in to take care of them.

There hadn't been more than fifty Indians, perhaps twenty warriors with their women and children.

Teela knew that because the rest of the party was forced to march through the Indian camp after the soldiers had gone in. In all her life she'd never been so shocked, so horrified. Bodies lay everywhere. The bodies of warriors.

The broken, battered, bloodied bodies of innocents as well.

She wasn't the only one who was appalled. She heard some of the soldiers riding with her whispering, and she heard what they said. It wasn't necessary, what had been done. God could never condone such murder, even if the Indians were heathens.

Teela rode rigidly, barely aware of the tears that streamed down her face.

But toward dusk, they stopped at last by a stream. Teela dismounted slowly while the men much more quickly broke up to make camp by the water's edge. Teela saw Tyler giving orders not far from where she stood and walked slowly to him. "Captain Argosy?"

"Teela?"

"Who led the attack on the Yuchis?"

"Teela, you can't involve yourself—"

"Tyler, who?" she demanded furiously.

A young soldier stood by Tyler. "Why, it was Captain Julian Hampton. He's right down there by the stream, ma'am," he said helpfully.

"Soldier, see to the tent!" Tyler commanded, but it was too late. Teela was already headed to where the young captain had come to bathe his face and drink from the cool water.

He stood as Teela approached, a handsome man with a fine curling mustache, hazel eyes, and a rich crop of mahogany hair. Teela walked straight toward him without stopping. When she reached him, she struck out at him instantly, taking him by complete surprise. Her fury was so great that her simple assault sent him flying back into the water.

He was quickly up, staring at Teela with disbelief, stroking his wounded cheek with his hand. Teela started toward him again.

"Ma'am, are you plumb out of your mind?" Hampton demanded.

She *was* out of her mind, she thought. She didn't care. She was ready to strike him again, but suddenly someone was holding her gently but firmly from behind. Joshua Brandeis was there, keeping her from Captain Hampton.

"How could you?" she raged. "How could you—*murder* babies?"

"Teela, come away," Joshua insisted.

"Teela!" Tyler Argosy had made it down to the stream as well. His hand firmly on her arm, he tried to lead her away.

"Wait!" Hampton cried. "Tyler, just wait with her one minute. Miss Warren, you see what you want to see, and you haven't seen the whole of it yet! White babies have been murdered, too. White women, young women, like yourself. You'll understand one day. You just wait until you've had one of those redskins standing over you with one of his knives, taking that red hair for a prize."

Hampton squashed his waterlogged hat back over his head and walked away.

"It's true, Teela, such things happen," Joshua Brandeis told her.

"I know that, but does it make it right for us to murder children?"

"No," Brandeis said after a moment. "It does not." He lowered his voice. "But you can't battle the whole of this army, my girl. And it's your stepfather giving the orders here. Come away, forget it."

"I'll never forget it."

"Come and have a good swallow of whiskey now. Go to bed, get some sleep."

Teela did that. Shaking, she drank whiskey with Joshua. When the tents were pitched, she retired to her own. She slept a troubled sleep. When she woke up in the morning, Michael Warren was standing over her.

He wrenched her to her feet, speaking before she could protest.

"We'll take this outside of the camp, daughter!"

She gritted her teeth while he half led and half dragged her through the field of tents. Most of the camp still slept. The soldiers on guard duty saluted Michael, and he and Teela hurried on until they were far downstream, with the breeze carrying their words away from the camp.

"Don't you ever interfere with my officers or my orders again, do you hear me, girl?"

"You ordered men to murder children."

She cried out as he suddenly slapped her with such a stunning blow that she was sent staggering down to the wet mud by the water's edge, her ears ringing, her vision blackening.

"You don't know anything about this war, or about right or wrong. All you know is what you've learned from being a little tramp with a half-breed. But I'll warn you on this, the next time you think to make a fool out of me, girl, I'll take a horsewhip to you in front of the entire army."

"Fine! Do it!" she cried.

He'd started to walk away, but at her words he paused, walking back to her. She leapt up, backing cautiously away from him, hatred burning in her eyes.

"You're out of Cimarron now. And Jarrett McKenzie and his half-breed brother may have their influence in this peninsula, but I tell you, the army is powerful, too, and I'm a powerful part of it. And do you want to know

why? White folks in Boston may bleed a little in their
hearts for a poor noble savage, but white folks in the
South want to move on down into this peninsula, and
they want the Seminoles out. The white politicians need
men who can accomplish that feat, and Teela, I am a
soldier above all else, a man to get the job done. And to
me, a half-breed is a breed, an Indian. James McKenzie's
almost as much trouble as that Osceola himself, and I'd
just as soon shoot that bastard breed as look at him.
Give me cause, Teela. Just give me cause, and I'll hunt
him down. I have hundreds of men behind me. I can
turn him into the worst criminal in the territory. I can
hunt him like a cougar. Just speak to me rudely once,
defy me one more time . . ."

"I've obeyed your orders. I am engaged to John Harrington—"

"And John Harrington is fighting in the field to the
south, girl. You're not his wife yet. You are my daughter
still. You speak to me politely, obediently. You know,
Teela, the soldiers are taking scalps as well now. Not
officially, of course. But they are taking scalps. And if
you embarrass me one more time, I will have James
McKenzie's, girl. If I have to call out the whole of the
army to do it. I ask you—are we understood?"

"Yes."

"Yes, what?"

"Yes, we are understood."

"Yes, *sir,* we are understood."

"Yes, *sir,* we are understood."

Michael Warren smiled, and he turned to leave her.
Beneath the shimmering sunshine she shivered. She was
stronger than he was, she told herself. She would be
stronger. She wouldn't falter or fail, and somehow she'd
best him in the end.

But to her dismay, her stomach churned. Her vision
blurred again. She stooped down to the water, dousing
her face with its coolness, praying the nausea would
leave her. At last it did.

And she stood, determined again that she would be

the stronger of the two of them. And she didn't give a damn what war they were fighting.

In the end, she was going to win.

There were many chiefs and many warriors who had come together in the grove southwest of St. Augustine. They had gathered from the various places they had been fighting, not many from the north now because the soldiers had so efficiently removed them from most of the fine ground just south of Tallahassee, the white capital, ironically named for the Indians who had abided there for thousands of years. They had been pushed east of St. Augustine, west of Tampa Bay, south of Ocala. Even the "good" Indians, the Spanish Indians north of the Peace River, were being attacked and pressed into the battle.

Since the massive escape of the warriors from the detention center at Fort Brooke, General Jesup himself, often a reasonable man if not a kind one, was rumored to have declared that no Indians could behave honorably. He liked to say that Osceola was a renegade who made agreements when he chose to for gain, then reneged upon his word.

There were many important warriors here tonight, drawn together around the bright yellow and orange light of their campfire. Some were alone; some were with their wives and family. There were no neatly hewn log cabins for them anymore. They built lean-tos and shelters—hooties, as they called them. Simple structures of pine branches and cabbage palms, whatever could give them some comfort against the elements. They had to be built quickly and with little effort because the white soldiers would soon come and push the Indians out and burn down whatever they had constructed.

Osceola was not a hereditary leader, but tonight, when they discussed the war, life and death, and simple survival, he held a very important position. He did, however, gaze into the fire remorsefully, waiting for James to read a letter taken from the bedroll of a fallen white soldier by a small band just days before.

James looked around the fire. Alligator was there, old Micanopy, Coweta, and Coacoochee, or Wildcat, the son of King Philip.

James glanced at the paper again and then told them, "The soldier was writing to his uncle. He asks about his family, then talks about General Jesup. Apparently, Jesup has asked the government for help against an Indian problem. Jesup wants help in recruiting other *Indians* to fight against us. He wants Shawnees, Delawares, Kickapoos, Sioux, and Choctaws." He looked up at the group around him. He never lied when he spoke with the Seminole leaders, even when he thought that a lie would sit better.

"General Jesup wants the U.S. government to pay these Indians to fight us as traditional enemies. He feels that they will kill the warriors without thought and take captive and enslave the women and children."

Wildcat let out a sound of disgust.

"Running Bear, tell us the rest," Osceola insisted quietly.

James shrugged. "That's all there is. He says that his rations are sad, his pay is poor, and that he will not reenlist."

"We will fight and kill the Sioux and the Choctaw and any other enemy as we kill the white soldiers!" Coweta said angrily.

"We will kill them, and more will come," Osceola said.

"We will kill them!" Wildcat cried.

"And more will come," James said quietly.

Wildcat was suddenly on his feet. He was a tall man, young, powerfully built, with strong, handsome, and ruggedly scarred features. He had gained his name from an entanglement he had survived with a panther he had inadvertently disturbed as a child. He stared at James, his fingers clenched into fists. "You speak as if you were

one of them. As if you would have us all surrender to
their demands."

James shook his head, rising carefully to lock eyes
stubbornly with Wildcat.

"I have never betrayed a friend. I have never fought
against any of my people. I have done my best to bring
terms and carry back demands in turn. I—"

"You don't understand, Running Bear, because your
blood is not pure and your mind is tainted."

James narrowed his eyes at Wildcat. "Osceola has
blood that may well be 'whiter' than mine. Within our
generation many men carry white blood. Don't challenge
me because of that fact."

"Your heart often lies with those of white blood."

"My heart lies where I see others who are in pain."

"You don't see!" Wildcat shouted. "You seek too
much good in the whites. Listen to me. They want us
gone. They want to remove us. If they cannot remove
us, they want to exterminate us."

"Not all white men wish to do so."

"White policy demands that the soldiers do so. You
fight with us only when a knife is but inches from your
heart!"

"I will not attack plantations!" James responded, reckless, angry. He swept a hand out, indicating the many
war chiefs. "I am told about the plight of our children.
Women smother their infants so that they do not starve.
Soldiers crack in little skulls, horses trample screaming
young ones. Well, I promise you this—my white brother
will not pick up arms, he will not fight alongside men
who injure Seminole children. His one surviving niece is
a Seminole child. My *white* sister-in-law once risked her
own life for my family. My brother and his wife believe
that my daughter who lives with them is innocent, trusting, loving. Beautiful. It is the same for me. My one
nephew is white. I will not take part in raids in which
white children die, whether from malice or careless accident. I have cradled a white child in my arms. My white
brother stayed with my Seminole wife and child as they

died, while others fled the fever. All that I am, all that I will and will not do, I have always stated it honestly. Would you call me a traitor for that?"

Wildcat, despite his occasional outbursts and ferocity, was learning to be a leader. He listened, then replied without haste. "I will not take this time to argue with your convictions, Running Bear." He slammed his fist suddenly against his chest. "We must fight to survive, to save our way of life. We must fight for our children, for a place for them. For their survival."

"We fight," Osceola said firmly, "and we continue fighting. When the soldiers follow us, we split and go in what directions we must go in to avoid them. We have come thus far because they cannot follow us into our secret hammocks. They have not won because we are an enemy capable of fighting and then disappearing. We mustn't forget that."

"Sometimes we must talk," Coweta argued. "Jesup has sent his messengers with great amounts of white cloth so that we may approach his chiefs in safety when we wish to talk."

Osceola stood up. "At this time we've nothing to say. Let General Jesup plan his great campaign. We will watch and wait. And fight on. As for me, when Running Bear comes to me asking that I allow certain women and children to capitulate to terms, I will not turn against those who are desperate now. I remind you, though, Running Bear, that there are those who would slay their families before letting them bow to the white men. Take care with what arrangements you make with the white soldiers—they may turn against you as well. That is all. If you come to me asking to talk to the soldiers, I will talk. But you should know this. I will fight until I can fight no more."

He wore a blanket that he wrapped tightly around his shoulders as he strode from the circle.

His words had been fierce, James thought. But Osceola still did not look well. In the middle of the summer he clung tightly to the blanket.

The group began to disband. James continued to stare

into the fire, weary of a war that showed no hope for an end, and weary as well of defending himself. At least the other men at this council knew whom they fought. Half the time he fought just to stay sane.

Long legs clad in bright red leggings came to a halt before him. He looked up. Wildcat stood before him, then hunched down.

"We were boys together," Wildcat said. "Friends a long time."

James nodded. "I am not your enemy now."

"Sometimes I am angry because you can see so much. Other times I know that you come to us to offer what wisdom you have when you might have turned your back on the people and lived the life of a white man yourself."

"I don't always know my part in this," James admitted. "I try to make all men see reason. It is a losing battle."

"No, my friend, you have not lost. Because you still see where you are trying to go."

"I hope you are right."

"I am right. But this loneliness is not good for you. Sunflower is now the widow of my cousin, Bird-in-Flight. As her husband's closest relative, it is my right to release her from her years of mourning. I will do so for you, Running Bear. Bring her the marriage gift. It will be returned, and your nights will not be so bleak in the hard days to come."

James looked up at Wildcat, who spoke so earnestly now. "Wildcat, I thank you, but—"

"She is very young and very beautiful," Wildcat said. He sounded indignant.

"Yes, and that is why I would not hurt her. She has suffered enough."

"There is rumor about you and a white woman. Do you turn Sunflower down because she is not white?" Wildcat demanded, his tone somewhat angry.

James kept his voice level. "You know that is not so. Naomi was Seminole, and I loved her with all my heart and being."

That seemed to mollify Wildcat, but his curiosity remained. "What about the white woman?"

"What red fool would love a white woman?" James asked, barely masking a trace of bitterness in his voice.

"One with white blood running beneath his red skin," Wildcat said. "And one who has come close to Warren's red-haired daughter, a rare beauty of her kind, like an exotic bird among sparrows."

Startled, James came to his feet, studying Wildcat's face. "What do you know of her?"

Wildcat smiled. "She is Warren's daughter. There are certain warriors who will care nothing about beauty or youth or innocence."

"Tell me, what do you know about Warren's daughter?" he demanded.

"Her hair is like flame. Gold and red and shimmering in the firelight. Very thick and rich. It's tempting to the hand to touch, even if she is white. She is slim as the reed in the field, yet with the curves of a woman. Her eyes are a green like the meadow after the rains."

He had to control his temper and his fear, James thought. It wouldn't help anyone's cause if he were to leap at Wildcat and go for his throat.

"Where have you seen her?" he asked firmly. Then, "Damn you, where?"

But Wildcat was determined to taunt him. He started to laugh. "I have described her well. You didn't know that others among us might know of her?"

"Wildcat—"

"She is lush, yes?"

And James did leap.

He caught Wildcat off guard, caught him with both fury and determination. His leap brought them both plummeting to the ground. Wildcat was no weakling. He bucked and tried to throw James; then the two men rolled together. The contest was in deadly earnest as Wildcat got a grip upon James's throat. James broke his opponent's hold and then rolled again. When they came to a halt, James had his thighs like a vise around Wildcat's. He slammed a solid fist against Wildcat's jaw, and was ready to strike again when Alligator suddenly came from the brush, angrily striding toward them.

"The soldiers will kill us soon enough!" he raged. "We do not have the white numbers, we need our warriors alive. The people need you both. Get up, get out of the dirt. You are not boys!"

James and Wildcat both went still, staring at each other. It was true. As children they had tussled. That had been long ago. There was a curious glint of shame in Wildcat's eyes that surprised James. There was no warrior fiercer than Wildcat. And it was true that many Indians had died at the hands of their own loved ones simply for hungering for survival—and capitulation.

James didn't want to kill Wildcat, and he was certain that Wildcat didn't want him dead, either. Pride was tremendous among the Seminoles—as the Indian agent Wiley had learned, dying at the hands of Osceola's men after having so foolishly humiliated the man.

Now he and Wildcat stared at each other, looking for an honorable way out of their fight.

James leaped from Wildcat, offering a hand to bring him to his feet.

Wildcat accepted his hand and stood up.

"My friend, I should have kept my temper. I beg your pardon. The argument was my fault," James said.

"I was at fault," Wildcat corrected. "I tormented my childhood friend."

"I beg to remain your friend," James told him.

"And I beg to remain yours," Wildcat said, and added quickly, "I saw Warren's daughter at the new fort. I saw her dancing. We thought to attack the fort, but it was too strongly built, and there were too many soldiers. From the trees beyond the clearing, I could see into the hall. She was different from the other women. Radiant with her wild hair and supple energy. She was in silk and lace. She danced with many soldiers. Smiled and laughed. She was very elegant, very beautiful. Very *white.*"

James felt white himself. Drained of all blood.

"It does not matter how beautiful she is, how elegant. She is not the right woman for you," Wildcat said. "You should consider Sunflower."

"I would not do Sunflower the injustice of marrying her when my heart is so heavy with so many matters," James said carefully, diplomatically. It was amazing to him that he could speak at all. It seemed that the whole of his body was tied into knots.

Wildcat nodded at him. "I understand."

"Sunflower lost a brave warrior who loved her beyond life itself, and she is very young and very beautiful. A warrior who deserves her, and can offer her all of his heart, will come for her soon."

"Perhaps it is so," Wildcat agreed. "My heart and my prayers go with you, my friend."

"And mine with you," James said. He turned to leave the council fire, certain that he could no longer manage the control to carry on a conversation when it felt as if he had just been ripped to shreds. He simmered with rage he could neither ease nor vent. One that would eventually explode or implode, destroying him either way.

What the hell was Teela doing, the little fool?

"Running Bear!"

James paused because Wildcat had called to him. As he turned, Wildcat hesitated, then walked firmly to stand before him.

"You are my friend, I understand you. Still, you should know. Even with your power and respect among the people, you do have enemies."

"All men have enemies," James said uneasily.

Wildcat's voice lowered still further, though Alligator was gone and they stood in the darkness alone. "The Mikasuki war chief, Otter, has sworn death to all whites, and that he will do to them what they have done to us. He will watch the soldiers at the fort and see that they are attacked along the trails any time they leave in small groups. He is waiting for Warren to leave; he covets his scalp. He is anxious for Warren's daughter to leave. He would rather have hers first, to send to Warren."

James extended a hand to Wildcat. "Thank you."

"If any of us comes upon the woman, we will take her for you, keep her alive. Even if she is wrong for you, and will bring down greater misery upon us."

"Thank you," James told him again.

He turned away. His rage was greater, churning with a fury, enhanced by a deadly fear.

He'd done everything in his power to see that she left the territory! At least at his brother's house she had been safe. Why had she left Jarrett's home, come eastward?

Warren, he thought, and he inwardly raged anew. Warren had come for her. And if Jarrett had refused Warren, he could have brought down the entire might of the army upon himself. He might have even risked Jennifer's safety, and Jarrett would have known that.

Teela would have known that.

But now, if Teela left the protection of the fort, she could damned well get herself killed.

James wound his fingers into fists, stiffening rigidly with his anguish and fear. By all the damned gods he could pray to, if he got his hands on her, he'd kill her himself. Surely she'd had ample chances to leave the whole theater of war, to sail home, to get out!

He strode to his makeshift shelter for the night and sat beneath its cabbage palm roof, looking up at the half-moon that rode the heavens.

He closed his eyes. She wouldn't leave the shelter of the fort. She was well aware of just how dangerous her position could be. She knew that Warren was hated, and that the Indians might well know her as Warren's daughter.

Warren's daughter ...

There was nothing that he could do now. Except watch and wait. And pray.

No.

He crawled out of the shelter, standing. Damn her! He didn't dare go to her.

But by every god in every heaven, he didn't dare stay away.

Chapter 15

Fort Deliverance had been kindly named, Teela thought, for there was really very little that the fort could deliver one from.

It was actually one of the depots made quickly and desperately in a chain against the Indians. It had been constructed by Tennessean and Georgian volunteers who had been promised that their stint in the Florida Territory would be over once a few such forts had been erected, and though it was a strong outpost in the wilderness, there were many day-to-day examples to demonstrate just how hastily it had been built.

The roof leaked in Teela's room. The wind ripped through gaps in the logs. The howling of wolves at night was loud, and seemed dangerously near.

But she did not mind such things so much. She minded the fact that she had come here with Warren, and she minded the horrors that she had seen along the way.

Standing atop the ramparts that ran the entire length of all four sides of the walled structure, Teela looked out over the land. They were thirty miles or so south of St. Augustine, yet they might have been a thousand, for there seemed to be nothing in front of her except strange, waving oceans of deep, rich green. Tall pine trees stretched out far to her north while there was swampland to the south and southwest, and bracken barrens to the east with the Atlantic Ocean not far beyond. There were trails out there somewhere, even a few good government roads. But to anyone walking just beyond the walls of the fort, it seemed that it was either a forbidden wild land or a very strange paradise, for there was nothing but the green of the foliage, the brown and tan of the earth, the bright blue of the sky, and the occasional deep turquoise of a creek or stream. Sometimes huge oaks shaded narrow trails from the heat of the day; there were exquisite copses where the boughs all seemed to join overhead right where a delightful little stream would tinkle by melodiously.

Fort Deliverance. Where the wind howled and the roof leaked. And men died daily, if not from bullets, knives, or arrows, from the scourge of disease.

Ah, yes, she was here. And sane, thanks to Joshua Brandeis and a few other men. She'd never ridden out with the men, but she assisted Joshua frequently in surgery, and with him she had created something of a hospital within the confines of the rickety fort. She suffered with the sick and injured men, but there was a sweet satisfaction in knowing that she aided them as well, and eased some of their suffering. She read to them, she wrote letters for them. Through her writing she learned how they felt about being consigned here. How they feared the heat and malaise, how they slowly became inured to the battle cries of the Seminoles. They were different, all of them. Some of them simply hated the redskins and didn't see human beings beyond the bronze faces. Other soldiers were fascinated by the wild and savage frontier created by the swamps and bogs and hammocks over which they fought, and by the lives of the men they fought day after day. Many had made friends among the Seminoles, and it seemed strange to Teela that they could fight those friends with such vigor and determination. Many prayed just to survive and go home. Some thought of it as nothing more than either a terrible or interesting step in their military career. Still, others saw the Florida peninsula as an Eden, a place where they might seek their own American dreams.

When she wasn't with the men, she spent a great deal of time with Joshua Brandeis. She liked him. She didn't really know his feelings about the Seminoles they fought, but where other men were concerned, he was always blunt, honest, and determined. He wasn't afraid of the officers, nor did he seek to antagonize them. He knew his own worth, and his goal was simply to save lives whenever he could. He taught her some of the incredible medical values of such simple things as sulfur, salt, moss, mud, herbs and roots that could be dug up almost anywhere. He admitted to her as well that there was so very little the best of doctors really understood about healing, fever, and infections, and he taught her that the will to live was almost always the best medicine. He was glad to have her; her hands were able, her mind was swift and competent. And she had the ability above all to give men the desire to fight and survive.

In all her life no one had ever so quietly and honestly valued her abilities. Even James seemed to think that she was ornamental and nothing more. It was odd to have finally met so many men who had such strong influence upon her life: John Harrington, who was all gallantry, protection, and charm; Robert Trent, so willing to teach about the place he so loved; Tyler, the perfect army officer; Joshua, who treated her as an equal; Jarrett McKenzie, who had been more like a father to her than Michael Warren, and welcomed her into his home and fought for her, even when he risked a certain danger there himself. And then . . .

Then there was James. And if she hadn't met him, she might have thought that John Harrington was charming. She might have found her liking for Joshua Brandeis very strong. She would never know. Because she had met James. And it didn't matter that John Harrington was right for her, or that she could spend hours in both silence and comfort working with Joshua. Nothing could be as strong as the simple feelings of passion and longing James had awakened within her.

Occasionally, the soldiers brought in a wounded Seminole. And each time she came to assist Joshua, her heart in her throat, praying.

She tried to tell herself that James did not seek to do

battle in the war, that he had probably gone far to the south to see to his mother's safety and happiness.

But that wasn't true. Somehow she knew it. He was near, because the forest was here, because so many of the war chiefs were near. Because he could speak for those chiefs, negotiate for them if a truce was called. He would want peace, an honorable peace. He would work for it ...

And if he was attacked, he would fight.

So she continued to wait, watch, pray. And to avoid her stepfather as best she could. Luckily, her performance with the sick and injured soldiers had brought such praise from the men that Michael had seemed satisfied enough to keep his distance from her.

"Teela!"

She turned from her study of the land with an instinctive stiffening as she suddenly heard his voice. *Dear God, what now?*

"Teela!"

Even as he snapped out her name a second time, she felt a sudden shivering seize her. She had the strangest feeling that her time of waiting was over. Something would happen. Soon.

Don't be an idiot! she mentally chided herself. She stilled her shivers and ruefully reminded herself that he made her flesh crawl every time he came near her. This time was no different.

Michael Warren was nearly upon her. He had climbed the wooden steps to the ramparts and now strode along them with the perfect military precision by which he lived. However, his efforts were wasted here. For the most part, the Florida militia men and volunteers dressed however they would, often in dun hunting frocks and plain breeches. These men were interspersed with those wearing tattered and ill-fitting uniforms of the regular army, navy, and marines, since so many seafarers had been assigned to land duty when the Indian wars broke out. But while other men grew more casual in the hammocks, heat, and swampland, Michael Warren grew more precise. His collar was starched and ironed sharp as a blade. His stance and walk were disciplined, his major's insignias neatly in place upon each shoulder.

"There's to be a dance tonight, daughter, right here, in the main hall of the fort."

Another dance, she thought wearily. So much for destiny churning into motion.

Another wretched dance!

They were very close to St. Augustine, where young ladies of good family lived, where some of the career soldiers had their wives and children now. Many young women were more than willing to risk the hazards of the trip into camp for the prospect of acquiring a good husband with a fine military career ahead of him. She had to admit that it was amazing to see what a wonderful effect such a thing had on the morale of the men. She had seen several of them who had been close to death's door arise at the promise of beautiful young women to touch, to hold, to charm.

She simply hated the dances herself. There were many soldiers she had befriended, but there were also those men she had seen kill with relish; those who thought that they hunted not human beings but lesser animals. She couldn't bear being touched by them, held by them, charmed by them, even under such circumstances as a simple dance. Besides, she had been tired lately, perhaps weary of it all. She hadn't felt exactly ill, but she hadn't felt particularly well.

And she simply hated Michael Warren. More and more.

She tried to keep a bitter smile from her lips, a taunt from her voice, "Sir, as you requested, I attended last week's party. But since John Harrington remains in the field and I know not where, I don't believe it would be proper for me to attend a dance again."

"This is to be a very special occasion. General Jesup himself is to be among our guests this evening, and you, my daughter, will be on hand. He has heard about you—

in glowing terms, I might add—and you will be there, daughter."

"Sir—"

"I am being sent out again tomorrow morning. If you wish to remain here in my absence, I would suggest your obedient attendance."

And she would obey him. It was either that or watch what he did when he rode with his men.

"The hardships on the march are many," he reminded her.

"I am not afraid of the hardships."

"It is me you fear?"

She shook her head. "I'm not afraid of you. What you wish to inflict upon me you will."

She was startled by the sudden torment and impatience that imbued his eyes and voice. "I have tried, by God, I have tried to be fair with you, to do my best for you, in Lilly's memory! It is God's will that a daughter honor her father, and you fault me at every turn. You should be locked away with the Good Book for nights without end to learn humility and obedience, girl, but as that is something I cannot enforce at this time, I will remind you that I am your master—until you wed young Mr. Harrington, at which point I will wash my hands of you! Now, you will attend the dance this evening, and you will make none of your rude remarks to the general, or you will tour this countryside with me strapped to the back of a mule!"

Thankfully, he didn't want a reply. He turned and walked away from her—with crisp, military precision.

He left her shaking. She fled from the ramparts herself, hurrying down to the small room that had been allotted her. She threw herself upon her cot, flushed, hot, afraid that she was going to be sick. The moment passed. Pulling herself up, she found fresh water in her pitcher, poured it into her washbowl, and soaked her face until she felt cooler. There was a knock on her door.

"Teela?"

"Yes, come in," she said, knowing the voice. It was

Katy Walker, wife of Lieutenant Harry Walker, second in command at the fort. She was a pretty woman in her late twenties, Teela thought, with a rich head of dark curls, rosy cheeks no matter what the weather, and a calm demeanor that defied all chaos.

Katy stepped in, closing the door behind her. She smiled. "I've just asked Annabella to bring us some tea," she said. "I saw you with your father. And I saw you run here. Are you quite all right? Oh, dear! I understand. Your handsome young man is out in the wilderness, and Michael is insisting you show your beautiful face at the dance again, is that it?"

"Er, well, something like that," Teela murmured. Katy had never shown her—or anyone else, for that matter—anything but kindness. How could she tell her that John Harrington had proven to be a wonderful friend, but that she spent her days and nights praying for a half-breed Seminole who wanted her out of his life?

There was a second knock on the door. Annabella, Katy's young black personal maid, arrived with a tea tray. "Thank you, Annabella, please set it . . ." She looked around for a place, but the room was sparsely furnished. There was a cot, a small set of dresser drawers, Teela's trunk, and a washstand.

"Set it there, please, Annabella, right in the center of the bed," Teela said.

Annabella grinned and complied. "Is there anything else, Miz Walker?"

"Not till later, Annabella. Why don't you take a rest now yourself till it's time for me to get ready for the festivities this evening?"

Annabella smiled, bobbed a nod, and left them, closing the door softly in her wake. Katy stared after her for a moment, then shivered fiercely. "Sometimes it just frightens me terribly, all that goes on here! You know, just months ago, the men brought down a tribe of warriors that were nearly all young negro men, and half of them slaves in St. Augustine just months before! Why,

I do tell you, the people were just terrified of total insurrection! Thankfully, the matter has been quelled."

"Has it?" Teela murmured.

Katy stared at her.

Teela shrugged. "Well, I understand that there are a number of abolitionists giving speeches now in the North." She hesitated. "Katy, you can't blame these people for wanting to be free."

Katy sniffed. "The Seminoles keep slaves themselves!"

"That's true, but most often their slaves become free men."

"And most often they live apart. Teela, you must see that the soldiers are not all vicious, and that the Seminoles are not all humanitarians!"

"Katy, I do see it. No good men, no bad men."

"Well, you must realize this. The blacks most often form their own bands. And they have suffered at the hands of the Seminoles as well. Many have come to the forts, turning themselves in."

"And often because they were starving, just as the Seminoles are starving!" Teela retaliated.

"No good men, no bad men," Katy said, then sighed and asked Teela, "Have I come here for a political debate?"

Teela shook her head, taking a seat cross-legged on her cot and extending a hand. "No, please. You came here to be a friend, and I appreciate it."

Katy sat opposite her, accepted a cup of tea, then shook her head. "Teela, I didn't come here to be a friend. I came here because I keep feeling that we've lost you somehow. Oh, Teela, you're not the only one who feels for the very savages we fight! Many of the military men have befriended certain chiefs—why, it was true that Osceola and Wiley Thompson were friends before Wiley so stupidly chained him and lost his fool life! But, Teela, don't lose sight of which side you are on."

"I can't help but be against the murder of innocents."

"Yes, I'm against the murder of innocents as well, including myself," Katy told her.

"I don't know what you mean," Teela said.

She thought that Katy was merely smoothing back her hair, but then Teela realized that she was removing a small hairpiece that blended in perfectly with her own rich brown hair.

Teela gasped in shock, covered her mouth with her hands, and felt tears spring to her eyes. She tried not to stare. She tried to apologize.

"Oh, Katy, I'm so sorry. I don't mean to stare. I, oh, my God, I can't imagine, I—"

"It's quite all right," Katy said, fitting the hairpiece back on her head. "I thought I was going to die. I nearly did. It happened very soon after the massacre of Major Dade and his men. I was visiting friends at a fine, working plantation just southwest of St. Augustine—the ruins aren't far from where we are now—and a band of Mikasukees attacked. They killed my friends, Jean instantly, Herb more slowly. And then they came for me. I was shot, but amazingly, the ball was deflected by a medallion I was wearing. They thought I was dying. I'll never forget the face on the man who ripped up my hair and head and took that swatch of scalp from me. His eyes were cold as ice, stygian dark. Perhaps the saddest thing about the attack was the fact that Herb was a fine and well-read Jewish man who had known persecution himself from 'civilized' folk. He'd come to the territory for a new life on the frontier. He believed that he owed the Indians for what we had taken from them, and that they should be left in peace. But when they came in for the kill, they didn't bother to ask what kind of man Herb was. Because it is war. The whites against the Seminoles."

"Oh, Katy!" Teela whispered in horror.

Katy smiled. "I lived, Teela. That's what matters. I never wished ill to any man, white, red, or black. But this is a war, and I know now which side I am on."

Teela sat her cup down on the tray. Her hands were shaking, and she was afraid her tea would spill.

Katy set her own cup down and turned to leave the

room. "Maybe you'll understand a lot of the men much better," she said hopefully. "Even your father."

Teela looked up at her. "Stepfather," she said softly, and she shook her head. "I do understand many of the men. I'm coming to understand war and fear and sometimes even courage, but I shall never understand Michael Warren."

"Pray for him then anyway, and for me." Katy stood, smiling. "Teela! You're an idealist, and if not a perfect world, you want a good one."

"Doesn't everyone?"

"Yes, I suppose so," Katy said. "But not everyone wants to see the good in others. I'm glad that you do. It's refreshing. And brave. You speak your mind to any man, and do it with dignity."

"Oh, Katy, you do show such tremendous courage yourself! I'm not always dignified, and I know I infuriate some of the men who have fought long and hard. It's just that I've seen what they've done to children! But now ... Katy, now I've seen what you've suffered. And I don't know how I would feel if I had been so cruelly injured and left for dead ... it's bitter, spiteful, absolutely hateful! But I do believe with my whole heart that there are many Indians just desperate to survive, and many more desperate to survive with some kind of honor. I know, too, that for every vicious monster Michael Warren has created in the ranks, there are dozens of good men in the army just doing their best to obey orders and protect our women and children."

"It's miserable to see both sides, isn't it?" Katy said.

Teela nodded. She smiled. "Absolutely wretched!" she exclaimed.

Katy rose and came around and sat beside Teela then, offering her a warm hug. Teela returned it with a deep surge of warmth and affection.

"Katy, where will it end?" Teela asked, shivering.

"I don't know. I truly don't know."

"How can you stand staying here? In the fort, so close

to where you were nearly killed?" Teela asked her softly. "You could be risking your life again."

"I stay here because my husband is here, because I love him. Because he is my life."

"Oh, Katy—"

"Besides, the risk is minimal. More warriors than whites are killed with each skirmish. They estimate that there are really only perhaps three or four hundred fighting men left among the Seminoles and their allies. We've hundreds of soldiers right here. The fort itself will not be attacked."

"I suppose not."

"Well, I'm going to go and rest and bathe and then prepare for the night's festivities!" Katy said cheerfully. She rose again and walked to the door, then turned back. "If you haven't found your good or perfect world, Teela, you should be content in knowing that you are a good person, and only people like you will ever create such a world."

"Katy, if there ever is such a world, you will definitely be part of it!" Teela told her.

Katy shook her head and winked. "Promise me, now. No trouble tonight. I don't want your stepfather angry with you."

"I promise, I'll behave, I'll be charming. But for your sake, and not for Michael Warren!" Teela said.

"For my sake," Katy said. "That will be fine."

Teela smiled. Katy grinned in return, waved a hand in the air, and left, closing the door behind her. Teela moved the tea tray to the floor and stretched out on her bed. She closed her eyes and wondered where James McKenzie would be that night. It seemed like a lifetime since she had seen him. Sometimes it even seemed as if knowing him had been nothing more than a dream.

Then sometimes the memories were so vivid they made her writhe, made her heart ache. She could see him so clearly in her mind's eye that she could almost reach out and touch him. She could see his eyes, feel their heat. Remember his hands, his long fingers. The way they had looked upon her pale flesh.

Then again, it seemed like forever . . .

Not quite two months had passed.

She closed her eyes and wondered with a mixture of anguish and bitterness how he could have closed her out of his life so completely when emotions had raged so fiercely between them. Unless her emotion had been fierce while his had not. He grieved for his wife; she knew that. His war came first; his brother had told her so. He had disappeared into the wilderness. He might even have another wife, perhaps even another two wives, since Seminole men often did so. Especially in times of war, when eligible young men became scarce.

She tossed, jealous, angry with herself for being so. She tried to put him from her mind without success. She was so tired, and tired of being tired, tired of worrying. At last that weariness seemed to steal upon her, and she dozed.

And dreamed.

She was running. Thrashing through underbrush, through swampland, over hammocks and pine barrens. Egrets shrieked and flew from the wetlands in front of her, filling the sky with sheets of white wings. They were coming for her. She could hear the horses, their hooves pounding the earth. She was heavy. She carried something, grasped it before her. It was hard to run, so hard. The ground sucked at her, threatened her. Saw grass scratched her flesh. She could hear her breath coming quick and ragged. Oh, God! It was so hard to run! But they were coming. They meant to cut her down with a bullet, or a knife.

She looked down, wondering what it was she carried that was so heavy, that weighed her down, and yet seemed such a precious burden.

It was just . . . herself. Her hands were clasped around her own abdomen. She carried a child, one nearly due. She carried it while she ran and ran, desperate to save her own life and that of the child.

Ran because they were after her. Ran because they would not care about the life of a woman or a child.

She gasped for breath. Turned back.

She could see them. The heat was rising off the ground in waves, distorting them, but she could see them, riding hard, coming en masse. She knew they meant to hunt her down. She inhaled with another deep, desperate gasp, and she started to run again. Sobbing, crying out . . .

She awoke with a start, bolting to a sitting position on her bed.

Her face was flushed, sheened with sweat. Her heart was still racing.

She was safe, of course. Quite safe. Nothing in the room had changed. The tea tray remained on the floor. Very little time had passed, and yet the dream had seemed so terribly real. Her heart was still pounding, she was shaking. She could remember it so vividly, see it!

Except that, awake or asleep, for the life of her, she could not see exactly who had chased her, seeking her death.

The Seminoles . . .

Or the soldiers.

Chapter 16

There were no more than forty members of the small Alachua band remaining. They had found their way to a high hammock on a small peninsula leading from the eastern side of the lake. There was only one trail that led to the encampment, and that same one trail led away from it.

James came upon the difficulty there because he had been riding away from Fort Deliverance with Wildcat when a scared Indian boy had found them. He barely spoke coherently.

"The soldiers are outside the trees. Near . . . too near. The bad soldiers. They ride with one who kills. There are too many of them. We can't fight them. Ten men can maybe fight. Ten are old. Two are already dying. The babies might cry and lead them to us. We will all die."

"We will have to fight," Wildcat said.

James shook his head slowly. "Two of us cannot kill a company of soldiers. We must go closer and study the situation. Boy, leap up here!" He reached down and caught the boy's arm, dragging him up in front on the saddle. "Lead us closer."

It was as the boy had warned. The soldiers were on a trail that led dangerously close to the Alachuas. They rode, then stopped, listening.

"The *mico*'s second young wife has a baby who cries," the boy said. "They will make her suffocate it, or else they will all die," he said flatly.

"Maybe," James said.

They had come around behind the soldiers. They were as silent as the breeze when the soldiers went still, and talked only when the soldiers started to ride through the brush again.

"And maybe not." James jumped from his horse, leaving the boy atop it. "I'm going across the water. I'll move those I can across to the copse there, where they can escape into the bush. When that is done, I will meet you back here exactly, and we must make a diversion to draw the soldiers in the other direction. They will ride forever without coming across another band in the forest."

Wildcat dismounted. "I am coming with you. The boy is young but bright. He will watch the young soldiers until we return."

"Wildcat, we are risking death if the soldiers move before we—"

"We can move people far more quickly if I come with you."

James didn't argue.

He and Wildcat swam the distance to the peninsula. Once there, they moved very quickly, speaking with the old war chief and arranging first to move his young wife and her half-starved and mewling infant across the water on a hastily fashioned raft.

James swam back to the glen, dragging the raft. He cautioned the girl again and again to stop the babe from crying. She tried.

When they reached the shore, silent tears streamed down the girl's pretty young face. The baby was quiet. She stared at James.

He felt a chill in his heart and wondered if she had succumbed to shame and smothered the infant.

She shook her head. "She sleeps. My baby sleeps."

He swallowed hard and nodded. "Take her swiftly into the woods. Go as deeply as you can and wait. If we can make the soldiers move on, it will be safe for you to go home."

She nodded and did as she had been bidden. James swam back.

Wildcat had enlisted the help of the five young boys in the small village. Between them all, the old chief was moved next with his first wife and two very old warriors. By the time they made a fourth trip with the hastily fashioned and very crude rafts, most of the village had been moved. As they were so good at doing, the Indians melted into the woods.

James returned one last time to make sure that no one had been deserted.

As he stood in the center of the now ghostly village, he heard a noise in the brush. He ducked swiftly behind one of the cabins, then followed the others around as he realized that a single young soldier was coming closer and closer to the cabins, scouting them out.

His heart sank. If he didn't kill the soldier, the man would sound an alarm. The hideout would be discovered. The Alachuas would have no homes to return to. No food to eat. They wouldn't be murdered in their own homes, but they might well die slowly of starvation when winter came again.

He hardened his jaw and his heart and skirted the cabins carefully, moving into the trees. If he went much farther, he would be in shouting distance of the entire company of men.

He saw the young soldier before him.

A very young soldier. Freckle-faced. He had barely ever shaved. He had wide, frightened green eyes and a few pimples on his chin.

It was evident that the soldier wanted to turn back. Evident that he wanted to live, but that he knew he was supposed to be brave as well and not fear death. The soldier kept walking, his back now to James. James moved silently in on him, damning himself. He slipped a knife from his waistband, knowing he dared not take a shot at the soldier with the others so close.

When he was about to strike, the soldier turned. He didn't cry out. He stared at James, at the knife above him, and he crossed himself. "Sweet Jesus!" he said softly, and closed his eyes.

James hesitated just briefly. Then he lowered his knife and raised his fist, slugging the boy with a force that sent him crashing with a thud to the ground. Then he hefted him up over his shoulders and started quietly through the brush.

He came as close as he dared to the soldiers, then went around and in front of them, carrying his burden until he had taken the young man in uniform far from the trail to the village. When he was certain he had taken him far enough, he laid him down. The soldier started to stir. His eyes opened and he stared at James with alarm, groaning, gasping, and trying to inch away at the same time. James hunched down beside him. "I'm not going to kill you."

"You're not?"

James shook his head.

"But I am going to knock you out again. Don't worry. They'll find you before dark."

The young soldier nodded emphatically. "Bless you. God bless you! Oh, but you don't believe in God right? Maybe I'm dead already, I think I'm talkin' English to an injun with blue eyes. You must have some kind of god up there, and he'll bless you. My ma will pray for you forever, honest!"

"How old are you, soldier?" James asked.

"Seventeen next month."

"You're too young to be in the army."

"I reckon so. We just needed the money back home, that's all."

"Go back home, boy," James said.

Then he took aim again, cracking the boy good in the jaw. He went out without a whimper. James left him beneath an oak.

He returned to Wildcat and the Alachua boy. They waited in the woods until the soldiers had passed on by.

The village had remained silent and undiscovered with everyone vacated from it.

The Alachuas would be able to return.

The day had passed without bloodshed. James should have felt good. But he felt wretched.

He had been to the fort with Wildcat.

And he had seen her.

Osceola stood in front of the communal cooking fire, stretching his hands before it, closing his eyes. The fire was kept burning through the night, a task for the slaves the Indians kept. A pot of sofkee with a large spoon remained hot over the fire, ready for a warrior whenever he was hungry.

But it was late, and Osceola stood alone.

He was a man of medium height, slim, wiry, with a well-muscled build. Except that the muscles were sometimes failing him now. And he was far slimmer than he should be. His wives knew that his strength sometimes left him, and when he looked at the moon at night and heard wolves howl, he sometimes felt a strange sense of destiny himself, as if his time was limited.

It was strange, but so often now he would remember the past. Think back to his boyhood.

Things had been so much different then.

He had been born a Creek, in the Upper Creek town of Tallahassee. He had first been known as Billy Powell, for his father, an Englishman. A white man.

Whites, he knew, debated his parentage. Was Powell his father, or had the man simply been married to his mother? It didn't matter. Powell had been a good man, but in the Creek wars now long ago, Powell had returned to Alabama while Osceola had come south to Florida with his mother's clan. Theirs was a matriarchal society. A son was of his mother's clan. He often learned from his mother's male relations, and it had been from an uncle of his mother, a man called Peter McQueen after her own Scots grandfather, that he had learned he must spend much of his life fighting for his very way of living it.

He had been a boy during the Creek wars. Young but

growing when Andrew Jackson had come to Florida. The wars had come, the battles. The "First" Seminole War. But it seemed that he could still remember peace. Waking in the morning to the warm caress of the sun, listening to the sound of the breeze that drifted through the *talwa,* the village. He could remember hunting with his bow and arrow, learning to shoot the plentiful game in the forest. Their way of life had been so defined then. The *mico* had received town guests, issued invitations, presided over the meetings. His aide, the *mico apokta,* had helped him in all things, while other men, the *micalgi,* had guided and counseled each village as well.

In times of battle, usually with the whites or hostile Creeks, the war speaker, the *holibonaya,* came before them all, shouting, gesticulating, preparing them for the fight. Young men longed to fight. The women cooked and performed most domestic tasks, while a young man was given such trivial chores as collecting sticks for firewood, tending pigs, or gathering roots and berries. He gained his prestige through a show of courage in either the hunt or in battle, and so young men longed for the chance to prove that they were brave and powerful and worthy of warrior status.

Many villages, many clans, many chiefs and their people, met every May for council meetings and then again in the summer for the Green Corn Dance. All things could be settled then. Marriages were sanctified, claims were settled. Young men and women played games, some together, some separately. They flirted, laughed, fell in love and in lust.

No Seminole was ever confined or chained, but crimes were punished. Adulterers were sometimes beaten; sometimes their noses or ears were clipped. Some crimes were minor, punishable by exclusion from tribal rites and rituals. Murder was severe, and many men decided upon a murderer's fate, sometimes a heavy payment, sometimes banishment, and sometimes execution. Sometimes life was harsh, sometimes good. But it had always followed a special way, a special path. Now each day seemed scattered, unpredictable. Their very independence hurt them at times. Battles took place, then warriors hurried home. They searched for food. They tried to plant crops even while they ran and hid. Warriors kept dying. Children perished.

He had known that they would have to fight. He had never been a hereditary leader like Micanopy; he had earned his station. The whites accused him of murdering Wiley Thompson after having befriended the man at times. They didn't understand. A Seminole could not be chained. Wiley had thought to break him. Wiley had not understood that you did not chain a Seminole.

There had been good days. He could remember so many good days ...

Now, too often, they all proved their fury and their power in battle. They died with it.

He had spoken with Wildcat, with others. They were all aware that their situation was grave. Osceola did not know if they could endure another year of fighting. He was ready to negotiate with the military again, under one of the white flags General Jesup had given them. Osceola was well aware that since the failed peace of March, Jesup was a sad man, now fighting a war of extermination since he did not feel he had a choice. He did not blindly hate the white men. Indeed, his relations with the military that March had been so good that he had slept in the tent of Lieutenant Colonel William S. Harney while some of the negotiations took place.

He had fought when it had been right to fight. He would still fight when he had to do so. But it was necessary that they talk again.

He heard footfalls behind him. They were almost silent upon the soft earth, but he could hear the quietest of footsteps. He turned around.

Otter stood there, his face as hard as if it had been cast in stone, so bronze, his eyes black and seeming to burn with an obsidian light.

"I have come to tell Osceola that I am riding with my men to my own *talwa* with the dawn."

Osceola nodded. "Our strength lies in our ability to fight and withdraw, and go so deeply into the swamps and hammocks that the soldiers cannot follow us."

"I don't withdraw!" Otter said fiercely. He slammed his fist against his bare chest. "I don't withdraw." He was nearly naked, wearing a breech clout only. The Seminoles had learned their ways of going into battle. They purged themselves with black drink often, and avoided the diseases of the bowels. They fought nearly naked because they had learned that bullet wounds sometimes brought threads and fabric ripping into flesh as well, and that such wounds often putrefied. Otter was shiny with bear grease. His plaited hair was a sleek ebony with it. He was ready for battle at any minute. No warrior had been more brave. Or more furious. More vengeful. His wife, infant son, and daughters had burned to death in a raid on his village. He wasn't afraid of death himself. Osceola thought that he was afraid of life.

"None of us here has given up the fight," Osceola said.

Otter gritted his teeth together, letting out a sound of disgust. He waved his hand in the air. "Osceola sees what he wishes to see. Many are giving up the fight."

"Many are weary."

"You have fought and killed not to give up the fight!"

"*I* am weary."

"You—!"

"Not weary enough to give up the fight," Osceola interrupted angrily, the old power in his voice. "But now the soldiers do not know where we are. I am hunting, I am making new weapons of war. I am gathering strength. And I am waiting to see what move the white man makes next."

Otter shook his head. "I will fight with you again, Osceola. But I am war chief of my clan, and I will make battle as I choose."

"It is our way," Osceola agreed. He was sorry for Otter, but weary of his anger. That was one advantage the white soldiers had. Discipline. Osceola knew that he was a leader in this war. But it was true that warriors chose to fight, sometimes chose to go home, and sometimes waged new, unwinnable battles on their own.

"You grow weak!" Otter cried.

"I grow more sensible. I seek to fight when I can win. I seek victories, not slaughters."

Otter slammed his fist against his chest again. "I seek death for the white men!" he cried.

"Remember, we seek our lives here. Our land. Our children. A future for them."

"It will not be allowed us."

"We will seek it until it is ours. Otter, you are a fierce and valiant warrior. We are all in your debt. Remember that we are all waging the same war!"

Otter stood very stiffly. "I remember," he said. "But even now white soldiers gather at the fort. More and more of them. They seek to find me. To find Osceola. I will find them. I will find Warren, and I will have his scalp. I will take the lives of all the men who leave the fort."

He inclined his head, respectful despite his words, and spun silently on his heel and disappeared into the line of pines beyond the fire.

Osceola turned back to the flames. He closed his eyes. He had fought, yes, he had fought! With fury, savagely, with cruel precision and wild abandon. He would fight again.

But tonight . . .

He was cold. So very cold.

Far from the fire, laid against an old, moss-draped oak, slept Riley Marshall, an old black man who had made his way south to Florida. Riley served the warriors and was protected by them. In good times he had worked for his Indian masters, but he had been allowed his own plot of land as well. He had been free to join the Negro Indian bands at any time, but he had been an old man at the war's beginning, and he had stayed close to Osceola's band.

Now Osceola woke him. "Ask Running Bear if he will come to me."

"Running Bear left to study the new fort."

"He is here tonight. He brought back a deer for the people to eat."

Riley did as he was bidden. Moments later, James McKenzie emerged silently from the darkness to walk toward Osceola where he stood by the fire.

Osceola had taken such a hard line himself so many times with others that both whites and Seminoles wondered at the friendship he shared with the half-breed. But there were things he knew about James that he could not say he knew of other men. If they were attacked, James would fight with them until his own death. The words that James spoke would be the truth. He would not betray a confidence, and he would not turn from his own people. Nor would he wantonly commit murder for any man. He would not attack whites, settlements, farms, plantations—or even soldiers. But he would bring food to various bands when none was to be had. He would share what he had to his last morsel. He would not lie; he would not cease to defend his brother and other white men of his ilk. He would fight until he fell to defend his position—or what was his.

And it seemed that the white woman at the fort was his.

"You have called me, Osceola?" James said. He stood about three feet away, bathed in the firelight. Osceola was of medium height himself. He had never doubted his own appearance as that of a fine warrior and chief. But this half-breed blood brother of his stood over six feet tall, his stance straight. His frame was hard, well-muscled, his shoulders broad. He wore a white man's form-hugging trousers along with a patterned cotton shirt. A single silver crescent hung from a chain at his neck, and an unadorned red band kept his black hair from his eyes. His bronzed face was taut and lean tonight, still striking but hard with a tension that burned a blue fire in the depths of his eyes.

"You've fed many mouths tonight with your fine buck. Such kills are harder and harder to find in the forest," Osceola told him.

Running Bear arched an ebony brow, a flicker of amusement passing across his features. "Osceola is an excellent hunter himself. He has hardly called me here to compliment a kill."

"I have heard that Major Warren's daughter is at Fort Deliverance."

No expression touched Running Bear's face. He shrugged. "She is."

It was Osceola's turn to feel a certain amusement. "My good friend, you are greatly mistaken if you do not realize that whispers and rumors travel the forest from band to band, borne on the breeze. Whether you abducted the woman or she ran to the shelter of your abandoned cabins is not known; that you have been involved with her is fact. For this reason I have called you. You have seen her? She is at the fort?"

"Yes. I have seen her myself. I moved through the bush with Wildcat, and observed the soldiers and the life at the fort."

"It is true that there are men and women I will not kill. At the first battle at the Withlacoochee, it was my order that the braves not kill a young soldier named Graham. They will not disturb your brother's home. There are others. I have commanded that Warren's daughter be brought here if she is captured. But you must understand, some braves run with hot blood. They have lost their own families. They have seen children lie in the crimson pools of their own lost lives."

"I am aware of this."

"Be aware then that you must watch Otter. He will attack any and all soldiers out of Fort Deliverance."

"I have been warned about Otter," Running Bear said. "But perhaps I will speak with him. Now."

Running Bear turned hard on his heel. Osceola watched him go. He wondered at the wisdom of his action. They could not afford to battle one another now.

But if they did not strive to live their lives in their way, with honor and integrity, then why did they fight so hard?

James knew where to find Otter. The Mikasukee *mico* had just returned to his makeshift shelter and lain upon his blanket.

The Seminoles had a tendency not to post guards through the night. James had warned the chiefs time and time again that the white soldiers always slept with a guard, and that nighttime was no deterrent if the whites chose to attack by darkness. But lifestyles were hard to change. When James leapt atop the platform where Otter had slept alone since the cruel death of his wife, he caught the *mico* quite by surprise.

Otter leapt to his feet, stunned, wary, ready for an attack. He saw James, and his wariness did not leave him.

"McKenzie," he said, spitting out the white name as he addressed James.

"I have been told that you wish to kill all the soldiers at the fort," James told him.

"I wish to kill all whites," Otter said flatly.

"There is a woman there who is mine."

"No white man cared about my woman."

"But I ask you as a chief of your people to respect my position—"

"As a half-breed?"

"As *mico* of my people. Through my blood right by my mother."

Otter strode to James, standing directly before him. He was a smaller man; it did not matter. He stared up at him with bitterness and hostility.

"You grew to drink the black drink; you learned the ways of our warriors. You learned to hunt and fight in breech clouts, to shoot your arrows straight and true, to wield a white man's musket with skill. Men listen to you and follow you. You have great power and great strength. You could lead men to great victories, slaughter the whites. But you fight with us only when a musket is aimed at your heart. Then you come to me about a white woman."

"She is mine, and I don't want her killed."

"If she is yours, take her from the fort, and the white men there."

James didn't allow the feelings in his heart to be betrayed in his features. God! The anguish and frustration within him seemed to eat at his insides, gnawing away. He could claim that she was his, but she was not. She was a white woman, in a white man's world. He could not claim her while she remained with Michael Warren.

"I'm asking you not to harm her."

Otter suddenly drew a knife from a sheath at his ankle and threw it so that the point lodged into the crudely hewn logs at their feet.

"Fight me, Running Bear. Fight for her. Decide her fate."

"Fight you? I do not seek your death—"

"Nor I yours. I wish to see you fight as I have fought, for what you love. What you covet. Life."

Before James could respond, Otter had plunged downward for the knife again. James leapt back, aware that the warrior meant to draw blood tonight, even if he wasn't seeking a fight to the death.

Otter charged him again. James caught the wrist that held the blade, but Otter's impetus caught him hard as the Mikasukee plunged into him. They both went down hard upon the platform, then rolled to the earth, caught in a deadly battle of strength.

Otter rolled atop James, fighting to draw his knife high and aim it downward. James could nearly feel the tip of the blade piercing his throat. His fingers tightened on Otter's wrist. He willed a greater strength into his arms and body, and managed to toss the smaller man from him. Otter landed on the earth about three feet away. James leapt to his feet. Otter was up as well. They circled each other. James let Otter attack again. This time he allowed himself to fall easily with the impetus, then he forced the roll as well. Otter tried to lunge with the knife, but James was prepared. He twisted his torso, then slammed down on Otter's arm, causing the knife to fly. He wedged an arm close on his opponent's throat, cutting off his breath, threatening to break his neck.

Staring up at him with hatred, Otter went still.

"Finish it. Kill me."

James shook his head slowly. "I didn't come to seek your death!" he said, exasperated. "Concede to me the white woman should you take her."

Otter was silent for a moment. James realized then that he could hear the quiet sounds of breathing, a slight motion of feet against the earth.

He looked up. Many of Otter's people had come to circle them. They would not interfere in the fight. They watched, they waited.

Otter was aware that they had come as well. James eased his hold, and Otter spoke woodenly.

"I do not seek to attack the fort. I will wage war against the men who leave it, against the men who seek out me and my people to exterminate us!"

"And the woman?"

"If I take her, you must come for her. And take her from me. I have told you, when you speak, men listen. We admire your strength—we seek it more for our cause."

James stood uneasily. Otter leapt up before him. "I travel toward my home in the south hammock in the morning. I will not attack the fort. Warren's daughter is only in danger if she leaves it. I will try not to forget that she is yours."

"I want your word, your promise."

Otter nodded.

James stood still in the moonlight for a moment, watching Otter. The Mikasukee suddenly sliced his palm, offering it to James. James took the knife and sliced his own as well, then gripped it hard to Otter's.

He could still feel the blood when he turned away. Hot, sticky. He could remember Teela's face as she had studied her own hands that last time he had seen her. So much blood, she had said. So much blood ...

And so much more would be shed.

He had battled Wildcat and Otter now. Fought his own people. He had become deadly enemies with Michael Warren.

And still ...

There was so little he could do to protect her.

"Running Bear!"

He had left Otter's shelter behind and stood in a copse in the moonlight. He could hear the slight stirring of the night wind and the gentle movement of the stream that rambled not far from where the council lean-tos and shelters had been erected. He turned.

Brown Rabbit, an old Mikasukee warrior with negro blood, had called him back.

"Otter means his word to you. He admires you, and is sorry that you do not fight with us with greater will and strength. He says that you could kill twenty men each battle, and rid us of many soldiers."

"I cannot fight as he wishes me to," James said simply.

"I know that. Many men know it. Otter cannot respect it, though I believe he intends to keep his word. But he means death to the whites. If this woman is yours, you must see that she does not leave the fort. And if she leaves it, you must come for her. Many things happen in the heat of battle. Many things that men may not intend."

"Thank you, Brown Rabbit."

Brown Rabbit nodded and turned hastily to return to his own band.

James stood in the moonlight. He cast back his head and stared up at the stars.

He had gone to the fort. He had climbed the oaks outside the clearing where the walls had been raised, and he had silently stared down into the yard, into the very heart of the military fortress.

He had seen her.

And his heart had been pummeled and his blood had

seemed to run both hot and cold. And he had been seared with both anger and fear, but in the end he had seen what Wildcat had. The Indians could not attack the fort. No matter how many warriors they gathered, the fort was too strong. They would not sacrifice themselves for a futile attack. Jarrett would have known how strong the fort was, how well protected, before he would have allowed Teela to go, no matter what arguments Michael Warren had used.

If she stayed within the fort, she was safe.

And if she did not . . .

His fingers knotted at his sides. What was she to him? he taunted himself. A white woman he had urged to marry a soldier friend. A sweet, lush body in the night, easy pain and tempest. She could be nothing more.

She was more. He could not claim her or command her, but she was his. In his blood. In his soul. He could not rid himself of her, of wanting her. Of longing to hear her voice again, see the flash in her eyes, listen to her words, soft or angry, warm or rebellious.

"Damn you, why did you ever have to come here?" he whispered to the moon.

Then he cast his head back still farther, his fingers knotted into his fists, and he let out a cry of anger and anguish to the moon.

It echoed around him.

And he moved in the darkness again, aware that he barely dared even sleep in the days that were to come.

Chapter 17

General Jesup, now in command of all forces in Florida, was a lean, tall, straight man. Teela had heard that he could be shifty, that he wasn't always to be trusted, but there were few men high in the military who didn't receive some kind of lambasting from their men. Teela didn't think that he looked untrustworthy. He had level, keenly intelligent eyes. And as she danced with him, she felt sorry for him.

"Were it up to me," he said, sweeping her very properly but just a bit stiffly around the room, "it would all be over now." He wasn't really looking at her as he spoke; he was brooding, and seemed sad despite the festivities of Robert's party. "We have fought a hard campaign here. When Governor Call held the reins of command before me, he fought a hard campaign as well. But when I fought in January, I came to see what they cannot see in Washington. I came to see that we could trek endlessly through brush and swamp and hammocks. No matter how hard we try, parties of warriors slip away. I came close to Osceola once, so close I nearly had that wretched war hawk in my grasp! But he slipped away. The prisoners taken in his pursuit informed us that he escaped our reach with just a few warriors. He'll come back again with a hundred. It is always the same. We catch our enemies, but always our enemies slip away once again."

"Why don't they just let the Seminoles alone, then, in the south?"

Jesup sighed, deeply troubled. "Would God that we

could! My frustration here has been so great that I pleaded to be relieved of duty. Then gossip hounds and political enemies cast such comments upon my abilities that I can no longer accept the relief I have so craved until I feel I have proven my competence. Good God! I would most gladly leave them to the wretched swamps. But it is the opinion of the United States government, especially that of Secretary of War Poinsett and apparently that of President Martin Van Buren, that we must not back down, that we cannot surrender our position, or we will but extend every fight we face across the whole of the country. I am but a servant of our government and therefore obey orders. I have suggested on more than one occasion that we just leave the Seminoles to the south of the peninsula." He was silent for a moment. "My orders leave me so little choice. The Seminoles must go, the Seminoles won't go; I am left to exterminate men I frequently admire. I tell you I am weary of this hellhole where the soldiers sicken constantly, where my regular army officers squabble incessantly with the militia commanders, and where disease plagues us all most pathetically. I am afraid to let the populace know just how many of our soldiers are ill, for they would be terrified to sleep at night. I tell you, it is a wretched, wretched war. Some men, of course, do thrive on it." He paused. "Your father is proving to be an admirable officer, never falling to sickness in the heat, following every trail relentlessly until he has hunted down his prey!"

"Yes, my stepfather is excellent at such maneuvers," Teela agreed. She could see Michael Warren across the floor, in conversation with Tyler Argosy and Dr. Brandeis. He watched her while she talked. For once in his life it seemed that he was pleased with her. Jesup's recommendations could bring about a promotion for him, and Teela knew that Jesup, whatever his personal dismay at the war he fought, was glad of the men who were winning the battles.

Eliminating the problems.

Jesup was looking at her gravely. "It is my understanding, Miss Warren, that you have befriended the hostiles."

Teela arched a brow at him, speaking carefully. "I don't know any of the 'hostiles,' sir."

"Your father has claimed that you were kidnapped by the half-breed, James McKenzie, that the man is dangerous, that his type will continue the war forever, threatening innocent women and children."

"I wasn't kidnapped by anyone, General. I met James McKenzie at a party finer than this one at his brother's house."

The general sniffed, on the verge of rudeness. He seemed a very bitter man that night.

"In my experience, I have met so many men who have not seen their brothers in years, and care not if they ever do so again! Then I come here, and Jarrett, a man who knows this frontier of Florida better than any other man, will not fight and seek out the deep-hammock hideouts of these wretches because he shares his father's blood with one of them. Then there is James himself! Articulate, well educated, fully versed in the white way of life, a man with that life opened to him, and he joins with the savages instead!"

"It has been my understanding that James has very frequently served both sides well—"

"As I've said, he's articulate and highly intelligent. He has the rare power to move men with both his example and his words, and a manner of reasoning that puts us all to shame." He sighed deeply. "I'm afraid I have become nearly as great a burden to many of those civilians I fight to keep alive as I am to the savages!"

"Surely, sir, you are greatly appreciated."

Jesup shrugged. "I think not, Miss Warren. But it is kind of you to pretend that it is so. Especially since it seems I am in charge of an effort you deplore."

"I'm not at all sure what I think anymore," Teela told him. "It is war and bloodshed that I deplore."

"Your stepfather rides out again tomorrow with a de-

tachment to follow a trail deep into the swamp. Both
your father and young Harrington will be gone. You
should perhaps leave this wretched territory. Go on
home, be safe."

Teela arched a brow. It seemed that everyone wanted
her to go home. If Jesup was suggesting she do so, perhaps Michael Warren would be bound to let her do so.

Her heart was pounding hard. She didn't think that
she wanted to go home. James was out there somewhere.

"General, you are kind, and I thank you for your con-
sideration for my health and welfare. But I don't think
I should leave without having a chance to speak with
John again."

She swept her lashes low over her cheeks, somewhat
ashamed of the lie, even if she had John Harrington's
blessing and encouragement to lie.

"Ah, young love!" the general said, smiling with a
faraway look to his eyes. Then he winked at her. "I
quite understand. What a commendable wife you will
make for such a promising soldier as your Mr. Harrington! I still say, my dear, if you've need of anything at
all while your men are fighting so bravely on the line,
you mustn't hesitate to ask."

"General, I will not," Teela promised.

Even as she spoke, there was a sudden commotion at
the door to the hall on the ground floor, where they
danced. The musicians stopped playing.

A soldier who had been on guard duty was the first
to break through into the room. He was young, freckle-
faced, with tawny hair. His flesh was very pale; his freckles stood out upon it. He was followed by two men who
held a muddied and bloodied companion between them.
Teela screamed, stunned, horrified to see that the blood
that streaked his face had come from a small spot on the
crown of his head where a patch of hair had been lifted.

"Sir, General Jesup, sir!" the man being held cried
out. "Captain Dixon, fourth volunteers, reporting."
Then his military protocol was lost, and he openly wept.
"We'd traced down Otter, sir. Oh, yes, we'd traced down

Otter. There were ten of us, and we thought we could surround his camp and surprise him and bring him in. We were so certain. But that damned Otter, sir, he wasn't in front of us at all. He was behind us. And he came around us just as we came into his village. For the love of God, sir, I crawled back here. They took me for dead, sir, lifted my hair, and by some miracle I did not cry out. But my men, my brave young boys, my beautiful boys. They're gone, sir. All gone."

General Jesup set a supporting arm around Teela, but Brandeis apparently did not see the action, or chose to ignore it. He came behind her, catching her by the hand. "Come, quickly."

She followed him, or more accurately, was dragged by him to where the captain stood, supported by the others. Brandeis quickly lifted the man's head and looked into his eyes. "Sir!" he said to General Jesup. "This man needs care promptly."

Jesup stood very tall and straight. "Indeed," he said quietly. "Captain, you are a brave man. Our prayers are with you, and your fine men."

Joshua pushed open the door, urging Teela and the men supporting the captain to hurry along behind him. They strode along the wood decking that led to the door into Joshua's surgery and hospital, and carried the captain into the back room where Joshua removed bullets, sewed up sword slashes, hatchet and knife wounds, and amputated destroyed limbs. He ordered the captain laid down.

"Teela, carefully clean the head wound. Get the sulfur. Have we ether?"

"Yes, we've a little left."

"Good, it seems his main wound is there, on the side. Open my bag, get me my scissors."

Teela hastened to obey him, her heart beating hard as the soldiers who had supported the captain stepped back, wide-eyed, looking as if they might be sick at last. Teela set out the bag with Joshua's instruments, quickly handing him the scissors so that he could rip open the captain's homespun shirt and hunting jacket. She started to order one of the soldiers to bring her hot water to bathe the poor captain's scalpless head, but Joshua glanced up and saw a bottle of whiskey on the table near his instruments and handed it to Teela. "This will do fine. Pour some on his head, then into his belly."

In the savage wilderness where supplies were sorely lacking, whiskey was a fine medicine. Except that Teela was convinced the captain could use a good swallow before feeling the sting of the alcohol upon his head.

He looked into her eyes with his own fine powder blue ones, read her mind. He reached for the bottle and consumed a good quantity in one long, hungry swallow.

He gritted his teeth, but didn't cry out when she then bathed his head with it. Amazingly, after all she had learned to do in the surgery, she felt tears stinging her eyes. She liberally applied sulfur to the wound, then helped remove the fragments of cloth from the captain's shirt. Joshua quietly requested her assistance, and she quickly gave it. Thankfully, the captain had not been riddled with bullets.

He had been slashed in a long line up and down his side. The whiskey wouldn't be enough. They did have ether. Joshua administered it; there were a few minutes of waiting.

The captain looked up at Teela with glazed eyes. She tried to smile, taking his hand. "Nothing will hurt you in a few minutes, captain."

He smiled. "I will hurt forever!" he said softly, then moaned. "My boys, my poor boys . . ."

She glanced at Joshua. He inclined his head toward the captain.

"Sir," she said softly. "Think on this, that they are gone now, in no pain, and abiding with God. They were volunteers, soldiers who knew the danger, glad to follow you, brave men. Captain, surely, you did all that you could!"

He closed his eyes, nodding. "All that I could . . ."

His eyes opened again. "But I have lived to see an angel, they have not."

"They are dancing with real angels now, sir!"

Once again the captain's eyes closed. His fingers squeezed hers. "Bless you . . ."

His eyes didn't open again. Joshua nodded and inclined his head toward the needles and silk thread they had been lucky enough to receive in their last shipment of supplies.

Nearly a hundred stitches were required.

She sat with the captain until it was very late. About two in the morning, Joshua came and looked at the captain, the whiskey bottle now in Joshua's hands. He pulled a long swig of it.

"He will make it, I believe. As long as no infection sets in. We tended him quickly enough. Come on, come into the office. Have a drink yourself. You need a drink, and you deserve one. Good, stiff whiskey, no sherry or the like."

Exhausted, Teela followed him into the small cubicle that served as his office. There were shelves loaded with books and medications. The desk was littered with supply forms, discharge papers, letters, and reports. He swept them to one side as he sat behind the desk, indicating that Teela take the chair before it. He opened the bottom drawer of his crude desk and drew out a glass, filled it with whiskey, and thrust it across the desk to her.

She took a sip of it and shuddered slightly.

"Oh, come now, down it in a gulp!"

She arched a brow to him, then did so. She shuddered fiercely, but she felt as if she had been warmed from head to toe.

"Better?" he asked.

She nodded. She set the glass down carefully. "He's a good man!" she said. "A very good man." She felt like crying again.

"And you hated the Indians like hell when he came in," Joshua said.

She arched a brow again and nodded as he poured her more whiskey.

"I hated the Indians. I thought of them all as despicable savages. Just like I hated Captain Julian Hampton the day that he massacred everyone in that village."

"It's a damned dilemma, isn't it?"

She nodded, inhaled and exhaled. "Oh, God, Joshua! I don't know why, I just keep thinking that I could do something here, but I can't. I thought that I could change things in some small measure. Oh, what a fool I've been! I'm humbled, and I'm tired. And I'm frightened. And I—"

"You don't want to see James McKenzie dead, and right now you're not certain you want to see him alive."

"Oh, dear Lord! Of course, I want him to be alive—"

"But sometimes he is one with those savage creatures who ripped this poor good man to shreds tonight!"

She stared down at her lap and nodded. "Just this evening General Jesup suggested I go home. And I didn't want to go home. I thought that I needed to be here. But now, so suddenly, I just want to be away. I do want to go home. I—please don't say anything. I'm going to wait until my stepfather has ridden out. General Jesup has told me that I can come to the military for help. I'll ask the commandant if I can leave as soon as possible. Perhaps ride north to St. Augustine when a detachment of men is going for supplies."

Joshua was silent. Teela stared down at her hands. She felt so numb tonight. So tired. So beaten.

"I'm sorry," she said after a moment. "I'm grateful to you, to John Harrington, to others. Perhaps I shouldn't go. I owe him, I owe you—"

"You need to go," Joshua said suddenly, fiercely.

She was startled by his vehemence. She felt her cheeks redden. She knew she was sometimes the talk of the stockade; everyone knew that she had pushed Julian Hampton into the water. Some of them mocked her as an Injun lover.

"If I've offended you—" Teela began.

"For the love of God! You've not offended me! I will miss you, but I pray that you will go."

"Will you explain to John for me?"

"John will understand."

"Perhaps he will be relieved."

"Teela, do not be a fool. Go on, get out of here, go home. If your fiancé does not love you, Teela Warren, I do. If you have lain with a thousand Indians, I don't care."

She stared at him, shocked, startled—and again glad of Joshua Brandeis because he was so blunt, because he spoke the truth, because he read into the hearts of men and women, and chose not to judge them. But tears stung her eyes because she was sorry to realize that she meant something to him that he did not mean to her.

"I haven't lain with a thousand Indians," she said softly.

"Only one."

"Joshua, it isn't that he is a Seminole. It's—"

"You're in love with him."

"It isn't that he is a red man, or a white man, or both. It . . ."

"I understand," he said with a slow sigh, picking up his whiskey bottle and swigging deeply again. "I understand, and I ache for you, and for James. What you cannot see is the unavoidable tragedy of it." He stared at her. "James McKenzie will not leave his war. Especially since he has been branded all but a true renegade now. Because of you."

"Because of me—"

"Rumors persist that you were kidnapped by the Seminoles, that James McKenzie abducted you from your brother's house. It is easier for most whites to believe that you were forced away from your father rather than that you ran away from him."

"Oh, God!" she breathed. "It seems that I have but added to everyone's misery."

"You couldn't have changed anything, Teela. Neither could he have done so. Many of us know James well.

Those of us who do understand. But if you leave this wretched place, it will be best for us all."

He set the whiskey down, rose, and came behind her. She felt his hands upon her shoulders. "Life is always ironic," he told her, as if that explained everything. She sat very still. He kissed the top of her head and lingered behind her just a moment.

"Remember, if ever, now or in the future, I can do anything for you, anything at all, don't hesitate to come back to me."

His hands left her shoulders.

"I'll pray for you," he said softly.

"You are a good man, too, Joshua. The best of men. I will be praying for you. And I will miss you."

"Go home. Be safe," he said softly.

Then he was gone, and she was left in his office alone, and in the whole of her life she had never hurt so badly. She hurt for Joshua, and for the good captain who had staggered into surgery tonight, scalped and alive. She hurt for the poor men who had served beneath him and met the savage fury of the Seminoles.

She hurt for the Seminoles. For the children with their wide, trusting black eyes . . .

For the babes she had seen so mercilessly battered, bloodied, and murdered in the woods.

And she hurt for James. But it seemed that there was nothing that she could really do, except watch the slaughter.

Joshua was right; James McKenzie was a part of the war. He would not leave it, could not leave it. He would stay until the bitter end. . . .

And she would do what he had wanted at last.

She *was* going home.

Chapter 18

Despite his better judgment, James had allowed Wildcat to talk him into joining him outside Fort Deliverance when the military commanders hosted their soiree.

They had been there all night. They remained still.

Every time he had come to the makeshift fortress on the hammock with the others, he had assessed the army's strength. Unlike Wildcat, he was grateful each time to note the thickness of the walls, the multitude of guards. The fort housed numerous soldiers, all of them preparing to ride to battle, of course, just awaiting Jesup's "pincer" orders, and the words of the spies who came and went, hunting down tribes within hammocks, marshes, and swampland.

From a thick branch of a tall, moss-draped oak, he had watched as the festivities took place. By early evening, a host of soldiers had arrived down the St. Augustine road with a multitude of young beauties. A soldier was not a bad catch for these ladies; just as in all times of war, the male population of the territory dwindled as a crop of courageous young beaus fell in the line of duty. These soldiers might soon perish as well, but the young ladies seemed to have determined one and all that it was better to die a widow than an old maid.

While they observed the party, Wildcat gave him a running commentary on the women, predicting which fair maid would one day be as fat as a house and which would quickly become a shrew. James had paid him scant heed, grunting now and then to pretend he was listening. Despite Wildcat's casual chatter, he sought any chink in the wood-and-flesh armor of Fort Deliverance while James sat in a cold sweat, hating himself for wanting a glimpse of her while longing to throttle her at the same time. He'd felt as hot and twisted as iron beneath a blacksmith's hands, damning her for being where she was.

Even what she was.

He'd seen her at last through the poor windows of the commander's house. Beautifully dressed, her gown hugging her upper body, cinching her waist, flaring at her hips, her sunset hair pinned elegantly high. She'd danced with a tall, older man, staring earnestly at him at first, growing animated as they spoke, even smiling. The twisted feelings inside him had viciously intensified.

It was Jesup she'd danced with. General Jesup, in charge of the entire removal operation now for the territory. Not a bad man, one weary of his struggle here. Anxious to let the Seminoles be, unable to do so because he was a military man, a servant of the United States of America who obeyed orders and did his duty.

Wildcat had suddenly motioned to him, wrenching him from his anguish. There had been a thrashing in the brush across the clearing and beneath them, by the walls that surrounded the fort. Wildcat had been ready to leap down from the tree; James had detained him.

A man, bleeding, falling, half dead, had made his way to the gate. His cry was answered. James had just made out his anguished words. "My boys, my boys, my God, my boys! It was Otter, Otter's men ..."

He was taken inside the gate. Through the windows they saw commotion within; the soldier was taken from the commander's house to the hospital, Joshua Brandeis and Teela close behind.

For long minutes James had strained to see within the hospital, watching as she moved, talked, worked over the soldier. When all was done for the man, she sat, and sat. Shared a drink with Brandeis.

And sat still.

All through the night, he had maintained his vigil in the tree. As the glorious pink and yellow streaks of dawn that could make the land a paradise began to stretch across the heavens, Wildcat shook his arm. "Look!"

The compound suddenly bustled with activity. Soldiers were racing out to a bugle call; men were mounting up.

Warren was among them.

James stared intently at the scene, trying to see if Teela remained at the hospital. She did. She came out to the wooden walkway in front of the hospital building and watched the activity as well. Her hair was straying from its pins. She wore a white apron decorated with blood.

The bugle sounded again and again. More and more men spilled out into the clearing before the buildings. Horses were led from their hastily built stables.

"He's leaving with at least two hundred men," Wildcat commented angrily. "A force we cannot hope to combat with the warriors I could gather."

James didn't reply. Wildcat was right.

He watched as the men said good-bye to wives and loved ones mounted up.

He saw Warren ride to his daughter. She stared at him, no expression in her brilliant eyes or weary features. Her fingers wound into the blood stained apron, her only outward sign of agitation.

They didn't touch; there was no fatherly kiss good-bye, no tear slipped from the daughter's eye. The slightest curve twisted her lip; she saluted Warren, and Warren rode away at the head of his troops.

James watched with relief as the gate opened, as Teela stood on the walk, watching the soldiers ride out. She wasn't leaving. She was staying within the fort. She would be safe.

He heard Wildcat swearing at his side. The soldiers were barely gone before Wildcat dropped from the tree.

James didn't slip down beside him at first. He watched Teela. Joshua Brandeis had come to stand at her side. He slipped an arm around her, leading her back into the makeshift hospital hut. James felt his fingers curling into a branch of the tree. Again the twisting within him. *Well? He had told her over and over again to marry Harrington, to get the hell out of the territory.*

But she hadn't left. And now he prayed for her safety. And *twisted* with the damned awful hunger and wanting and jealousy.

He forced himself to slip to the ground with Wildcat. She was safe for the time being, not riding with Warren.

"I will kill him! I will find a way to kill him!" Wildcat said savagely.

"But not in the fort," James murmured.

Wildcat looked at him sadly. "Not at the fort."

They found their horses where they had been tethered deeper in the brush, mounted them bareback, and rode inland. James looked back, shaking off an uneasy feeling. Fort Deliverance stood strong beneath the rising sun. Still, he would ride far distant from it, he told himself.

He did not accompany Wildcat toward the hammock where Osceola had taken up his temporary residence. He rode to a place deep along a trail by a small lake he had known as a boy. Where pines carpeted the ground. Where, as yet, peace could be found.

And solitude.

From the whites . . .

From the Seminoles.

And the world torn between them.

Warren had been gone no more than twenty-four hours before Katy sought out Teela in the hospital.

"My dear, General Jesup has given word that you're to travel out with Captain Mayerling tomorrow. He and his company are riding north to St. Augustine, and there will be a ship there, the *Bonne Brianne,* to take you straight home to Charleston."

So soon! Teela thought with a moment's panic. So soon! She *had* wanted to go, she reminded herself. Ever since she had seen Otter's work, she had felt exhausted, weary, unable to keep living on hope. She had wanted to leave this place of death and disease and torment behind.

She had told Joshua she wanted to go, and Joshua had made her feelings known to Jesup. And Jesup was going to explain to both her father and young John Harrington that he had insisted that she leave.

"Oh, Teela, you've been such a sweet friend. And I do love you dearly and will just miss you so terribly!" Kathy said, offering her a firm hug. "But, my dear, though some of the men do love you, too, there are those still angry with your sympathies for the enemy. Home will be the best place for you."

Home. She loved Charleston. Charleston was beautiful. She would always love Charleston.

But it was so far away.

And here . . .

James was here. Somewhere. The man who didn't really want her. Her soul was here, her being was here. Watching, waiting, always in a tempest.

She couldn't go.

She had to go.

"How wonderful," she told Katy. She tried to smile. Yes, she was going home. Far, far away. Maybe she would see things differently while walking along the Battery, where everything was beautiful and civilized and manicured.

Maybe at home she could nurse her wounded heart and soul. Learn to forget him. She hadn't heard a word from him, about him, in so very long. He might have even forgotten her name.

"Teela?" Katy asked worriedly.

"Katy, you're a dear. I'm going to miss you so very much, too. And I will pray for you, daily. I guess I'd best—pack," she said. She started to hurry from the hospital, then hesitated, turning back. "Mayerling . . . Captain Mayerling? Isn't he . . . ?"

"A tremendous Indian fighter, my dear! He's taken down entire villages. Indeed, he's cleared out entire hammocks for the military! A brave and dedicated man. You'll be safe with him."

Safe . . .

Yes, safe. She would pray the ride went swiftly. Mayerling was very much like her stepfather; in fact, he would surely have been her stepfather's choice as an escort for her. He had indeed killed many Indians. Young ones. Women. His men boasted of their exploits. Other soldiers—even fierce Indian fighters among them—whispered of his brutality.

It didn't matter. She had made the decision to go. Warren was not here to stop her. She would ride in the morning, be gone by evening's tide.

James slept without really sleeping, dozed while listening.

In the night he heard the bird's cry that wasn't a bird's cry.

He rose quickly, moving from the hidden shelter of the hootie he had built by the lake. He returned the cry and waited.

A second later, he heard a horse moving through the brush. He strode forward to greet Wildcat.

"I have come thinking myself a fool. Yet a fool who is a friend to one who I believe would give his life for his people, no matter who those people be."

James nodded, acknowledging the compliment. "What has happened?"

"Within the next hour a party is due to leave from Fort Deliverance. Captain Mayerling will be leading the party."

Mayerling. Despised among all braves. Otter would surely be moving like the wind if there was any opportunity to reach the man.

"How many in his party?" James asked.

"Two companies. Fifty, sixty men."

"Otter will massacre them," James said softly. His heart was cold. The men were doomed. He felt a sense of bereavement and pity, yet one of justice as well. Mayerling deserved death. He collected ears from the infant Indian children he killed. Yet some men would surely travel with him who would not deserve their fate.

"Your red-haired witch is riding with them," Wildcat said.

James stared at him, cold to the bone.

Then he said no more, racing back to his bay. He hadn't a single second to spare.

It was difficult to say good-bye to Katy, more so to say farewell to Joshua Brandeis. She never realized just how deeply he felt for her until he held her close, a hug good-bye. One that lasted just a few precious seconds too long.

She had never realized, either, just what he meant to her. The pity was that she loved him as a friend. A good friend, a best friend, one she would love for life.

Captain Mayerling was impatient to be under way, his words polite as he urged her to mount up for the ride.

"Dawn's breakin', Miss Warren. We'd best be on our way. The men and me will have a long enough ride back with supplies this evening."

Joshua released her. "You want to come back, you write now, eh?"

"Of course."

"I shouldn't allow you to come back. No man in his right mind should allow you to come back. I'm grateful as all hell that you're leaving."

She smiled. "Thank you!"

His smile deepened. He kissed her on the forehead, then spun her about, setting her up on her horse, a handsome black cavalry gelding that would be returning that evening along with the men.

The gates to the fort opened. She rode out in the center of the men. They walked their horses in silence. Dreary hour after dreary hour. She closed her eyes. Sweat trickled down her back. The landscape seemed to stretch on endlessly. The silence was heavy and oppressive. . . .

All at once, the most ungodly screeching seemed to tear the very air, ripping apart the silence.

"Attack!" someone shouted.

"Dismount! Battle formation!" Mayerling ordered. The words had barely left his lips when the sound of gunfire exploded around them.

Mayerling fell dead from his horse.

Again gunfire exploded, ricocheting through the air, so loud it was unbearable.

Her horse reared. She fought to steady it. Men leapt down from their mounts, taking shelter behind the trees that lined the road and copse from where the first fire of the ambush had come.

More shouts exploded. War cries whooped out, a cacophony of voices as the Indians burst upon them. So many of them! Turbaned, bare-headed, most of them half naked, armed with rifles, knives, bows and arrows . . .

Her horse suddenly went down. Shrieking, Teela slipped free from her mount, rolling before she was crushed. She tried to rise.

And then she saw a brave rushing for her. She had no weapon! She ducked down for a handful of dirt, threw it into his eyes, started to run.

Screams filled the air. She tripped over a body. She shrieked in panic, nearly falling upon a brave in the very act of stripping the scalp from a young, blond, and thankfully dead, soldier.

She turned back. The brave was closing in on her.

"No!" she gasped, racing harder.

A hand fell upon her, spinning her around. She barely saw the man at first. All that she saw was the knife and the trail of crimson blood that dripped in a stream from its razor-honed edge. . . .

The carnage taking place in the copse was horrible. James had seen battle before, more often than he had wanted. He had tasted blood and steel and fear. But these soldiers had already been bested; those who were not dead would die soon, and blessedly. He couldn't even spare a thought for those dying such wretched deaths. He could only pray that Teela was not yet among them. As he rode more deeply into the scene of battle, he desperately searched for her.

He saw her across the copse. She'd been backed up to an old, half-fallen cypress tree. She stared up at the knife about to spill her blood, sever her life. She stared at the warrior about to slay her with hot defiance. Her hair streamed in its fiery splendor down her back, her eyes glittered in contempt for her attacker, never defeat. She was white, so very white, and startlingly beautiful here in these bloody surroundings, her features so delicate, chin so high. In those few brief seconds in which he saw her, the whole of his body seemed to constrict and knot with a burning fever. He hated her, wanted her, feared for her. Felt he would die without her, knew he could never have her. Because of this. This carnage. Even if he could save her life, they must never meet again.

The knife was plunging toward her.

Otter. Otter was about to kill her. Otter, who had forgotten his promise.

James reined in his pony and shouted in Otter's first spoken language, the Hitichi of the Mikasukee. "Otter, stop! By your word! Her death will mean yours!"

Not only did Otter pause in his act of murder, but the whole of the glade seemed to still as James dismounted swiftly, and strode toward Otter. The cries of victory and triumph and *massacre* went silent.

Teela did not seem to recognize that rescue was at hand. He heard her shout in fury.

"Bastard!"

Otter still had his hands in her hair. She didn't seem to care. She offered the brave a savage kick against belly and groin.

A good, solid kick. It must have been, because Otter cried out furiously in pain.

Damn her! Whatever influence James might have borne over Otter, he held no more. Otter had already caught her arm and swung her back around. In a matter of seconds Otter's blood-drenched knife would fall with full force into her heart.

James catapulted across the clearing in the road, heedless of the dead that lay strewn upon the ground between them. There would be no reasoning with Otter; James's only hope was his superior strength.

Before that blade could fall.

James cried out again, a cry of warning and of fury, then pitted himself against Otter, catching the warrior's muscled arm, the one that held the knife, and wrenched it back with all his strength, causing Otter to spin. Enraged, Otter wrenched free, raising his knife again with deadly intent against James. He leapt at Otter, bearing him down to the ground beneath him. His fingers wound around Otter's wrist. He slammed Otter's arm and hand against the earth until the knife fell free from his fingers. Otter stared at him with a deadly hatred. "You'd kill me for the white woman, for Warren's daughter? Your brains, your pride, lie in your cock, traitor!"

James sat up swiftly, hurtling the knife away. The world around them had come back to life. Braves again gathered rings from the fingers of the fallen, food from their haversacks. "I'm not killing you, Otter. And you'll not interfere with the white woman again."

Otter continued to stare up at him. James had no choice but to leap to his feet, disdaining Otter. And go for Teela.

Sweet *Jesu*! She had risen from the cypress and run and was now halfway across the copse, racing back along the trail. He shouted to her, then realized he did so in the Hitichi he had spoken with Otter. It didn't matter. He would terrify her now as much as any other warrior here—yet it was imperative that he get her away from here as quickly as possible, before his own position could be forgotten by Otter's warriors, before they both went down in a rain of carnage.

She deserved to be terrified. His fury at her rose along with his fear that they might not make it out alive.

The running speed he had never fully appreciated became his greatest asset that day. He all but flew after her, winding his fingers into the skeins of vibrant red hair that flared behind her, the hair she had so nearly lost to Otter's lust for vengeance against Warren. She shrieked, still trying to fight, flailing, kicking, pummeling. He dragged her down to the earth, desperate to make her not just see him but obey him.

Swearing beneath his breath, he straddled her, catching her wild-flying fists, pinning her wrists above her head with one hand. She continued to twist and writhe with a savage energy that threatened to defy his strength. He swept the tangle of hair from her face, staring down at her. She was gasping for breath to scream again, yet the scream did not come to her lips.

She stared at him, closed her eyes, lay still and trembling.

"Look at me," he ordered curtly.

She did. Her eyes flew open, filled with ice and hatred. It had been a long time since they had met face to face. A lifetime in this hell that was the world between them.

"So you are a part of a war party now," she stated coolly. "Kill me, then, and have done with it! Slaughter me, slice me to ribbons, as your people have done with these men."

"It was a fair fight!" he countered angrily. Was it? He didn't know, he hadn't been there. There was no fair fight left to be had here. She knew that. She knew what the battle was here, knew that women and children died on both sides.

She had merely never been under attack before herself. Feeling death's whisper against her cheek.

"It was an ambush!" she spat at him.

He felt a coldness in his heart. She had been living in her world. Living among the soldiers. Attending dances, sipping champagne. Well, she belonged in her world, he told himself with all the contempt he could muster. But he meant still to force the truth of everything that went on here down her throat. "The captain leading this party ordered the direct annihilation of two entire tribes, Miss Warren, men, women, and children. Babes still within their mothers' wombs. Yet you say these soldiers should have been shown mercy?"

"I know that there is none within you! There is no mercy to be found in this wretched hell, I am well aware, so do whatever you will! End it!"

He leaned closer to her, longing to shake her, make her see, make her realize . . .

What? He wasn't a murderer. Yet he was a part of these people now stripping fallen bodies. He gritted his teeth, arching a taunting brow to her. "End it? But we do so enjoy torturing a good victim!" And how had she become such a victim? She should have been at Cimarron, safe. She should have listened to him.

"What were you doing with these men?" he demanded. His words were incredibly harsh, he knew. They had to be. She wasn't answering him. Shaking inwardly and praying not to show her any of his own fear, he shouted the question again, "What were you doing with these men?"

"Leaving!"

His heart slammed like a rock against his chest. "For where?" he demanded.

"Charleston."

Charleston! Charleston! Damn her, now she was running home, when running was deadly! He'd told her to go home before, but she'd defied him, stayed. Seeped into his very blood, obsessed him, until . . .

He leapt to his feet, reaching down for her. She was already trying to rise, trying to run from him again. Incredulously, he reached for her, slamming her with a savage force against his body, determined to let her realize they still faced danger.

"Fool! You will not be going anywhere now!"

"You're the one who has always told me to leave!" she reminded him fiercely. "You'd have thrown me off your precious land were it possible. You *told* me to go—"

"And you didn't listen."

"I was trying—"

"Apparently, you didn't listen in time," he snapped. "Leave my side now and you are dead, Miss Warren, don't you see that?"

A scream suddenly split the air. A scream that came from a white man not quite dead as a piece of scalp was sliced cleanly from his head.

Teela trembled in his arms even as her eyes continued to defy him. Her eyes glittered with a fresh fever. Tears. She was trying so hard not to shed them.

James called out in his own Muskogee, not looking around, keeping his eyes on Teela. "Warren's daughter is my captive; I am taking her now!" He caught her firmly by the upper arm, aware that he didn't dare loosen his grasp for an instant, yet aware that she could too easily see the tragedy strewn on the ground around them. "Don't look down and don't look back!" he ordered sharply.

Thankfully, he had managed to keep the bay, a gelding raised at Cimarron, well enough fed that the horse was a good and decent mount, able to carry them both swiftly from the scene of the carnage.

Still, he offered his horse little mercy, forcing it at reckless speeds over the trails, across marsh, through the bush. He wanted to put as much distance between them and the massacre as quickly as possible.

He didn't speak to her, didn't slow his gait, until they had traveled to his shelter within the hammock. There he dismounted, setting her quickly down before him.

She stared at him, very stiff and straight. *Regal.* The perfect white southern lady. Without blinking, she turned coolly from him, walking to the water.

He was grateful that she was alive.

He was furious that she had been nearly killed. Furious that he still shook with fear, furious that he had nearly been too late.

"So you were leaving," he drawled contemptuously. "Going back to graceful drawing rooms, charming company, and the elegance appropriate to such a well-bred young lady."

"I wasn't trying to go back to anything," she replied, perfectly composed.

He wasn't going to have it. She had nearly died. She was a fool, and she needed to be shaken until she realized what a dangerous little fool she was.

"You were just trying to leave this barbaric wilderness?" he taunted.

She spun around, staring at him. He wished that her eyes weren't so brilliant, her skin so silken white, her hair such a tantalizing shade of pure fire. "I was trying to leave the wretched battles and the horror and the— death! Your friend meant to slit my throat!"

Yes! Otter would have gladly killed her. A knife seemed to be slicing into him. "I'd have killed him very slowly had he done so."

"How reassuring! I could have cheered on your efforts from heaven."

"Or hell!" he said, eyes narrowing. Then his fury seemed to erupt within him. "Why did you leave my brother's house?"

"I had no choice."

"Jarrett would never have cast you out."

"I had no choice!"

Defiant. Still defiant. Stubborn and fighting to the end. He could best white enemies, red enemies. He could not best her.

Again his fury erupted within him. He strode to her. She tried to back away, but there was nowhere for her to run. He set his hands upon her, not knowing what he meant to do, wanting to shake her. Fire seemed to rip and tear throughout him. Heated iron, bolting, bending, twisting. He clutched her hand, dragged it against his bare chest. Words spewed venomously from his lips. "You left Cimarron, but not for home then, when you could have sailed right out of Tampa Bay. You forged across the territory! What then? Did sense come to you at last? Did you run from the war?" he demanded harshly. "Or did you run from *this*? Bronze flesh, copper flesh, *red* flesh?"

She wrenched her hand away with such vigor he couldn't stop her.

"I'm not afraid of you!" she cried out. "I'm not afraid of you, you—"

"You should have been afraid! You should have been afraid a long time ago. You should have run back to your *civilized* Charleston drawing room the second you set foot in this territory. Damn you, you should have gone away then!"

"Go to hell!"

"I think I shall get there soon enough," he snapped back quickly, his temper soaring again. He didn't know quite what he was doing, but he was suddenly touching her again. Touching her. The anger was hunger, gnawing at his soul, eating away at his loins. His fury was passion. He didn't know what it was about her, what so obsessed him. He knew that he had watched her through the windows of her life long enough. His torment would come to an end for this night.

He set his hands upon her shoulders, backing her along the riverbank until she was forced against an old, gnarled cypress. His whisper was as hot against her as the tempest raged within him. "Weren't you sufficiently warned that there was a war on here? Didn't you hear that we pillaged, robbed, raped, ravished, and murdered? That red men ran free in a savage land? Didn't you hear? Or didn't it matter? Was it tantalizing to play with an Indian boy? Touch, and back away, before you get burned?"

"Anyone who touches you is burned!" she spat at him. "Burned by your hatred, your passion, your bitterness. Anyone is burned—"

He could bear no more. His fingers dug bitingly into her shoulders, a promise there would be no escape from him now. "Then, my love," he warned her, *"feel the fire!"*

And it was a blaze, wretched, demanding, ruthless, that filled him. With any sanity he'd never be so rough. But sanity was lost. The rapacious hunger in his blood seized hold. He touched her, and fabric split and tore. He ground his lips down upon her mouth, tasting, questing, searching, demanding. Her hands were against his chest. He fought the violence within himself. She writhed and kicked, slammed her fists against him. He didn't care, couldn't care. He swept her up and cast her down upon the soft, damp earth, carpeted there by a bed of pines. He hated her. Hated himself. Hungered all the more.

He straddled her, caught her wrists. And she ceased to struggle. She stared at him, eyes liquid and glittering with fury.

He eased his hold from her wrists.

Her hands did not move against him again.

The tempest, the passion, stayed with him. Yet his fury suddenly seemed lost on the gentle breeze that swept around them. Her hair was a pool of fire against the green earth. Her flesh was absurdly beautiful against the rich and verdant ground. Theirs was a hell neither had created; it was an inferno that ignited the instant they had first set eyes on each other. There was no explaining it, and no denying it.

"What in God's name am I going to do with you?" he whispered.

And he touched her. Touched the rise of her breast, the hardened nipple, the fullness of the mound.

He nearly cried aloud. Desire shot through him like rifle fire. The sweetness of touching her was almost unbearable. His lips found hers again, and there was no protest to be found there. . . .

"Bastard!" she whispered.

Yes. Indeed.

"Perhaps. But tell me to leave you be. Say it with your eloquent words, and mean it with your soul!"

"Bastard!"

"I know, I know," he agreed, shuddering with the feel of her, the wanting.

He threaded his fingers through her hair, found her lips. Found more of her, inhaling the scent of her, breathing her in, tasting her. His lips traveled every-where, teased, hungered, teased, tasted. Ruthlessness filled him again, but ruthlessness tempered now by tenderness, by the desire to evoke within her a hunger to match his own. Her soft cries increased the desperation of his urgency and desire. There was no intimacy he would spare her, needing more and more of her. Nothing would deter him. Nothing but ...

She cried out suddenly, fighting him again. Yet fighting him because of the sensations exploding within her, sensations she longed to deny. Ruthless again, he took that moment to thrust deeply within her, sinking into a field of ecstasy with the simple act, shuddering before feeling the maelstrom seize hold of him. She'd been in his dreams too long. Haunting his sleep, taunting his days. Now she was his, encompassed in his arms. She touched him. Held him. Moved with him. He felt as explosive as a cannon, charged with a desperate, urgent desire, so glad to hold her, wanting to caress her forever, so damned on fire that he could not hold back the bursting climax rocketing from him. Into her. Again, again, until he was empty and she was filled.

He lay back, half ecstatic, half ashamed.

She stirred beside him, ripping her hair from beneath him. She tried to gather the pieces of her dress to-gether—impossible. She cast them aside, rose naked like a goddess, and walked to the water. He rose restlessly and followed her. Stooped down to gather the water up in her hands, she would not look his way. "Feel the fire!" she whispered softly. "I am well burned!"

Shame constricted within him, along with the haunting jealousy he had not been able to help but feel when he had watched her within the fort. "You should have known better than to play with an Indian boy from the very beginning."

She stared at him. "I never played," she said with dignity, and rose again. She walked away from him, staring down at her destroyed clothing. "It will be a cold night."

A damned cold night, he thought. He stood, walking back to her. "I will warm you through it. In the morning we'll worry about something for you to wear." He'd be damned if he'd let her hear any kind of apology in his voice.

"I don't intend to stay the night," she informed him in her most regal tone.

The hell she wasn't staying. And the hell with her tone.

"You wanted to play the game. It is well under way. You didn't run to your drawing room soon enough. Now, Miss Warren, you will be my guest."

"Prisoner, so it seems."

"Whatever, you will stay."

She stood there stubbornly. With an impatient burst of violence, he swept her up from where she stood. He carried her to his small shelter in the woods, setting her down without much gentleness, silently damning her all the while. She wouldn't leave when he had told her to do so. When she might have done so safely. She had played her game. And now that game was so well and deeply engaged, she was going to have to see it through.

She shivered, and he set one of the fur blankets around her. He realized that he had taken her from the road, from near death, and all but raped her. Staring into her eyes, wanting her, hating her, refusing to believe that he loved her, he offered her a drink of water from a leather gourd. She accepted it in silence, drinking, then told him, "You'll never keep me if I choose to take my chances and leave. I came from a drawing room, but I've learned your jungle well."

What had he done to deserve her amidst this jungle of red and white, right and wrong? If she tried too hard to get away from her only salvation within the deadly terrain, he might as well kill her himself and get it over with!

"A challenge? Then let me assure you, if it is my choice, you'll never escape me."

"Damn you—"

"Teela, would you escape me to meet another brave

anxious for the beauty of your hair—ripped away along with your scalp?"

"I'd escape you to find freedom from this travesty. Not all Seminoles are barbarians—"

"What a kind observation, Miss Warren," he commented. He could feel anger growing within him again.

"Nor are you any more a Seminole that you are a white man! Don't tell me about the bronze of your flesh—even your mother carries white blood in her veins, indeed, you are actually more white than Indian—"

"Teela, one drop of Indian blood suddenly turns the color of a mans' flesh, and you are worldly enough to know that it is so. Look at my face, and you know that I am Indian."

"I look at your face and know that you are a creation of two worlds!"

"Then know this—life has made me Indian in my heart, and you must not forget it."

Was he angry that she was *not* Indian? Could not be part of his world? He wondered if it was so.

"Life is making you cruel—"

His temper exploded. "Enough, Teela. Enough for tonight!" he warned her.

Surely, she saw that he was frayed and weary. She gritted her teeth hard, her eyes glittered with fury. But she said nothing more. She turned her back on him and lay down in silence.

He stared at her back. At the soft white flesh rising above the fur. At the tangle of red hair streaming around her.

Leave her! Walk away! he commanded himself.

Tonight, he might as well will the moon to fall from the heavens.

He lay down beside her and took her firmly into his arms.

He couldn't have her, couldn't have her . . .

All the more reason to hold her, possess her, while he could. Feel her nakedness against him. Cherish it.

Chapter 19

When Teela awoke, it was barely dawn.

The colors filtering through the trees, cypress, pine, and moss-laden oak, were both delicate and striking. Just as the sun set with majestic palette, it rose in splendor as well. Shades of gold and pink and mauve entered the sky, in hues both soft and vivid. Light dazzled through tree limbs, catching little dust motes that rode upon the air. Dew covered much of the earth, creating a diamond pattern against it. Morning kept the insects at bay. In the distance an elaborate spider web spanned two branches, as dazzling with morning's moisture as if it were decorated with thousands upon thousands of precious jewels. The air was sweetly cool, clean, kissed with a breath of freshness. The sun would rise soon, hot and punishing, but for the moment the morning was completely and without doubt glorious beyond measure.

Morning . . .

She was awakening in a savage territory where the colors of morning and night were equally fed with the crimson of spilled blood. She had set out yesterday with over fifty soldiers. Every one of them must surely lie dead. She should be dead herself.

She half rose to discover that James had apparently awakened some time before her. He was dressed in a pair of form-hugging cotton trousers, probably homespun out of Cimarron, and his doeskin boots. Leaning against a structure pole of the hootie, he chewed a blade of grass, studying her reflectively.

She sat up uneasily, dragging the blanket of furs with her, meeting his gaze.

"Sleep well?" he inquired politely.

"Remarkably so. Amazingly so," she added, her eyes faltering, "for someone who saw so many murdered not twenty-four hours ago."

He made an impatient sound, tossing down the blade of grass. Three long strides brought him down beside her, balanced on one knee, his eyes intense as they challenged hers. "What did you call it when Mayerling went into Indian villages? War?"

"I called it murder as well, for that is what it was! That you all massacre one another with vicious brutality does not make it right for anyone! Don't defend those warriors who want my hair because of my father's actions. They are no better than he is!" she informed him heatedly.

He arched a brow at her slowly. "Perhaps not," he said. "Perhaps not. Except that you must remember, the military has come here to remove or exterminate the Seminoles. We've never assumed to remove or exterminate the entire white race."

She rolled away from him, frightened by passion and fury that seemed so alive within him still. "I'm sorry. If you wish to blame me for the war, I'm just too tired to listen."

She was startled when the blanket of furs was suddenly ripped from her, leaving her naked and shivering on the bare ground. She was instantly very awake, leaping to her feet, quite ready to do battle with him again.

"Tired, Miss Warren?" he inquired incredulously. "But you chose to stay here—"

"I was trying to leave when I was so nearly murdered yesterday!" she reminded him.

"Ah, but too late. I warned you time after time to go. I told you to stay at my brother's house. I do vividly recall stumbling upon you on a battlefield and warning you to keep out of the warfare! Did you ever heed a word I said? Alas, no. So here you are now, my prisoner, preferable, I do pray, to being a hairless corpse on the trail. But, my dear Miss Warren, you may be too *tired* to direct a servant after a Charleston soiree. Seminole prisoners are never too *tired* to pay heed to their captors."

The morning air was damp and cool. He knew her as no other human being on earth, and she had certainly stood her ground often enough with pride. But she was both cold and humiliated at the moment, and very resentful of the fact that he frequently didn't even seem to consider that they were the same species.

"Go to hell, Mr. James-Running-Bear-McKenzie. Fill the air, the water, sea, space, fill it all with your violence and mockery and cruelty. You can't force me to listen, you—"

"Coffee," he snapped suddenly.

"What?"

"Coffee. Our women awaken and work, Miss Warren. Always. There is something to do. There has always been work, of course, but since your people came it is a harder life than ever our women lead. Preparing what food they can gather, what little can be grown, what can be hunted. And when the Seminoles are forced to run, the women pack what little they possess and carry it on their backs. They are forced to fight. To practice infanticide."

"What has this to do with coffee?"

"I'd like some."

"Good for you."

A strangled sound escaped her because he was suddenly all but on top of her. He'd captured a wrist, drawn her close. His eyes seemed like twin blades of steely fire, about to slice cleanly through her.

"You're a prisoner, Miss Warren. Ah, but you can't appreciate that luxury. We used to take prisoners. We didn't seek to slay all women and children. We brought them back with us. Some grew to stay among the Seminole by choice. They learned our ways. Some even came to love their captors, and discover that they were not as savage as they might have imagined. In fact, many realized they had seen more viciousness and savagery in some of the finest drawing rooms in their own nation."

"Let go of me."

"I shall have to, won't I, if you're to make the coffee?"

"Isn't coffee a white man's luxury?"

"If so, we have been trading for it for a very long time, and I am a spoiled man in many things, and like coffee for breakfast. The basic structure for the fire is to the left of the shelter; the river water is fresh and sweet, and you will find the rest of the fixings in the haversack to the rear of the hootie."

"So you say!" she hissed, ripping free her hand from his grip. She was shaking from more than the cold. This time yesterday she had thought never to see him again. Now he stood just inches from her, his bare chest brushing her naked flesh. She told herself that she absolutely hated him for his judgment and mockery; yet again, he had not failed her when her life had been in the gravest jeopardy. Nor did such complex emotions matter under circumstances such as these, for just his proximity was enough to make her heart race, thunder with such speed and fury against her chest that he must surely see its beat beneath the white wall of her flesh. "I won't make you coffee!" she cried.

He pulled her flush against him. His fingers splayed into her hair at either side of her head. His lips found hers with heat and fever and force, his hands then sliding through the length of her hair, over her shoulders, down to her buttocks, cupping them. She tried to draw her fists between them. Her fingers pressed against the muscled barrier of his chest. He drew her down to her knees, whispering against her lips.

"I don't want coffee anymore," he informed her. She was pressed down. To the earth. The morning-fresh scent of it filled her. His scent swept into her, a part of him, his warmth, his vitality.

"Wait! I will make coffee!" she began desperately.

But his hands were all over her, his lips, his teeth. "Always too late, Teela," he told her. "You ran for home when it was too late. You chose to obey me when it was far too late."

Too late . . .

She had dreamed of him, night after lonely night. Longed for him, longed for this. His touch on her. She hadn't imagined the moss- and pine-strewn earth as her bed, the sky was her canopy. The raw, rough feel of dirt against her back, the golden streaks of the sun shining down with an ever greater brightness on her nakedness. Hadn't imagined how wild it could be, how lonely in a deep green glade, how she might hear the ripple of the nearby water one second and nothing but the heavy tenor of his breathing the next. He touched her everywhere. Leaves rustled beneath him. She twisted to elude him, to avoid complete surrender. To no avail. His teeth gnawed gently at her nipple as his tongue bathed it. "I make—very good coffee!" she gasped, clinging to his head, trying to dig her fingers into his hair. Stop him. Have more of him. Love him. Be free of him.

"But you do this better!" he hissed softly, rising above her.

She whispered the word no. Surely, she did. But he didn't hear her. And she didn't mean it. Her legs were parted; he was within her. The rising sun touched her flesh with a wicked heat that nearly matched that of his ardor. Again different sensations caught and filled her. The flight of a bird far above their heads, the increasing intensity of the sun. The feel of his hands on her hips, rough, urgent, his kiss, his stroke, the earth beneath them, soft, cushioned by the moisture of the nearby river, and hard cradling her against the momentum of their rhythm. Then all blended together, and it seemed that the sun's rays had exploded inside her, liquid gold, warming and filling her body, radiating throughout it. She blinked, and the sun was still overhead. He was beside her, his weight eased from her, the scent and feel of him still touching her.

He rose abruptly, walked naked to the river, and plunged into it, walking and then swimming into the depths. She crossed her arms over her chest and looked up at the uncanny blueness of the sky. How was it possible to know such ecstasy and misery at one time? To long to be with him. To hurt and ache inside and feel so wretchedly hopeless?

A moment later, he was standing over her, river water dripping from his flesh.

"You need clothing," he told her abruptly.

She arched a brow at him. "Imagine! Perhaps you should have thought of that last night, Mr. McKenzie!"

"Ah, but Miss Warren. I hadn't seen you in some time. Foolish me. I had completely underestimated the enemy."

"The enemy?" she challenged furiously, leaping to her feet. "Enemy! As if I might have brought any of this about, as if I ever attempted to seduce or flatter you, as if—"

He caught her, drawing her close, laying a hand across her mouth, yet doing so gently. "You are the enemy, Miss Warren, because you don't know your own strength. Nor do you recognize my weaknesses." The words, so softly, almost tenderly spoken, brought a string of tears to her eyes. Half sobbing, she laid her head against his chest. He held her, fingers gently moving through her hair. His body was wet and very warm, rippling with muscle. It was oddly comforting to be there, leaning against him, held against him, both naked and somehow vulnerable beneath the endlessly blue sky in a place so devoid of other men and women and creature comforts that it might have been the first design of Eden.

He lifted her chin, kissed her lips gently.

"I'll make us some coffee," he said huskily.

"I don't mind making coffee."

"I'll build the fire."

"I'll get the water."

In a few minutes, coffee was nearly on. He had expertly stoked a cooking fire within a circle of rocks. His coffeepot was, indeed, of European design. His coffee, however, was chicory, very strong and somewhat bitter. She sat by his side, looked longingly at the river as he hunkered down and set the pot on a wire-mesh camp stove above the flame.

"Want to go in?" he asked.

"Is it safe?" she asked nervously.

"Only a few alligators," he said.

She shivered violently.

He smiled, looking downward. "Quite honestly, there's no guarantee that 'gators will not be in any Florida waterway, but they are surely scarce here. And actually," he added, "you're not natural pray for a 'gator. He prefers birds and small mammals. With most wild creatures, you keep your distance, they'll keep theirs." He cocked his head. "Perhaps that's something you should have learned by now."

She smiled. "Are you, then, a wild creature?"

"Haven't you made that determination, Miss Warren?"

She shook her head slowly, gravely. "I reserve my judgment until I have weighed all that I have seen as fairly as I may."

He lowered his head. She thought that he smiled ruefully to himself.

"Want me to protect you from the wild things in the water?"

"Would you?"

"Yes."

"Are you afraid of the water?"

"No."

"Do you swim?"

She hesitated. "A little. Years ago, when I was very young, my father used to take me to the creek by my home. It's been awhile."

"You'll remember."

"You'll come with me?"

He nodded, reached for her hand, and drew her along with him.

It was wonderful. The water was so beautifully clear and refreshing. Fed by underwater springs, James told her. She could see beneath it, shake out her hair beneath it, plummet down and rise up. At first she stayed near James, not venturing out where the water was deep. But she did remember, and it was wonderful to swim. She wanted to explore, to feel the coolness of the water, the heat of the sun. She didn't think that she had ever felt such a sense of freedom.

And she was a captive. So she had been told.

James, surely far more accustomed to such sweet and natural freedom, tired of the water more quickly than she. "Come in!" he called her.

Treading water, she smiled and shook her head.

"Miss Warren!"

"No!"

She dived under again. She nearly shrieked, inhaling a lungful of water, when she felt something tug her foot. She kicked madly for the surface, and when she broke through it, she spun to see that it had been James.

She might have remembered how to swim, but he was an expert at it. "I called you to come out!" he snapped.

"And I wasn't ready!"

"You forget that I am the captor here, and you my prisoner."

"A pity, then, for prisoners must attempt escape at all costs," she said, still treading water.

"And if there was danger in the water?"

She arched a brow. He was lying. "What, sir, you now resort to scare tactics?"

He smiled. "Look down."

She looked. Good God, he wasn't lying. There were two massive creatures swimming beneath him. She shrieked, throwing herself at him, though to what avail she didn't know, for he was treading water as well. Indeed, her impetus sent them both hurtling downward, right toward the monstrous animals.

"Get out, get out!" she cried, but he was laughing, holding her close in his arms, treading the water for them both. She hadn't seen him laugh so easily in a long time. No, she hadn't seen him really laugh so ever before. He was changed, entirely. He was a young man. A very handsome one. The curve of his smile was completely charming. Her heart slammed against her chest. So monsters were about to eat them. It was all right, because James was smiling, and no monster could come upon them that was a greater evil than the warfare that stretched before them.

"You've never seen them before?" he queried.

"Sea monsters? No! Why aren't you moving? Don't you care in the least—"

"Tara never mentioned them to you? Why, she is crazy about the beasts."

"I'm beginning to think that you're all mad beasts!"

He arched a brow but still smiled. "They're sea cows, as gentle as can be, and just like 'gators, they inhabit many of our waters. They're rather like ... well, they're mammals. They're like dolphins."

Teela shuddered. "Damned ugly dolphins!" she whispered vehemently.

"All right, my love, so perhaps they're more like cows in appearance, big and squat and hardly graceful. Never fear them, though. They wouldn't dream of feasting on any kind of meat, and certainly not human flesh."

He had leaned back, a strong and accomplished swimmer, able to backstroke with her weight half atop his chest, her arms still clinging around his neck. As he moved, she tentatively ducked her head into the water, watching the sea cows swim on by. There was a mother and a baby, so it seemed. Swimming together, oddly graceful despite their funny faces and heavy bodies. The mother was a good eight to ten feet long, mottled gray. The baby was perhaps four feet and a slightly softer color.

Teela surfaced, lying her head against his chest, feeling the ripple and movement of his muscles as he swam toward the shore.

"How odd," she said softly.

"What is odd?"

"That it can be so hard to tell sometimes by appearance what to fear—and what to trust."

"Fear everything," he warned her. "Trust no one."

"You trust your brother."

"That's different. He's my blood."

"White blood."

"Teela—"

"You're lucky."

"I'm lucky?"

She nodded earnestly. "You share that blood and something very special with your brother. I never had that with anyone. I loved my father, and he died so young. I loved my mother, and I lost her, too. Then I had Michael Warren."

He had reached a point of the river where he was standing, she realized, but he still leaned back, holding her. He smoothed back a piece of her wet hair. "Perhaps you don't realize, Miss Warren, how quickly you have made friends here."

"Friends . . . ?"

"Both my brother and Tara adore you. Robert Trent would defy the wind for you, and young Harrington is head over heels. Joshua Brandeis as well. Of course, the later three would certainly desire much more of you than friendship . . ." His voice trailed away, a slightly bitter note to it once again. He shrugged. "Unless, of course—"

"Don't you dare accuse me—"

"Accuse you? I've told you to save us all grief and marry Harrington!"

She tried to kick away from him; his hold around her tightened, his arms enveloping her. Then suddenly he was whispering fiercely, words tumbling out with passion and fever. "Listen to me, and listen to me well. Don't ever think that I don't desire you more than anything in all the world, or that I do not dream of holding you in my arms, feeling, breathing the sweetness of your flesh when you are away. Don't think I don't long to kill any man when I watch you dance with him, laugh with him. The jealousy in my heart and blood is like something alive and dark and terrible, ready to riot, tear me apart. Yet I say to you with all truth that yes, I wish you to wed Harrington, because I wish life, peace, and happiness for you. And God, yes, sometimes I'm bitter, so sorry, so damned sorry that I can't say, yes, my father was a white man, a rich white man. I can't buy my place in the white world and turn my back on these people. They are mine. It is their plight, my plight. My world is starvation, and yours is a night dining on fine china to the sweet sounds of violins. Mine is running, yours is dancing. Mine is the rough earth, while yours is a feather bed. You cannot survive without your world. I *must* survive without it."

She pulled back from him, amazed at his words. Amazed at his fever. He had almost said that he cared for her. That he wanted her. For more than just the passing of a frantic night, a fleeting, heated passion. She stared at him, at the emotion in his eyes, the harsh, rugged beauty of his features, and she wanted to cry out with an agony greater than death. "And what if I cannot survive without *you*?" she asked.

He pulled her close again, shuddering fiercely, holding her. He held her for the longest time, and she was grateful for the river, glad of the water that drenched them both, for it would hide the silent, damp tears that streamed down her face.

"You can and must survive without me."

"What is survival if the soul perishes?"

"I had thought my soul had perished long ago," he informed her very softly.

"James—"

"Have you ever made love in the water?" he whispered to her suddenly.

His words angered her, shattering the closeness of the past moments. She felt as if she was choking. She tried to free herself from his hold. "My God, James, you would know!" she cried. "You would know!"

"Shh! Shh!" he whispered, and he was laughing again,

she realized, and when she met his gaze, there was a tenderness in his eyes unlike any he had offered her before.

"Damn you!" she hissed, but with no conviction.

"Since we've not shared the pleasure ..." he murmured. He kissed her. Long and deeply. The water felt chill. Her body seemed ablaze.

He began to make love to her in the water.

They drank the strong, hickory coffee. He clothed her in one of his large cotton shirts.

He caught fish for their dinner. She learned to skin and debone it, and cook it over the open fire. He talked about being a boy and visiting Charleston, where Jarrett's mother's family had hailed from. She told him how the city had changed.

Night began to fall. They sat on the riverbank and watched the sunset. Watched the colors in silence, felt the breeze touch them while the golden orb of sun flattened and stretched out, spreading tenacles in bright red, orange, yellow ... then a softer crimson, a mauve.

Darkness blanketed the landscape. Coolness seeped in along the river. He built up the fire, and they sat before it. He taught her a few words in Muskogee and then Hitichi, explaining how the languages differed, how white men had labeled the Creeks for the bodies of water they lived along. She told him how she had come to love medicine, what a thrill it was to treat a man and see him heal. She caught him watching her intently over the campfire, and she flushed and told him, "Any man, James. I love to see any man heal, be he white, red, or black."

He nodded, reached across the campfire, and kissed her. Then he rose, sweeping her up, carrying her to their makeshift bed within the crude hootie. He made love to her again, his desire never sated, just newly awakened as he learned each new smile she could offer him.

There was a war on. Hundreds had died, she had nearly perished. She hadn't even the clothes that had been on her back. She lay in the wilderness, without even solid walls around her.

She had never been happier in all her life.

In the middle of the night she awoke slowly. So slowly. He had been arousing her, awaking her, his finger stroking down her spine. His lips, tongue, following it its wake. He rolled her swiftly, his kiss suddenly searingly intimate. She caught her breath, crying out a soft plea, shuddering with the hot sweetness that soared through her as he entered her. Moving. Oh, Lord. Moving slowly, more swiftly . . .

Dimly, she heard the cry of a bird, and realized that dawn was nearly upon them.

Again, the bird.

"What's that?" she whispered, suddenly pressing against him.

"Nothing!" he muttered, but he paused. He hesitated, then stood. The moon had risen. Naked, slick, shimmering in its glow, he walked down to the water. He stood there for a moment, as striking as some pagan god in the mystical light of moon with the sun just beginning to touch the horizon. Then he turned, disappearing into the brush.

Teela shivered, pulling the furs around her. Birds cried again. She listened intently, frightened that she would hear some rustling in the brush. She heard nothing.

She gasped as she felt a hand upon her shoulder, spinning with alarm. It was James. She hadn't begun to hear him return from behind her.

"What is it?" she demanded anxiously.

"Nothing," he told her.

"But what—"

"Nothing!" he repeated firmly, pressing her down. Covering her with his body and warmth and strength. Sexuality and seduction.

When he moved again within her, something was different. He made love with an even greater passion. Reckless, almost ruthless. He held her with a greater fervor. A greater urgency.

It seemed that he would never let her go.

* * *

Major General Joseph M. Hernandez stood quietly by his tent. A hundred and seventy men had set up bivouac in the ruins of Dunlawton Plantation. Night was falling. Peaceful time, pretty time. He loved dusk, the soft coating of shadow that added a muted beauty to his surroundings.

He was a Floridian, and did not mind his duty here in the territory. Of Hispanic descent, he had a fine, subtle sense of humor and a liking for humanity in general. He had befriended many of the Indians, and was often torn with pity for them. He knew the enemy he fought, and often wondered if the war could possibly ever end.

"General!"

John, a young aide-de-camp, approached him quickly across the overgrown lawn of the once beautiful plantation. He saluted quickly, and Hernandez saluted in return.

"We've gone with the Negro, sir, and spotted the Indian camp. It appears easily assailable now that it is discovered."

"Ah!" Hernandez nodded. Well, if the Seminoles did not suffer enough from the whites, they had their own numbers and rebellious Negroes to deal with as well. They were here tonight because a servant to the Mikasukee chief, King Philip, had grown weary of life in the scrub. Actually, it was the man's wife who had grown weary. Life was increasingly burdensome among the Indians. They were constantly on the run. Seeking poorer and poorer shelter. Seeking more and more desperately for any food to still their hunger, that of their children, their servants.

King Philip's man had promised to lead the whites to the chief's camp. And now he had done so.

"Sir?" John said.

Hernandez sighed deeply. "Ready the men. We will surround the camp, watch our enemy, attack by first light."

"Sir!" John acknowledged.

The order to march was sounded.

The dusk was too quickly gone. They marched by darkness, finding their positions around the Indian camp by midnight. He split his troops, ordering groups of volunteers to encircle the encampment on three sides. His regulars remained mounted, ready to ride in at first light.

No dog barked, no guard called out. Deep in the hammocks, too often the Indians slept with no guard. It had long been their way. The battle tactics of the whites were not easily accepted or realized, even when it brought terrible destruction upon the Indians.

By the first faint light of dawn, Hernandez gave the order for the troops to attack.

No alarm ever sounded. The soldiers ran over the encampment.

There was no battle. None of the Indians was slain, only one escaped, the rest were captured. There had been no chance to fight under the circumstances, and the Indians had known it. They were scarcely dressed; they'd scant time to pick up weapons.

"Royalty!" a soldier called, guffawing loudly. Shouts went up. Hostile cries from the Indians, jeers from some of the men.

Hernandez came forward, brushing past an army surgeon, Dr. Motte, who seemed ready as well to snicker at the sight of the man before him.

The Indian was not large in stature; indeed, he was covered in dirt, for he had run, probably for his weapons, and been dragged down. He was naked as a jaybird, except for the small breech clout covering his loins.

"A dirty king at that, eh, General?"

Hernandez, a striking, imposing man, turned with distaste to see who had called out. He didn't judge the Seminoles; he didn't judge his own men. They'd seen too much of disease and grisly death. He turned back to the man who, naked and dirty and not large at all, still managed to stand with tremendous pride before him.

"King Philip?" Hernandez said.

The Indian nodded in acknowledgment. Interpreters

stood by, but the *mico* had apparently understood his name.

"You are my prisoner, sir. Perhaps things will go better for you if you send out for your followers. Have them come in. Talk with us."

The interpreter repeated his words. Philip stared at him. Hernandez thought he smiled. Philip spoke in his own tongue to one of his people at his side.

"King Philip will send out runners for his allies."

"Tell him to bring in his son, Coacoochee. Known to the white men as Wildcat."

Philip again appeared to be smiling. He said something to a man at his side.

"What was it?" Hernandez asked John softly. He had learned many words himself in the Indian tongues, but John had a gift for language and spoke Philip's language fluently.

"He said, sir, indeed, he will send for the 'Wildcat.' And he says that white men should take grave care. He cannot know what manner of creature will come once a wildcat is summoned."

Hernandez nodded, acknowledging Philip's importance. He turned on his heel, aware that the night wasn't over. Another captive, called Tomoka Jon, had promised to lead them to another camp.

He should have been glad, proud of his leadership, proud of his troops. In all the time they had battled so far, he had just made one of the most important captures ever, that of King Philip. The more leaders they brought in, the more they would break the resistance.

He had Philip. And Philip could bring him Wildcat. And other wild denizens of the forest as well perhaps. Smart, dangerous creatures. Like an Alligator—or a Running Bear.

He felt weary, not elated.

The Indians, it seemed, were far wiser than many of their white enemies realized.

Wildcats and other creatures of the forest simply could

not be kept in captivity. They couldn't be tamed, and they couldn't be chained.

God alone knew what blood and fur might fly when they were accosted.

Chapter 20

The days passed strangely for Teela and James, as if time had somehow stopped within the copse, gone still. It had not, of course. Beyond the green shade of their hammock, the world, and the war, were going on. But here, for the time, it didn't touch them.

At first James seemed somewhat subdued, brooding. And almost determined to make Teela see that she couldn't endure the hardships of life in the hammock.

He told her that they had nothing to eat; she said that she wasn't hungry. He found roots that could be ground for a starch stew or porridge; she learned to grind roots. He told her that the Seminoles always kept a sofkee pot going, so that any visitor or man or woman within the tribe might eat when he or she was hungry. He told her Seminole women served their men.

She told him she wasn't Seminole.

Two mornings she was wretchedly sick, and determined he wouldn't realize it. He did see it, damned himself, and collected some wild berries and some squash and potatoes from an abandoned plantation. He killed a rabbit, which she annoyingly and expertly prepared over a spit, according to his directions.

His temper eased. His brooding gave way to a simple thoughtfulness.

And finally, in the privacy of the copse, they managed to cease being white and Indian, and simply be.

James didn't mention what he was going to do with her; Teela didn't ask. They swam, they fished, they lay in the sun, they slept beneath the moonlight. They made love at any hour. They saw no one, they wished to see no one.

The best times, Teela thought, were those when the sun was setting. When the sky was etched in magenta, when cranes and egrets streaked across the heavens and came to rest upon gnarled roots by the water. Sometimes then James lay propped against the trunk of a fallen cypress, and she lay curled within his arms, and they both watched the sky and talked. One day when they had spent nearly a week in their haven, there had been rain, and the sun was just beginning to fall with an extraordinary beauty. Teela told him about Lilly, about how her mother had thought that marriage to Michael Warren would be so wonderful, fitting, and proper. Lilly believed with her dying breath that Warren had been a fine father for Teela. "I don't think she ever loved him. I think she loved my real father, but then . . ."

"Then?" James queried.

Teela shrugged. "Well, marriages are often arranged in Charleston. She'd known most of her life she was going to marry my father. I used to love to dream about them, though. To imagine that he had been the great love of my mother's life, that they'd shared a passion beyond bounds. Children want to believe those things, though, don't you think?"

"Sometimes they're true. In that, I was lucky. I know that my father adored my mother." He hesitated a moment. "He was willing to give up everything for her, not that she asked him to."

"She must miss him."

"She has missed him a long time," he said softly, his hand moving gently over her arm as he spoke. "He was quite a man, my father. When Jarrett's mother died, he grieved terribly until he found a new interest in life. Indian culture. He was intrigued, fascinated, by other cultures and people. He was twice blessed. He met my mother, and she adored him, and Jarrett." He smiled ruefully. "At times, I believe, she is actually more fond of Jarrett than me. I accused her so once, in good humor, really, and she told me that she'd had Jarrett longer than me."

Teela laughed. "Jealous little ruffian, eh?"

He smiled, shaking his head. "Mary has a tremendous capacity for love. She might still marry again, who can say? She was sixteen when I was born, and gives the appearance of a young woman even now. She has mourned Father a long time and I imagine—" He broke off suddenly.

"What?"

"She might indeed marry again. If any men are left alive to marry when this is over."

Teela drew slightly away from him. "I don't want to talk about *this*."

He hiked his weight up, half leaning over her. His eyes were grave. "Eventually, we're going to have to talk about what we're going to do."

"We could stay here," she said stubbornly.

"Not forever."

"Why not forever?"

"Warren will hunt us down and you know it. And though I honestly wouldn't mind a chance to rip him to shreds, he'd kill so many others in the process of finding you that their lives would be on our conscience."

"So what will you do?" she demanded.

"I don't know yet," he said evasively.

"Go back to war," she accused him.

"And have you a better suggestion?"

"Yes! Quit fighting, live at Cimarron with your brother and your daughter, and—"

"Trade my life for my honor and the debt I owe my mother and her people?"

"What about the debt you owe your father, your brother, your friends?"

"They are not threatened with extermination."

"You've said you will not raid plantations—"

"And I will not, you know that."

"Then walk away from the war!"

"Do you think it will be so simple now?"

"What do you mean?"

"Never mind."

"Damn it, James—"

"Never mind!"

"You need to explain yourself and listen to me in return. The war will eventually be lost. The army will come, and come again in droves."

"Mark my words, Teela, you are wrong. This war will not be lost. One Indian standing firm can defeat a dozen exhausted soldiers, hungry, weary, and riddled with disease."

"The Seminoles are hungry, and many have died of malaria and measles."

"Teela—"

"James, if you just—"

"Stop."

"But I—"

"Enough!"

Enough, enough! He spoke, and she was supposed to obey.

She startled him by leaping up, her hands on her hips, looking like a very feminine pirate in his white cotton shirt, tied at her waist with a dyed red band of rawhide. She glared at him through narrowed eyes. "*Enough! Enough!* What is that, Mr. McKenzie, your favorite word? Order? Command, rather, I should say! Well then, you're damned right. I've had *enough*!"

She spun away from him, the wild length of her hair flying behind her. Shoulders straight, head high, her posture suddenly again that of the well-bred southern lady she was, she stalked away from him.

He watched her for a moment, vexed. Then he smiled slowly, because her appearance was so at odds with her bearing. His shirt chastely covered her shoulders, back, and rump, but there stopped, revealing the slim and delicious length of her legs. Her carriage was prim; her movement was unbearably evocative. He watched her another moment, making her barefoot way a good distance from him along the water. Where she was going he didn't know. That she was never going to reach her point of destination was a dead certainty.

He closed his eyes briefly. Their time was limited. He knew it well. It seemed they'd found a hidden paradise. But Wildcat had always known this place. Jarrett knew it as well; they had sometimes come across the territory as children; they had come for conferences; they had celebrated the Green Corn Dance with other tribes and factions. They had played here, a refuge for them then, a refuge for them now. Luckily, only those he trusted completely—whites and Seminoles—did know of this place.

Wildcat knew he was here. He had come briefly in the night to tell James that Otter had conceded Running Bear's right to the woman. She would be safe from Otter in the future. Otter was pleased that his attack had been so perfectly planned. Only a few soldiers had escaped the slaughter. Wildcat had spoken very quickly, warning James that white soldiers were rumored to be in vast numbers all around St. Augustine. Though James was safe from Otter, he had best take care on all other fronts.

Wildcat was a strange friend for James. No one, not even Osceola, was more determined to dig in. He could battle and kill without blinking and speak his mind clearly no matter what the opposition or consequence. He was a man of integrity who could also keep completely quiet when necessary, and in the bonds of friendship he could be utterly trusted.

So much for Otter and Wildcat.

He didn't need thoughts of either man to warn him anew that his time in this strange haven was limited.

She was still walking. With such dignity. Yet still, she . . . swayed. She was so angry, aloof, disdainful, proud . . .

Delectable.

He rose swiftly, agile, silent. It was true that his silent speed was uncanny.

Yet she heard him. In the split second before he

caught up with her, tackled her, and brought them both down to the earth.

"Enough!" she shouted to him, gasping for air, struggling furiously against his hold. "Enough, enough, enough—"

"Enough!" he agreed, his fingers lacing with hers, forcing them against the damp earth.

Yet as his body straddled hers and his lips silenced any further argument, he realized with a sinking feeling of anguish that it would never, ever be enough.

They had to talk with the white men. Another parley. The events taking place recently demanded that it be so.

Staring into the fire, seated before it, Osceola thought these things with a great deal of pain in his heart.

Yes. He had to talk. The children were starving. The women were bones. The warriors themselves were little more than skeletons. Some temporary truce must be made.

If he went in to talk, he realized, he might never walk away again. He had done things the whites did not understand and would never forgive. He had waged the war against them that they had waged against him and his people.

He was interrupted in his weary thoughts by the sudden arrival of Otter. The warrior stalked with his typical fury to stand before the fire opposite Osceola.

Osceola refused to acknowledge him, so Otter sat before him.

"We need Running Bear. Now," Otter told Osceola. "That he fought me I will accept, for I challenged him to do so. That he took a white woman whose scalp might now hang from my rifle, I accept, for he fought for her. I have granted his right to her, sworn her safety from me. But he stays deep in the hammock now when he is needed. He stays with the white woman, forgetting us. You know where he is. Tell me. I will go for him now."

Osceola looked up at Otter. Yes, he knew where Running Bear had gone. Wildcat had been to see him very early one morning, before the dawn had begun to brighten the sky. They had spoken briefly. Running Bear had the problem now of the white woman, but he trusted Osceola, and Osceola would not betray that trust.

Wildcat could not go to Running Bear again. Wildcat had felt he had no choice when his father's messenger had come to tell him that the whites had demanded King Philip bring in his son or perhaps face the hangman's noose. So Wildcat, a fierce warrior they needed badly, was a captive of the whites.

But there were others who could be trusted to summon Running Bear. Despite Otter's words of honor, Osceola could not trust Otter with directions to the secret copse.

Osceola was suddenly very tired.

There were days when he could rise and feel as well as he ever had, days when it seemed that strength and sun and life came with swift energy to his limbs. Then there were times when he believed that he dreamed those days, for some mornings when he woke, he could almost imagine that death slept atop him like some dark, blanketing form. As it did so often lately, Osceola's mind drifted back in memory.

Wild Orchid had been so beautiful then. The best that three shades of men had to offer. Her skin was deeper than copper, her eyes darker then black. Her hair was like the wing of a raven, curling beautifully from her Negro heritage while her white blood softened her features. He had warned her often enough when they had been young to keep clear of the soldiers, but she had loved life. Loved to move, to dance, to run, and so, long before his run-in with Wiley Thompson that had become so well-known, he had become enemies with the man. Because Wild Orchid had come too close to the whites, and she had been seized as a runaway slave. It hadn't mattered that he had explained the beautiful mulatto was his wife. She had been taken from him, and he hadn't had the strength or the power then to fight and demand that she be returned to him. He had been able to do nothing but follow behind through the bush as the soldiers had taken her, chained, to St. Augustine. All along the way he had looked for a chance to attack the whites and rescue her. They had been too strong. He had all but wept with fury and frustration. Then he had waited for word of her sale, and he had learned that she had been stripped down on the block and sold to a gaunt-faced white man who intended to take her to a plantation near Tallahassee. They had laughed while she stood on the block. They had commented on what fine sport she would make in a white man's bed, how lush and erotic her flesh would appear against the whiteness of cotton sheets.

He had been sickened, knowing then that to wage a war would mean sure death for him and so many others. They hadn't planned as yet. They hadn't gathered rifles and gunpowder. They were too weak. Yet even as he waited just south of St. Augustine, desperately plotting and planning, he had heard a woman's joyous cry, shouting his name in greeting. And through the brush she had come running to him. Behind her, leading the pony she had ridden, were the McKenzies. Running Bear and his white brother. They had known, they had heard of the injustice, and they had gone to the overseer and persuaded the licentious bastard to sell her to them. At an exorbitant price, Osceola was certain, but neither brother would ever comment on it.

Now neither of his wives was so very young or fragile, but neither had he forgotten what that first hunger and passion of love could be, denying all reason and logic. Wild Orchid had been precious to him all these years, as had Morning Dew. He loved his children by both wives; he knew the strength and support of his family, all begun by love.

He could not deny James McKenzie his passion. Especially, he thought with a certain humor, since he had seen the red-haired woman himself.

"You will leave him be one more night," Osceola said. "Let him watch the sun go down in his hammock one more time, see the colors streak the horizon, feel the kiss of the dew upon his flesh with the coming of the dawn."

"Osceola, you forget the events that have taken place! We need him—"

"One more night will not change the war, not the history of our world or theirs. I will send for him myself come the morning," Osceola said.

He would let McKenzie have one more sweet taste of his savage paradise before the world exploded upon them all.

General Thomas Sydney Jesup sat at his desk, studying again the war orders from Secretary of War Joel Poinsett. He closed his eyes morosely, damning his Florida duty. In fact, for the moment, damning the military altogether.

Let them come down from their high horses in Washington! he thought angrily. They had ignored him. Ignored his plea that they leave the Seminoles alone. Let them flee south. Live out their pathetic, starving lives in the no-man's land that filled so damned much of the mosquito-infested peninsula.

He was a military man, a hard-core soldier. He had come to Florida from battling the Creeks, and he knew how to fight Indians. If he had ever said anything negative regarding any of his predecessors as to their stint of duty as commanders in Florida, he had let it be well-known that he retracted such statements. This was hell. A war that couldn't be won. He had quickly, painfully learned that the Seminoles could split their numbers and disappear into the terrain while his men floundered in hammock and swamp. He had come expecting to round up the Seminoles with all speed, and send them west to live. Poinsett was an able man, an incredibly able man, in Jesup's opinion. But Jesup damned him just the same. Poinsett had left him no choice but to exterminate the Indians.

Jesup sighed, running his fingers through his white hair. His bitterness extended toward the enemies. Before the escape in June of the nearly seven hundred Indians from the center at Tampa, he had believed he had broken the resistance, that his war was all but over. But then those seven hundred had disappeared, with the wily Osceola at the head of it, or so it seemed.

He slammed a fist against the table. The Indians deserved no decency on his part. They knew nothing of any code of honor. They were slippery, cunning, treacherous.

If he had to use treachery against them in return, then so be it.

He set aside the missive from the secretary of war. He picked up his quill and began to pen the orders he would give in turn to General Hernandez.

His hand shook as he wrote. He set his quill down. And still his hand shook. A chill fell over him. He shook it off. He refused to admit that his ill feelings might forebode the damning consequences of his own actions, setting the cry of treachery upon himself for his lifetime, and all history yet to come.

The day had been a good one. They'd awakened to a powder blue sky, puffs of clouds moving across it. Teela had been ecstatic to catch a fish herself, spearing it through with lightning speed. He'd skinned it, they cooked it and ate it with nuts and fruit.

Now they played in the river. Teela had become an excellent swimmer. The water was filled with an abundance of sea cows, and Teela took great pleasure in them. She'd even decided that they weren't ugly anymore. There were adorable, as charming as otters, as gentle as puppies.

"There!" she cried to James suddenly.

"Where, what?" he asked, turning.

She dove beneath the surface, caught his foot, dunked him thoroughly, then swam away with a practiced speed that startled even him. He sputtered to the surface. "Playing with fire again, eh, my love?" he shouted, swimming hard to pursue her. Damn. She was getting good. She reached the bank and raced out of the water, laughing and shrieking. He followed her. Despite the fact that she was a quick learner and swam very well indeed now, she hadn't a chance against him on dry land. Yet even as he sped after her, he suddenly ground to a dead halt, staring past her to the entrance of the secluded copse.

There was a rider there, a very old black man on a gaunt gray mare. It was difficult to determine which was more pathetically thin, the man or the horse.

Osceola's old servant, Riley, had come for him, he realized, the air all but sucked out of him with the knowledge that the days he had clung to so desperately had come to an end. That Riley had come already indicated trouble, for if things were normal, Wildcat would have been the one to come.

Teela had been looking back at James as she ran. Still laughing, she whirled around and shrieked in sudden terror as she nearly crashed into the black man who had dismounted from a horse. James found motion again, running swiftly enough to be there when she backed away from Riley, trembling. Perhaps Riley was a startling visage. He dressed in buckskin trousers and a white man's shirt. A turban of bright cotton and egret plumes sat atop his dark head and cascaded down his back. It was a magnificent headdress, a gift from Osceola to a faithful servant. It made him appear, however, to be nearly seven feet tall.

James wound his arms around Teela, then eased her behind him. Her hands set upon his hips, the fullness of her naked body pressed against him as if he were a barrier of steel.

"Riley," he said quietly. "Teela, it's all right. It's Riley. He offers us no harm."

She was shaking still, but it occurred to him then just how greatly she trusted him.

"Don't be afraid," he said softly.

"I'm not afraid. I'm—I'm naked James."

"Riley will take his clothes off, too, if you want."

She slammed a fist against his back.

"Riley, have you something there Miss Warren might wear?" he asked.

Riley nodded gravely, tossing a satchel he carried down to James.

"Real clothing," James muttered, bending down to open it. Teela quickly ducked down behind him. In the bundle he found a full, flared indigo-dyed skirt and a colorful pullover blouse. He turned and offered both to Teela, who scrambled into the items quickly and awkwardly, refusing to rise behind him until she was dressed.

"Coffee, Riley?" James suggested. His breeches were back by the cypress log, and it didn't seem that Riley had brought anything for him.

"Coffee would be fine fittin', Master James," Riley said. The old man's usage of both the Muskogee and Hitichi languages was fluent, but he had always addressed James by his English name and in the English tongue.

"Well, let's all come along, then, shall we?" James said, starting back to his pants and their shelter.

"Did you come alone?" Teela asked him.

"I did, Miss Warren."

"How did you know where we were?" Teela demanded.

"Osceola knows this place. Wildcat came before and talked to James. We knew where James would be when the time came."

James winced, stiffening his back for a moment.

"Wildcat was already here?" Teela asked sweetly. "And we didn't know?"

James found his breeches and scrambled into them. When he turned, old Riley was grinning and Teela looked flushed. "Master James, he knew. He knew."

Teela turned her stare on James. Accusingly. He brushed past her to get water for the coffeepot. "We always knew that our time here was limited," he told her.

She followed him to the water. "Your friend, this Wildcat, was the bird, right?" she demanded in a furious whisper. "I was, we were—" she sputtered. "And he was there!"

He sighed. "Wildcat was discreet. Since he did rather interrupt us in the middle of something."

"Bastard!" she hissed.

"He has seen far more," James said with a shrug. "Besides, it was dark."

She started to shove him. He caught her hand and warned her harshly, "Teela, he came, he went. He didn't mean to interrupt. He came to tell me we were completely safe from Otter. Now, my love, you behave, or I'll have to paddle you black and blue to keep my standing—and perhaps my life—among the people. Riley is a good man but a damned talkative one."

He didn't give her a chance to obey or disobey, keeping one hand and a firm grip upon her arm and another on the coffeepot as he rose and headed back toward the hootie. Old Riley had already laid out some of the delicacies he had brought them, smoked deer meat and cornmeal cakes. Dragging Teela with him, James quickly had the chicory coffee going. As the fire lapped beneath the pot, James asked Riley, "What news?"

"Soldiers seized all of King Philip's camp. King Philip was betrayed by his servant, whose woman was unhappy." Riley paused to glance at Teela, silently warning against the evils of female influence. "Wildcat has gone in to the whites for his father's sake. There is to be more talk. Osceola has sent messages to General Jesup, and General Jesup has said that there will be a meeting again. Running Bear, Coa Hadjo will speak for Osceola, but Osceola has asked that you accompany him and the others when they meet."

James bowed his head. "He knows that I will come."

Riley hesitated. He looked at Teela again. "Osceola says that you must know there is talk that you are the most dangerous of all Indians, a white Indian."

"Why this talk?" James demanded, frowning.

"The white soldier, Warren, has said that you planned

the murder of many men in order to steal his daughter. Warren says that you should be hanged."

Teela gasped, horrified. "He is a liar!"

"There are many who will believe his lies," James said quietly.

"But I'll tell them all that he's a liar—" Teela began.

"Tell them what you will," James said. "Some men will believe you, and some will not."

"Then you can't go in with Osceola!" Teela said. "James, you must stay hidden!" she insisted fervently.

"I have to go."

"You cannot! You—"

"Teela!" he warned her, his voice low and grating, a harsh command that she stop.

Riley said, "You can keep your camp here until morning. Then Osceola asks that you meet with him tomorrow, behind the soldiers' road that leads to the east."

James nodded. "That will be fine."

"That will not be fine—" Teela began.

James clamped a hand over her mouth, dragging her hard against his chest. "That will be fine," he repeated.

Old Riley poured himself coffee and rose. "I will sleep behind the copse," he told James. James nodded. Teela was fighting like a scalded wildcat against his hold. He gave her a firm shake, not daring to release her until Riley had made his way from the copse.

"You can't go! You can't go!" she told him, tears blinding her eyes.

He stared down at her, not replying. "You can't, you can't, you can't!" she said, slamming her fists against his chest, beating him, pummeling him. He didn't stop her. She kept it up until her blows were soft, until her words were sobs.

"We've a last sunset," he told her.

"You can't go. You can't—"

He hushed her with a slow, tender, heartbreaking kiss.

Yet as darkness came, she was the one to refuse tenderness. To hold him fiercely. Make love with a wild, wicked, violent abandon.

But with sobs, not words. Now her very violence brought her to exhaustion. When at last she slept next to him, he cast a fur around his shoulders and left the copse, coming to Riley.

Awake, resting against an oak, Riley smiled grimly, as if he'd expected James.

"I must make arrangements for Teela. Osceola knows this."

"Osceola has sent word to Jarrett McKenzie, and he and the young soldier Harrington will come for your woman."

James nodded, feeling a twist like a knife in his abdomen. "Sleep, Riley," he told the old man.

He returned to the hootie and stared down at Teela. Her cheeks were liquid with tears. Her hair was a fan around her, beautiful in the moon glow, red, radiant. She was almost ivory in her whiteness, her naked body as perfect as porcelain. He lay down beside her, intending to let her sleep.

But their last sunset had already fallen.

He woke her. Silenced her words, her protests. Made love tenderly, fiercely, tenderly . . .

Indeed, their sunset was gone.

And dawn was coming. A red dawn. A bloodred dawn.

Chapter 21

Teela was subdued during the ride early the next morning.

She kept her distance from him at first, and he thought that she was feeling ill again. He didn't attempt to comfort, though he worried at the many deadly diseases she might fall prey to. No matter what emotions and desires tore at his heart, it was not just necessary but good that she was going to be back in his brother's care. Harrison's care, even. Out of the territory, with any luck!

She swam without him, using sand for soap as he had shown her, and dressed without a word in the strange new outfit Riley had brought her. He longed to seize hold of her, defy the bleak future. He turned away. He couldn't hold her tightly enough to change the future. He braced himself as he did so, wondering if this was the last time he would ever see her. A million different things could go wrong. Osceola's parley could turn into a desperate battle. Warren might have already made arrangements for Running Bear to be seized and hanged upon first sight. Yes, Teela was best far removed from him. There was nothing that she could do.

"Teela! Come along!" he told her when she hesitated by the water, watching the sun rise. She turned back to him. Her hair was as soft as angel's wings, floating freely down her back, its exotic color wildly at odds with that silky softness. Her eyes were brilliant, beautiful. She lowered her lashes, though, and came to him. Riley had mounted. James put his hands on Teela's waist to lift her atop his bay. She caught hold of his shoulders, eyes blazing into his. "Don't go!" she whispered.

He held still for a moment, wishing with all his heart that he could oblige her, very nearly doing so.

Despite the fact that they were riding double, they made good time, both Riley and James knowing the land so well. The sun rose swiftly, but it was a beautiful day, just kissed by a hint of the coming of fall. The trees dappled green light over their heads. They made their way through swamp and pine barrens.

Toward noon, James paused, seeing that the trail had recently been used. His brother was near, he was certain. He felt Teela jump when he let out his bird's cry, a perfect imitation of a loon. Jarrett McKenzie came riding out of the bush toward them. He was accompanied by Robert Trent and a few of his plantation men, including some of the Indians who had long worked for him.

He didn't dare speak to Teela. He dismounted from the bay. Jarrett dismounted from his horse as well, and the brothers greeted each other in the pathway with an affection neither man made any attempt to hide, embracing, then stepping back at last.

"My daughter?" James asked.

"Sends her love. She is very well."

"Let's walk for a moment, shall we?" James asked. Jarrett nodded in agreement, and the two turned, heads lowered in private conversation.

"I hear Warren has stated that I was behind the attack on the companies out of Fort Deliverance."

Jarrett nodded grimly. "The good news is that General Jesup and most sane commanders know you too well. They don't believe the story. Also, as you must know now, King Philip and his people were taken, and then a group of Yuchis—Blue Snake and Yuchi Billy among them. Philip sent for Wildcat, and Wildcat is a prisoner now as well."

"Yes, I know."

"Wildcat has told the generals in quite disdainful terms that they are fools. That Warren's daughter would have been dead for simply wearing his name were it not for your interference."

"Well, that's good, for it seems Osceola has arranged a meeting with the military."

"Yes. Some speculate that he has agreed to meet so that he can discover some way to rescue Philip and the others. Jesup has not forgotten the seven hundred men Osceola freed in June."

James shook his head. "He has moments when he is strong, but he is sick. Really sick. I don't think that the military commanders realize just how sick he is."

"That may be. I hope that the next meeting will bring peace, but I feel uneasy about it."

"What do you know?"

"Nothing—I am no longer trusted by our military friends."

"I'm sorry."

"Don't be. We are both at a loss in this war."

James nodded, turning toward Jarrett, extending a hand to his brother. Jarrett gripped it. "Thank you," James told him.

Jarrett shook his head. "There is nothing to thank me for. We are both our father's sons. Perhaps the time will come again when we can be like a normal family. I pray for it. I hold your property against that time. I beg you to take care, and live to let us touch that time again."

James grinned, nodded. He glanced toward Teela.

"Take care of her. It's a heavy burden I set on you, I know, but please try to keep her out of trouble."

Jarrett hesitated. "I think I can do so. Tara is in St. Augustine with the children. We've taken a house there for the fall and winter so that I can, perhaps, be nearer the present theaters of operation and step in if I am needed. It's my understanding that Osceola's council is going to be set not far from Fort Peyton, just seven miles south of the city. I'll be near." He hesitated. "John Harrington is stationed at Fort Peyton at the moment. I'm hoping he'll prevent any confrontation that might occur once Warren rides back into the picture."

"Where is Warren now?"

"Still in the interior, south of us now, I believe. Hunting down more women and children. If he follows his orders, he should not come around to hound us at least for a few months."

"That's a relief," James murmured, glancing back toward Teela again. She looked so stoic, seated atop the bay. She would probably remain so, as still and silent as a statue, even if Robert approached her. James lowered his head, glad. Robert was one of the best men James knew. He had the ability to make anyone feel at ease, to draw out conversation, even laughter, when there was none to be drawn.

He looked back up at his brother. "Jarrett, you have to give me one promise."

"What's that?"

"You don't risk your life for mine."

"James—"

James set up a hand. "If things go badly, interfere only if I ask you to do so. Things are more deadly now than ever before. My association with you could bring daggers into your back from your white friends, as could your influence on my part hurt me among the people at this time. I beg of you, don't interfere now. If you can help me at any time, and safely so, I won't hesitate to call, I swear it, big brother. Now, I want your word."

Jarrett, dark eyes somber and unhappy, hesitated. "James, these are difficult times—"

"Your word, big brother. White Tiger."

Still Jarrett hesitated. "My word," he agreed grimly at last.

"Take Teela to safety. Send her away. Make her marry Harrington if that is what it will take."

Jarrett crossed his arms over his chest, arching a brow at James. "How many things have you managed to make that woman do, little brother?"

James smiled slowly. "Well, a very few. The key is never to let her know that there are any weaknesses in men.

"Hell, if it comes to it, drug her. Drag her down an aisle rolled in a blanket if need be. Just keep her from harm. Perhaps you can put her on a ship out of St. Augustine. That was what she intended to do when she was traveling north before Otter's band attacked the group. That would be best. Try to make her leave. Please."

"My word again. I will do my best."

"Thank you."

"But . . ." Jarrett began.

"But what?" James asked, crossing his arms over his chest as he stared at his brother warily.

"Well, you have chosen this life."

"I didn't choose anything. I was born with this!"

"And which parent would you rather not have had?"

"Neither, of course—"

"You could build a plantation on the land you own right outside Cimarron."

"Under these circumstances—"

"Right. You cannot refuse to be part of this. So therefore you choose to be a part of it. Perhaps she has chosen the same."

"Well, she can't. She's got to go, dammit."

Jarrett lowered his head, lifted his hands.

"She could be risking her fool life."

"Some people choose to do so."

James let out a growl of irritation.

"Jarrett—"

"I will do my best. My word."

James inhaled deeply. "Thank you."

"You do something for me. Your word," Jarrett said.

"What is that?"

"Keep yourself safe."

James smiled, nodded. "That's it, I guess."

"Another good-bye."

They turned in unison, heading back toward the others and the horses. James went straight to Teela, lifting her down from the bay. The warmth of her body fell against his, slid against it as he lowered her to her feet. Her eyes were on his, glittering. She drew her hands from his shoulders even as he set her down. Jarrett cleared his throat discreetly. He, Robert, and his men moved ahead in the clearing, followed by old Riley. For a moment they were alone in the strange peacefulness of the clearing.

"You're not going to ask me not to go again?" he inquired.

She shook her head. "You've already made the decision. What does it matter what I say? You're going."

He nodded. "Jarrett will get you to St. Augustine. You were ready to leave the territory. Now you must go."

"Must I?"

"You said yourself that it was your course of action to leave the territory when Otter and his band attacked you and the soldiers."

"Yes, but . . . so much has changed."

"I told you to go—"

"You've also told me to marry John Harrington."

"Teela, dammit, don't argue with me—"

"Why? Everything in your life must be so neat and tidy. It's time to go to war again, so you put Teela away, you cannot play with her any longer."

He suddenly couldn't bear the parting, or that glitter, cold and disdainful, that had come into her eyes. He wanted to shake her. He drew her hard into his arms, pressed his lips to hers one last time, determined to taste and remember. He wanted her to feel his fury and his anger, know the harshness, feel again that what she had said herself was true—his bitterness made him a fire, a fire that burned others . . .

When he released her, she was shaking. Her lips were swollen and red. Her eyes were alive with a blaze of their own. "Yes, damn you, I'm done playing with you!" he snapped.

He didn't dare look at her again. He leapt, an Indian, bareback, up on his bay.

And rode away from her as quickly as he could.

* * *

With Jarrett and his men, as with James, it was possible to move very quickly through the landscape.

Jarrett was exceptionally eager to do so. Their small party was heavily armed, and if Osceola was still wielding any power, they were safe, but he wasn't eager to take any chances.

The men were incredibly polite to Teela, constantly solicitous. She was grateful. James's last stinging words remained in her heart. He did not mean them, she told herself. She had taunted him into them. But throughout the day she was chilled to the bone. She felt the pain of losing him as she might feel the pain had some piece of her been cut away. The worst of it was that she was so afraid he would be killed. He was a strong man. But no man was stronger than a bullet. Yes, he could probably best a number of soldiers, but if her stepfather came against him, he could command more and more soldiers. No one could stand up to battle forever. Any man could be tricked, fall prey to treachery.

They rode very late and made no fire that night. Jarrett didn't want to attract parties of either Indians or soldiers. He was hoping to bring her into St. Augustine quietly, and give them all time to adapt before she was forced to talk to any of her father's friends in the military.

When they did stop, Jarrett and Robert created a bed for her from a tarp and blankets, with a saddle for a pillow. Jarrett sat down beside her, leaned against an old oak, his rifle at his side. "You can sleep," he told her. "You'll be safe, I promise."

"I have no fear with you or James," she assured him.

He was quiet a few moments, then said, "Teela, this war is going to go on and on. I see no hope for a solution. If new boundaries are created, the settlers will overstep them again. The Indians will send out their hunting parties when the food in their poor sections runs scarce. Many of the generals think they can stop the war by capturing the chiefs. There will be more chiefs. Young warriors will grow to cunning leaders."

"Why are you telling me this? These things I already know," she said softly.

"Because I know your intentions regarding my brother now, Teela. You are in love with him. With no prejudices and no reservations. But you shouldn't be. The world will not allow what lies in your heart. You need to sail away as you were going to do. Forget everything and everyone here."

Teela sat up, hugging her knees to her chest. "You have told me my intentions—or what I feel at least. Now tell me about your brother. He saved my life. I never planned what I feel. I'm like the arrow of a compass, ever pointing north, and he is north. And when I'm with him, I cannot give a damn about the rest of the world. Yet, sometimes, it is as if he has come to dinner at your house, enjoyed the fullness of a meal, the feel of soft white sheets against his flesh—and then ridden away, needing no more. He can be brutal—"

"James has hurt you?" Jarrett queried, his voice gruff.

She shook her head. "Only with his words. So tell me, where is the truth in him?"

"The truth, Teela, is that he is obsessed with you. But he knows what I have told you is the real truth—this war could go on forever."

"He loves you and Tara and his daughter. You all love him in return. So—"

"We all know that he could be killed any day. We accept that in our hearts. Do you, Teela?"

She lowered her head. "He has told me to leave, or marry John Harrington. Does he mean it?"

"If you were to marry Harrington, he would probably want to slash Harrington's throat and have you drawn and quartered. But yes, he means it."

She lay back down, tears stinging her eyes, and not wanting Jarrett to see them. She was startled when she felt a soft shifting of her hair from her face, and felt a very light, paternal kiss on her forehead. "He wants you to marry Harrington because he loves you, little fool," he said softly. And that was all. He sat back against his

tree, his rifle at the ready. The night breeze moved very
gently around her, and she slept for the few hours left
before first dawn.

They were back on the road incredibly early. They
were not far from the city of St. Augustine, but Jarrett
wanted to slip in before most of the citizenry awoke.
Teela had never been to the city, but even in Charleston
she had heard stories about it and the Spaniards who
had founded it. They had always been seeking gold and
the fountain of youth Ponce de Leon had been promised
by the early Indian tribes, decimated now, that he had
found within the peninsula. The architecture was charming, old government buildings with balconies and arches
interspersed with more modern dwellings, some in wood,
some in masonry. She did not look long, though, for as
they passed through an old cemetery, Jarrett pointed out
the giant Castillo de San Marcos, Fort Marion, rising off
a spit of land against the water. "Let's not run into soldiers now!" he told her, and they hurried down the
streets to the old Spanish house he and Tara had taken.

Once they arrived, it was wonderful for Teela to see
Tara, Jennifer, and little Ian McKenzie again. Wonderful, even, to soak in a very hot tub, sip sherry, wrap up
in a soft cotton nightgown provided by her hostess.

It had been a hard ride, and she was exhausted.

But she was glad of Tara's company after her bath.
Glad to have Tara by her. She was brought a rich red
steak with corn and a fruit garnish, and she had to admit
that the dinner was absolutely delicious. When she finished eating, she was still weary, but content to sit back
in a heavy upholstered chair and have Tara brush the
snarls out of her hair.

"Newspaper reporters may soon be after you," Tara
warned her. "Anything to do with Indian abduction and
captivity always intrigues readers."

"I wasn't abducted! Surely, Tara—"

"I know that, of course. But that's my point. You
should speak with a reporter. Let him know that James

McKenzie saved your life. It's amazing what sway public opinion can sometimes have over the army."

Teela swung around, catching Tara's hand and meeting her gaze. "Is James in greater danger because of me?"

Tara sighed. "Well, he is an outlaw at the moment, most certainly. But it is not because of you. It is because Warren is a treacherous liar. If you'll allow me, I can see to it that you speak to the right person. Warren's lies will be disarmed. You should do so soon, before your ship leaves."

"My ship?"

"Well, you were returning to Charleston?"

Teela swallowed hard. "I—I'm not ready now."

"But perhaps you should," Tara suggested softly.

Teela shook her head stubbornly. "I've caused trouble for James, but now perhaps I can change that."

"And what are you going to do? Run out and shoot down both the Indians and the army?"

"I'm going to give your reporter the story," she said firmly.

"And when your father does come out of the interior, he'll do something horrible to you."

"I can't go—yet. Please, don't you be against me, too."

"No one is against you. I just think that maybe, for both you and James, it would be best if you did go home soon."

Teela felt something bubbling in her stomach. She leapt up, biting her lower lip.

"What—?" Tara said with alarm.

"The chamber pot!" Teela said. Tara found it in the nick of time. Spasms seized Teela until she was weak. She soaked her face and hands in the fresh water Tara brought her.

"Are you all right now?"

"The food was delicious, too good. I don't think I could handle so much so soon. I shouldn't have wolfed it down like that."

Tara looked at her strangely.

"You should try to get some sleep. We'll talk again in the morning."

Tara left her. Teela had never felt more drained or exhausted. She curled up on the soft four-poster bed in the room with its clean white sheets. She slept.

Tara came downstairs and went into the library of their rented home. It was quite a wonderful place, built in the mid-1600s by a wealthy don for his beloved bride. There was a beautiful mantel hewn from the same coquina shell they had used to build the fort. It was still owned by one of the don's descendents, a charming man with a Spanish name and an English accent, since his family had retained ownership through the years when the territory had passed from the Spaniards to the English, back to the Spaniards, and on to the Americans. He'd been happy to offer the home to a family, just as Tara had been happy to come to the Atlantic side of the territory. She found St. Augustine to be charming, a mixture of the cultures that had passed its way. There were well-stocked general stores, and there was the military base at the ancient fortress, rising on the horizon with a tremendous magnificence. It hadn't actually ever withstood any attacks. Perhaps it was too foreboding to attack.

The city was long established, filled with many languages, the social elite of different cultures, military, slaves, free blacks, even Indians—remnants of decimated tribes and those who had simply embraced white ways.

Jarrett had suggested that they come for a change of scenery and a bit of a social scene throughout the fall and winter. Tara knew, of course, that he didn't give a damn about scenery or society. He had come because he feared for his brother, and seemed to think that he could be of greater help here.

As she walked across the tiled floor of the library, he looked up from the ledger he had before him on the heavy old Spanish desk. "Is she settled?"

Tara nodded. "Sleeping by now, I think. She was very tired."

"There are a number of ships stopping in Charleston that leave here soon."

"There will always be ships leaving St. Augustine," she murmured, perching on a corner of his desk. "She's going to speak with a reporter."

Jarrett folded his arms across his chest and leaned back in his chair, watching his wife. "Two men escaped that slaughter. Both of them told reporters that James McKenzie was not the leader of the band that attacked them. Warren's story was surely a better one."

"But not the truth."

"Lies often catch the public imagination."

"But Teela will be able to make a better story of it, I'm quite certain."

"But should she?" Jarrett murmured, looking out the window. They could see the water from the house, a very blue inlet of the Atlantic.

"My God, of course—"

"Then Warren will tear her to ribbons."

"Jarrett, he won't dare. It will be done before anyone sees him again. And then she can be gone."

"She doesn't want to go."

"Well, she may not have a choice!"

"Are you ready to drag her, kicking and screaming, onto a ship?" she asked him. Then she smiled slightly. "Never mind, what a question! There's very little I put past you, my love, in the pursuit of right as you see it. But I'm warning you, she won't go otherwise."

Jarrett sighed with exasperation. "Then what? Shall I send for Harrington? Should we insist she marry the poor fellow if she's so determined to remain? Harrington would probably become a groom with the greatest pleasure, but would it be fair?"

Tara looked down at the desk. "No, I don't think that sending for Harrington would be a good idea at this point. Jarrett, she's sick."

"With what? Should we quarantine her? Get her away from the children as quickly as possible?"

"No, no. She hasn't a fever or the like. She's—sick. To her stomach."

Jarrett tapped a finger upon his desk thoughtfully. "Oh, dear. I think she was ill along the way as well. She refused, of course, to let me see that she felt poorly in the least. She's determined that she will forge through the territory without a complaint, come what may."

"You don't understand," Tara murmured.

"My love, I understand this situation far more than I wish! Tara wants to stay near my brother no matter what, and though he covets her pathetically, he wants her gone! Perhaps she really should marry John, then—"

"Jarrett, trust me, you don't understand!" Tara repeated. She leapt off the desk and came around, kneeling beside him and taking his hands in hers. She had that strange half smile on her face that meant that men didn't really ever understand anything.

He smiled in return, a brow arched. "What is it, Tara?"

"She can't marry Harrington."

"Tara, Warren remains her guardian—"

"Jarrett, she's expecting."

"Expecting what?"

"Oh, my God. A baby!"

He felt like an idiot. He simply hadn't been prepared for a bomb to be thrown in what was already a dangerous battleground.

"Oh, good God!" he groaned. He clutched his wife's hands more tightly. "How can you possibly tell? I mean, you can't possibly know this for fact. He didn't rescue her from that slaughter in the woods that long ago—"

"It must have happened back in June. When he slipped back to our house after the massive escape of the Indians from near Fort Brooke. Remember the day of the skirmish down the river, when Teela met Harrington and Brandeis and James came back that night?"

"Yes, I remember the night. It was the last time I had seen him until today. But just because she's been sick—"

"Jarrett, I was just in the room with her. While she was bathing."

"Yes?" He arched a brow suspiciously.

"She's changed."

"You were looking at another woman that closely?"

She made a fist of her hand and slammed it on his knee. "Jarrett! I didn't need to stare!"

"Oh, God!" he repeated. He stared at his wife. "James doesn't know."

"I don't think Teela even knows."

An ink dark brow rose on his forehead once again. This time, he realized, he was probably giving her the male look that indicated women were far less than sane and never rational in the least.

"I didn't know for the longest time about Ian," she reminded him. "You get caught up in life, in the worries from day to day—and she has certainly had enough going on around her! Time goes by—and she's been living under such strange circumstances."

Jarrett reached into the bottom desk drawer for a brandy bottle and glasses.

"She doesn't know, but you're certain."

"I've had a baby. I know the signs." She counted on her fingers for a moment, showing him. "Middle of June, end of September. Mark my words. It will be evident to all of us very soon."

Jarrett was about to pour the liquid into a glass, then brought the bottle to his mouth instead. Tara took it from him. "You might share!" she admonished.

He took the bottle from her, poured an equal amount into both glasses. "Sorry, my love," he said, and raised his snifter to her.

Tara picked up her glass. "Thank you, McKenzie."

"Well, congratulations, we are about to become an aunt and uncle once again."

Tara clinked her glass to his, but didn't sip from it. "Indeed, my love, congratulations. Oh, dear Lord! We will need no longer worry about Major Warren. He will die of rage and apoplexy upon receipt of the news."

"We can only hope. But now, Tara McKenzie, since you are so certain about this impending event, when do you think we should share the information with the happy mother-to-be upstairs? And then, for the love of God, where do we go from there?"

"I'm not sure," Tara murmured. She glanced up at him, setting her snifter down on the desk and pushing it from her.

"What now? You did just insist I share."

"Yes, but actually, it doesn't go down well at all. I haven't been feeling quite as robust myself the last several weeks."

"Tara," he began frowning, "are you trying to tell me—"

"Yes, I am," she said. She looked up at him, smiling ruefully. "If nothing else, these cousins will be very close in age."

Jarrett scooped up his wife, set her upon his lap, and held her very tenderly. "I am delighted, of course," he said huskily. "Ian is still so young—"

"He, too, will be close with his new brother or sister."

Jarrett smiled, breathing in the scent of her, cherishing the moment they shared. "Have I told you recently that I love you more than anything in the world?"

"Actually, you are quite wonderful, and say such things at least once a month, and not always in the absolute heat of passion," she teased him.

"Alas, you remain a vixen!" he sighed with mock despair. "Hmm. Now our lives are made easier. We need only hide Teela until March. We can say that we have become the proud parents of twins, the war can go, and those nearest and dearest to us can continue running around the bush."

"We've one little difficulty with that scenario," Tara said, contentedly leaning against him.

"What's that?"

"Your brother can be amazingly like you. He has your

father's eyes. But no one will mistake his child for ours, because the baby will have Indian blood."

"Well," Jarrett mused, "maybe it will not be such a bad thing if Warren dies of apoplexy after all."

She smiled again, closing her eyes, glad to be with him. "God forgive me for saying this, but it's quite a pity that he will surely not do something so convenient for us all any time soon!"

"So what do we do?" Jarrett asked softly, his whisper against the golden softness of her hair.

"Pray."

"For Warren's death? Does God answer such prayers?"

"If he knows Warren, perhaps!"

Chapter 22

Osceola had a look of the spirit about him when he met James. He was seated on one of his war ponies, and he was dressed in full, splendid array with a plumed turban, red leggings, colorful shirt, and fringed jacket. Coa Hadjo, a subchief and wise man for Osceola's band, was close at his side while a half-dozen near-naked warriors surrounded him

"Thank you for coming when I have called you."

"I'm anxious to hear what news you have, what parley you wish to make."

"We will talk at our council," Osceola told him, leading the way along the trail. They moved swiftly across high ground, then plowed more slowly through the marsh, disappearing through the dense brush that flanked the swamps until they reached a pine barren. There the warriors were greeted quietly by the women and some of the boys not quite ready for warfare. Their horses were taken, food was brought, and they sat cross-legged before an open fire built in a clearing.

"You know what has happened?" Osceola asked him.

James nodded. "All of King Philip's people have been taken. A Yuchi village was invaded right after, and Blue Snake and Yuchi Billy were seized along with others. Wildcat has gone in to the whites as his father sent for him, and is now a prisoner as well."

"Word has been sent to General Jesup that we will parley again," Coa Hadjo told James.

"I am very tired, but also wary," Osceola said. "Coa Hadjo will speak for me when we go for our talks with the whites. But you must be another set of eyes and ears for me. You must help me understand the white men's words, see what really lies beneath them."

"I will be happy to be with you, Osceola. What do you seek to gain from your council with the military?"

Osceola lifted his hands. "I have not wished to rob the whites. I have never sought to massacre their women and children, though I do not deny that they have died. I have always sought true boundaries. I want to draw lines again. I want to let the whites live in peace, and I want my people to be left to live in peace."

"There is speculation among the whites that you wish to see their strength and learn what you can about how and where they are keeping Wildcat, Philip, Blue Snake, and the others prisoner."

Coa Hadjo and Osceola exchanged glances. Coa Hadjo shrugged. "Men always talk to gain new information."

James grinned. "That is true."

"I seek no battle, Running Bear. That I swear to you by the Great Spirit."

"I have never doubted Osceola's word."

Osceola stood. He seemed to tremble as he did so, and his color was ashen. James and the others stood quickly as well. "Thank you for being among us," Osceola told him briefly.

"I am glad to be with a friend," James replied, but as he watched the war chief, he was worried. Osceola had looked well during the day; he looked as if he was ill again by night.

He left them, and the others moved away, except for Coa Hadjo, a power in his own right, who watched James.

"In truth, what do you think of these new talks, Running Bear?" Coa Hadjo demanded.

James sighed. "I think that men have talked and talked. And that most of the talk has been lies. From both sides," he added sadly.

"What truth is there except that which each man sees in his own heart?" Coa Hadjo asked him.

"Osceola is gravely ill," James said flatly.

"And very, very tired," Coa Hadjo added.

"And what does that mean?" James asked him.

"It means he tires of war," Coa Hadjo said. "Good night, Running Bear. I have never feared for my own safety. I am glad to speak for myself, and for Osceola. But I am glad that you will be with us as well."

James nodded in acknowledgment. Coa Hadjo went his own way. James stared at the fire, then went to find the shelter he had been provided there in the barrens. It was a simple platform raised above the ground a few feet, covered with cabbage palm. The air was cool circulating in and around it. Being elevated, it protected the inhabitants from the creatures that preyed upon the ground at night.

He lay down, weary. He closed his eyes. And all that he could think was that she was gone. He had slept so well beside her. He had felt her warmth, her fire, her heat. Now there was cold and loneliness. He wanted to cry out in the night. He wanted to close his eyes, sleep and dream.

And in his dream there would be no war, nothing savage, and nothing civilized, and nothing red or white. The sky would be alight with a brilliant red dawn, and she would be laughing, running to him, and when he captured her, and spun her beneath the sun, he would never need to let her go again. . . .

He tossed, cold, stiff, uncomfortable.

It was a dream.

Just a dream. And in this wretched world it could never come true.

There was no way to hide the fact that Teela Warren was with the McKenzies, in their home. Teela was very anxious to set the papers straight about her capture and so-called kidnapping. At Jarrett's suggestion, certain of the reporters from Florida and the nation who had swept down upon St. Augustine to cover the Indian wars were invited to the house. Both Tara and Jarrett were with her when the five invited interviewed her.

She was amazingly composed and relaxed, relating her story from the moment she had left Fort Deliverance to the time of her capture.

"That anyone has accused James McKenzie of any evil or treachery in this entire affair is pathetic and laughable," she informed them. "He saved my life."

Thomason, of a Washington paper, demanded, "But what of your captivity, Miss Warren? You were seized by a savage and held against your will—"

"My brother-in-law is not a savage!" Tara interrupted, as fierce as a terrier.

"I'm sorry, Mr. and Mrs. McKenzie," Thomason said hastily, stroking his white-bearded chin. "What I meant is, there was a certain time in which you were kept in the bush. Was no danger, no offense forced upon you? What will your fiancé think and feel? Have you spoken with Lieutenant Harrison since your ordeal?"

"John Harrison and James McKenzie are the best of friends. I know that John will be grateful, as will anyone who is pleased to see me still alive, that James came to my rescue. Sir, I cannot even condemn Otter, the chief who so craved my death, because his own family was cruelly murdered in this war."

"Preposterous!" the heavily jowled fellow from St. Augustine muttered.

Teela rose. "Sir, if you find the truth preposterous, there is nothing else I have to say. Now, if you will all forgive me ..."

She didn't care if they did or didn't. She was suddenly exhausted. She turned and headed for the stairs. She was incredibly grateful for Jarrett McKenzie's stern admonition that the men were now to leave his residence.

In her room, she stretched out on the bed. She could hear the reporters talking among themselves outside the house, nearly below her window.

"It's disgusting! A decent woman would be horrified

by all that has occurred—" one man began. Evans, from an Atlanta paper.

"Ah, but through history they tend to fall under the influence of their captors," another man asserted.

"Gentlemen!" It was Thomason speaking. "You're forgetting that the man involved is a McKenzie, half white, brother to one of the most influential man in the state. Both have been highly respected for years; they have both acted as negotiators often enough in this sad fracas."

"What, are you an injun lover, too, Thomason?" Teela was sure it was that vile Evans speaking again.

"There is right and wrong, my friends. And I have seen right and wrong on both sides of this affair. You tell me, sir, would it be better if young Miss Warren was today a dead woman yet a *decent* corpse? Her life was saved, quite simply. That is the story, the way I will print it."

"Ah, but it isn't what Warren believes. The half-breed McKenzie is one powerful buck, so rumor has it. Warren believes his daughter feels a fascination for this man. Perhaps he slaughtered the troops, yet she gave him promises of wicked pleasure if he should spare her!" Evans theorized. He would have spoken again when Teela heard something like a choking sound. And it was Jarrett's voice she heard next.

"May I suggest, sir, that if you wish to discuss *my brother* in such slanderous terms, you do so far from my home. Otherwise, I might be the one to give you some very savage behavior to condemn within your text!"

"Mr. McKenzie, you're hurting me—" Evans gasped out.

"Indeed. Get off my property before I kill you!"

Teela heard a door slam. A scurrying. And then ... blessed quiet. She rolled over, heartsick, wondering how she could feel so exhausted when she had slept so deeply the night before.

There was a tapping on her door. She sat up, trying to straighten the damage she had done to her pinned hair by lying upon it. "Come in!"

It was Tara with a tea tray in her hands. She set it on

the morning table by the window. "You did very well," Tara assured her.

Teela sighed. "I heard them talking afterward. It didn't really matter what I said. They all have their pre-conceived notions."

"No, you spoke very well." She paused reflectively, pouring the tea. "You were very good. Jarrett let his temper get the best of him. No matter, he's been accused of everything in the world already. Come over here now. You must eat something."

"Oh, Tara, thank you so much, but I'm just not hungry."

Tara sighed, looking at her in perplexity. "Teela, you are actually losing weight."

"Am I?"

"You must come eat."

"But—"

"Oh, you little fool!" Tara cried at last in exasperation. "Don't you want a healthy child?"

Teela felt a sudden surge of energy and bounded to her feet, staring at Tara. "What?"

"The most casual of observers will soon notice your condition, and yet you have not considered the possibility yourself!"

She had not. Oh, God. Sweet Jesus, she had not.

Why not?

She had been so busy. Men had been dying. She had patched them up. She had lain awake nights at Fort De-liverance, praying that she would not get word that James McKenzie, *Running Bear,* was dead. Praying that she would not find him maimed and dying on the operating table. And then ...

"Teela?" she dimly heard Tara's cry.

But that was all. She was spared any more of the initial shock and trauma of the revelation.

The room misted to shades of red and gray.

And she saw no more.

A strange period of peace and inactivity settled over Osceola and his warriors as the time passed before the

agreed-upon date for the parley. James worried more
and more about Osceola. The chief had days when he
looked fit and well, and days when chills and fever seized
him. He liked to talk during those periods about his
boyhood, about the life he had spent, always fighting, so
it had seemed.

"They think that I have waged a war against their
people," Osceola told him. "The whites—they think that
I have wished to kill them all, as they have wished to
rid the land of us. They are wrong. I fought and I killed
just so that we could have our piece of this great land.
I know what the white newspapers tell people. I know
that there are those in the great cities who consider this
a battle against a people they would rip from their heart-
land, their blood land. And there are those who say the
whites have more right to this peninsula than we do,
that we *Seminoles* are new here. Yes, I am Creek, yes,
many of my brothers are what *they* call Creek. But we
have come here now in waves for well over a hundred
years. We have shed our blood here; we have fed the
land here with it. I have always fought only to stay, only
for our right to the land we have bled upon for our
heritage. There are many among your father's people I
have called friend. Young John Graham, your brother,
others in the military. If only they could make a treaty
and keep it!"

James stared at the fire without replying. But Osceola
smiled. "Many of them have said that I cannot keep a
treaty. That I make promises, come for the white food
and supplies, and then run again. Sometimes I have done
so. I could not watch my children starve."

James looked at him. "I am uneasy about this parley
to come."

"Why?"

He shrugged. "I don't know. I feel it. Like we feel the
footsteps of others when they are near. Like a scent on
the wind. I fear for you."

Osceola was quiet for several long seconds. "The parley will take place. I am resigned."

* * *

The date came. Osceola, Coa Hadjo, many of the others, were dressed in their finery for the talks that would take place.

The army was coming to the Indians. In a copse not far from Fort Peyton, Osceola and his warriors raised a huge white flag above their camp.

James had dressed neither to suit his Indian heritage nor his white, but chose his usual dark breeches, cotton shirt, strip of red fabric around his head to keep his hair from his eyes.

He was on his way to find Osceola when he heard the cry of a bird.

One he had not expected. He answered in kind.

Jarrett stepped from the foliage but beckoned to him. "Follow me out some. The soldiers are coming here even as we speak."

James quickly did as his brother bade him. He almost felt as if they were boys again, running wildly through the forests and marshes, learning, laughing. Jarrett had taught him to hunt, to fish. Through their mothers they had differed. Through their love of their land, they had forged a bond deeper than blood.

They were older now. Jarrett was gasping somewhat as he paused next to an old oak. "General Hernandez left St. Augustine early this morning for the parley. Jesup will not be with him; he is so nervous that he awaits the results at Fort Peyton. Altogether Hernandez will have a force of nearly two hundred and fifty well-armed men. James, this is not to be a talk. Jesup believes that Osceola has betrayed him again and again. He plans to capture him under a flag of truce. You shouldn't be here. Teela has given a statement to the newspapers—"

"Teela is still in the territory?"

"She is safe, she lives with us, and Harrington has been the best of friends, escorting her about town so that they can be seen together. There is more about Teela that I must tell you, but pay heed to me about this first. Most men believe that you are the noble if half-savage negotiator you have been throughout the conflict, but there are those still eager to hang anyone associated with any attacks on whites."

"Do they plan on hanging Osceola?" James asked.

"No, there is no such talk. The Indians are to be escorted to Fort Marion. You know, the old Castillo de San Marcos." Even as Jarrett spoke, James became alarmingly aware of motion on the trails near them. He dragged Jarrett down low beside him as they watched the mounted men of Hernandez's force riding by on the trail nearest them.

"Jarrett, I've got to go back."

"You'll be imprisoned with the others by association."

"Perhaps. And perhaps I will speak for myself and clear my name before your military friends. Jarrett, all I know is that I must be with Osceola now. He—"

"He what?"

"I think he's dying. I have to go. If I need you, I swear, I will send for you. If not, brother, I have to pave my own way in this world. You must get out of here before you are condemned as a traitor for coming to me!"

"Wait! I have to tell you—"

The more horses that rode by, the more James worried. For his brother now, not himself. He turned, ready to run back the way he had come. "Go!" he commanded his brother, and disappeared back into the bush himself.

He ran harder than he had come. Too late. He slipped through the back of the copse even as the first of the military men entered the Indian camp with its high-flying white flag. There was nothing that he could do.

He stood back in uneasy silence, watching as the white soldiers came around them. General Hernandez was at the head of the delegation. As Jarrett had told him, General Jesup was not among the soldiers. James studied the uniforms of the men around Jesup. There were Florida mounted men with him, dragoons on foot.

Scents on the wind . . .

He suddenly knew that they were completely surrounded by white military, just as his brother had warned. There was nothing that he could say or do; any cry of alarm on his part now would bring all the white guns blazing against them before the Indians had a chance to raise their own weapons. He saw that Osceola seemed to be choking. He went forward with Coa Hadjo at his side. General Hernandez stepped forward with his black interpreter at his side. He greeted Osceola and Coa Hadjo with all courtesy, then said, "I thought there would be more of your number among you. Where are Alligator, Micanopy, Jumper, and Cloud?"

"Ill," Coa Hadjo said. "Disease—the spotted disease, measles—has laid many of our people low."

Hernandez saw James then, arms folded over his chest, watching. He nodded in acknowledgment, flushing. Hernandez was a good man, James thought. In the quick glance Hernandez had cast him, he thought he saw many things. It was true that this was pure treachery. Jesup had planned it; Hernandez disagreed with it. He was following his orders.

"I am your friend," Hernandez said. "Tell me, why have you come to talk?"

"For the good of all," Coa Hadjo replied.

"Why?"

"We have had word from King Philip through the messenger of his son, Wildcat."

"Have you come to surrender to me?"

"No, that was not our intent. We had not understood that we should do so. We have kept our peace during the summer."

"Ah, but there have been incidents—"

"Ah, friend! Not by us. We have sought peace. Just as the generals have not always been able to control the slaughters by the farmers settling the land, neither can we always control a renegade warrior."

"Have you brought back stolen property!"

Here Coa Hadjo hesitated. "We have brought in the negroes many call their property."

Again Hernandez looked conflicted. "I wish you all

well," he said. The words were repeated by the interpreter. "But we have so often been deceived. I am afraid
that you must now come with me. I will promise that you
will be treated well. Here, I have brought Blue Snake of
the Yuchis to speak with you. He will tell you that you
must come with me."

Blue Snake, his leathered face weary, stepped from
out of the soldiers and came forward. "General Hernandez, it was not my understanding that any who spoke
would be seized."

Hernandez looked surprised at Blue Snake's defiance.
He made a movement, the slightest movement. The
troops that surrounded them surged forward.

The trap was sprung.

Every single warrior saw what James had seen. Though
they carried rifles, they could not get off a shot before they
would all be mown down like corn in autumn.

James looked at Osceola. His expression was unread-
able. Hernandez continued to speak with them. It was
to be as Jarrett said. They were to march the seven miles
to St. Augustine to the fort there. They would be well
treated. They wouldn't be harmed or killed.

Osceola and two others were brought horses. James,
his arms still crossed over his chest, watched the proceedings until Hernandez rode to where he stood.

"It was treachery," James said quietly.

"It was necessary."

"You seized a man who is already a legendary chief
while he waited under a white flag of truce."

"And I shall live to rue the day, surely," Hernandez
said wearily. "I can excuse nothing to you, James. I am
sick myself with what we have done, yet I see that Jesup
believed he had no choice. He thinks if he can stop
Osceola, he can stop the war."

"He won't stop the war. He will create a martyr."

"God forgive me, I just pray to stop the bloodshed
for a while. James, I say again, I can offer no excuse. I
can but give you a chance to slip into the woods if you
so desire."

James looked up at him, slowly smiled, and shook his head. "Thank you. I appreciate the offer, and the friendship. But I must go with Osceola now."

"But—"

"Am I in danger of being hanged?"

"No. You are in danger of being classified a renegade."

"Surely, I have been classified as worse already. Again, I thank you, but I have to see this through."

"I'll see that the men find your horse—"

"All right. But I feel the need to walk."

They began the trek to the fort. The take for the day had been brilliant, James mused. Osceola, Coa Hadjo— and seventy-odd warriors, six women, and a few Indian Negroes. Someone would have already ridden hard to Jesup to tell him that his treachery had paid well.

James didn't think as he walked the distance. It felt good to move hard, to work the tension and fury from his limbs, bones, and soul.

They came to the city with tremendous commotion and fanfare. People had lined the streets to watch the soldiers, mounted and on foot, lead in their haul of savage prisoners. Men and women called out, laughed, sneered, pointed. James walked, looking straight ahead.

He heard whispers.

"Dear, isn't that the half-breed McKenzie?"

"Turned savage, indeed! Blood tells in the end, no matter how his brother dressed him up in white frilled shirts."

"He was quite the rage for a season—"

"No decent man would allow his daughter near him, surely! Even if he is rich as Midas!"

"Rich?"

"Half the McKenzie land is his."

"But he's a savage ... so very good-looking, but a savage nonetheless ..."

The words didn't matter. He had heard them before. He walked with prisoners because he had chosen to do so, because they were his people, too, because he still had to do what he could. No stares, no words, could hurt him. He continued to keep his head high, his bright blue gaze focused before him.

But then ...

He saw her. She was by the roadside. She wore a blue flowered day dress, and yet somehow she had never appeared more elegant. Her fiery hair was swept into a perfect twist at the back of her head.

She was standing with young John Harrington, her hands gripping his arm as she watched the wave of Indians and soldiers come and come.

There was something different about her.

Of course. He had last seen her in the swamps. She had been naked half the time, her hair as wild and free as her spirit. They had been the same.

Now they were different.

Now she was white, and he was that half-breed McKenzie no decent white woman would go near. *Bitterness.* It tore at him even when he knew he was proud of his heritage, glad of his red blood, the honor and pride that were a part of his people, just as much as the starvation and misery....

But she was one of them. She couldn't understand.

It wasn't just that. She was indeed different. Staring at him with pity, turning away. He couldn't bear the pity, and he couldn't bear the way she turned from him. In shame? She clung so tightly to Harrington's arm ...

Yes, she was different! There was something very different about her indeed! More than the way she looked at him, more than the pity, more than the shame.

It was subtle. So subtle, at this stage.

But it was *physical*.

Yet striking into him with alarming speed, with staggering force. Suddenly it felt as if everything inside him began to wind into a tight, burning coil. It felt like a braid of emotions, the bitterness he longed to fight, doubt, fear, envy, jealousy ...

He looked at the way she stood with Harrington. Stared. *For the love of all the gods,* he mocked himself, *hadn't he told her to marry Harrington? Hadn't he all but thrown her from himself again and again . . . ?*

It didn't matter. He wanted to tear himself from the rows of walking men, leap through the crowds, grab her, shake her. Ah, yes, let them see how blood told what kind of a savage he was!

She was going to have a child—and not a child she had conceived just weeks ago. She must have known it when she had been with him in the private cove. She hadn't said a word. Hadn't told him . . .

Told him what?

That she had tired of staying at his brother's, waiting for him, because there were *white* men in the world? How many had she admitted she liked well? Robert Trent, Harrington—even the physician Joshua Brandeis?

His fingers knotted into fists; he looked straight ahead again and kept walking. *Is the twisted fear of a man so accustomed to prejudice that he cannot accept the times when it may* not *exist? But if she knew, if it was* my *child, why didn't she tell me?*

Was she all a lie? Everything they shared except for their desire—savage desire?

Stop! he told himself, but the doubts and the fury had taken hold, eating into a heart weary with the treachery just practiced upon Osceola, the band, and himself.

Just whose child did she carry?

He felt someone walking quickly by his side. Old Riley, face forward, marched beside him.

"Warren's daughter is in the crowd," he informed James softly in Muskogee. "Perhaps she will try to see you—"

James swung on old Riley. "If she is smart, she will keep her distance!" he lashed back furiously, then paced on ahead swiftly, angry with himself.

He knew there was no sense or logic to it, but his pride suddenly seemed to be rubbed raw.

And he couldn't help but wonder how many men, warriors and whites, watched him as he walked.

A prisoner, accused.

While *she* watched on a white man's arm.

Chapter 23

Teela raced into the house, shouting for Jarrett. He didn't appear, but Tara came flying down the stairs. "Teela! What is it, what's wrong?"

"They've brought a large group of Indians in ... to the fort!" She gasped for breath. Hurrying along behind her, John Harrington stood panting, almost doubled over. "James is with him. He's—in chains!"

Tara stood still, clutching the banister, going very pale. "Where's Jarrett?" Teela asked.

"He rode out very early; he's not back yet."

"Teela," John said, "he's going to be safe in the fort, you needn't be so disturbed. He can't be going into battle—"

"No, but battle can come to him!" Teela said. "If my stepfather returns—"

"He is on campaign," John reminded her.

"Campaigns end."

"But—" John began, but at that moment the door opened and closed behind them. Teela spun around.

Jarrett had returned. He had been out riding. He had come in sober and thoughtful, and looked up to discover the three of them staring at him. Teela rushed to him. "They've taken James! They've taken your brother! They just marched him into the Castillo."

"Yes, I know."

"You know!" Teela gasped, horrified. "Then, you must get him out, Jarrett. Surely, you've the power—"

"I've the power, not the right."

"What?" Teela demanded, stunned.

"He could have escaped before the prisoners were taken. He chose not to do so. He has made the choice for reasons of his own, and I have sworn not to interfere."

"But—" Teela protested.

"He is in no danger," Jarrett said.

"But if my stepfather returns—"

"He has not done so yet."

Teela approached him, still unwilling to accept that Jarrett wasn't ready to drag down the heavy walls of the fortress. "There may be some other man—a guard, perhaps, who hates all Indians—"

"Well, he will have plenty to choose from, then."

"But what if he wants to kill an Indian who he believes has brought about the deaths of many soldiers—"

"Then he would start with Osceola, wouldn't he?"

"Jarrett, damn it—"

"Teela, my hands are tied. I gave my word. There is nothing I can do. And you underestimate my brother. He is strong, intelligent, and well capable of looking after himself."

"Jarrett—"

"I have given my word."

"Well, I have not!" she announced furiously. She spun around, hurrying out of the house. She marched to the small carriage still waiting in the street and climbed into it. By then John had come running from the house behind her. "Teela, wait—"

"I can do this alone," she said.

"And I can help. I am military, remember?"

She waited. When he sat down beside her, she smiled ruefully and kissed his cheek. "Truly, you are the world's best friend."

"Maybe I am the world's biggest fool. Maybe I think that you will turn to me if something does happen to your magnificent warrior."

"You don't mean that."

"Well, I do—and I don't. Don't make me maudlin, now. You were in such a hurry, let's move on!"

She smiled and flicked the reins. A few minutes later, they were in front of the Castillo. John helped her down. There was tremendous confusion around the place, now called Fort Marion. Townspeople still milled around the coquina-shell walls, watching the guards on the walks, curious for every bit of news called down to them, anxious to see another glimpse of the warriors in their splendor.

John managed to usher Teela through the waiting crowds and into an office. John kept explaining that they had come to see a well-known white-Indian, James McKenzie, taken by mistake.

But they met with a sour-faced clerk, a man with iron gray hair and a long, slim face, one side of it scarred from forehead to chin.

He had been writing on a pass when he paused, staring at them both.

"No visitors."

"What?" Teela demanded, rising.

"Your white-Indian is not so innocent."

"How dare you—" Teela began.

"He's guilty of murder and kidnapping."

"That's one hell of a lie—"

"Teela!" John gasped in warning. All right, so she shouldn't have cursed. She'd lived in a military fort too long, in the wilderness too long, and it just didn't seem to matter to her too much anymore what young women should and shouldn't say. But this soldier would think her ill-bred. Actually, she was dying to tell him that he belonged in hell—she even wanted to tell him what to do with himself before he went there—but she managed to restrain her tongue. "James McKenzie is innocent of any such charges. I am the woman he supposedly kidnapped, and I can swear to you—on a dozen Bibles, if you so choose!—that he did no such thing. I was also a witness to the massacre—"

"So you watched him kill people?"

"You pompous ass!" Teela hissed.

"No visitors. The Indian Running Bear clears himself by witness of the surviving soldiers, and that's that!"

"You think that's that!" Teela cried. "Just you wait! I'll create such a stink about what you've done here today that—"

"Teela?" John interrupted.

"Just a minute, John. Now, you pay me heed—"

"Teela!" John insisted.

She stopped, staring at him. He caught her by an arm, pulled her close, and whispered softly. "His name is Clarence Higgens. He has ridden with your father and been attacked by Osceola's band, *and* barely survived to tell the tale. We must retreat for now."

"I will find someone to overrule you, soldier," Teela stated coldly, ready to quit for the time being, but never to give up her fight.

The scarred Lieutenant Higgens stared at her. "I can send into the interior for your father if you wish?" he taunted.

Teela did tell him then that he could go straight to hell. John started to urge her out, but just as they were leaving the outer passage, she saw old Riley being escorted along by a young sergeant. "Riley!" she cried. "I've being trying to see James. I—"

She broke off because Riley was shaking his head. He lowered his voice. "Don't see James."

"But—"

"Miss, don't see James." He lowered his voice, trying to take care not to be heard by anyone other than her. "Give him time. He would tear your heart out. Stay far away."

"What? Why?"

"He is betrayed."

"By the military!"

"And you. Please, don't try to see him. You will bring more trouble down on everyone."

Riley hurried on by her with the soldier. Teela felt her eyes stinging.

Good God, what in heaven was the man talking

about? She quickly blinked against her tears. James was a royal bastard, and that was that. He'd said that he was done playing.

And he meant it.

"Teela—?" John began.

"Let's go."

She drove the carriage back to the house in silence. When they reached the front, she leapt down, anxious to reach her room.

"Teela, we can still manage to see James—"

"James can rot for all I care!" she assured him, and ran up to her room as quickly as possible.

Their conditions of capture were not so cruel. Captain Morrison, in charge of their imprisonment at Fort Marion, allowed the Indians free movement within the walls of the fort. The only difficulty was that there were so many imprisoned, the "necessary" stations built directly into their cavernous cells were not nearly enough, and fever caught and spread quickly.

The good was that they were all fed. Osceola sent out for his wives and children, and some of the other warriors sent for their families as well. Many of the children came in looking beyond the point of help, but they were hardy little creatures and ate hungrily all that was given them.

James had asked Jarrett not to interfere. He knew that it was probably tearing at his brother to do something about his situation, but he chose to wait. He was in no danger while in the camp. He saw many friends among the military who assured him that Warren was still in the field, determined on his own brand of warfare. A Dr. Weedon, who was beginning to spend a tremendous amount of time at the fort treating the Indians, had come to meet James, specifically interested in him. It was through Weedon that James learned that two of the soldiers who had been with Teela's escort when Otter attacked had been recuperating from wounds all the way over at Fort Brooke, Tampa Bay. Hernandez had sent for the men, determined to have them clear James.

He intended to be cleared.

James was seated against the stone wall of one of the large rooms within the fort. Wildcat approached him, sinking down beside him. "The white captain has said that you and I are invited to a party in St. Augustine. We are to be released under escort to go. I imagine you are invited because you are sometimes one of them. I am invited because I am Wildcat, Coacoochee, and they want to look at me."

James smiled. Wildcat was right. The whites wanted to see him. He had earned himself quite a reputation. Despite the scratches on his face—or perhaps even partly because of them—he was a handsome man, young, with incredibly deep, arresting eyes. He was so swift that he had often been able to stop when soldiers were in pursuit of him during battle, laugh at them, and take flight again, disappearing, perhaps to ambush the same soldiers just minutes later. He was the type of Seminole that appealed to the romance of the public, a true "savage" in their minds, yet somehow as well a wild prince of the forest.

"They want to see me," Wildcat repeated. "I want to see them."

"My friend, you go. I have no heart for a party."

"Running Bear, you must come. I'm not sure I will still be invited and let out if you do not attend."

"Wildcat, half these people merely wish to gape at us."

"Then they shall gape. I am as curious about them as they are about me. I wish to go. I beg of you, attend with me. Let me know what they are saying about me."

"Wildcat—"

"Perhaps your woman will be there."

The very words set his insides burning again. He had wanted to shriek at the sight of her on Harrington's arm, roar like thunder.

She would be there. He could talk to her. Find out the

truth. But he didn't want to talk, he wanted to shout and shake her. Thoughts of her had plagued him through the long days and endless nights. And the more he thought about, the more doubt slipped in to taunt him. She had been so damned obviously *rounded* in the month since he had seen her. He was not mistaken. He was already the father of two children and well aware that a woman did not change so in the course of weeks. So she had very definitely been expecting the babe before.

Since when?

The question seemed to scratch into his heart every time he breathed. He could remember himself talking to her that day in the river. *Have you ever made love in the water?* And she had been angry. *You would know. You would know . . .*

But she had been away from him a long time before then. Endless days, nights, weeks, when they hadn't spoken. He relived their entire relationship in haunted silence, staring at the walls of the fort in his endless hours of captivity.

She had run away from Warren, escaped into the woods. But then she had ridden from his family's ghost village with John Harrington. Pretended an engagement with him. James had next seen her in the thick of battle, with Joshua Brandeis. They'd had a night. One night. But then he'd gone back to the interior, and she'd ridden with the military. Been with Tyler and Brandeis, in her own society, with men who killed Seminoles for their livelihoods. She'd lived at Fort Deliverance. Laughed with the soldiers, danced with the soldiers, treated the soldiers.

Until she'd come to him.

And she'd not said a damned word to him about a child!

Nor had she made the least attempt to see him since he had come here.

Had she decided to attach herself to Harrington in truth? Had she done so for a reason? Had there actually been something between the two of them other than the feigned engagement? Had there been someone else in her life? A deeper involvement with Joshua Brandeis, the physician she admired so much?

She had definitely turned her back on him since he had come here. Perhaps it was just the stigma of who he was, *what* he was. She had seen him marched into the fort, a prisoner. A Seminole prisoner. A renegade, an outcast.

Damn her.

He had to see her, talk to her—even if he did yell at her. He had to end the constant torture he heaped upon himself, penned and staring at the walls.

"All right. I will attend," he told Wildcat.

Wildcat smiled, pleased. "The food will be very good, I imagine. I will taste everything and remember it all when I fight again."

James wondered if Wildcat would ever have the chance to fight again. He refrained from saying so out loud, but Wildcat must have sensed his thoughts. "I am the son of King Philip, a *mico* of the Mikasukee. My mother is the sister of Micanopy, a *mico* of the Alachua band. I am a born leader, James. Sometimes Osceola has mocked me. He has considered himself the best leader, and he has brought us to glory and victory at times. He has said that I am good to send out to raid small parties, while he has battled the greatest generals. You will see. My time is nearly here. I will not remain a prisoner, I swear it."

"Perhaps you will not."

"I will have you escape with me."

James hesitated. "I came in to be with Osceola."

"Well and good," Wildcat warned, "but you never know when you will *need* to escape." Wildcat left him where he had found him.

Dr. Weedon found him later that same day and asked him to walk with him. James had never felt more thoroughly studied and examined in all his days. The doctor was a man of medium height and coloring, mild in his manner, not young yet certainly not yet old. He had an

attractive wife and young children who sometimes came
to the fort, but since there had been another outbreak
of measles, the children had stayed away. "Osceola is
very sick," he told James.

"I know."

"It is difficult for me to treat him. He lets his tribal
medicine men rule him."

James shrugged. "It is his way."

"He is an interesting fellow," Weedon said. "Fascinating, really. I love to watch his movements when he
speaks, listen to his voice. He has humor and warmth. Of
course, he is completely uncivilized. Any type of formal
education would have been entirely wasted on the man,
but I do find myself in deep sympathy with him."

James stopped walking and stared at the doctor. "How
curious, sir. I've had every manner of formal education
offered me. I remember rebelling often enough against
lessons as a child, but in retrospect, I can't think of a
wasted moment."

"You, sir, are half white. You've lived among civilized
people. There is a difference."

"Is there?" James arched a brow at him. "Osceola,
Billy Powell, as many call him, has white blood as well."

"There is a difference," Dr. Weedon said firmly. "But
I beg you, if you've any influence with him, see if you
cannot manage to let me examine him and treat him."

James nodded, not trusting himself to speak. He
should have appreciated that Weedon did feel such sympathy for the "savage." He found instead that he was
furious to realize that the good doctor considered himself a better man with a greater capacity for learning—
because of the color of his skin.

Tara walked into Teela's room, smiling. "I have a
surprise."

Teela, staring at the flames burning in her fireplace,
looked at Tara curiously. Her host and hostess tried so
very hard to make her happy. Especially in such a tense
time, and despite the fact that she had been feeling ex-

tremely confused about James since the day she had gone to the fort. Jarrett, she knew, was wrapped in his own turmoil regarding the situation. He had promised James that he would not interfere, and he would not do so.

James had contacted Jarrett, but only with a brief letter to say that he was well and ask that his brother convey his love to his daughter.

Not a word had been said about her.

Teela clamped her hands together in her lap, her anger reawakened. He'd stared at her with such fury, and then Riley's words had been like the final nail in the coffin. She couldn't forget the way he had looked at her. As if Riley had been right, and James would just as soon rip her heart out as say hello. He had told her when he left her that he was done with her. Well, he couldn't be. Like it or not, he couldn't be.

But why was he so furious? Because she had remained here? Or because she had seen him brought in as a prisoner when he was such a proud man?

Had he somehow realized that she was expecting a child? Was he angry because of it, as if it was something she had planned to make his life more miserable?

She felt well. Better than she had felt since she had first set foot in the territory. She was never sick in the mornings anymore—if she suffered at all, it was because she felt like such an idiot for not realizing her condition. Sometimes she didn't even care what James's reaction would be. There were moments when she was so happy and thrilled over what was surely only nature but seemed like a miracle that nothing else in the world mattered. She couldn't wait to see the baby. She would love it with all the strength and intensity within her.

Every once in a while she did pause to fear what Michael Warren might do if he discovered the truth. Sometimes she even thought that Tara and Jarrett were right, that she should get away and protect the babe from Warren. She could go to Jarrett's mother's family in Charleston—close to her own home but, she hoped, just far enough away. In May she would reach her own majority, when Michael Warren could no longer force her to do anything.

She had seriously considered leaving when she had first come to St. Augustine, but then the prisoners had been brought to the Castillo.

And he had looked at her.

And she had known that nothing on earth would induce her to leave when he was so close. Even if he did refuse to see her and wretched dolts in the military saw fit to threaten her. She lived comfortably with friends she loved. Ian was a delight, growing daily. Tara was expecting another baby again as well, and though Tara was nicely, legally wed and had the right to be as excited as she was, Teela was still glad to share the experience with her, to know that their children would be cousins. She was also able to be with Jennifer. Her relationship with the little girl was very good. She knew she loved Jennifer, and she was certain that Jennifer loved and trusted her in return. They spent a lot of time together. Teela read to her constantly, fairy tales, special stories, tales of adventure and intrigue. She was as honest as she could be about James's current situation, always assuring Jennifer that prison was a very safe place for her father to be for the moment.

John Harrington was always near, ready to help her in all things. Even though he remained stationed at Fort Peyton, he managed to come into the city often enough, and he never lost patience with her.

He hadn't seen James, either, though, as he'd had to return to duty the day after the prisoners had been brought in. He was due for a few days' furlough again shortly, and would come calling, she knew. She felt guilty every time she caused him a bad moment. He offered her his undying friendship and support, never commenting on her condition, always being both honest and supportive. She prayed that someday there would be a way to thank him.

She would actually be living a happy life if it wasn't

for the emptiness she felt inside. She feared sometimes that she was desperate for the love of James's family because she could not have love from the man himself.

She grated down hard on her teeth, thinking of James's desertion, but managed to smile pleasantly for Tara.

"A surprise?"

"A party."

"Oh, Tara! I don't think I should go to a party. My condition isn't that evident, but I know that some of our town's good matrons are looking down their long noses at me quite frequently. And there's always the chance that someone will decide to send a soldier or scout into the interior of the territory just to find Michael Warren and see to it that he does ride to St. Augustine."

"Jarrett's friends will see to it that we're advised when Warren is returning," Tara reassured her.

"A party will still be uncomfortable. I'm telling you, the society matrons do disapprove of me."

Tara wrinkled her nose. "They don't dare—even if they are jealous old biddies. No matter what he does, Jarrett *is* Florida society."

"Tara, I don't think—"

"I've heard that James is going to be there."

"What?" Teela demanded.

"I thought that might draw your interest," Tara said dryly. "John has sent a message that he will be available that evening, and he will be more than happy to escort you. Teela, I thought you'd be anxious!"

"Umm. I am anxious," Teela assured her. "Very!" Inside, she was already simmering. She was anxious. She definitely had a few things to say to James.

The soiree was held at the home of Mrs. Virginia Tenney, widow of retired army Brigadier General Wilfred Tenney. James and Wildcat came along with several of the commanders of the fort. Wildcat was in full array with his bright leggings, shawl over one shoulder, and blue calico shirt. He wasn't a particularly tall man, but he was remarkably agile.

The military commanders needn't have feared trouble from their guests of honor. The last thing James wanted to do was offer the citizenry of St. Augustine any chance to feel that—in civilized society or not—Seminoles were not worth *educating*. And Wildcat was simply too curious, too busy taking it all in.

The home was beautiful, a typical southern manse with a huge breezeway and all doors thrown open. Violinists, harpists, and pianists had been hired. At first Wildcat stayed close to James, wanting the security of a friend who spoke both languages well. But he was soon quite the center of attention. As James found himself greeting more old acquaintances—a few he would term friends—among the company, he was edged away from Wildcat. He was surprised to see that with his current reputation, he drew his fair share of attention, and much of that from families he had known through Jarrett. Apparently, he thought wryly, there remained a mystique about a man who ran in the forest. And oddly enough, he was urged to the dance floor with many a sweet young belle by her own father.

The food was delicious. He sampled delicate pastries, spiced vegetables, potato melees, and more. He found himself beside Wildcat again, who was complimenting a plump matron on her wonderful corn muffins. A young half-breed interpreter in an army uniform was repeating Wildcat's words. The matron blushed with pleasure. Wildcat said, "You must tell her husband that he has taken a very good wife even if she is built like a house."

The interpreter flushed. James stepped into the breech, managing to remember the man's name. "Mr. Hubley, my friend has said that your wife's cooking is excellent, that you have made a wonderful choice of a wife to love over the decades."

"Oh, I am so glad that the poor wild man is enjoying himself! He must have been starved!" the matron beamed.

With all the charm he had ever learned in the best drawing rooms, James kissed the woman's hand, nodded in acknowledgment to her husband, and quickly swept Wildcat away.

"You cannot tell these men that their wives are fat," James told him.

"It wasn't an insult!" Wildcat said. "I said that she cooked so well it did not matter that she was fat, she was a good wife."

They were stopped next by Captain Morrison, who was leading a young aide-de-camp and his new, buxom bride about the room. The fellow was new, a raw recruit to Florida, James thought.

"Ah, Mr. McKenzie, Mr.—Wildcat," Morrison said lamely. "May I present Lieutenant Anderson and his bride."

James shook hands. "A pleasure," he murmured. He had been right. People had come to gape at them. Mr. Anderson's well-endowed beauty was quite plainly assessing them both.

"Why, the pleasure is mine!" the lady said, brown eyes very large, words drawled out as thick as molasses. "My, but the forest does keep these savages fit, now, isn't that true, sugar?" she said to her husband.

"What did she say?" Wildcat asked him.

The interpreter was standing behind them. Apparently, despite his army uniform, he was taking offense at the words of the white woman. He repeated her words to Wildcat.

Wildcat smiled boldly, glancing at the woman with his dark eyes in a way that made her blush. "Oh, my . . ."

"Tell Mr. Anderson—and do tell him . . . never mind!" Wildcat said in Muskogee, deciding to speak in his own broken English. "Pretty now," he commented. He shook his head. "But once she has babies, she will be *all* fat!"

"Excuse us, will you?" James said quickly, leading Wildcat away once again. "Damn you, I didn't want to come. You talked me into it—"

"I'll stop," Wildcat said with quiet dignity. "But my words were true."

It didn't matter to James anymore. Dancers had moved across the polished hardwood floor. He saw Teela. She was on Harrison's arm. Her hair was very elegantly swept up with a few tender trails of red escaping to dust her shoulders. She was wearing a rich green velvet gown, and it enhanced the beauty of her vibrant coloring, eyes and hair, and the ivory quality of her flesh. Her breasts strained against the scooped bodice of her evening dress, a fashion reminiscent of the recent Empire mode. It hid the rounding of her figure, so he wondered if anyone who did not know her slimness so well would note even now how her curves had changed.

"I tell you—" Wildcat was saying, but he broke off. "Ah, there she is! Warren's daughter."

"Yes," James said, starting to walk across the floor.

Wildcat stopped him. "We are to be civilized savages, remember?"

"Yes."

"Bring me. Introduce me to her."

He had no choice but to allow Wildcat to follow him. John Harrington was the first to see him coming. He beamed with a broad smile, walking forward to greet James with a massive bear hug, then setting him arm's length away. "James, my good fellow, my, but it is good to see you! You seem in fine health, all bones, but that happens in this place, eh? I attempted to see you, you know, but I didn't quite have the rank to deal with the cantankerous old fellow on duty. Jarrett has also informed me that there are matters now you wish to deal with yourself. But be assured, if there is anything at all that I can do—"

"You're doing it," James said, wishing he could bite back the coldness in his tone. Harrison honestly looked incredibly glad to see him. "You're looking after Warren's daughter."

"Yes!" Harrington said. "We go everywhere together. Warren will not be able to offer us any trouble, though he had much of it planned for you, my friend! A hangman's noose at that!"

"Indeed."

"Wildcat!" John said, smiling at the warrior who stood behind James. John switched into a halting Muskogee. "You are most elegant, sir! Are you enjoying yourself here?"

"As much as a prisoner may," Wildcat assured John.

John kept smiling, clearly delighted. "Wildcat, I face you at a party! We are neither negotiators or combatants. I must say, I enjoy this! Ah . . ." he said, noticing that James was looking behind him.

That he was staring at Teela.

"Please, sir, if you will, have a dance with my fiancée."

His fiancée. Harrington's fiancée. Warren's choice for his daughter. Teela. Was it mockery, teasing, or truth? He wanted to shout at Harrington, ask if he was blind or a fool or both, or worse?

"James?"

"Yes. Oh, indeed, I would very much enjoy a dance," he said, stepping forward. She was exchanging words with a silver-haired colonel. James nodded to the man in acknowledgment, then caught Teela's hand.

Her eyes fell on his, burning with a strange heat. A wild, wicked fury. He tugged her hand; she tugged back. He was stronger.

Into his arms.

And into the heat of the simmering flame that had burned so searingly into his heart since he had seen her last.

Chapter 24

He brought her spinning out onto the floor.

"Bastard!" she hissed to him.

His brows arced. He lowered his lips to her ear. "Bitch."

"Ill-mannered—" she began, but he propelled her into the waltz rather than allow her to complete the thought. He was an accomplished dancer, and he drew the attention of many—despite, or because of the fact that Teela was determinedly struggling against him with every sweeping step they took. At last she ceased to struggle. She followed his lead, moved with the music, to his touch, yet avoiding his touch as much as she might, studying his face with wary anger, her lips pursed, face taut with outrage.

"Let the hell go of me, McKenzie. Unless you want a scene on the dance floor."

"Are you threatening me?"

"Ah, sir, but you are perceptive for a savage!"

"Ah, lady, what you dish out, I promise to return. And now, where to begin? How very lovely to see you, Miss Warren."

"What a liar you are!"

"But I'm not lying. Not really."

"Then you're a hypocrite and an ass—"

"Careful, my love—"

"And you are a rude, rotten savage."

"Your opinion has become quite clear. Yet I would say you were the hypocrite. You've returned to civilization with the absolute greatest of ease. You are *la belle femme* indeed, rich in lace and satin. Forgetting—"

"Forgetting nothing! Especially not a man who would just as soon strangle me as look at me! When he is the one with the most atrocious behavior—"

"You've not looked at me and wondered what games I play with others—"

"I need wonder nothing! Your reputation has preceded you in all things, McKenzie."

"As has yours, Miss Warren. But how remiss I am. You look lovely in green."

"Why are you making it sound as if I chose the color for sheer decadence?"

"The gown is positively decadent."

"I beg your pardon."

"Cut nearly to your navel."

"If you're going to spend the evening insulting me—"

"My only purpose in coming here was to see you," he told her.

"Ah! Am I to swoon at the chance to talk with you now? How amazing when you have not wanted to see me before!"

"Oh, I've wanted to see you. Out of earshot from others!" He swung her around the floor with such speed and purpose that he managed to bring them out upon the rear porch. There he went still, his fingers biting cruelly into her shoulders, eyes a blue fire as they stared into hers.

"Whose child is it?"

"What?"

"You heard me quite clearly. I said, whose child—"

She inhaled on a strangled gasp. "You bastard!"

"I said—"

She slapped him. Very hard, and with incredible speed. Then she spun around, head high. She didn't go back into the house, but away down the back lawn.

"Teela, damn you—" he began.

"Go to hell. Go back to prison. You're right, you are

a savage, and I want no part of you in my life!" she cried, spinning to face him once again, her fists in knots.

He started to run after her. "Stop, damn you!" he hissed.

"Leave me be!" she cried out. Loudly.

All of a sudden, from inside the house, he was aware of a commotion.

"He's escaping! The Indian is escaping!"

Wildcat, he thought first. Oh, God, Wildcat was choosing now to make the escape he planned.

But then he realized that *he* was the Indian who was escaping. Soldiers were running from the house, and they were after him.

Teela was still stalking away down the lawn.

He couldn't let her go, let the words between them stop, not now.

"Damn you, Teela, come back here!" he ground out. In seconds he could catch her. He bolted after her, and was startled when someone seized him. He didn't know the fellow, had never seen him before in his life. "Soldier, let me go!" he warned.

The man dug in. "I've got him, I've got him!"

James slipped free and cracked the young man in the jaw. But there were another two soldiers who fell on him, and when he struggled free from them, there was a foursome to throw their weight against him.

Shots were suddenly fired into the air. James went still along with the soldiers. Captain Morrison walked in among them, shaking his head. "James McKenzie, what in God's name has gotten into you? I thought we'd have trouble with Wildcat, but that pure-bred boy is in there seducing half the ladies while you're out here in the middle of a brawl!"

"I intended no fight, Captain. These men waylaid me when I needed to move."

"Mr. McKenzie, you can't move off these grounds tonight! You're a military prisoner. Sir, I'm sorry, but I must escort you back to the fortress now."

There was no fighting the situation, unless he wanted

to kill one of the boys here who were really not at fault at all and then be shot down in turn. He nodded his head. "Captain, I am your prisoner. As you direct."

But he seethed. Anger simmered inside him all the way back to the fort. She had slapped him and turned away from him, run when he could not run after her. Instead he'd been dragged to the ground, a prisoner indeed.

He couldn't wait to get his hands on her. And, he determined, he would never talk to her again when other men might have the power to interrupt what he had to say, and the answers he would demand in return.

When Wildcat found him later that night, James had but on thing to say to him. "When your escape is planned, let me know."

"You'll come with us?"

He had to see her again. On his terms. *Had to.* But there was still the matter of Osceola and the others. If nothing else, James knew that he was the best interpreter of what was going on within the walls of their prison.

"When your escape is planned," he repeated, "let me know."

As it happened, when the time came, there was no choice but for him to go.

"It was quite a spectacle," Tara murmured, pulling off her gloves as she came into Teela's room. "Jarrett was never even able to say a word to James. Everyone was whispering as we arrived. According to the most wildly circulated story, you and James had a terrible argument. James tried to assault you, you escaped him. He came after you again, but you made your escape—and it took a good eight soldiers to bring him down. Shall I take this to mean that things did not go very well?"

"He is a wretched bastard," Teela said. "Oh, God, was anyone hurt?"

"Well, those boys will not feel wonderful come morning. James throws quite a punch."

Teela gnawed lightly on her lower lip. She had been right, she was quite certain. Yet she worried now that she had caused real harm by walking away. She had heard shouting, but she had never turned back. "He— he asked me who the baby's father was!" she said indignantly.

Tara was silent a minute. "Well, then, he quite deserved whatever you did," she said brightly. With a smile she started to leave the room.

"Tara!"

"Yes?"

"What happened to James after I left?"

"They took him back to the Castillo. He was too wild to enjoy a civilized white party."

"Well, he was," Teela murmured.

"Let him simmer and brew for a while. Perhaps it will teach him manners."

"Perhaps ..."

Teela was suddenly afraid. She felt a strange quivering within her. But she was in the right—and he was locked in the Castillo. And he did deserve whatever punishment he got. He had behaved with something worse than savagery, and he could damned well rot a prisoner before she attempted to see him again.

"He may take his uncivilized manners straight to hell!" she assured Tara.

Smiling slightly, Tara left the room once again. She closed Teela's door, leaning against it. James and Teela were both too stubborn and too proud. The situation had to be resolved. Time, it seemed. They needed time. She hoped that they had enough of it.

It was nice, in a way, to worry about her brother-in-law and yet know at the same time that he was actually safe for once—even if he was behind bars.

He couldn't get into mortal danger where he was.

"You've studied the layout as I have?" Wildcat demanded anxiously. He spoke in a whisper, though none of the guards near them knew a word of Muskogee.

James, walking in the yard of the fort, nodded, gazing to the southwest. That angle of the coquina fortress was considered to be escape-proof. Because of that fact there were no guards posted there. On a dark night silent figures could reach the parapet walk unaccosted, and slip downward over the side of the wall.

They could escape. The small opening they sought was a good fifteen feet above the ground. It was five feet high but only eight inches wide, cut through the six-foot thickness of the walls. There were two iron bars across the opening, but James, Wildcat, and another of the warriors, Coweta, had determined that they could break the shell around the one bar and remove it while using the other as the anchor they would need to reach the opening. They could then drop down into the ditch behind the walls and from there disappear into either the ocean or the land.

"We'll take turns each night, chipping at the shell to loosen the bar," James said.

Wildcat nodded. "It's very high. We've nothing to use to reach the wall—"

Coweta, a strong Indian with Negro blood, entered the discussion. "We have one another. We will manage the task."

Four days later, they were nearly ready to lift the bar, though they would not do so until the time of escape arrived, lest they alert someone to their intentions.

Warriors had made a human pyramid, and James was atop them, chipping the last little bit of the wall away to clear the bar. He was startled when Wildcat's husky whisper suddenly urged him from his task.

"Running Bear!"

"What?"

"We must talk. Quickly."

He had pressed against the bar. It moved. The task was done.

He climbed down the ladder of bodies in silence. One by one the Seminoles leaped from their perches atop one another. James, hands on his hips, stared at Wildcat, frowning.

"It's done."

"And none too soon."

"Why? What has happened."

"Come with me."

James quickly followed Wildcat through an archway to the adjoining cell. Osceola was there with his family. He motioned to his first wife, Morning Dew, to leave them in peace. James sat before Osceola while Wildcat hovered behind him.

"They have been fairly free with old Riley here, you are aware of that?" Osceola said.

James nodded, frowning. "Yes, why?"

"He is able to give the white soldiers our requests, to ask them questions for us. They have used him in return, making more of a servant of him."

"They often seek to return black men to their evil masters, you know that."

Osceola waved a hand. "Riley is among us," he said dismissively. "The point is that he hears the soldiers talking often. One of the soldiers who works with the papers in this place was talking to another."

"And?"

"This soldier once rode with Michael Warren."

"Yes?"

Osceola lifted his shoulders as if he had already explained things fully. He rubbed his thumb and forefinger together. "Papers ... letters. This man has sent out a message to Major Warren. To let him know that you are imprisoned here. Where Warren is, he didn't exactly know. How long it might take a letter to reach Warren, the soldier didn't know. But a man on a good, fast horse can travel fifty miles a day at least, eh?"

James nodded thoughtfully. "Yes, you are right."

"So, though you worry about me and the others, though you let yourself be taken for me and the others, you must now go. Your heart has been soaring over these walls many days now. Your spirit has been gone while your mind has fought to remain for the good of the people here. Now there can be no war within you. I am not afraid. I am resigned. What will come, will come. But you must go."

"Osceola, Warren cannot just walk into this place and shoot me down—"

"My friend, both of us know that he would not even need to do so! Guards could come in the night, food could be poisoned. Who knows? You could kill yourself with a rope that happened to be in your cell. A tragic suicide. A half-breed, battling all his worlds. Many will suspect. None will be able to prove anything. James, you must go."

James nodded slowly. "As you say, great *mico*."

Osceola smiled, drawing his blanket more closely around him. "Warrior. I was a great warrior, eh?"

"You are a great warrior."

Osceola nodded, not arguing the point.

That night, James stood with Wildcat beneath the opening, studying it.

"Will we make it through that little space? There lies our challenge," James said.

"It will be easy for me, more difficult for you. But you are determined. We will slick our bodies with grease and twist and turn until we are free. We have starved often enough because we haven't had food, and now we have starved to make ourselves smaller. It is still your desire to do so? You could most probably call upon your white brother and be free."

"I have asked my brother not to interfere. I will not put him or his family in jeopardy for helping me. I will be coming with you," James said. He knelt down by Osceola, who sat against the wall, ready to tell them good-bye. "Perhaps I can be a better friend from the outside."

There was no question of Osceola joining the escape. He hadn't allowed the whites to realize how sick he often felt. Some of the warriors had tried to talk him into coming. His escape would be a just revenge for the whites who had behaved so treacherously bringing them all in. But Osceola had made his decision. He was, as he had told James, resigned.

Now he placed a hand on James's. "I am proud that you will keep fighting. I will tell my captors that I could have gone with you, but that I chose not to do so." He lowered his voice. "You, James, know that I cannot go. I will slow you down, bring disaster upon you. I will pray to the Great Father for us all."

James clasped his arm. "I will never be far from you. I will seek to help you from the outside when I am cleared of Otter's guilt in the massacre of the soldiers. And ..."

"When you have settled that fire in your heart, eh, my good friend?"

"Yes, great *mico*. When I have settled the flames that eat upon my soul."

He stood again, very tired yet grateful for his own health. There had been so much sickness. Yuchi Billy had died just four nights ago and been buried under the supervision of the medicine men and priests. Others had already perished as well. James was now ready to leave. His way. With no outside help.

It was very late, and the sky darkened even further as a cloud slipped across the moon. It was time to go.

Eighteen of them had determined to risk the escape, sixteen men and two women. They worked together in unison and in silence. The chiseled-out bar was removed. A rope was cast and anchored over the remaining bar.

The hardest part of the escape was slipping through the narrow opening. For the women it was easy. They were very small and slim. James knew that with the size of his shoulders and torso, it was going to be most difficult for him. He had been aware of that fact from the beginning.

He forced himself to think of Teela. Her face, her form—and the way she had walked away from him, leaving him to be tackled by the soldiers. His skin was well greased. He twisted and strained harder, then sought to make his muscles and bulk smaller, all but shearing the flesh from his body. He clamped down hard on his jaw, knowing that he could not let out a sound.

And at last he was through. He joined the others.

Wraiths, they stood in the darkness and the breeze. Free.

They knew how to move in silence, all of them. One by one they shinnied down their stolen line the twenty-one feet to the ditch below.

It was there that he parted with Wildcat and the others.

"I must go my own way now," James told him.

"The white way."

James shook his head, though he knew full well that he was not going to become a part of the war against the whites, no matter what accusations Warren conjured to throw against him. He had never fought willingly; he had only fought for the survival of those around him.

"I have always tried to remain at peace with my father's people and my mother's. I want to find peace again."

"Perhaps it cannot be found when there is a war being fought."

"Peace is something we may have to find in our own hearts," James told him. "But I promise you this, I will never betray my *Seminole* brothers."

Wildcat smiled. "Neither of your peoples, eh? The Great Spirit be with you. When you tire of the pasty-skins, find me. I will fight the war again, by our lives and blood!"

They embraced briefly.

Wildcat went his way, raising a hand to indicate that the rest should follow him. He was there a moment, a dark shadow barely visible in the dark night, then he was gone, silently disappearing with his people. James scampered through the darkness until he reached the water of the inlet. He plunged in. Thanks to Dr. Weedon's interest in half-breeds and talking, he knew where his brother's family was lodged, even though he'd yet to see Jarrett since his capture.

It was well past midnight when he found the house. Yet he was in luck. As he stood dripping on the wood-planked sidewalk before it, staring up at the second floor, Teela sat at a dressing table. He could just make out her form through the filmy white curtains in the flickering glow of her candlelight.

She blew out the flame.

He smiled.

He was naked save for a breech clout. His body had been greased down to allow for his escape, but the salt water had washed away the grease. His hair was queued at his nape with a leather band. Dressed so, he could move with the same ease of any creature who preyed in the forest.

He climbed the wall with the help of a trellis and slipped onto the balcony, then through those telltale flimsy curtains and into the darkened room. He made his way to the bed, kneeling swiftly down by the woman there and clamping his hand over her mouth. He lowered his mouth to her ear even as he heard her muffled squeaks of protest, and cast his weight against her to keep her still.

"All right, now, my love, just whose child is it?"

To his amazement, a large, dark shadow moved on the side of the bed by the woman.

"Mine!" snapped the shadow.

Chapter 25

James leapt back from the bed, stunned but instantly wary, prepared to fight. But no one attacked him, and he was startled to hear the shadow speaking and to recognize the voice.

"Mine—and there's no damned question about it. And what the hell are you doing in my bedroom at this time of night?"

A match was struck, a candle lit. James found himself staring at his brother and sister-in-law, both seated in their bed with the covers drawn up around them and looking at him expectantly.

"I—" he began, then lifted his hands. "I'm sorry, Tara."

"I think you've got the wrong room," his sister-in-law said smoothly. "You want to be down the hall and to the left," she informed him.

"Of course, you could have just knocked on the front door," Jarrett said, studying his appearance critically.

"I can't stay long," James said simply.

"Maybe you should stay long enough to talk," Jarrett suggested.

"He doesn't need to talk to us. He needs to talk to Teela, as is evidenced here," Tara said.

"Yes," Jarrett said, "and no matter what your circumstances, I want to know what's going on before you leave."

"Fair enough," James said, turning to leave their room.

"There was an escape, I take it?" Jarrett said.

"Yes."

"And you led it?"

James paused, shaking his head. "I did not. I merely joined it." He hesitated. "I had no choice. I've had word that Michael Warren was informed of my presence at the Castillo. It was suggested to me that I might not survive imprisonment if I didn't leave quickly."

"Warren knows you were imprisoned?"

"If he does not know now, he will soon."

"You know, then, that you don't dare stay here long?"

"I'll be gone by dawn, before it's discovered that there has been an escape."

"So has Jesup lost Osceola?"

James shook his head again. "Osceola is dying," he said quietly. "He may have some time left. Weeks, months, I don't know." He started out of the room and then paused. "Jesup thinks that this will win the war for him. But it won't."

"I know," Jarrett told him.

James nodded, stepped out, and quietly closed the door behind him.

Jarrett looked sternly at his wife. "Should we have allowed him to do that? He's liable to give the poor girl a heart attack."

"She's stronger than that, but she will be ready to kill him," Tara said complacently. Her husband was staring at her as if she'd gone mad. "He will deserve it, definitely, and as you know, they must solve their own problems."

"The problems may be greater now than ever. He has just escaped from a military prison!"

"They had no right to hold him, and James was right. Warren probably would have had him murdered within the Castillo. James is not just an innocent man. He has saved the lives of both white men and Seminoles."

"That's your feeling on the matter."

"He should just stay here—"

Jarrett groaned softly, "Tara, don't you see? He can't

possibly stay. This is the first place they'll come to look for him!"

"But—"

"Tara, leave it be."

"But—"

"Tara!"

"Jarrett—"

He sighed, and kissed his wife. It was the only way to silence her, he had long ago discovered.

She was having the dream again.

She knew that she was somewhere deep in the interior of the territory. It was no place she knew well. The trails were narrow, nearly nonexistent. She could hear the constant buzzing of flies and mosquitoes. She could hear something else as well. Her own breathing.

She was running.

Running so hard. And she was carrying the weight in her arms. Desperate to reach safety, desperate to hide. She was being chased.

The footsteps kept falling and falling. She couldn't run fast enough. The green trees were overshadowing her. She heard a hissing sound and nearly cried out, startled as a snake nearly struck out at her from a low-hanging branch.

The runner was gaining on her. Coming closer and closer. She looked down at the weight in her arms. It was a babe. Dark-haired, so tiny. Newborn, helpless.

The footsteps, pounding against the earth, were almost upon her. She turned, opening her mouth to scream. Someone was coming to kill her. Her and the babe.

She couldn't see her pursuer through the trees.

She didn't know if she was being chased by a white man or a red man, a soldier or a Seminole. She only knew one thing.

He wanted her—and the baby—dead.

James hurried down the hallway, finding the door on the left and stepping through it.

The windows were open from the balcony. Soft white linen curtains floated with ghostlike grace, allowing in more moonlight than his brother's room. Halfway across the room he could see her, and knew that this time he had come to the right place. The waves of her hair spilled against the white sheets like tendrils of the deepest, darkest fire in the night. She slept restlessly, her breathing shallow. She wore a gown of frilled white cotton, absurdly chaste—other than the fact that her breasts, definitely enlarged, strained against the lacy bodice. He walked closer to the bed, standing very still as he stared down at her, oddly at war within himself. He discovered he was as fascinated with her as he had been that very first time he had seen her in his brother's house. She was exceptionally beautiful, and knowing her made her even more so, because the fire that filled her spirit was even greater than the vibrant glow of her hair and eyes, the marble perfection of her flesh. He felt his heart hammering against his chest, and he wanted to touch her in the most tender way, and he wanted to shake her because he was afraid. Perhaps because he had no right to doubt her; and yet perhaps because he did. He knew her so well, so intimately, and yet he didn't really know her at all. He had sent her away so many times.

With no choice, he reminded himself.

And what now? he silently mocked. What now? He was more the renegade than ever. It hadn't occurred to him until Jarrett had asked him about the escape that he might be accused of masterminding it, and that Jesup himself would want his head.

Should he walk away without waking her? Leave her in her restless sleep without ever touching her, speaking to her? Go on the run once more, this time forever?

She stirred as he watched her; her eyes suddenly flew open. It seemed that she had been alarmed before she even awakened. She jumped up to a sitting position, inched to the headboard, and flattened herself against it.

She was about to scream, he realized, while remembering his own appearance, deeply bronzed, half naked.

She had nearly been stabbed to death once by a man with a very similar appearance, he remembered. Otter. Any second she might start shrieking, waking not just the household but the entire neighborhood. He dared not let her cry out.

He took the step to the bed before she could scream, leaping upon it, silencing her with his hand. Her eyes widened with greater alarm, then shock, then fury.

"You son of a bitch—" she began with a hiss.

Anger bred anger. "Whose child is it?" he interrupted just as heatedly.

She inhaled sharply and tried to slap him. He caught her hand, but didn't deter her wrath. Her teeth sank into his wrist, and he cried out softly with surprise. She wasn't done. He had met men in battle without half her furious strength. Coming to her knees against him, she pummeled his shoulders and chest wildly. She came at him with such a force that he fell back, and she glared at him. "Wretched, pompous, despicable ass!"

"Teela, isn't this where we left off last time? I warn you—" he began.

But she threw herself against him again so hard that she sent them both flying from the bed. He managed to twist to buffer her from their fall, but she didn't seem to notice at all. "You really are one scurvy, detestable bastard. You—"

"Teela!" He managed to catch both wrists. "Teela, damn you, enough—"

"Don't you dare say that word to me! Enough! Nothing is ever enough for you, everything is your way. You're demanding, unreasonable—" She broke off breathlessly because he had managed to roll her weight from him. He rose, dragging her up with him. She instantly began the fight again, ripping an arm free from his clutch to aim a fist right for his jaw. He ducked and she swung into his arms. He plucked her up and threw her back to the bed. When she rose to fight again, he was quick and ruthless, wrestling her down and pinning her wrists to the bed as he straddled her.

"Whose child is it!" she spat out. "Don't you even think about asking me that question again!" she warned him.

"How could I not? You lived among the soldiers and whites far longer than you have been with me! You all but had a death grip on Harrington when you watched me being paraded by toward the Castillo. You were *with* Harrington—"

"Who has been nothing but the nicest man in the world, the best friend imaginable to both of us! How dare you doubt him? How have you the damned bloody nerve to doubt me—"

"Nerve! You walked away from me, ran away from me! Knowing damned well that for once I couldn't catch you!"

"My lord! What a shame!"

"You could do what you pleased because you knew a dozen soldiers were ready to shoot me if I defied an order."

"Did they shoot you? Obviously not!"

"They stopped me, they—"

"And the poor fellows are all beaten black and blue and sorely bruised for their efforts while you look none the worse for wear, McKenzie."

"You wanted me dragged back to prison."

"It was a fitting place for you!"

"Why, you little witch! You—"

"I didn't even know about it!" she spat out.

"I was humiliated," he informed her tensely.

"Good! You need to learn a little humility."

"I might have died for you!"

"Why not? You are willing to die for everyone else."

"But I might have died just to hear an answer from your lips."

"To a question you've got no right to ask!"

He was floundering, he thought. "You wouldn't fight your own battle!" he accused her lamely.

"I'll fight you anytime!"

"Will you? Just try to scream again and see if the soldiers won't come back and take care of things for you now!"

"Oh!" she cried furiously. She had the strength of a wildcat and almost managed to dislodge his hold on her arms. She tossed her head, trying to find some flesh to sink her teeth into again.

"My love, that's hardly civilized—"

"Well, how does one deal with a savage!" she countered, wrenching one wrist free. She tried to strike out at him; he just barely managed to catch hold of her again. She was far more wily, swift, and determined than many a man he had met in battle. "Get off and get out, you wretched—" she began, then stopped, gasping. She went dead still, staring at his face yet seeming to see nothing at all.

"James!"

"What?" he cried, his sudden fear heavy in his voice. In the passion of their argument, he'd forgotten the babe. If he'd hurt her, hurt it ... "What? Damn, Teela, talk to me. Are you ill, have I harmed you ..." His voice broke to a whisper. "The babe ... ?"

"Oh, James, it's moving!" She caught his hand, dragging it down to her abdomen. At first he could feel nothing. Then a ripple like a tiny hand seemed to stretch across the inner length of her womb, slight, scarcely discernible, but there, so completely there.

"Our child," she said suddenly. Her voice broke with emotion as she added, "You really are a wretched bastard. How *could* you doubt me?"

"It's not that!" he whispered fiercely, his hold on her easing as he sat back on his haunches, holding his weight from her. He smiled ruefully, swept with a soreness different from any pain he had known, fully aware that his behavior had been less than exemplary many times. He battled forces he couldn't begin to control, and thus did come across too bitter and too hateful. He had accused the whites of grouping the Indians as one kind of human being, of not realizing there were those who respected life, learning, and happiness, those who loved children and would sooner die themselves than harm a child. He hadn't been able to accept the fact that Teela could really love him for what he was, and that John Harrington could be a friend and not a rival. Very, very gently he moved a wild strand of hair from her face, his fingertips just brushing the softness of her cheek. "I all but threw you away," he said softly. "Then despised the fact that you might have gone."

She lay still, staring up at him, her eyes slowly taking in his appearance. Tears suddenly glazed her eyes. "It's your child. Yours. And whether you are glad or not and seek to throw me away again or not, *I* am glad. I will love this baby, and I won't teach it hatred or bitterness. I will let it know every possible thing *that is good* and wonderful about both races. I'll—"

He silenced her with a kiss. Salty tears mingled with the unbelievably sweet taste of her. When he lifted his lips from hers, he took both hands and placed them around her rounded abdomen.

He shook his head. "Teela, I don't know how to make you understand. In my heart I wanted you to love me. But by all sense and logic, I truly wanted you gone, away from here, away from the danger. Away from Warren. When I walked through St. Augustine, a prisoner, I heard what people said. About the Indians, about me. I am proud of all that I am, but I hated them for what they said. Hated them for being white, for being so prejudiced. And I couldn't believe then that you could really want me ... my life ... once you had tasted all that went with being white once again. It was perhaps one thing to feel desire, excitement for a brief time in the wilderness ... but that is so very different from a lifetime. And you didn't tell me. That's what triggered every evil thought within me. You didn't tell me about the baby. In the copse."

"I didn't realize!" she whispered in return. "I would have told you. It's just that I didn't know. Honestly. I—"

"I've been afraid," he told her quietly.

"Afraid? I've never seen you afraid of anything."

"I've been afraid of wanting you, knowing that I can't have you."

"But you do have me."

"How?" he demanded. "How do I have you? What have I done but give you an illegitimate child. A red one at that. Ruin you in society. It isn't as if I'm a lawyer or a doctor having difficulty paying his bills. I'm an Indian. *Red.*" He caught her hand, brought it to his chest as he had once before. "Feel the red, my love, because you'll be burned by it, yet it's as if you haven't the sense to feel the pain."

"I feel pain when you're gone. When I am in fear for your life. When I don't know—"

She broke off. They were both startled by the sounds of hoofbeats on the streets below them.

"Horses!" she whispered. She stared at him then. "My God, James, how can you be here? As you are . . . in the middle of the night? You escaped—you broke out of the Castillo!"

"I had to."

"Why? If they've discovered that there has been an escape, they'll be hunting you down!"

James jumped up. He walked quickly to the open balcony window. How long had he been here? It appeared that the first streaks of dawn were just filtering into the sky. It wasn't the middle of the night anymore. It was nearly morning. And there were horsemen coming.

In military uniforms.

He had to leave his brother's home, and do so without delay. Even as he realized his dire situation, the door burst open. Jarrett, in a long robe, stood there.

"Sweet *Jesu,* James, you've got to get out of here, and fast."

"I'm not going to be afraid of the military. I'm not going to run from them now," he decided. "I'll turn myself in to you, and you can bring me to Hernandez or Jesup and we can tell them that my life has been threatened at the Castillo. I intend to clear my name on

Warren's ridiculous charges that I led the massacre against his men."

"James, you don't understand. It's not just the military now," Jarrett said. "It's Warren, and his men aren't army, they're cutthroats."

"Warren!" James said incredulously. "Warren has returned to St. Augustine, discovered the escape, and come here so quickly? It can't possibly be Warren—"

"James, you knew he'd been informed that you were here," Jarrett reminded him. "And I'm telling you, I recognize the man! I don't know how he has managed to move so quickly, only that he has. Perhaps he arrived at the Castillo with his troops just as the escape was discovered. What difference does it make? He is here, riding toward this house right now."

"Oh, my God!" Teela breathed. She stared at James. "You knew that he knew you were in St. Augustine? You shouldn't have come here! You fool, you shouldn't have come—"

"I had to come," he told her.

She leapt to her feet, racing across the room to the place where he stood by the window. "You've got to go quickly, please! He'll kill you."

James hesitated. "And what will he do to you?"

"Well, he can't *kill* me," she stated, and added bitterly, "Not in front of witnesses."

"But he can take you from Jarrett's house."

"James, you've got to leave us. You have to go," Jarrett said.

"I should have this out with him!" he cried passionately. "He hasn't the right to his cruelty, his determination to destroy so many lives."

"James!" Teela pleaded, "don't be insane. You can't talk to him rationally. You can't fight an entire company of men. You've got to go."

"Wait—" James said.

"For the love of God, go!" Jarrett exclaimed.

"Please!" Teela added.

He didn't want to go. The greatest feeling of unease

was ripping through him, and not because Warren could have him fired upon by a half dozen rifles at once. He didn't want to leave. He didn't want to leave Teela.

But it seemed that she and his brother were right; he would only invite disaster if he stayed. With no logical argument, he couldn't fight Jarrett and Teela, and it was certainly true that he couldn't tackle Warren and all his men alone and bare-handed. He stared at Teela one last time, then turned and ran silently for the balcony. He leapt over the rail, balling his body to fall to the ground with a spring action, then stayed hunched low behind the shrubbery as he watched the riders approach, stopping in the front.

He saw the first man on horseback, saw him as he reined in.

Saw Warren.

The man's eyes seemed alight with a fanatical glow. He had the greatest zest for a chase, a pursuit.

For murder.

"Surround the place, men!" he ordered. "See that no one goes in or out. Pay me heed! That renegade half-breed will not hide behind his brother's white flesh tonight!"

James counted the men. Ten of them with Warren, all of them armed with rifles, knives, and bayonets. As they scattered, Warren observed the house with that same gleam, seeming to grow brighter in the night.

"Indeed!" he said softly, almost to himself. "Tonight that McKenzie half-breed will pay the price of his wretched audacity—with his blood. With his blood, by God, I swear it!"

With that, Warren dismounted and started for the house.

Chapter 26

James slipped along the flower bushes growing beside the walk, keeping very low. Warren's men had all dismounted. James could have stolen a horse and disappeared quickly into the night—except that he knew he wasn't going anywhere, not until he had seen what Warren had in mind.

He didn't leave the yard. He crawled quickly to a heavy branch of a very old oak in the yard and climbed it. From where he perched, he could see dimly into the parlor of the house, and into Teela's room above it. He heard a rustling below him as Warren's men surrounded the house, two to the back, two in front, and two to each side—two, with their guns loaded and aimed, had entered the house with Warren. The fellow on James's side of the house was all but beneath him, guarding a window.

Candlelight suddenly blazed throughout the house. James heard Warren, demanding entry and the right to search the place. He heard Tara speaking next, her voice outraged. He strained to listen as others spoke. Jarrett warned Warren in no uncertain terms that he would have words with the governor, General Jesup, and even Martin Van Buren if Warren didn't get himself and his men out of the house.

"Your half-breed brother staged the disappearance of some of General Jesup's most important captives! If you think that Jesup will overlook your brother's part in the escape, McKenzie, you are sadly mistaken."

"This is private property, Warren. My property. And I want you off it."

"I can't oblige you, sir. Now stand aside, or I will shoot."

"You shoot me, and I can guarantee that you'll go on trial for murder. If you live that long. The half-breed you're hunting would find a way to slit your throat."

"Ah, yes, McKenzie, you know his violence as well as I do!"

"I know *your* dishonorable violence."

"Let him search the house if he wishes, Jarrett," Tara said. "We can speak to his superiors about him at a later time."

"I'll start in my daughter's room," Warren said. "Newman!" he barked out, addressing one of his men. "If he moves to stop me, shoot him!"

"I'm not going to stop you. Search your daughter's room. My brother isn't there."

James quickly drew his gaze to the second floor. He saw through Teela's window as Warren came bursting through her hallway door.

"Well, daughter!" Warren stated, a wealth of venom in the two simple words.

"Warren," Teela said in return. "You've returned alive and well from the bush."

"Indeed!"

"What a pity, sir, for all those who will continue to die because of you."

James did not hear Warren's next words, for the man lowered his voice to a deadly quiet pitch.

And he didn't hear what Teela had to say in return, but he definitely heard the venom Warren spilled out after. "Injun-lovin' *whore*! Vilest bitch seed I've ever seen thrown out of woman ..."

Warren was suddenly across the room, one of his hands in Teela's hair, holding her taut by a thick hank of it.

"I'll kill you, girl! At the very least I'll kill that brat bastard you're carrying!"

* * *

Kill you, kill you, kill you, kill the brat ...

She wasn't in the forest, or the swamp. On a pine barren, or anywhere that might have been called wild or dangerous. Yet here it was. Her nightmare.

She had run and run, and heard the footsteps after her all the while. Because there had been nowhere to run. Warren was the monster in her life. The savage.

The one who meant to kill her babe.

She shouted out expletives to him, words she hadn't realized that she knew ...

Kill the babe, oh, God, no. She couldn't let him, couldn't let him. But she had no weapons. He was strong. A military man. A well-trained savage.

She had to fight him.

For the baby.

Their baby.

James tensed, ready to spring. Teela didn't even scream, she just gritted her teeth, her nails digging into Warren's hands with such force that he shouted, freeing her. She started to back away from Warren. He caught her with so stunning a blow she fell backward against the wall. Then he started to hit her. Again, and again.

James saw red. Blood red.

Reason deserted his mind; no thought of the possible consequences deterred him. He leapt down from the tree and headed for a trellis to skim up the wall to Teela's balcony.

One of Warren's men, guarding the window, stepped toward him. "Halt!"

James kept going.

"Halt, or I'll shoot!"

"You ass! He's beating his daughter!"

"He's her father; it's his right!" the man defended.

James moved so swiftly the soldier was never able to raise his rifle. He knocked the man unconscious with a solid blow to his jaw. He flew to the balcony, then propelled himself swiftly into the room—and onto Warren.

He caught the man by the throat, spun him around, and slammed his fist into his face. He heard a crunching that assured him he had broken the man's nose. Warren swore, trying to lash out in turn, but a vivid, hot anger, unlike anything he had known in all his life, seized hold of James.

He had killed men before. Killed them in battle. Killed them because they would have killed him first.

He had never wanted to kill.

Now he did.

He beat Warren, and beat him again, until he fell to the floor. Then he crawled atop the man, ready to smash in more of his face.

But he heard Teela's voice, crying out to him.

"No, James! God, no! They'll call it murder. They'll want to hang you for it. James, you can't kill him. You just can't do it."

Her hands were on him, long fingers digging into his arm. He barely heard her at first. The whole of the room seemed to be spinning in red.

He stopped and looked at her. Her hair was wild; she was flushed. Yet there were no marks on her face. If she'd been seriously hurt, she gave no sign.

"Teela, you—"

"I'm fine."

"Our child?"

"Fine. Please, James, don't kill him! You didn't cause the massacre or kidnap anyone. You don't stand condemned now. But if you kill Warren, you will be hunted for murder. Please, James, he's not worth it! I tell you, he isn't worth your spit, and he's not worth the rest of our lives."

He stood, dragged to his feet by her. He stared down at Warren, still seized by that consuming, heated anger.

"For you," he whispered, tenderly setting his hands upon her shoulders, kissing her forehead. "For you, he lives."

"For us!"

Yet even as he pressed his lips quickly against her

forehead once again, the door to Teela's room suddenly burst open. Soldiers streamed quickly into the room, all of them with rifles aimed at Teela and James.

"The savage has done in the major!" a young man shouted.

"Not—done in!" Warren gasped, trying to rise. Men rushed forward to aid him. "But the savage surely did try to finish me off!"

"We'll have him in custody, sir—" another of the men began.

"Custody, hell!" Warren raged. "We'll hang him here and now, out on the oak. Take him!"

Teela screamed, trying to grasp James as the soldiers rushed in on him, but even as Teela was dragged away, James fought. He punched, kicked, gouged, threw his fists again and again. The men fell back, injured. Wailing.

But they kept rising. They kept coming. He kept fighting.

Then he heard a shot, fired into the ceiling. He stopped fighting, because Warren had a Colt repeater pressed against Teela's skull. "Her or you," Warren said flatly.

"Sir!" began one of his men.

"Silence! Her or you!" Warren raged.

James didn't trust the man not to put a bullet through her skull, even if it did mean he would pay with his own life. James went still. He lifted his hands in surrender. Soldiers surged around him again, grappling him by the arms.

Jarrett was somewhere, he thought, not believing that he could die here. Lose the sweet taste of life to a man so wretched and treacherous as Warren. Warren could not get away with this atrocity.

One of the soldiers pressed the muzzle of his gun against James's throat. "Your hands, Mr. McKenzie," the man said. He was shaking. He was afraid of James.

"Mr. McKenzie!" Warren spat. "Running Bear, *breed.*

He is no 'Mr.', son! Now bind his hands and be quick about it."

Maybe the young soldier was every bit as afraid of what he was doing as he was of James.

James had no choice. He offered up his hands. The soldier was still shaking as he tied James's hand behind his back. The man did a poor job of it. James was not at all securely tied. However, it wasn't his place to let his captors know it. He remained still, staring at Warren.

"Let's head for the oak," Warren said.

"No!" Two of the men had taken Teela's arms and pressed her to the wall across the room. She shrieked with a wild fury, freeing herself from the soldiers to throw herself at Warren, scratching, clawing, slamming against him. "No, you'll not get away with this. You'll—"

Warren whipped his Colt against her head. She fell to the bed with barely a whimper. James started to surge forward. The gun muzzle pressed against his Adam's apple.

"Did you want her to watch you die, eh, injun?" Warren inquired. He tried to wipe the blood from his face. His nose was smashed. Tomorrow he'd have two huge black eyes. The whole of his face would be swollen and bruised.

Pity I won't live to see it! James thought.

And Teela had offered Warren mercy!

Well, he might die himself, James determined, but if he did so, Warren was going with him. Teela was going to be free. And she would love their child, and Jennifer. And there would be a future for the three of them, at least.

"Let's go!" Warren barked. He was obviously still in great pain.

The men began to usher James toward the door, down the hall, and toward the stairs.

He found his brother at last, and realized that Jarrett had never been given a chance to come to his aid. He lay slumped down on the bottom step with Tara kneeling

over him. A soldier stood over her, gun aimed at her.
She gasped, looking up as she saw James coming down
the stairs. Tears were streaming down her face. "You
fools! You've already injured my husband, and I swear,
you'll have the devil to pay. Stop this, stop this!"

James burst free from his retainers, hurrying toward
Tara and his fallen brother. He fell to his knees at the
bottom of the stairs, trying to see Jarrett's face, to ascer-
tain what had happened to him.

"Tara—"

"Jarrett will be all right. He's knocked out," Tara assured him quickly. "He tried to run up the stairs when
he heard the shot, and this big brave soldier here"—she
mockingly indicated the man with the gun—"slammed
the back of his head with his rifle butt. James, where
are they taking you, what are they doing?"

"It's all right, Tara, stay with him."

"James, what—"

"Tara, stay with Jarrett. See to Teela when you can."

"Teela—?"

"These big, brave men treated her the same way."

The soldiers had come again and were tugging his
shoulders, dragging him back to his feet and toward the
door. One ran by him, quickly exiting the house and
securing rope and a horse. A noose was hurriedly fashioned. James stood calmly in the center of the soldiers,
watching as Warren stepped forward, slipping the noose
over his head. He stared at Warren with undisguised
hatred.

"One more dead Indian," Warren gloated. "One, and
then another, and another. And finally all the Indian
boys will be dead. And you'll just be forgotten dust, a
bad dream. Beaten to the core."

James shook his head. "You're wrong. Kill one of us
in front of you, and another will appear. Chase us until
there is no land, and we will fight in the swamp. You
cannot beat us. In the end you will die and go to hell,
and we will remain undefeated."

"You're going to die now, boy. So say your prayers

to whomever you call God, and be quick now. Bring the horse!" he roared.

The horse, a well-fed army roan, was brought up. Except for the two soldiers who were to be his executioners, the men, along with Warren, remounted their horses for the show. James was thrown atop the horse by the two men, hands still tied behind his back. The end of the rope was thrown over the oak and quickly secured.

"Make your peace with your Maker!" Warren cried, coming closer to him. He smiled. "I want to see those blue eyes of yours bulge out of your head as you die, boy. Everything in the kidneys goes, too, after a hanging. Smells bad, real bad. You won't be such a good-looking Indian boy then, huh?"

He spat at Warren, but the man edged his horse back just far enough to avoid the insult.

James fought to control his temper. He had but one chance and he knew it, and that chance was slim. He had to free his hands to catch the noose, and use the very rope that would have hanged him to make a bid for freedom. There were no guns upon him now. All the soldiers had lowered their weapons, laid down their guard, to watch him hang. Their rifles were back in their saddle holsters. Their knives were sheathed.

"You know, Warren, I don't think this is legal, do you?" James said, working at his hands.

"This is war against the Seminoles. You're a Seminole! You led an escape from the Castillo, and then you tried to murder me in cold blood. I am justified in my actions, and I am surrounded by witnesses!"

James had worked the ropes around his wrist entirely free. If he could only catch the noose before his neck was broken . . .

"Hang the red bastard!" Warren shouted.

She had come to with a murderous pounding in her head. The pain, in fact, was so intense at first that it clouded her mind.

Then she remembered. *They'd taken James.*

She leapt up, racing to the window. *They were going to hang him. Oh, God, at any second now, he was going to swing . . .*

She tore down the stairs, reaching the landing just as Tara was helping Jarrett struggle to his feet.

"They've a rope around his neck!" she cried. She flew past Jarrett to the hallway closet, aware that he kept a double-barreled shotgun there. Jarrett had lived in a raw, new land for far too long not to keep such a weapon ready and close. She dragged it out, only to find Jarrett already at her back, plucking the weapon from her grasp.

"Give me the damned thing, it's loaded—"

"He's about to hang!" she cried tearfully. She spied a Colt repeater hanging from a holster by the door and drew it out. John Harrington had always said it was a weapon that might misfire.

She didn't care. She grasped it firmly in her hand and turned to fly after Jarrett.

Even as she did so, she froze.

Shouts were rising from the front of the house. Oh, God, he might have already . . .

She nearly passed out. She ran instead.

James heard the sound of a switch slammed hard against the roan's haunches. So hard that the animal let out a pitiful whinny before rearing high and racing off into the night.

It was the horse that saved him, he thought. That, and the cruelty of a man who would strike an animal with such fervor. When the horse reared up, the noose and rope loosened, and James had the split second he needed to seize hold of the noose.

When the rope pulled taut, he was able to swing his body toward Warren before escaping the noose. Warren didn't have time to move his horse back fast enough. James's weight caught him, slammed him off his horse. Warren shouted, seized his knife from the sheath at his side, and tried to plunge it into James as they rolled.

"Major!" One of his men shouted, but James and Warren were already rolling, engaged in a battle to the death, and if the soldier had a rifle, he couldn't possibly have aimed it with any precision at James.

James grappled Warren's arm, fighting to loose the knife from his fingers. He slammed Warren's wrist against the ground. Warren twisted, and James caught his jaw, ramming it hard against the earth.

He heard a strange crunching again, and at first, in the desperate fight for his life, he didn't recognize the sound. Then he realized that Warren had ceased to fight, that the knife had fallen from the man's fingers. And then he knew.

Something else had broken.

The man's neck.

His first thought was that Teela was free.

He didn't realize his own continued danger then, but closed his eyes in misery.

Now he was damned.

He'd had no choice. No choice at all. But any hope he'd ever had of finding his own peace, a place between the world of the Indian and the white man, seemed doomed.

"*Jesu,* he has killed the major this time!" someone shouted.

"Up, up, Indian, get off the man before we fill you full with bullet holes!" cried another soldier.

He started to rise, slowly. He might at least get a military trial now, a chance to see his daughter and Teela once again.

"Kill him!" one of them shouted. "Kill him. He's killed Major Warren."

Rifles were lowered. He was ready to make a diving drop, roll and run, and somehow pray to evade a score of bullets.

But then he was startled—just as startled as the soldiers before him—as a resounding shot was fired over their heads.

Jarrett was standing in the front door, Tara at his side.

He held a double-barreled shotgun in his hands, aimed at the fellow who had last spoken. "Gentlemen, I want you off my property now. You're trespassing. You had no right to become a lynch mob."

"The major is dead! The savage—your brother killed him, Mr. McKenzie!" one of the men sputtered.

"The man half killed his own daughter first! This hanging was illegal in every way, shape, and form, and I swear that I will see to it that every man jack one of you pays if you don't turn around and ride away now! You want my brother? Yes, sir, one of you can shoot him. But I guarantee at least two of you will have big holes for guts before your bullets make their mark!"

Before anyone could reply, a second voice called out from the porch, feminine but incredibly fierce.

"Your bullets will never, ever reach their marks, I guarantee it!"

He almost smiled. Teela had come to the porch as well. She stood on Jarrett's other side—and she was aiming one of his brother's repeating pistols at the soldiers. She was still in her white gown. Her hair was a fire-red mane about her shoulders. She stood very tall, proud—and barefoot.

"Mr. McKenzie, Miss Warren!" It was the young officer who had been shaking so badly when he'd tried to bind James's hands. "There will be no shooting here tonight. There's plenty of fight and danger left for all of us, boys!" he cried to the men before looking gravely back to Jarrett. "We're not savages." He glanced at James and added softly, "I been out in the bush nearly two years now, and I admit I ain't never seen no one so savage as Major Warren. And tonight—savage against his own daughter. We're riding out. Men, we are riding out!" he insisted.

"Take your major's body with you. It isn't wanted by his next of kin," Jarrett suggested.

Warren's body was duly thrown over the back of his horse. The soldiers started down the street, with the young man at the head of the group.

But the fellow who had so nearly been James's executioner wasn't ready to give it all up so easily. He twisted in his saddle, calling back to them. "Jarrett McKenzie, you'll go to jail for this as well! Wait till Jesup hears what's gone on here tonight! There won't be no rest, no place to hide."

"I won't be hiding!" Jarrett called.

The young soldier suddenly rode back to where James stood. "My name is Noonan, sir. You need a witness, you call on me."

James smiled slowly. Nodded. "Thanks, Noonan."

"Your brother and your, er, Miss Warren can't hold soldiers off forever, McKenzie. You'd best hightail it quick."

"Thanks again."

Noonan smiled, saluted, and turned his horse, quickly catching up with his retreating company.

In a few minutes, the sounds of hoofbeats faded. James turned to his brother. "Thanks. And I'd thought they'd really cracked you in the head. You're a damned good brother. You came back to consciousness in—in damned good time!"

"Almost too late." Jarrett halfway grinned. "I have never seen anyone escape a hangman's noose before."

James shrugged. "They tied lousy knots." He smiled at Teela.

"Now, you . . . you are surely the fiercest fighter I have yet to come across. She could maybe end the war, don't you think, Jarrett?"

"Or start up another one," Jarrett teased gently, then sobered. "Now, will you listen to me this time? You really do have to get out of here."

James nodded. He stared at Teela. "The fear will be over," he told her softly, then turned back to his brother. "Teela and the baby will be safe," he said.

"Of course they will be. But I'm not real sure about your status at the moment, baby brother, and I know I can't shoot the whole army. Will you please get the hell out of here?"

Tara suddenly came running down the steps, hurrying toward James. She flung her arms around his neck and kissed his cheek. "James, he's right! Dear God, you're alive, you're safe—and in danger again! Get out of here like he says before they come and arrest you."

"Yeah, yeah, I will." He hugged her quickly in return. "Jennifer—"

"You haven't time to see her. Trust me, we love her and will keep her well."

"Teela—"

He broke off, staring at the porch, realizing that she was gone. "Where's Teela?" he asked.

Jarrett swung around as well, unaware that she had disappeared until that moment.

"James, you mustn't worry," Tara assured him. "We love her, too—"

"James!"

He stared back to the porch. Teela had returned. Red hair a cascade that seemed to fly in the wind behind her, she came hurrying down the steps toward him. She had changed from her frilled white nightgown and now wore a gingham day dress and riding boots.

She ran to James and threw herself at him, holding him. She crushed his head between her palms and kissed him with a wonderfully savage, hungry, passionate splendor.

He caught hold of her. "Teela, I've got to run—"

"I know."

"Have you realized that your father is—"

"My *step*father is dead. James, you're alive!"

"Then you realize, I've got to go—"

"I'm coming."

"What?"

"I'm coming with you."

"Teela, the road for the time being will be very rough. You're carrying our babe. You—"

"I'm as tough as any road, James McKenzie. I have told you many times, I can survive much, but after this

I am afraid to see you go. I can survive anything but losing you again."

"Teela, you don't understand—"

"James, I do understand."

"But our babe . . ."

"James, I'm strong. Our baby is strong. I know it. I wouldn't endanger a life I cherish so desperately!"

He cradled her against him, looking over her head to Jarrett and Tara helplessly. "What do I do?"

"Seems to me Teela knows her own mind," Jarrett said.

"And she is darned tough," Tara said.

"Amazingly so," Jarrett commented wryly.

James grabbed Teela by the arms, holding her from him, searching out the startling beauty of her eyes amidst the flaming sea of her hair.

"We may have to run night and day. We may starve. We may not be able to come close to any civilized society for years. We'll live and sleep in the woods and the swamp. You would do this . . . to be with me?"

She nodded.

"James, the more time you take . . ." Tara warned.

"You've got to hurry—one or both of you. Go around the back—take horses from the stables and ride quickly, for God's sake!" Jarrett said.

James took Teela's hand. "Well?" he challenged softly. Did she mean it? Would she run with a renegade, cast all hope of comfort and peace aside?

Perhaps not, for she was suddenly very still, holding pat when she might have followed him.

"Teela, I don't expect this of you!" he whispered quietly. "You are finally free of Warren. I will come back when I can. I will love our child—"

"Then say it to me."

"What?" he queried, confused. "I've just said I will love our child—"

Her chin lifted; her head was proudly high as she interrupted him. "Not the child, James. Me. I will go anywhere with you, James McKenzie, Running Bear. I will sleep in any forest, any swamp, and do so gladly. But just once, say it! Say that you love me!"

He offered her a very slow and crooked smile. He felt the breeze stir, and his heart suddenly lighten.

"I love you, Teela," he said softly. "I've been so afraid of the way that I love you, but I do. With all my heart, for all time. More than anything in the world. More than hatred, more than war, more than any of the pain that has blinded me. I love you. I need you. And I am not so sure that I can survive any more without you."

She smiled at last, closing her eyes in sheer bliss. "Oh, God!" she whispered. "I would follow you to hell were you to ask!"

"It might well be hell!" Jarrett said, interrupting the moment. "If you two don't get going."

James caught her hand, shaking his head once again. "Teela, still, you can not imagine the wilderness—"

"I have been there!"

"James!" Jarrett warned. "Once they come, Tara and I can buy you some time, but my God, you've got to let us try to get out the truth of all this."

"Go!" Tara pleaded.

Teela's eyes were on his, brilliant, determined. He thought that he would always remember her as she stood before him, hair wilder than any flame that had burned in the territory, her pride greater than that of any commander in the field of battle, her heart stronger than that of any warrior. Her beauty like that of the land, vivid as the sunset.

He took her hand.

"Let's get the horses!" he said. He glanced to his brother and sister-in-law, lifted a hand good-bye.

And together he and Teela began to run.

Chapter 27

It was nearly dawn when they left, and though James was worried about the strain he was putting on Teela, he knew that he had to put some distance between them and the city before full daylight.

He rode inland at a swift but controlled speed toward Palatka, determined to pick up supplies from caches along the way before heading farther south. He found a cabin that had been deserted early in the war, one out in a pine barren that could be reached only by those who knew the trails through the marshland. He told Teela they would rest there during the day before heading southward once again. A clear spring provided them with plenty of drinking water in a pretty, shaded copse.

When they had bathed their faces and drunk their fill, James told Teela that he'd fix her a bed in the old cabin where she could sleep until it was time for them to ride again.

She placed a hand on his arm. "James! I'm all right."

He shook his head, wincing. "I already know that this is madness. I shouldn't have brought you. You're not all right, you're expecting a child."

"Indian women have children."

"They are used to running."

"James!" On her knees she came to him, brought his hand to her heart. "Feel it! Feel the beat of it. It's strong, James. I'm strong."

He wound his fingers with hers, his hand still against the swollen softness of her breast. "Today we have shelter, and sweet, pure water. But we will travel where the

mosquitoes vie with the fleas for bites of human flesh.
We'll travel through swamp and slush, places where the
water rises to our knees, where the horses will bolt,
where—"

"James, I'm not afraid."

"You never seem to have the sense to be afraid," he
reminded her.

She smiled, hesitating. "James, I am alive when I am
with you. This life is more precious than any safety. I
am with you, I am not afraid. And at the moment I
am not tired. James, you said that you love me! You
did, remember?"

He nodded, a slow smile brightening his face despite
the situation. "I remember."

"You did mean it."

"I did."

"Then . . . show me."

"Teela . . ." He frowned, lifting his hands. "Teela,
we're in flight. You've cast your fate with a renegade, a
murderer—"

She placed a finger against his lips. "James, he would
have killed me, our child, and you, given the chance. He
stole everything of my father's. His cruelty brought
about the deaths of countless others. I don't want to
speak about him ever again. I want to forget cruelty and
hatred. I want to discover love."

"But, Teela . . . the babe!"

She stood, walking to the water's edge. With a slow,
leisurely sensuality she sat upon a rock, removing one
boot, then the other. Then her stockings, very slowly.
She glanced back at him, lips curving in a secret smile.
"Is the Indian boy McKenzie not quite the man he
thinks?"

He found himself on his feet, wondering at her ability
to provoke him.

And arouse him. Her clothing was making a pool at
her feet. Sturdy skirt and bodice, more fragile chemise,
petticoat, and pantalettes falling atop them. He paused,
even as the fire burned through him, staring at her as

she stood tall, totally naked and uninhibited by the spring's edge, as if she belonged there. Despite the porcelain quality of her flesh, its very white perfection, she was strong. And changed, of course, far rounder than even he had realized until now, yet somehow all the more sensual for it. She did appear the epitome of health, she was radiant. Her pregnancy seemed to add to both her strength and her beauty.

"The Indian boy may just manage all right," he drawled, and started moving toward her.

Teela smiled and executed a swift dive into the water, delighting in the feel of it. The weather was perfect with fall, warm without being brutal, the water cool from beneath the earth's surface, refreshing and exotic against her flesh. She cut across it swiftly, glad that she had learned to swim with such graceful ease, grateful that in this element she was James's equal.

Yet as she reached the center and spun around, seeking him, she frowned, for he was nowhere in sight. She cast her face up to catch rays of light striking through the green leaves of the trees above. She felt a hard tug on her feet, inhaled deeply, and went slicing downward through the water, only to meet James beneath its surface. His body slid along hers, hot as a flame, hard as rock. His mouth formed over hers, his kiss a deeper heat. His hands began to move over her. Touching her. Her breasts. Her hips, rounding around them, pressing her closer. His mouth lifted from hers, allowing her to shoot above the water's surface once again to breathe, to drag in air . . .

Yet he stayed below the surface, his kiss a liquid flame that undulated with the wave and twist and movement of the water, touching her. Here . . . lower . . . there . . . everywhere.

She tried to struggle, tried to drag him to her. Finally she shot beneath the surface again herself, catching him, dragging him back against her. He slipped an arm around her, pulling her back to the grass and mud embankment, barely bringing them out of the water before

he was atop her again, his intimate kisses stoked by the
breeze that waved over the slickness of their wet bodies,
creating erotic sensation atop erotic sensation. He teased
her unmercifully, tantalized, until she cried out in their
strange, abandoned pine haven, and still he stroked,
kissed, teased . . . cherished her. And when she thought
at last that the searing fires within her would never be
satisfied, he rose above her, brushing her lips, whispering, "I love you, I love you, I love you, Teela, I love
you . . ."

Just that and nothing more.

And it was everything.

He was gentle, gentler than she had ever known him
to be, yet making love had never brought her a greater,
sweeter satisfaction. He lay with her long past the time
when the fury of climax had seized them both, and his
words were still soft, tender.

"I love you, Teela."

He wanted her to sleep, to rest. She did so. When she
awoke, twilight was almost upon them. To the west the
sun was setting, a giant orb in crimson, crashing into the
earth with rays spilling from it in fantastic colors. Teela
rose upon her elbows, just watching the colors. She realized that James was awake beside her, watching it as
well.

"My God, it's breathtaking. The most beautiful sunset
I've ever seen."

"The world itself is simply more beautiful today," he
told her.

She flashed him a quick smile.

"Oh, God!" he exclaimed, and she looked into the
crystal blue fire of his eyes, smiled, and found herself
drawn back into his arms, the heat of his body, fierce
now against the coming of night. His lips bathed her
breasts, the tip of his tongue laving over her nipples,
creating sensation she could scarcely bear. His mouth
then hovered over hers.

She caressed his face, lowered her hands down the

lean muscle and sinew of his body. Stroked his sex. Met his lips again.

Dimly, with her peripheral vision, she was aware of a great blue heron suddenly shooting out of the water, toward the sunset. She felt that she flew with it, that she felt the red and the gold and the fire of the sunset.

And with it she sweetly burned.

As he had warned her, the days grew harder.

Sometimes they passed Indian lands, and he would not light a fire lest they draw down the wrath of the Seminole bands.

Worse, sometimes he was convinced that they were near white troops. Upon occasion he would leave her resting in a copse and ride out.

When they had been on the trail a few weeks, he returned one afternoon to tell her that he was afraid they were following a large body of Indian troops—as well as a large movement of soldiers.

"Jesup has been planning a pincer movement. We've known that. I've known that, the Seminoles have known it. Fortunately, the army regulars are the least familiar with the terrain down here," he said. He'd caught a rabbit that day and determined that it would be all right that afternoon to light a cooking fire.

Though Teela had admittedly found the trail harder and harder—one afternoon the mosquitoes had been so bad that she pleaded that they ride rather than rest— she had also learned to manage rather well. There were many abandoned Indian camps, and occasionally there were crops to be discovered that had never been harvested.

There were the ruins of plantations as well. They offered cooking utensils, salt, sugar, and spices upon occasion. Sometimes they discovered blankets, bullets, and medical supplies. She knew how to fashion a bed at night from a simple tarp that would keep her warm and dry and, for the most part, the insects away.

Sometimes they traveled ground where even James was wary of dangerous snakes.

Yet though it was hard going, Teela was amazed to discover just how happy she was. If only they could live without the fear that he could be hanged at any time, she didn't think she'd care if she ever had more than what they did simply traveling with each other.

That would change, of course, with the baby.

She was fascinated more and more by the movements their son or daughter made, and though James would smile and laugh with her, he would often seem his most worried after such occasions, lying on his back, staring up at the sky. He would talk about Jennifer then, about how he missed her.

And how he had wronged her.

And Teela would tell him, naturally, that he had not, that Jennifer was well, a loving child. If she suffered from the world around her, she did so because she was very mature for her tender years. They wove dreams about a place where they would live one day, all of them, Jennifer, the new baby, James and Teela.

"Jennifer is more Seminole than I am, and this baby will hardly have Indian blood at all, yet ..."

"Yet?"

He rolled to her. "One drop of Indian blood can create a red man—*less* a man—to many whites."

"But there are those who know that there are no barriers between men, and they will be our friends."

"You live in a fantasy world."

"There is no other."

Now, after he had scouted the countryside for both soldiers and Seminoles, and snared the rabbit, he told her that he was convinced that they were riding parallel with a large body of the army and several bands of Indians.

"Should we stop and let them pass us?" Teela asked. She could expertly skin a rabbit, and she was proud of herself as she spitted the nicely plump creature and roasted it slowly and evenly over James's fire.

He shook his head. "I was thinking of getting past them," he told her.

She agreed. They ate. They lay together watching the stars.

It poured that night. A violent rain with slashing lightning and pounding thunder. It was barely midnight when the weather became so vicious that they dared travel no farther. There was no way to keep dry.

James sought shelter, but there was little to be found. He quickly built a hootie with what supplies he had, but after a few hours, the ground began to flood. He took to the trees, holding Teela against him. Toward morning, the rain stopped. She slept against his arms.

There were vicious bug bites against her neck and breasts. She never mentioned them, she never complained. Her flesh was warm. He was afraid the rain had given her a fever. He laid his head back against the tree, damning himself for having brought her with him. She awakened, her eyes bright, her smile warm. "I love you," she told him.

He smiled. Kissed her. "I love you, too," he whispered, and damned himself again. He loved her, but he risked her very life with every day that they rode.

"Do you know what?" she asked him softly.

"What?"

"It's Christmas."

"And you are in a savage wilderness where there is no belief in Christ."

"It is the first Christmas in years in which I will be able to awake completely happy."

"And sick," he worried as she sneezed.

"James, I have been sick in Charleston as well."

"I have nothing to give you."

"At this moment I have everything."

He eased her from him, leapt from the tree, and helped her down. "We've traveled too slowly so far. I've been afraid to go faster," he told her. "Jarrett and I have kept cabins on the bay property my father left us. If we can just reach it . . ."

"Fine. Well, move more quickly."

That afternoon, they came around a trail that skirted Lake Okeechobee. James reined in his horse, looking around uncomfortably.

"What is it?" Teela demanded.

"Indians." He pointed at hoofprints she could barely make out before them. "Horses . . . unshod. Lots of them. Then, there . . . prints from skin boots. There are a lot—I mean a lot!—of Seminoles very near us." He stared at her suddenly. "I'm taking you to the copse right up there. Stay there, no matter what, until I come for you."

"But, James—"

"Teela, you must. I don't know what we've stumbled upon. Please, no stubborn action, listen to me this once. Swear it."

"I—swear it. But where will you—"

"I've got to find out what's going on."

For once Teela didn't argue with him. He found her high, secluded ground within a hammock near the lake, and in that ground he found an old oak with perfect, sprawling branches where she could await him. He kissed her lightly when he prepared to leave her; she drew him back, clinging to him.

He took a silver amulet from around his neck, setting it around hers. "I am not in danger here, but you may be. I'm taking the horse away so that no one will find you, though this piece of silver should keep anyone who wished you harm from hurting you. But, Teela, if you stay in that tree and are not seen, I can promise that no one will harm you, so do as I say."

"Yes," she whispered. "James?"

"Please . . . remember, it is Christmas. You be careful. Let your life be your present to me, please!"

He held her again, then helped her up within the tree, hurrying to his horse immediately before he could delay further. About a half mile from Teela, he tethered her horse in a pine copse. Then he followed the trail of hoofprints until he came to a clearing where he halted, suddenly aware of just what they had stumbled upon.

In the whole of the theater of war as he had known it, nothing had ever appeared so big; nor had Indians ever prepared so carefully for battle. The lake was to the rear, a high hammock just in front of it. In front of the hammock, mud, mush, and saw grass stretched in all directions. Some of the saw grass had been mown down to allow for clearer rifle fire. Even as he stared at the field before him, he saw movement to his left. Dismounting from his horse, he silently pursued the movement, catching up with a breech clout-clad Indian and tumbling him to the ground. Straddling the young warrior, he saw that it was Racoon, a young man of Coacoochee's tribe.

"Running Bear! You've come to fight!" the boy exclaimed with surprise. "I thought you were a solider. I am to lead them here. There are many. Another commander comes against us. Zachary Taylor. Wildcat says that he is the general that he will best!"

"Wildcat fights, who else?" James demanded.

"Arpeika—you know, Sam Jones. And Alligator is here with his warriors. We are nearly five hundred in number."

Startled, James arched a brow. "What of the white troops? I know they've come this way. How many?"

"Over a thousand, we believe. But it doesn't matter. We will kill them as they cross the swamp. Blood will mingle with the mud."

James crawled off the boy, helping him up. He looked at the sky in time to see that the sun was already up. It had to be around noon.

He heard the sudden sound of fire and turned.

They were coming, indeed.

The soldiers were making a frontal attack despite the swampland and saw grass they would have to traverse. Guns were loaded, guns were fired. Horses couldn't possibly navigate the swamp, and the men came on foot.

Out of the hammock the Indians responded. They fired their weapons in return.

They let out their terrible war cry. *Yohoehee . . . yohoehee . . .*

The sound of it was enough to make skin crawl. "Get out of the line of fire, Racoon!" James commanded the boy.

"I'm not afraid—"

"Then live to be free!" James commanded him. "Go!"

The young man started slipping through the saw grass. James saw the first ranks of the soldiers draw in, fall back, regroup.

Another regiment was brought forward. Traversing the swamp. Firing, stopping, reloading, firing, stopping . . .

Falling, bleeding, dying . . .

James fell back, watching the action, hurrying for his horse. He mounted, moving more quickly as he realized that another regiment was being sent in to attack on the right wing.

Watching the way that the soldiers moved around, James realized that there would be hand-to-hand combat all around the hammock.

Even in the high ground where he had left Teela.

Teela heard the first gunfire and nearly leapt down from the oak. James had told her to stay. He knew how to fight. He knew how not to die. She had to obey his command in this.

Yet the fire came closer, closer. She heard men shouting, first in Muskogee. She had learned some words but not enough to begin to understand what was being said. And the voices were excited, fast . . .

Screams. There were screams as bullets found their marks. There seemed to be quiet for a while, and then . . .

More fire. And the awful, hair-raising shrieks of the warriors as they cried out before an attack.

Near her, she suddenly heard English.

"Careful now, men, we've been cut off. To the high ground, use the trees for cover. Reload and prepare to fire at my command!"

To her amazement, she knew the voice, knew it well.

She knew the tall, harried, muddied, dirtied, even bloodied young man who suddenly led a dozen men into the
copse directly beneath her.

John Harrington.

His men quickly scampered into position, pausing to
load their breech-loading weapons with uncanny speed
for the action required, teeth ripping into powder bags,
the slide of metal against metal as they tamped down
their shot.

Suddenly, the Seminole war cry was let out again.
Teela nearly froze in her tree, then gasped back a
scream of horror as naked, painted Indians came flying
toward the hammock.

She heard a roar of fire; three Indians went down.
Another roar of fire . . .

Three Indians behind the first to arrive had awaited
their chance to fire.

A boy below Teela shrieked, struck in the shoulder.
John swore vehemently, hit in the arm. Another soldier
fell without a word or a whimper.

The Indians were all over the copse. The combat was
hand-to-hand, the soldiers fighting desperately with bayonets, swords, knives . . . even using their rifle butts as
clubs. The Indians kept coming.

The soldiers fought bravely. Indians and white men
fell together.

John stood before the oak, shouting a command to
his men. "Retreat, behind me, eastward toward the main
body of troops. Men, march!" he roared.

Those still standing did as he commanded. Two of the
remaining Indians chased them.

Two of them stared at John, smiling slowly. John, with
only one good arm, raised his rifle high like a club. He
faced certain death.

He began to waver, then he fell.

The Indians let out one of their hideous, bone-chilling
cries, and started for him.

Teela didn't think, she reacted, slipping from the tree
in desperate horror. She threw herself over John's fallen

body, rising to meet the startled eyes of the two warriors
men she'd never seen before. Terror filled her, and sh
wondered at her own reckless action, for it seemed tha
not only would they finish off John, but they would kil
and scalp her as well.

"No!" she cried out, leaping to her feet, warily keep
ing her place in front of Harrington's fallen body.

John began to come to, struggling up. "Teela! Teela
for the love of God, the savages will kill you! How ca
you be here? I must be dead already."

"You're not dead! Shush!"

She lifted from her chest the amulet James had give
her, showing it to them. To her amazement, they paused
Then one came forward, fingering the silver crescent
She held her breath in terror as they spoke to eac
other. Yet when one voice grew loud and she recoiled
there was a sudden thunder upon the ground.

James burst into the clearing on his horse, leaping
from it, surging forward, his knife aimed at the chests o
the men who would accost her. He shouted somethin
in his Muskogee language, fierce, commanding. H
moved the knife, showing the men they must leave.

His words were so harsh! Yet she felt him shaking a
he held her, drew her back, forced her behind him. Joh
staggered to his feet. "James, my friend, get Teela ou
of here—"

One of the Indians lunged at James. He shoved Teel
hard back to John, ducking the blow that was comin
his way. He slammed the Indian in the gut, then lifte
him over his head, throwing him against the tree. Th
man crashed to the ground, either dead or unconsciou

The second Indian let out a cry and came flying a
James. He braced for him, half stepping aside and lettin
the man's own impetus bring him down hard to th
earth. A fierce knife battle followed with the two o
them rolling. Teela grabbed up John's rifle, shaking a
she loaded it, then discovered she was unable to tak
aim at the moving, confusing target.

But then the battle suddenly ceased with an awfu

sound. The warrior let out a howl, and Teela realized that James had broken the man's arm to force him to relinquish his knife. James leapt up, shouting at the warrior as he dragged him back to his feet, and let him go. After a moment of stunned disbelief, the wounded brave turned, disappearing into the brush.

"You saved my life, both of you," John whispered, falling against the oak. From there he fell to the ground again, unconscious, almost on top of the fallen Indian.

"You left the tree!" James roared at Teela.

"I had to, James! They would have killed John."

James fell to his knees beside his white friend. Teela came down beside him. "He was wounded in the arm, then he passed out. He's lost a terrible amount of blood."

"Let me rip up your hem ..."

"I've still some sulfur left if you can clear the wound and we can see the damage."

James had the strength to rip John's uniform and clear the arm. Teela tenderly ascertained that the bone hadn't been shattered or chipped, and between them they fixed a tourniquet to stanch the flow of blood.

"What did you say to them?" Teela demanded. "How did you get them to leave?"

"I told them that the soldiers were coming."

"How brilliant."

"How true."

Teela leapt up, staring from him to John. "Oh, God, what do we do? We can't just leave him here. What if they do go on by him? What if they don't find him? He'll die without immediate care!"

"Yes, he'll die."

"But ... but we've got to go ..."

"We're not going," he said firmly.

"What?" Teela cried with incredulous alarm. "Oh, you are a madman! We have to figure out something else. You can't be taken. We must go, we must go—"

A madman? He might be one, James knew, but he had suddenly—and very determinedly—made his decision.

"No, we're not leaving. I'm sorry, my love. We both

know that we cannot leave John to die. And there is
more."

"What more?" she whispered.

"I'm hurting you, Teela. I'm hurting our unborn child."

"But—"

"I cannot do so anymore. It isn't that I wish to make
my home anywhere else. I just don't wish to run any
more. Once I felt that running was my only chance. Even
with Osceola gone, the Indian chiefs know that I am not
their enemy, and more—they know that I am worth far
more alive than dead, and I do not betray my promises.
Now I intend to stand my ground with the whites. War
ren is dead. And I am innocent of the accusations that
have been made against me."

"But," Teela cried, "you still remain accused of terrible
deeds, and we stand in the middle of a battleground—"

"And I will stand before those who accuse me and
show everyone that their words are lies."

"James," Teela whispered. "You will still be judged!
You can't know—"

"But I can *believe*," he told her very quietly. "Because
of *you*," he assured her softly, "I can believe. Believe
that there is justice in men, and that the justice in them
isn't dependent on their color."

She appeared stricken. He pulled her closer. "I will
make a life for us, Teela. I will prove myself. I believe
because of you. Now you have to believe in me again.
Believe that I can be as strong in your world, against
your *civilized* savagery, as I can be in the wild."

She stared at him and slowly smiled. She came up on
her toes to kiss him. *"I believe!"* she whispered. "Oh,
God, yes, *I believe*!"

And even as she did so, they heard the sounds of
hoofbeats.

Soldiers were coming.

"Call them, Teela!" he commanded her softly.

"I believe!" she whispered again. Then loudly she
called out, summoning the soldiers to John's aid.

Chapter 28

Though the Battle of the Okeechobee could hardly be called a conclusive victory, the day's commander, Zachary Taylor, fairly new to the Florida war, would receive accolades for the action, and more—military advancement.

It was one of the largest battles, since the Indians had learned, from the beginning, that they hadn't the superior numbers, and striking quickly and disappearing into the bush usually gave them far more success. They had thought they had a battleground on which they could win. In the end, however, their flank had been broken. Still, they had caused more casualties to the whites than they had sustained themselves, and therefore, though the soldiers had made quite a haul in captives and Indian cattle, the engagement was at best a stand off.

John had come to in good time, telling those who found him that James had not been among the Indians, but had fought to save his life. Joshua Brandeis was on hand in the field hospital where John was brought. While James's fate was still in the air, he discovered himself helping with the wounded along with Teela.

He was surprised to find himself treated not just well, but with respect by the majority of the commanders and the soldiers. He met with Hernandez and Zachary Taylor, who assured him he would have a fair hearing in St. Augustine.

"One thing, Mr. McKenzie," Taylor told him.

"Yes, sir?"

"You might do well for yourself to marry Miss Warren

in a Christian ceremony before coming to a hearing. Do
you have a problem with such a ceremony, sir?"

"I? Not in the least. Most especially if the lady is
willing."

Apparently, Teela wasn't informed as to why she was
being brought from the hospital to the command tent,
because she entered with a very anxious expression. Her
relief was such that when a stern Zachary Taylor asked
her if she was willing to marry one James McKenzie, er
known to be the father of her expected child, she began
to pass out.

James caught her. "Would you have them hang me
on the spot?" he teased her, fanning her awake.

"Marriage . . . James! We'll really be married?"

"Once you agree to the ceremony."

"Oh, I agree."

The regimental chaplain came in, a lean, kindly man
who believed in God's good will to all men. They were
married quietly and quickly, and allowed to engage in a
long kiss that brought a swift barrage of applause from
all present. Then—under the circumstances—Teela went
back to the hospital, and James was again under guard.

Finally, they returned to St. Augustine. And on the
day James came before the military commanders for his
hearing, he was ready to speak in a way that he prayed
would be honest to all that he was, to the mother he
still loved and the father he had adored. The brother
who would be his ally for life.

And now his wife. His expected child. His daughter.
Even his memories of Naomi.

"Before I was born, my father came to this land, came
to live among her people. They welcomed him here, they
gave him solace for the loss of a beloved wife he grieved.
Gentlemen, I've heard it claimed that the Seminoles are
not native to this land any more than the white man,
and therefore there should be no hesitance on behalf of
the white citizenry to cast us out. There you are wrong.
For when my father came to Creek country, our people

had already been running south for a century, already running from the white man.

"Some white men have always come to learn; some men come to take. By my birth, I am saddled with the horror and trauma of this war. It is not hatred of either side that drives me, but rather, it is love for both. When war broke out, I felt as if a stake began to be driven into my heart, for at the very beginning I felt as if I was doomed within the conflict of the two worlds. There was only one way to survive it, and that was to follow my own conscience. It is true that I have refused to take up arms against any Indians, but it is equally true that I never joined with any band to attack my brother's people. I consider myself a friend to such war chiefs as Osceola; I have also met with many of you at my brother's home, and there are among you many I call friends. I've heard some whisper that I came here today to beg for mercy; I have not. I have come to demand justice. I was innocent of the massacre outside Fort Deliverance— my only action there was to save my wife's life. And though I admit to having caused the death of Major Michael Warren, I plead extenuating circumstances. A dozen witnesses can tell you that I killed the man in self-defense."

He stood in a makeshift military courtroom between St. Augustine and Fort Deliverance. General Jesup himself—as sad and weary-looking as an old bulldog—sat at the table before him along with General Hernandez, Captain Morrison, and a young military lawyer named Lieutenant Pete Harding. John Harrington, bandaged to the gills, had been brought in on a litter.

General Jesup had ordered the proceedings closed, but somehow word of the hearing had gotten out, and despite Jesup's greatest determination, the room was filled with not just military men but citizenry down from St. Augustine and a host of newspaper reporters. When James stopped speaking, he could hear the sounds of lead pencils moving over paper as sketch artists captured his likeness.

He had decided to don his customary apparel, indicative of all that he was, European-cut trousers, boots, headband, and a silver medallion Osceola had given him years before, the same medallion he had given Teela to wear to keep her from harm. Jarrett had reminded him that he meant to prove he could fight in a white world, and he had somewhat amended his appearance, adding a frock coat and white shirt to the mixture and queueing his hair back. He knew he was an articulate speaker, and he knew that he was capable of presenting a good appearance. Yet more than anything he might do for himself, he believed that Jesup's current difficulties would weigh in his favor.

The press had ripped into the man. Many whites who previously might have decried the savagery of the Seminoles were appalled that Jesup had taken Osceola beneath a truce flag. There had been an outcry across the country, one that was continuing even as this hearing went on.

"I demand justice, as justice is my right. But to receive it I will not promise to seek out Indian leaders like a bloodhound; nor will I betray those who come to me for help. Just the same, gentlemen, neither will I ever betray a white confidence or friendship, as I believe many here will testify. Gentlemen, my fate is in your hands. My soul remains my own."

He ceased to speak. For a moment there was absolute silence in the room. Then there was chaos.

Before he had spoken, he had been accused of both the murder and the massacre. Jarrett had spoken in his defense, and the young soldier Noonan had done likewise, as had the survivors of Otter's massacre against the whites. Still, he knew that his life had rested in his own hands, and it was thus that the crowd now shouted and went wild. He had friends in the room.

He hoped he had enough.

Jesup banged upon the table, shouting for order. He conferred briefly with those around him, then rose.

He opened his mouth as if to give a long lecture, then seemed to decide against it.

"As to the matter of the death of Major Michael Warren, there will be no charges brought against James McKenzie, as we deem the incident justifiable self-defense—Major Warren had no authority to hang anyone. As to the matter of the military attack outside Fort Deliverance, we deem Mr. McKenzie completely innocent. Due to the fact that Mr. McKenzie's father was a white man with legal title to property within the state, we can hardly suggest that he leave the territory. Therefore, Mr. McKenzie, you are free to come or go as you should choose."

Again there was chaos. He heard a shriek, a cry of happiness, and had to ease his way through a congratulating crowd to reach his wife.

Wife . . .

The word was sweet to him.

She threw herself into his arms, kissed him before the crowd. There were reporters all around them, wanting to know everything. What had Teela's relationship been with her stepfather? What did she think of the war, of Jesup's capture of the chief, Osceola . . . ?

"I think," she informed them charmingly, "that my husband would like to see his daughter."

Jarrett and Tara were there, doing their best to get through the crowd. Despite the fact that his brother had just been freed, Jarrett seemed somewhat somber. When the four of them had cleared the courtroom, Jarrett quickly led them to their carriage. Tara kissed James and hugged Teela. Jarrett embraced his brother and promised champagne as soon as they reached the house in St. Augustine.

It felt good to be in his brother's rented home. Not that the place mattered; what was good was that he had family again. Jarrett and Tara were with him, Ian, and for once now, against so much time of separation, he could be with Jennifer. She was a beautiful child, her eyes such a perfect soft hazel as her mother's had been, her skin a light burnished copper, her hair rich and thick and with a McKenzie wave. Jennifer was growing to be everything Teela had said, beautiful and loving. She had scarcely let him go since he had come to the house.

And then there was Teela. The woman who put everything together for him. Teela, with a capacity to love that knew no boundaries of color or creed, and allowed no obstacle to defeat it.

And soon the family would be larger. Ian would have a little sister or brother, as would Jennifer.

Jarrett waited until late at night, then met James in the library.

"Everything seems perfect today," James said, raising a brandy snifter to him. "Thank you."

Jarrett nodded, smiling with a crooked twist. "I wish things were perfect."

James sat forward, his heart thundering. "Mary—"

"Your mother is fine. I've told you that."

"You didn't lie?"

"James—"

"Of course you wouldn't," James said. "Then—"

"I've taken the liberty of arranging a trip for us to Charleston."

"Charleston? Is someone in your family ill? Is there a problem with Teela's property—"

"Osceola has been taken there, to Fort Moultrie, along with a number of the Seminole prisoners. He is near death, James. He has asked for you."

The end was very near. James was well aware of that fact from the time he came into the room where Osceola lay dying. Osceola was aware of his own impending death; he had been aware of it for a long time, and now knew that it was nearly upon him. He was dressed in his finery—magnificent feathers adorned his turban and dress; rows of silver medallions were displayed down the length of his chest.

James slowly approached the chief, thinking that Osceola might have already breathed his last, but he had not. He must have sensed James there, and he summoned the energy to open his eyes, and even to smile before he closed them again. He lifted a finger, indicating James should sit at his side, and James did so, taking his hand.

"Not a death for a warrior, eh, my friend?" Osceola asked softly.

"Death comes as rest for a great warrior who has led his people in a quest for freedom."

"A weary man."

So many people had died. White, red, black. Osceola's grip was suddenly very strong, like the handshake many Seminoles had learned to offer the whites they had befriended. Osceola had been known at one time for such a hardy grip, taking a man's arm firmly, nearly jerking it from the socket in a determined shake. Osceola had killed many men, befriended many men. He remained an enigma even to James in many ways. He was ready for death. A warrior who knew death well. Yet James clenched his teeth hard, fighting the sudden pain in his heart that stung hot fire behind his eyes.

"Artists—white artists—have come to paint me, you know," Osceola said. His eyes remained closed, his lips curled into a smile. "Many men. I have posed for them all. I liked the one they called Caitlin the best. He is familiar with many Indians, many different places. He interested me."

James nodded. "Your likeness will be everywhere."

Osceola opened his eyes again. "I have heard about the newspapers. They call Jesup a treacherous man, a coward, for the way that I was taken."

"Yes, there are many whites furious with what happened. Many who find you noble and courageous. That's why so many men have come to sketch and paint you."

"He thought that the war would be over when I was gone," Osceola said. "But it will not be over. Young warriors grow to men. The mosquitoes may best the white men in the end. There are places we can go they cannot follow. But I will be dead. I will not be a part of it."

James tightened his hold on Osceola's arm. "You will be the greatest part of it. You are famous, even among the whites. They will see your picture, and they will know for eternity that you were a proud warrior, brought in only by the use of treachery. You will live on forever."

"I will die undefeated," Osceola said, and James thought that he saw the trickle of tears beneath his dark lashes.

"Undefeated. But you will not die, Osceola. To the whites and the Indians, you will live on. You are even now a legend among all the people. Even in death you will be a great warrior. Men throughout history will remember your name."

Osceola was silent, pleased with his friend's words. He squeezed James's hand. "And you, my friend? The war is over for me. What will it be for you?"

James sighed softly. "It is over for me, too. I had thought I could help. I cannot."

"You will leave Florida? Become a white man?"

"I don't know what I will do right now. I have married—"

"The wild, red-haired white vixen, Warren's daughter. So I have heard. Had she been a part of this war, we might have been beaten long ago!"

"Except that she doesn't wish to beat us," James said.

"But she is your wife; you have killed Warren, and a child is due. So what does this mean?"

"I don't know yet. Maybe I will stay here, in Charleston, for a while. Or perhaps I will go home."

"Ah, but will you live happily among the whites where battle still rages?"

"I'd go south. Jarrett and I own property down in the southeast section of the territory."

"Near Fort Dallas? There are soldiers there."

"And bands of Seminoles nearby. I don't believe there will be much conflict because it is so remote, and because they will have to keep their eyes on each other. Maybe, sometimes, I will still be able to intercede on occasion."

"Maybe. Hmm. So the whites have set you free." Once again Osceola's large dark eyes opened gravely on James. "And you may go home."

"And I may stay here."

"You will go home, I think." He smiled. "You are very eloquent, Running Bear. You always have been. I heard you were quite magnificent in court. That though your life was at stake, still you defended our people. The war may be over for you. You can fight no more, for there is no battle you can win. You are a man with integrity. You have found your own heart and soul once again. Don't ever look back, my friend. You were a true friend to us all. We never bested you, and neither did the whites. Like me, my good friend, like many of our people, you have remained among the undefeated. Now go, Running Bear. Leave me to my wives and family. Go to your new wife and your new home. And in the years to come, help create a world where we all can live."

"Osceola—"

"Go now. You have made my heart glad."

James rose and left the room. Wheedon nodded to him, and reentered the room, along with one of Osceola's Seminole priests and his younger wife and one of his baby daughters.

Past the antechamber, in the walled hallway, he found Teela waiting for him. She arched a brow at him and nodded when he shook his head. They walked in silence from the fort to the water, and there waited in silence again for the navy boat scheduled to take them back to Charleston.

When they reached the Battery, they walked, looking out on the fort on the water, feeling the breeze pick up and blow around them.

"I don't think he can live another twenty-four hours," he said at last.

She slipped an arm around him. "I'm sorry, for I know you loved him."

"I loved him," James said softly. "Some will mourn him more deeply than I will—and some may very well be glad that he is gone. Some of the chiefs have resented his rise to power, and blamed him for much of the misery the Indians have suffered. What no one has realized as yet is that the war will go on with an ever greater fervor. Osceola will become legend to the red men and the white. Wildcat will fight on, Arpeika—the white men call him old Sam Jones—will fight on. If they are caught, the tribes who have already run deeply into the Everglades will fight on." He turned to her suddenly. "The question is *you*. Us. What do we do? Our child is due soon. This is your city." He turned, indicating Charleston with a sweep of his arm. "It's beautiful. Cultured, with such lovely homes. So many conveniences . . ."

She smiled. "You would never be happy here."

"I have friends here. Jarrett's mother's family are wonderful people—"

"You would never be happy here."

"Our babe is due in perhaps eight weeks—"

"I love Charleston, and will always love Charleston, and yes, it is a beautiful city, and we own a beautiful home here. I will want to visit, and we'll have to come and keep up the plantation. One of our children will want it one day, or if we no longer want to keep it, we'll want to make a profit on it. But I want to go home."

"*You* are home."

She shook her head. She smiled softly. "Not anymore, I'm not. Have you ever made love in the water? On an evening just at the time that sunset is coming? When the sun itself is like a golden orb, almost within reach yet sinking on the horizon in a mist of crimson and mauve, orange and yellow? Have you felt the breeze beneath the palms at that time . . . heard the sway of them, watched a pure white egret fly across the sun's reflection in the water . . . ? James, home is where you are, where we found each other, where our dreams lie, where we'll create our own life."

"But, Teela," he said, lifting his hands, "I've told you, the war will not end."

"And what will that matter, since, at the least, the battle is over between us?"

He laughed softly, turning against the breeze to cradle her against him. "Now, in truth, I'm not so sure that war will actually end, either, seeing that you are incredibly hardheaded and stubborn and—"

"Ah, but my love! How else does one deal with a savage?" she interrupted, pressing against his chest to stare into his eyes with her demand.

He began to laugh again.

And he knew that though his life might continue to be rich with conflict, it would be rich.

And it would be sweet.

Because with Teela, it was love that would always remain undefeated.

Epilogue

Southeastern Florida, 1842

John Harrington rode along the beach, picking his way around small tree stumps, trying to keep his mount walking along the hard-packed sand.

He had come to the right place. Through an endless trail of pines he could see the house in the distance, a one-story structure built strong from what they were now calling Dade County pine—since this was now a county, and it had been named after Major Francis Dade and the pine was exceptionally fine and durable. It was a wonderful home, not as lavish as Cimarron, but as comfortable in a different way. The kitchen was inside, and the first room opening off from it was a huge dining area. The family ate there, and welcomed travelers to this remote area while the children could play and be seen at all times.

"John!"

Jennifer, now a very mature and willowy girl nearly eleven years old, called to him. She was sitting on a pine stump with a book, watching over her little brothers Jerome, now nearly five, Brent, three and a half, and sister, baby Sydney, almost two, laughing away as she threaded sand through her fingers.

"Ah, 'tis the lot of you McKenzies!" John said, happily dismounting from his horse. He hugged Jennifer, offered her an elegant ivory-handled comb that caused her to squeal with delight, then gave the boys little drum sets and little Sydney a doll.

"John," Jennifer said, the lady of the house now, "the presents are lovely, but you know, we are desperate for news these days . . ."

"Well, the news is this. The war is over. Worth—the general in charge now—says that it is over."

Jennifer gasped, delighted. Then she sobered. "Have—have my people *surrendered*?"

The war years had been brutal. Osceola had died on January 31, 1838, then lived on to become legend, and though Congress had fought and politicians had screamed about costs and the Americans at large had been outraged at times, the battles had gone on and on. Zachary Taylor had taken the reins from a weary and disgusted Jesup. Walker Keith Armistead had followed Zachary Taylor, and then William Jenkins Worth had come in.

Many Indians had been forced west. Even fierce, flamboyant Wildcat had come in at last and talked others into taking the trail west. But others had stayed.

Others would never leave.

Something called the Armed Occupation Act, by which Congress had allotted huge quantities of Florida land to those who would settle on it, had kept the population of the peninsula soaring, despite the small but fierce battles that had continued on long after the big battle at Okeechobee.

And now . . .

Well, there hadn't been a major battle, no fanfare at the end. The last of the Indians had not surrendered. It had just been declared over.

John smiled at Jennifer. "No, sweetheart, your people have not surrendered. Your grandma's band is still south, and Mary herself says she'll be here in time for your next birthday. It's just . . . come to an end. Your dad will understand, I think. Know where he and Teela are?"

"They took a walk to the lagoon. My father was gone for a while, to see my grandmother's people. Then he stopped by the settlement near Fort Dallas for some supplies. He hasn't been home very long, and Teela asked if I'd watch the children for them." She said it with grave maturity. John lowered his head to hide his smile.

"The lagoon?"

"Yes. You'll stay for dinner? I'll tell Cook."

"Yes, I'll stay for dinner."

He walked around the house toward the sunken lagoon that lay to the rear of the property. James hadn't built on the bay but on an inland waterway, with wonderful little shallow inlets on the western side of it.

He rounded the corner, then heard her laughter.

He stood very still.

Teela stood upon a tree stump above the aqua water of the lagoon, naked, red hair flaming in a wet fall so long it nearly made her lack of apparel somehow decent. He felt his heart lunge a bit, yet not so badly now, for, with the war over, he was going to marry a girl he'd met in Tampa recently and, he hoped, buy a piece of land from James and bring her here.

This area was the future! Just because no one else saw it yet didn't mean that it wasn't so!

Again the laughter, jolting him back to the present.

"Jump!" he heard James call. Pitch black hair, ebony against his copper features, James stood in the shallow water, commanding her to come down to him. As naked as his wife, he remained as tautly, strongly built as ever. The two of them seemed to refuse to age.

"Jump! What if you don't catch me?"

"And when have I not?"

She smiled.

"Come on, jump!" he encouraged.

She did so, landing perfectly in his waiting arms.

"I believe!" she whispered to him.

He kissed her.

John Harrington smiled and quickly, quietly turned away, hurrying back toward the house.

Dinner would be plenty of time to talk.

Florida Chronology

1492	Christopher Columbus discovers the New World.
1513	Florida discovered by Ponce de Leon. Juan Ponce de Leon sights Florida from his ship on March 27, steps on shore near present-day St. Augustine in early April.
1539	Hernando de Soto lands-on west coast of the peninsula, near present-day Tampa.
1564	The French arrive and establish Fort Caroline on the St. Johns River.
	Immediately following the establishment of the French fort, Spain dispatches Pedro de Menendez to get rid of the French invaders, "pirates and perturbers of the public peace." Menendez dutifully captures the French stronghold and slays or enslaves the inhabitants.
1565	Pedro de Menendez founds St. Augustine, the first permanent European settlement in what is now the United States.
1586	Sir Francis Drake attacks St. Augustine, burning and plundering the settlement.
1698	Pensacola is founded.
1740	British General James Oglethorpe invades Florida from Georgia.
1763	At the end of the Seven Years' War, or the French and Indian War, both the East and West Florida territories are ceded to Britain.
1763–1783	British rule in East and West Florida.

1774	The "shot heard 'round the world" is fired in Concord.
1776	The War of Independence begins; many British Loyalists flee to Florida.
1783	By the Treaty of Paris, Florida is returned to the Spanish.
1812–1815	The War of 1812.
1813–1814	The Creek Wars. "Red-Stick" land is decimated. Numerous Indians seek new lands south with the "Seminoles."
1814	General Andrew Jackson captures Pensacola.
1815	The Battle of New Orleans.
1817–1818	The First Seminole War. Americans accuse the Spanish of aiding the Indians in their raids across the border. Hungry for more territory, settlers seek to force Spain into ceding the Floridas to the United States by their claims against the Spanish government for its inability to properly handle the situation within the territories.
1819	Don Luis de Onis, Spanish minister to the United States, and Secretary of State John Quincy Adams sign a treaty by which the Floridas will become part of the United States.
1821	The Onis-Adams Treaty is ratified. An act of Congress makes the two Floridas one territory. Jackson becomes the military governor, but relinquishes the post after a few months.
1822	The first legislative council meets at Pensacola. Members from St. Augustine travel fifty-nine days by water to attend.
1823	The second legislative council meets at St. Augustine: the western delegates are shipwrecked and barely escape death.

The Treaty of Moultrie Creek is ratified by major Seminole chiefs and the federal government. The ink is barely dry before

Indians are complaining that the lands are too small and white settlers are petitioning the government for a policy of Indian removal.

1824 The third session meets at Tallahassee, a halfway point selected as a main order of business and approved at the second session. Tallahassee becomes the first territorial capital.

1832 Payne's Landing. Numerous chiefs sign a treaty agreeing to move west to Arkansas as long as seven of their number are able to see and approve the lands. The treaty is ratified at Fort Gibson, Arkansas.

Numerous chiefs also protest the agreement.

1835 Summer. Wiley Thompson claims that Osceola has repeatedly reviled him in his own office with foul language and orders his arrest. Osceola is handcuffed and incarcerated.

November. Charlie Emathla, after agreeing to removal to the west, is murdered. Most scholars agree Osceola led the party which carried out the execution. Some consider the murder personal vengeance, others believe it was proscribed by numerous chiefs, since an Indian who would leave his people to aid the whites should forfeit his own life.

December 28. Major Francis Dade and his troops are massacred as they travel from Fort Brooke to Fort King. Wiley Thompson and a companion are killed outside the walls of Fort King. The sutler Erastus Rogers and his two clerks are also murdered by members of the same raiding party, led by Osceola.

December 21. The First Battle of the Withlacoochee—Osceola leads the Seminoles.

1836 January. Major General Winfield Scott is ordered by the Secretary of War to take command in Florida.

February 4. Dade County established in south Florida in memory of Francis Langhorne Dade.

March 16. The Senate confirms Richard Keith Call governor of the Florida Territory.

June 21. Call, a civilian governor, is given command of the Florida forces after the failure of Scott's strategies and the military disputes between Scott and General Gaines. Call attempts a "summer campaign," and is as frustrated in his efforts as his predecessor.

1837   June 2. Osceola and Sam Jones release or "abduct" nearly 700 Indians awaiting deportation to the west from Tampa.

October 27. Osceola is taken under a white flag of truce; Major Sidney Jesup is denounced by whites and Indians alike for the action.

November 29. Coacoochee, Cowaya, sixteen warriors, and two women escape Ft. Marion.

Christmas Day. Jesup has the largest fighting force assembled in Florida during the conflict, nearly 9,000 men. Under his command, Colonel Zachary Taylor leads the Battle of Okeechobee. The Seminoles choose to stand their ground and fight, inflicting greater losses to whites despite the fact they are severely outnumbered.

1838   January 31. Osceola dies at Ft. Marion, South Carolina. (A strange side note to a sad tale: Dr. Wheedon, presiding white physician for Osceola, cut off and preserved Osceola's head. Wheedon's heirs reported that the good doctor would hang the head on the bedstead of one of his three children should they misbehave. The head passed on to his son-in-law, Dr. Daniel Whitehurst, who gave it to Dr. Valentine Mott. Dr.

Mott had a medical and pathological museum, and it is believed that the head was lost when the museum burned in 1866.)

May. Zachary Taylor takes command when Jesup's plea to be relieved is answered at last on April 29. The Florida legislature debates statehood.

1839   December. Because of his arguments with federal authorities regarding the Seminole War, Richard Keith Call is removed as governor. Robert Raymond Reid is appointed in his stead.

1840   April 24. Zachary Taylor is given permission to leave command of what is considered to be the harshest military position in the country. Walker Keith Armistead takes command.

December 1840–January 1841. John T. MacLaughlin leads a flotilla of men in dugouts across the Everglades from east to west; his party becomes the first white men to do so.

September. William Henry Harrison is elected president of the United States; the Florida War is considered to have cost Martin Van Buren reelection.

John Bell replaces Joel Poinsett as secretary of war. Robert Reid is ousted as territorial governor, and Richard Keith Call is reinstated.

1841   April 4. President William Henry Harrison dies in office: John Tyler becomes president of the U.S.

May 1. Coacoochee determines to turn himself in. He is escorted by a man who will later become extremely well known—Lieutenant William Tecumseh Sherman. (Sherman writes to his future wife that the Florida war is a good one for a soldier; he will get to know the Indian who may become the "chief enemy" in time.)

May 31. Walker Keith Armistead is relieved. Colonel William Jenkins Worth takes command.

1842 May 10. Winfield Scott is informed that the administration has decided there must be an end to hostilities as soon as possible.

August 14. Aware that he cannot end hostilities and send all Indians west, Colonel Worth makes offers to the remaining Indians to leave or accept boundaries. The war, he declares, is over.

It has cost a fledgling nation thirty to forty million dollars, and the lives of seventy-four commissioned officers. The Seminoles have been reduced from tens of thousands to hundreds scattered about in pockets. The Seminoles (inclusive here, as they were seen during the war, as all Florida Indians) have, however, kept their place in the peninsula; those remaining are the undefeated. The army, too, has learned new tactics, mostly regarding partisan and guerilla warfare. Men who will soon take part in the greatest conflict to tear apart the nation have practiced the art of battle here: William T. Sherman, Braxton Bragg, George Gordon Meade, Joseph E. Johnston, and more, as well as soon-to-be president Zachary Taylor.

1845 March 3. President John Tyler signs the bill that makes Florida the 27th state of the United States of America.

*Don't miss the magnificent
continuation of
Heather Graham's
Florida series,*

REBEL

*On sale from Topaz
in the Spring of 1997.*

*Turn the page for a
special advance preview. . . .*

The spy stared at the fast approaching coastline. *Almost home!* the Mocassin thought, and was glad, for the war was a wearying effort, more trying than ever recently. Frequently, the spy was sorry to have ever become the Mocassin and begun such a dangerous game.

It was just that the spy believed, passionately, in the Southern cause. In states' rights. The Confederacy was fighting for the right to independence, for the pursuit of life, liberty, and happiness. If only others understood . . .

There would be no war.

Still, the pain plagued the spy. And still, too often now, the fear.

The Mocassin had been thinking a very long while now that it might just be time to curl up like a ball python—and quit. So far all that had been done was good. Rebel lives had been saved. The spy's information had been sound. But that was changing. The spy wasn't making the same discoveries anymore. Perhaps it might be possible to slither into the water . . . and disappear into legend and history.

And have a life again. Bitter now, perhaps, but one touched by hope. If only . . .

In the small inlet, just before they might have run aground, the ship was brought to a slow, smooth halt.

"Cast dinghy!" the captain ordered. He was a good, gruff old man who had sailed the seas as a scavenger before the war and the Cause had caused every able man with so much as a rowboat to try to best the Union forces and break the blockade. The Mocassin had sailed

with this captain many times. They were close; good
friends, old friends. Neither had ever sought riches from
the war. Although the spy's usual contraband was qui-
nine or laudanum and the spy's main determination was
to save lives, serious mischief had been caused, and the
Union broadsides pasted up in every possible Yankee
port advised that the Mocassin was far more deadly than
any regular snake, and was to be hanged or shot without
mercy if captured.

The Mocassin didn't dare think about such threats—
or the fact that they would be carried out. Without
mercy. Fear made it impossible to function. From the
beginning, the Mocassin had known a spy must function.

Tonight, the spy wore a face-concealing, dark slouch
hat and a large, encompassing greatcoat with frocked
shoulders and numerous pockets. The pockets were
filled with correspondences, gold and hard Yankee cur-
rency, and laudanum. The weight of the coat was such
that it would be easy for the spy to drown if cast over-
board, but it would be equally as easy for the spy to cast
off the coat if necessary, and, if possible, retrieve the
coat at a later time.

But things should go smoothly this evening.

This was a no-man's land, inhabited by mosquitos and
snakes. Thus, the Mocassin. And staring toward the land
with sharp eyes, the spy could see nothing amiss. The
moon kept creeping behind clouds, but when the bil-
lowing puffs burst apart, a strange yellow glow illumi-
nated the earth. The water, with or without the
moonlight, seemed black. Trees and trails were encased
in silent shadow. In a sudden burst of yellow moonlight,
the Mocassin scanned the shore. Nothing. Nothing, except . . .

"Wait!" the spy said, and the captain, about to order
a man to row the spy in, paused.

"You see something?" the captain demanded, frowning and trying hard to peer into the night.

Yes, something. Something had moved in the shadows.
The Mocassin was suddenly filled with dread. Twin red

lights suddenly seemed to peer from the trees. The Mocassin felt a tightening grip of panic begin, but then breathed more easily again, nearly laughing aloud with relief.

"What?" the captain asked anxiously.

"A little deer," the spy said.

"Ah . . . ! A deer. You're certain?"

"Yes."

"Jenkins, bring the Mocassin in," the captain ordered one of his young seamen.

"Yes, sir!" Jenkins said, saluting.

The captain turned to the Mocassin. "Be careful. Please, be careful."

"I will, sir."

"Remember, your life is far more valuable than your cargo, no matter how precious it may be. *You* cannot be replaced. You must remember that."

"I will remember."

"You must."

"I will, and I must go now, sir."

The captain nodded. He appeared unhappy, as if he struggled for more words to say, but could not find them. As if he, too, had suddenly been filled with the same sense of dread.

For a moment the Mocassin was made uneasy by his manner, and felt a strange chill, one as foreboding as the haunting night with its strange, eerie, uncanny yellow moon glow.

"Be careful," the captain said again, gruffly.

The Mocassin nodded, hiding a smile, eyes averted downward. "I know my business, sir."

"We should move now," Jenkins said uneasily. He believed in his duty, and he'd die in this war if the good Lord called for it. But he hailed from Jacksonville, and he hated swampland, and he hated this southern region of the state where a deceptively beautiful coastline was but a slender thread of land that bordered the dense watery jungle of the Everglades.

The Mocassin nimbly scrambled over the starboard

side of the ship, following Jenkins down the small drop ladder to the dinghy waiting below. Jenkins quickly slipped the oars into the water, and the dinghy shot across the night-black sea. The coastline loomed ever closer.

"Stop!" the Mocassin whispered suddenly, overwhelmed by a feeling that all was not well. No more flashes of eyes made red by the moon's sudden reflection peered out, yet he was certain they were being watched. That something awaited them. The heavy breathing of some great, horrible creature seemed to echo in the darkness. The trees were too still. Nothing stirred; no insects chirped.

Jenkins ceased to row; the dinghy, caught by the impetus of his previous strength, continued to streak through the water despite Jenkins's efforts to position the oars to come to a standstill.

Then the trees came to life. The moon was gone, darkness had settled, but the Mocassin heard the sounds as men slipped from the trees, rifles aimed at the dinghy.

And dreaded words in a more dreaded voice were suddenly issued:

"Surrender! Come in peacefully. Your lives will be spared, you've my guarantee!"

The moon slipped free from the clouds. Eight men in hated Union blue had come from the trees. They were in formation at the water's edge: four on their knees, four standing, all aiming their rifles directly at the occupants of the dinghy.

"Lord A'mighty!" Jenkins swore. He didn't even glance at the Mocassin; to him escape was impossible. He'd rather face a Union bullet a hundred times over before daring even his big toe to the water here.

The Mocassin stared at Jenkins with both panic and contempt.

The Mocassin could not surrender.

"We surrender—!" Jenkins began.

But before he could finish, the Mocassin had already dived deep into the water.

* * *

"Damn the wretch!" Ian McKenzie swore, shedding his cavalry jacket and swiftly unbuckling his scabbard while kicking off his boots. "Men, keep your guns trained. Get the Reb in the rowboat and watch the surface for our friend emerging from the shallows. Gilbey Clark—" he said, and hesitated just briefly. Gilbey was his new man. But a good man. "Gilbey, take the trail up a hundred yards; Sam, follow him at fifty. Sharp eyes on the water!"

He turned, running out into the shallows, then leaping into a dive that took him into the depths near the dinghy. Fool spy—they all carried their contraband in their clothing. This idiot would go down like a leaden ball.

But though he dived and surfaced in the area of the dinghy again and again, he could find no trace of the spy.

Nor did a body float to the surface.

It was night, and though he had excellent vision in the darkness, even he was nearly blinded. Yet he instinctively believed that the spy was not dead; the spy had dived into the water because he was someone who knew how to swim, how to manage the water and the shore— even in the darkness.

He didn't dare think beyond that.

He made one last dive and came up triumphant: the spy's heavy-laden coat. Dragging it along with him, he swam toward shore, then came to his feet to wade the rest of the way in. His sodden cotton shirt was plastered to his chest, making his skin clammy; his wool uniform pants felt even worse.

"There! There!" came a sudden shout.

Ian forgot his discomfort and ran to the shore. Up ahead, he could see a shadow rising from the water; Gilbey Clark had seen the apparition as well.

"Halt, or I'll shoot!" Gilbey called out, raising his rifle.

But Gilbey didn't shoot. Ian came behind him, bursting out of the blackness of the night. He laid his hand upon Gilbey's rifle, lowering it. "No shooting. I'll take the spy," he said, adding softly, "alive."

He raced past Gilbey with speed and agility, heedless of the ground against his callused bare feet, determined only to catch the figure that had just emerged from the water—and realized that pursuit was just feet away. He heard a cry which should have been a final warning to him that all he had feared secretly within his heart but hadn't wanted to believe, was true. It didn't quite register, he was so intent on the pursuit. In a little spit of sand between tree roots and shore, Ian caught up with the Mocassin at last. He threw himself upon the spy with a fierce burst of speed, grappling, intending to bring the enemy down, winded, before he could be knifed or throttled in turn.

The catapulted weight of his body forced the spy down to the ground easily enough.

They were soaked with sea and sand. Ian caught his balance, easing from the figure beneath him and rolling his enemy face forward at the same time. Without missing a beat he straddled the spy.

At last the Mocassin was pinned to the sand.

The moon's light was suddenly abundant.

Even with soaked hair tangled in seaweed and lashed about her face, the Mocassin was exotically beautiful. Neither night nor water could completely dim the shimmering gold of her hair, and the glowing moonlight only helped illuminate the unique color of her eyes, a hazel so fused that the color was not green at all, not brown, but nearly as gold as her hair. Her lashes and brows darkened to a honey. Her face was delicately formed with a small, straight nose, elegantly high cheekbones, a stubbornly square chin, and a beautifully shaped, generous mouth. Her cheeks were usually flushed to give a warmth to her coloring; her lips were naturally tinged a cherry except that now they were held in a thin, grim line, and they were a mixture of white from tension and blue from the cold.

She was really quite amazing.

"So you are the Mocassin," he said, and his anger was so deep that his words and body shook with his effort to remain still. To control the sweeping range of emotions that tore at his heart and soul. Remembrance, fear, rage, pain.

And the desire so suddenly and wildly awakened by the brutal physical force of those other feelings tearing so viciously into him. *For she remained Alaina. Curved, warm, vital, and alive, beneath him. Alaina, with her cat-like eyes, her smile, her laugh, her temper. Her reckless-ness. Her dedication, her passion ...*

The Alachuas would be able to return.

The day had passed without bloodshed. James should have felt good. But he felt wretched.

He had been to the fort with Wildcat.

And he had seen her.

Osceola stood in front of the communal cooking fire, stretching his hands before it, closing his eyes. The fire was kept burning through the night, a task for the slaves the Indians kept. A pot of sofkee with a large spoon remained hot over the fire, ready for a warrior whenever he was hungry.

But it was late, and Osceola stood alone.

He was a man of medium height, slim, wiry, with a well-muscled build. Except that the muscles were sometimes failing him now. And he was far slimmer than he should be. His wives knew that his strength sometimes left him, and when he looked at the moon at night and heard wolves howl, he sometimes felt a strange sense of destiny himself, as if his time was limited.

It was strange, but so often now he would remember the past. Think back to his boyhood.

Things had been so much different then.

He had been born a Creek, in the Upper Creek town of Tallahassee. He had first been known as Billy Powell, for his father, an Englishman. A white man.

Whites, he knew, debated his parentage. Was Powell his father, or had the man simply been married to his mother? It didn't matter. Powell had been a good man, but in the Creek wars now long ago, Powell had returned to Alabama while Osceola had come south to Florida with his mother's clan. Theirs was a matriarchal society. A son was of his mother's clan. He often learned from his mother's male relations, and it had been from an uncle of his mother, a man called Peter McQueen after her own Scots grandfather, that he had learned he must spend much of his life fighting for his very way of living it.

He had been a boy during the Creek wars. Young but

growing when Andrew Jackson had come to Florida. The wars had come, the battles. The "First" Seminole War. But it seemed that he could still remember peace. Waking in the morning to the warm caress of the sun, listening to the sound of the breeze that drifted through the *talwa*, the village. He could remember hunting with his bow and arrow, learning to shoot the plentiful game in the forest. Their way of life had been so defined then. The *mico* had received town guests, issued invitations, presided over the meetings. His aide, the *mico apokta*, had helped him in all things, while other men, the *micalgi*, had guided and counseled each village as well.

In times of battle, usually with the whites or hostile Creeks, the war speaker, the *holibonaya*, came before them all, shouting, gesticulating, preparing them for the fight. Young men longed to fight. The women cooked and performed most domestic tasks, while a young man was given such trivial chores as collecting sticks for firewood, tending pigs, or gathering roots and berries. He gained his prestige through a show of courage in either the hunt or in battle, and so young men longed for the chance to prove that they were brave and powerful and worthy of warrior status.

Many villages, many clans, many chiefs and their people, met every May for council meetings and then again in the summer for the Green Corn Dance. All things could be settled then. Marriages were sanctified, claims were settled. Young men and women played games, some together, some separately. They flirted, laughed, fell in love and in lust.

No Seminole was ever confined or chained, but crimes were punished. Adulterers were sometimes beaten; sometimes their noses or ears were clipped. Some crimes were minor, punishable by exclusion from tribal rites and rituals. Murder was severe, and many men decided upon a murderer's fate, sometimes a heavy payment, sometimes banishment, and sometimes execution. Sometimes life was harsh, sometimes good. But it had always followed a special way, a special path. Now each day

seemed scattered, unpredictable. Their very independence hurt them at times. Battles took place, then warriors hurried home. They searched for food. They tried to plant crops even while they ran and hid. Warriors kept dying. Children perished.

He had known that they would have to fight. He had never been a hereditary leader like Micanopy; he had earned his station. The whites accused him of murdering Wiley Thompson after having befriended the man at times. They didn't understand. A Seminole could not be chained. Wiley had thought to break him. Wiley had not understood that you did not chain a Seminole.

There had been good days. He could remember so many good days . . .

Now, too often, they all proved their fury and their power in battle. They died with it.

He had spoken with Wildcat, with others. They were all aware that their situation was grave. Osceola did not know if they could endure another year of fighting. He was ready to negotiate with the military again, under one of the white flags General Jesup had given them. Osceola was well aware that since the failed peace of March, Jesup was a sad man, now fighting a war of extermination since he did not feel he had a choice. He did not blindly hate the white men. Indeed, his relations with the military that March had been so good that he had slept in the tent of Lieutenant Colonel William S. Harney while some of the negotiations took place.

He had fought when it had been right to fight. He would still fight when he had to do so. But it was necessary that they talk again.

He heard footfalls behind him. They were almost silent upon the soft earth, but he could hear the quietest of footsteps. He turned around.

Otter stood there, his face as hard as if it had been cast in stone, so bronze, his eyes black and seeming to burn with an obsidian light.

"I have come to tell Osceola that I am riding with my men to my own *talwa* with the dawn."

Osceola nodded. "Our strength lies in our ability to fight and withdraw, and go so deeply into the swamps and hammocks that the soldiers cannot follow us."

"I don't withdraw!" Otter said fiercely. He slammed his fist against his bare chest. "I don't withdraw." He was nearly naked, wearing a breech clout only. The Seminoles had learned their ways of going into battle. They purged themselves with black drink often, and avoided the diseases of the bowels. They fought nearly naked because they had learned that bullet wounds sometimes brought threads and fabric ripping into flesh as well, and that such wounds often putrefied. Otter was shiny with bear grease. His plaited hair was a sleek ebony with it. He was ready for battle at any minute. No warrior had been more brave. Or more furious. More vengeful. His wife, infant son, and daughters had burned to death in a raid on his village. He wasn't afraid of death himself. Osceola thought that he was afraid of life.

"None of us here has given up the fight," Osceola said.

Otter gritted his teeth together, letting out a sound of disgust. He waved his hand in the air. "Osceola sees what he wishes to see. Many are giving up the fight."

"Many are weary."

"You have fought and killed not to give up the fight!"

"*I* am weary."

"You—!"

"Not weary enough to give up the fight," Osceola interrupted angrily, the old power in his voice. "But now the soldiers do not know where we are. I am hunting, I am making new weapons of war. I am gathering strength. And I am waiting to see what move the white man makes next."

Otter shook his head. "I will fight with you again, Osceola. But I am war chief of my clan, and I will make battle as I choose."

"It is our way," Osceola agreed. He was sorry for Otter, but weary of his anger. That was one advantage the white soldiers had. Discipline. Osceola knew that he

was a leader in this war. But it was true that warriors chose to fight, sometimes chose to go home, and sometimes waged new, unwinnable battles on their own.

"You grow weak!" Otter cried.

"I grow more sensible. I seek to fight when I can win. I seek victories, not slaughters."

Otter slammed his fist against his chest again. "I seek death for the white men!" he cried.

"Remember, we seek our lives here. Our land. Our children. A future for them."

"It will not be allowed us."

"We will seek it until it is ours. Otter, you are a fierce and valiant warrior. We are all in your debt. Remember that we are all waging the same war!"

Otter stood very stiffly. "I remember," he said. "But even now white soldiers gather at the fort. More and more of them. They seek to find me. To find Osceola. I will find them. I will find Warren, and I will have his scalp. I will take the lives of all the men who leave the fort."

He inclined his head, respectful despite his words, and spun silently on his heel and disappeared into the line of pines beyond the fire.

Osceola turned back to the flames. He closed his eyes. He had fought, yes, he had fought! With fury, savagely, with cruel precision and wild abandon. He would fight again.

But tonight . . .

He was cold. So very cold.

Far from the fire, laid against an old, moss-draped oak, slept Riley Marshall, an old black man who had made his way south to Florida. Riley served the warriors and was protected by them. In good times he had worked for his Indian masters, but he had been allowed his own plot of land as well. He had been free to join the Negro Indian bands at any time, but he had been an old man at the war's beginning, and he had stayed close to Osceola's band.

Now Osceola woke him. "Ask Running Bear if he will come to me."

"Running Bear left to study the new fort."

"He is here tonight. He brought back a deer for the people to eat."

Riley did as he was bidden. Moments later, James McKenzie emerged silently from the darkness to walk toward Osceola where he stood by the fire.

Osceola had taken such a hard line himself so many times with others that both whites and Seminoles wondered at the friendship he shared with the half-breed. But there were things he knew about James that he could not say he knew of other men. If they were attacked, James would fight with them until his own death. The words that James spoke would be the truth. He would not betray a confidence, and he would not turn from his own people. Nor would he wantonly commit murder for any man. He would not attack whites, settlements, farms, plantations—or even soldiers. But he would bring food to various bands when none was to be had. He would share what he had to his last morsel. He would not lie; he would not cease to defend his brother and other white men of his ilk. He would fight until he fell to defend his position—or what was his.

And it seemed that the white woman at the fort was his.

"You have called me, Osceola?" James said. He stood about three feet away, bathed in the firelight. Osceola was of medium height himself. He had never doubted his own appearance as that of a fine warrior and chief. But this half-breed blood brother of his stood over six feet tall, his stance straight. His frame was hard, well-muscled, his shoulders broad. He wore a white man's form-hugging trousers along with a patterned cotton shirt. A single silver crescent hung from a chain at his neck, and an unadorned red band kept his black hair from his eyes. His bronzed face was taut and lean tonight, still striking but hard with a tension that burned a blue fire in the depths of his eyes.

"You've fed many mouths tonight with your fine buck. Such kills are harder and harder to find in the forest," Osceola told him.

Running Bear arched an ebony brow, a flicker of amusement passing across his features. "Osceola is an excellent hunter himself. He has hardly called me here to compliment a kill."

"I have heard that Major Warren's daughter is at Fort Deliverance."

No expression touched Running Bear's face. He shrugged. "She is."

It was Osceola's turn to feel a certain amusement. "My good friend, you are greatly mistaken if you do not realize that whispers and rumors travel the forest from band to band, borne on the breeze. Whether you abducted the woman or she ran to the shelter of your abandoned cabins is not known; that you have been involved with her is fact. For this reason I have called you. You have seen her? She is at the fort?"

"Yes. I have seen her myself. I moved through the bush with Wildcat, and observed the soldiers and the life at the fort."

"It is true that there are men and women I will not kill. At the first battle at the Withlacoochee, it was my order that the braves not kill a young soldier named Graham. They will not disturb your brother's home. There are others. I have commanded that Warren's daughter be brought here if she is captured. But you must understand, some braves run with hot blood. They have lost their own families. They have seen children lie in the crimson pools of their own lost lives."

"I am aware of this."

"Be aware then that you must watch Otter. He will attack any and all soldiers out of Fort Deliverance."

"I have been warned about Otter," Running Bear said. "But perhaps I will speak with him. Now."

Running Bear turned hard on his heel. Osceola watched him go. He wondered at the wisdom of his action. They could not afford to battle one another now.

But if they did not strive to live their lives in their way, with honor and integrity, then why did they fight so hard?

James knew where to find Otter. The Mikasukee *mico* had just returned to his makeshift shelter and lain upon his blanket.

The Seminoles had a tendency not to post guards through the night. James had warned the chiefs time and time again that the white soldiers always slept with a guard, and that nighttime was no deterrent if the whites chose to attack by darkness. But lifestyles were hard to change. When James leapt atop the platform where Otter had slept alone since the cruel death of his wife, he caught the *mico* quite by surprise.

Otter leapt to his feet, stunned, wary, ready for an attack. He saw James, and his wariness did not leave him.

"McKenzie," he said, spitting out the white name as he addressed James.

"I have been told that you wish to kill all the soldiers at the fort," James told him.

"I wish to kill all whites," Otter said flatly.

"There is a woman there who is mine."

"No white man cared about my woman."

"But I ask you as a chief of your people to respect my position—"

"As a half-breed?"

"As *mico* of my people. Through my blood right by my mother."

Otter strode to James, standing directly before him. He was a smaller man; it did not matter. He stared up at him with bitterness and hostility.

"You grew to drink the black drink; you learned the ways of our warriors. You learned to hunt and fight in breech clouts, to shoot your arrows straight and true, to wield a white man's musket with skill. Men listen to you and follow you. You have great power and great strength. You could lead men to great victories, slaugh-

ter the whites. But you fight with us only when a musket is aimed at your heart. Then you come to me about a white woman."

"She is mine, and I don't want her killed."

"If she is yours, take her from the fort, and the white men there."

James didn't allow the feelings in his heart to be betrayed in his features. God! The anguish and frustration within him seemed to eat at his insides, gnawing away. He could claim that she was his, but she was not. She was a white woman, in a white man's world. He could not claim her while she remained with Michael Warren.

"I'm asking you not to harm her."

Otter suddenly drew a knife from a sheath at his ankle and threw it so that the point lodged into the crudely hewn logs at their feet.

"Fight me, Running Bear. Fight for her. Decide her fate."

"Fight you? I do not seek your death—"

"Nor I yours. I wish to see you fight as I have fought, for what you love. What you covet. Life."

Before James could respond, Otter had plunged downward for the knife again. James leapt back, aware that the warrior meant to draw blood tonight, even if he wasn't seeking a fight to the death.

Otter charged him again. James caught the wrist that held the blade, but Otter's impetus caught him hard as the Mikasukee plunged into him. They both went down hard upon the platform, then rolled to the earth, caught in a deadly battle of strength.

Otter rolled atop James, fighting to draw his knife high and aim it downward. James could nearly feel the tip of the blade piercing his throat. His fingers tightened on Otter's wrist. He willed a greater strength into his arms and body, and managed to toss the smaller man from him. Otter landed on the earth about three feet away. James leapt to his feet. Otter was up as well. They circled each other. James let Otter attack again. This time he allowed himself to fall easily with the impetus,

then he forced the roll as well. Otter tried to lunge with the knife, but James was prepared. He twisted his torso, then slammed down on Otter's arm, causing the knife to fly. He wedged an arm close on his opponent's throat, cutting off his breath, threatening to break his neck.

Staring up at him with hatred, Otter went still.

"Finish it. Kill me."

James shook his head slowly. "I didn't come to seek your death!" he said, exasperated. "Concede to me the white woman should you take her."

Otter was silent for a moment. James realized then that he could hear the quiet sounds of breathing, a slight motion of feet against the earth.

He looked up. Many of Otter's people had come to circle them. They would not interfere in the fight. They watched, they waited.

Otter was aware that they had come as well. James eased his hold, and Otter spoke woodenly.

"I do not seek to attack the fort. I will wage war against the men who leave it, against the men who seek out me and my people to exterminate us!"

"And the woman?"

"If I take her, you must come for her. And take her from me. I have told you, when you speak, men listen. We admire your strength—we seek it more for our cause."

James stood uneasily. Otter leapt up before him. "I travel toward my home in the south hammock in the morning. I will not attack the fort. Warren's daughter is only in danger if she leaves it. I will try not to forget that she is yours."

"I want your word, your promise."

Otter nodded.

James stood still in the moonlight for a moment, watching Otter. The Mikasukee suddenly sliced his palm, offering it to James. James took the knife and sliced his own as well, then gripped it hard to Otter's.

He could still feel the blood when he turned away. Hot, sticky. He could remember Teela's face as she had

studied her own hands that last time he had seen her. So much blood, she had said. So much blood . . .

And so much more would be shed.

He had battled Wildcat and Otter now. Fought his own people. He had become deadly enemies with Michael Warren.

And still . . .

There was so little he could do to protect her.

"Running Bear!"

He had left Otter's shelter behind and stood in a copse in the moonlight. He could hear the slight stirring of the night wind and the gentle movement of the stream that rambled not far from where the council lean-tos and shelters had been erected. He turned.

Brown Rabbit, an old Mikasukee warrior with negro blood, had called him back.

"Otter means his word to you. He admires you, and is sorry that you do not fight with us with greater will and strength. He says that you could kill twenty men each battle, and rid us of many soldiers."

"I cannot fight as he wishes me to," James said simply.

"I know that. Many men know it. Otter cannot respect it, though I believe he intends to keep his word. But he means death to the whites. If this woman is yours, you must see that she does not leave the fort. And if she leaves it, you must come for her. Many things happen in the heat of battle. Many things that men may not intend."

"Thank you, Brown Rabbit."

Brown Rabbit nodded and turned hastily to return to his own band.

James stood in the moonlight. He cast back his head and stared up at the stars.

He had gone to the fort. He had climbed the oaks outside the clearing where the walls had been raised, and he had silently stared down into the yard, into the very heart of the military fortress.

He had seen her.

And his heart had been pummeled and his blood had

seemed to run both hot and cold. And he had been
seared with both anger and fear, but in the end he had
seen what Wildcat had. The Indians could not attack the
fort. No matter how many warriors they gathered, the
fort was too strong. They would not sacrifice themselves
for a futile attack. Jarrett would have known how strong
the fort was, how well protected, before he would have
allowed Teela to go, no matter what arguments Michael
Warren had used.

If she stayed within the fort, she was safe.

And if she did not . . .

His fingers knotted at his sides. What was she to him?
he taunted himself. A white woman he had urged to
marry a soldier friend. A sweet, lush body in the night,
easy pain and tempest. She could be nothing more.

She was more. He could not claim her or command
her, but she was his. In his blood. In his soul. He could
not rid himself of her, of wanting her. Of longing to hear
her voice again, see the flash in her eyes, listen to her
words, soft or angry, warm or rebellious.

"Damn you, why did you ever have to come here?"
he whispered to the moon.

Then he cast his head back still farther, his fingers
knotted into his fists, and he let out a cry of anger and
anguish to the moon.

It echoed around him.

And he moved in the darkness again, aware that he
barely dared even sleep in the days that were to come.

Chapter 17

General Jesup, now in command of all forces in Florida, was a lean, tall, straight man. Teela had heard that he could be shifty, that he wasn't always to be trusted, but there were few men high in the military who didn't receive some kind of lambasting from their men. Teela didn't think that he looked untrustworthy. He had level, keenly intelligent eyes. And as she danced with him, she felt sorry for him.

"Were it up to me," he said, sweeping her very properly but just a bit stiffly around the room, "it would all be over now." He wasn't really looking at her as he spoke; he was brooding, and seemed sad despite the festivities of Robert's party. "We have fought a hard campaign here. When Governor Call held the reins of command before me, he fought a hard campaign as well. But when I fought in January, I came to see what they cannot see in Washington. I came to see that we could trek endlessly through brush and swamp and hammocks. No matter how hard we try, parties of warriors slip away. I came close to Osceola once, so close I nearly had that wretched war hawk in my grasp! But he slipped away. The prisoners taken in his pursuit informed us that he escaped our reach with just a few warriors. He'll come back again with a hundred. It is always the same. We catch our enemies, but always our enemies slip away once again."

"Why don't they just let the Seminoles alone, then, in the south?"

Jesup sighed, deeply troubled. "Would God that we

could! My frustration here has been so great that I pleaded to be relieved of duty. Then gossip hounds and political enemies cast such comments upon my abilities that I can no longer accept the relief I have so craved until I feel I have proven my competence. Good God! I would most gladly leave them to the wretched swamps. But it is the opinion of the United States government, especially that of Secretary of War Poinsett and apparently that of President Martin Van Buren, that we must not back down, that we cannot surrender our position, or we will but extend every fight we face across the whole of the country. I am but a servant of our government and therefore obey orders. I have suggested on more than one occasion that we just leave the Seminoles to the south of the peninsula." He was silent for a moment. "My orders leave me so little choice. The Seminoles must go, the Seminoles won't go; I am left to exterminate men I frequently admire. I tell you I am weary of this hellhole where the soldiers sicken constantly, where my regular army officers squabble incessantly with the militia commanders, and where disease plagues us all most pathetically. I am afraid to let the populace know just how many of our soldiers are ill, for they would be terrified to sleep at night. I tell you, it is a wretched, wretched war. Some men, of course, do thrive on it." He paused. "Your father is proving to be an admirable officer, never falling to sickness in the heat, following every trail relentlessly until he has hunted down his prey!"

"Yes, my stepfather is excellent at such maneuvers," Teela agreed. She could see Michael Warren across the floor, in conversation with Tyler Argosy and Dr. Brandeis. He watched her while she talked. For once in his life it seemed that he was pleased with her. Jesup's recommendations could bring about a promotion for him, and Teela knew that Jesup, whatever his personal dismay at the war he fought, was glad of the men who were winning the battles.

Eliminating the problems.

Jesup was looking at her gravely. "It is my understanding, Miss Warren, that you have befriended the hostiles."

Teela arched a brow at him, speaking carefully. "I don't know any of the 'hostiles,' sir."

"Your father has claimed that you were kidnapped by the half-breed, James McKenzie, that the man is dangerous, that his type will continue the war forever, threatening innocent women and children."

"I wasn't kidnapped by anyone, General. I met James McKenzie at a party finer than this one at his brother's house."

The general sniffed, on the verge of rudeness. He seemed a very bitter man that night.

"In my experience, I have met so many men who have not seen their brothers in years, and care not if they ever do so again! Then I come here, and Jarrett, a man who knows this frontier of Florida better than any other man, will not fight and seek out the deep-hammock hideouts of these wretches because he shares his father's blood with one of them. Then there is James himself! Articulate, well educated, fully versed in the white way of life, a man with that life opened to him, and he joins with the savages instead!"

"It has been my understanding that James has very frequently served both sides well—"

"As I've said, he's articulate and highly intelligent. He has the rare power to move men with both his example and his words, and a manner of reasoning that puts us all to shame." He sighed deeply. "I'm afraid I have become nearly as great a burden to many of those civilians I fight to keep alive as I am to the savages!"

"Surely, sir, you are greatly appreciated."

Jesup shrugged. "I think not, Miss Warren. But it is kind of you to pretend that it is so. Especially since it seems I am in charge of an effort you deplore."

"I'm not at all sure what I think anymore," Teela told him. "It is war and bloodshed that I deplore."

"Your stepfather rides out again tomorrow with a de-

tachment to follow a trail deep into the swamp. Both your father and young Harrington will be gone. You should perhaps leave this wretched territory. Go on home, be safe."

Teela arched a brow. It seemed that everyone wanted her to go home. If Jesup was suggesting she do so, perhaps Michael Warren would be bound to let her do so.

Her heart was pounding hard. She didn't think that she wanted to go home. James was out there somewhere.

"General, you are kind, and I thank you for your consideration for my health and welfare. But I don't think I should leave without having a chance to speak with John again."

She swept her lashes low over her cheeks, somewhat ashamed of the lie, even if she had John Harrington's blessing and encouragement to lie.

"Ah, young love!" the general said, smiling with a faraway look to his eyes. Then he winked at her. "I quite understand. What a commendable wife you will make for such a promising soldier as your Mr. Harrington! I still say, my dear, if you've need of anything at all while your men are fighting so bravely on the line, you mustn't hesitate to ask."

"General, I will not," Teela promised.

Even as she spoke, there was a sudden commotion at the door to the hall on the ground floor, where they danced. The musicians stopped playing.

A soldier who had been on guard duty was the first to break through into the room. He was young, frecklefaced, with tawny hair. His flesh was very pale; his freckles stood out upon it. He was followed by two men who held a muddied and bloodied companion between them. Teela screamed, stunned, horrified to see that the blood that streaked his face had come from a small spot on the crown of his head where a patch of hair had been lifted.

"Sir, General Jesup, sir!" the man being held cried out. "Captain Dixon, fourth volunteers, reporting." Then his military protocol was lost, and he openly wept. "We'd traced down Otter, sir. Oh, yes, we'd traced down

Otter. There were ten of us, and we thought we could surround his camp and surprise him and bring him in. We were so certain. But that damned Otter, sir, he wasn't in front of us at all. He was behind us. And he came around us just as we came into his village. For the love of God, sir, I crawled back here. They took me for dead, sir, lifted my hair, and by some miracle I did not cry out. But my men, my brave young boys, my beautiful boys. They're gone, sir. All gone."

General Jesup set a supporting arm around Teela, but Brandeis apparently did not see the action, or chose to ignore it. He came behind her, catching her by the hand. "Come, quickly."

She followed him, or more accurately, was dragged by him to where the captain stood, supported by the others. Brandeis quickly lifted the man's head and looked into his eyes. "Sir!" he said to General Jesup. "This man needs care promptly."

Jesup stood very tall and straight. "Indeed," he said quietly. "Captain, you are a brave man. Our prayers are with you, and your fine men."

Joshua pushed open the door, urging Teela and the men supporting the captain to hurry along behind him. They strode along the wood decking that led to the door into Joshua's surgery and hospital, and carried the captain into the back room where Joshua removed bullets, sewed up sword slashes, hatchet and knife wounds, and amputated destroyed limbs. He ordered the captain laid down.

"Teela, carefully clean the head wound. Get the sulfur. Have we ether?"

"Yes, we've a little left."

"Good, it seems his main wound is there, on the side. Open my bag, get me my scissors."

Teela hastened to obey him, her heart beating hard as the soldiers who had supported the captain stepped back, wide-eyed, looking as if they might be sick at last. Teela set out the bag with Joshua's instruments, quickly handing him the scissors so that he could rip open the

captain's homespun shirt and hunting jacket. She started to order one of the soldiers to bring her hot water to bathe the poor captain's scalpless head, but Joshua glanced up and saw a bottle of whiskey on the table near his instruments and handed it to Teela. "This will do fine. Pour some on his head, then into his belly."

In the savage wilderness where supplies were sorely lacking, whiskey was a fine medicine. Except that Teela was convinced the captain could use a good swallow before feeling the sting of the alcohol upon his head.

He looked into her eyes with his own fine powder blue ones, read her mind. He reached for the bottle and consumed a good quantity in one long, hungry swallow.

He gritted his teeth, but didn't cry out when she then bathed his head with it. Amazingly, after all she had learned to do in the surgery, she felt tears stinging her eyes. She liberally applied sulfur to the wound, then helped remove the fragments of cloth from the captain's shirt. Joshua quietly requested her assistance, and she quickly gave it. Thankfully, the captain had not been riddled with bullets.

He had been slashed in a long line up and down his side. The whiskey wouldn't be enough. They did have ether. Joshua administered it; there were a few minutes of waiting.

The captain looked up at Teela with glazed eyes. She tried to smile, taking his hand. "Nothing will hurt you in a few minutes, captain."

He smiled. "I will hurt forever!" he said softly, then moaned. "My boys, my poor boys . . ."

She glanced at Joshua. He inclined his head toward the captain.

"Sir," she said softly. "Think on this, that they are gone now, in no pain, and abiding with God. They were volunteers, soldiers who knew the danger, glad to follow you, brave men. Captain, surely, you did all that you could!"

He closed his eyes, nodding. "All that I could . . ."

His eyes opened again. "But I have lived to see an angel, they have not."

"They are dancing with real angels now, sir!"

Once again the captain's eyes closed. His fingers squeezed hers. "Bless you . . ."

His eyes didn't open again. Joshua nodded and inclined his head toward the needles and silk thread they had been lucky enough to receive in their last shipment of supplies.

Nearly a hundred stitches were required.

She sat with the captain until it was very late. About two in the morning, Joshua came and looked at the captain, the whiskey bottle now in Joshua's hands. He pulled a long swig of it.

"He will make it, I believe. As long as no infection sets in. We tended him quickly enough. Come on, come into the office. Have a drink yourself. You need a drink, and you deserve one. Good, stiff whiskey, no sherry or the like."

Exhausted, Teela followed him into the small cubicle that served as his office. There were shelves loaded with books and medications. The desk was littered with supply forms, discharge papers, letters, and reports. He swept them to one side as he sat behind the desk, indicating that Teela take the chair before it. He opened the bottom drawer of his crude desk and drew out a glass, filled it with whiskey, and thrust it across the desk to her.

She took a sip of it and shuddered slightly.

"Oh, come now, down it in a gulp!"

She arched a brow to him, then did so. She shuddered fiercely, but she felt as if she had been warmed from head to toe.

"Better?" he asked.

She nodded. She set the glass down carefully. "He's a good man!" she said. "A very good man." She felt like crying again.

"And you hated the Indians like hell when he came in," Joshua said.

She arched a brow again and nodded as he poured her more whiskey.

"I hated the Indians. I thought of them all as despicable savages. Just like I hated Captain Julian Hampton the day that he massacred everyone in that village."

"It's a damned dilemma, isn't it?"

She nodded, inhaled and exhaled. "Oh, God, Joshua! I don't know why, I just keep thinking that I could do something here, but I can't. I thought that I could change things in some small measure. Oh, what a fool I've been! I'm humbled, and I'm tired. And I'm frightened. And I—"

"You don't want to see James McKenzie dead, and right now you're not certain you want to see him alive."

"Oh, dear Lord! Of course, I want him to be alive—"

"But sometimes he is one with those savage creatures who ripped this poor good man to shreds tonight!"

She stared down at her lap and nodded. "Just this evening General Jesup suggested I go home. And I didn't want to go home. I thought that I needed to be here. But now, so suddenly, I just want to be away. I do want to go home. I—please don't say anything. I'm going to wait until my stepfather has ridden out. General Jesup has told me that I can come to the military for help. I'll ask the commandant if I can leave as soon as possible. Perhaps ride north to St. Augustine when a detachment of men is going for supplies."

Joshua was silent. Teela stared down at her hands. She felt so numb tonight. So tired. So beaten.

"I'm sorry," she said after a moment. "I'm grateful to you, to John Harrington, to others. Perhaps I shouldn't go. I owe him, I owe you—"

"You need to go," Joshua said suddenly, fiercely.

She was startled by his vehemence. She felt her cheeks redden. She knew she was sometimes the talk of the stockade; everyone knew that she had pushed Julian Hampton into the water. Some of them mocked her as an Injun lover.

"If I've offended you—" Teela began.

"For the love of God! You've not offended me! I will miss you, but I pray that you will go."

"Will you explain to John for me?"

"John will understand."

"Perhaps he will be relieved."

"Teela, do not be a fool. Go on, get out of here, go home. If your fiancé does not love you, Teela Warren, I do. If you have lain with a thousand Indians, I don't care."

She stared at him, shocked, startled—and again glad of Joshua Brandeis because he was so blunt, because he spoke the truth, because he read into the hearts of men and women, and chose not to judge them. But tears stung her eyes because she was sorry to realize that she meant something to him that he did not mean to her.

"I haven't lain with a thousand Indians," she said softly.

"Only one."

"Joshua, it isn't that he is a Seminole. It's—"

"You're in love with him."

"It isn't that he is a red man, or a white man, or both. It . . ."

"I understand," he said with a slow sigh, picking up his whiskey bottle and swigging deeply again. "I understand, and I ache for you, and for James. What you cannot see is the unavoidable tragedy of it." He stared at her. "James McKenzie will not leave his war. Especially since he has been branded all but a true renegade now. Because of you."

"Because of me—"

"Rumors persist that you were kidnapped by the Seminoles, that James McKenzie abducted you from your brother's house. It is easier for most whites to believe that you were forced away from your father rather than that you ran away from him."

"Oh, God!" she breathed. "It seems that I have but added to everyone's misery."

"You couldn't have changed anything, Teela. Neither could he have done so. Many of us know James well.

Those of us who do understand. But if you leave this wretched place, it will be best for us all."

He set the whiskey down, rose, and came behind her. She felt his hands upon her shoulders. "Life is always ironic," he told her, as if that explained everything. She sat very still. He kissed the top of her head and lingered behind her just a moment.

"Remember, if ever, now or in the future, I can do anything for you, anything at all, don't hesitate to come back to me."

His hands left her shoulders.

"I'll pray for you," he said softly.

"You are a good man, too, Joshua. The best of men. I will be praying for you. And I will miss you."

"Go home. Be safe," he said softly.

Then he was gone, and she was left in his office alone, and in the whole of her life she had never hurt so badly. She hurt for Joshua, and for the good captain who had staggered into surgery tonight, scalped and alive. She hurt for the poor men who had served beneath him and met the savage fury of the Seminoles.

She hurt for the Seminoles. For the children with their wide, trusting black eyes . . .

For the babes she had seen so mercilessly battered, bloodied, and murdered in the woods.

And she hurt for James. But it seemed that there was nothing that she could really do, except watch the slaughter.

Joshua was right; James McKenzie was a part of the war. He would not leave it, could not leave it. He would stay until the bitter end. . . .

And she would do what he had wanted at last.

She *was* going home.

Chapter 18

Despite his better judgment, James had allowed Wildcat to talk him into joining him outside Fort Deliverance when the military commanders hosted their soiree.

They had been there all night. They remained still.

Every time he had come to the makeshift fortress on the hammock with the others, he had assessed the army's strength. Unlike Wildcat, he was grateful each time to note the thickness of the walls, the multitude of guards. The fort housed numerous soldiers, all of them preparing to ride to battle, of course, just awaiting Jesup's "pincer" orders, and the words of the spies who came and went, hunting down tribes within hammocks, marshes, and swampland.

From a thick branch of a tall, moss-draped oak, he had watched as the festivities took place. By early evening, a host of soldiers had arrived down the St. Augustine road with a multitude of young beauties. A soldier was not a bad catch for these ladies; just as in all times of war, the male population of the territory dwindled as a crop of courageous young beaus fell in the line of duty. These soldiers might soon perish as well, but the young ladies seemed to have determined one and all that it was better to die a widow than an old maid.

While they observed the party, Wildcat gave him a running commentary on the women, predicting which fair maid would one day be as fat as a house and which would quickly become a shrew. James had paid him scant heed, grunting now and then to pretend he was

listening. Despite Wildcat's casual chatter, he sought any
chink in the wood-and-flesh armor of Fort Deliverance
while James sat in a cold sweat, hating himself for wanting a glimpse of her while longing to throttle her at the
same time. He'd felt as hot and twisted as iron beneath
a blacksmith's hands, damning her for being where she
was.

Even what she was.

He'd seen her at last through the poor windows of
the commander's house. Beautifully dressed, her gown
hugging her upper body, cinching her waist, flaring at
her hips, her sunset hair pinned elegantly high. She'd
danced with a tall, older man, staring earnestly at him
at first, growing animated as they spoke, even smiling.
The twisted feelings inside him had viciously intensified.

It was Jesup she'd danced with. General Jesup, in
charge of the entire removal operation now for the territory. Not a bad man, one weary of his struggle here.
Anxious to let the Seminoles be, unable to do so because
he was a military man, a servant of the United States of
America who obeyed orders and did his duty.

Wildcat had suddenly motioned to him, wrenching him
from his anguish. There had been a thrashing in the
brush across the clearing and beneath them, by the walls
that surrounded the fort. Wildcat had been ready to leap
down from the tree; James had detained him.

A man, bleeding, falling, half dead, had made his way
to the gate. His cry was answered. James had just made
out his anguished words. "My boys, my boys, my God,
my boys! It was Otter, Otter's men ..."

He was taken inside the gate. Through the windows
they saw commotion within; the soldier was taken from
the commander's house to the hospital, Joshua Brandeis
and Teela close behind.

For long minutes James had strained to see within the
hospital, watching as she moved, talked, worked over
the soldier. When all was done for the man, she sat, and
sat. Shared a drink with Brandeis.

And sat still.

All through the night, he had maintained his vigil in the tree. As the glorious pink and yellow streaks of dawn that could make the land a paradise began to stretch across the heavens, Wildcat shook his arm. "Look!"

The compound suddenly bustled with activity. Soldiers were racing out to a bugle call; men were mounting up.

Warren was among them.

James stared intently at the scene, trying to see if Teela remained at the hospital. She did. She came out to the wooden walkway in front of the hospital building and watched the activity as well. Her hair was straying from its pins. She wore a white apron decorated with blood.

The bugle sounded again and again. More and more men spilled out into the clearing before the buildings. Horses were led from their hastily built stables.

"He's leaving with at least two hundred men," Wildcat commented angrily. "A force we cannot hope to combat with the warriors I could gather."

James didn't reply. Wildcat was right.

He watched as the men said good-bye to wives and loved ones mounted up.

He saw Warren ride to his daughter. She stared at him, no expression in her brilliant eyes or weary features. Her fingers wound into the blood stained apron, her only outward sign of agitation.

They didn't touch; there was no fatherly kiss good-bye, no tear slipped from the daughter's eye. The slightest curve twisted her lip; she saluted Warren, and Warren rode away at the head of his troops.

James watched with relief as the gate opened, as Teela stood on the walk, watching the soldiers ride out. She wasn't leaving. She was staying within the fort. She would be safe.

He heard Wildcat swearing at his side. The soldiers were barely gone before Wildcat dropped from the tree.

James didn't slip down beside him at first. He watched Teela. Joshua Brandeis had come to stand at her side. He slipped an arm around her, leading her back into the

makeshift hospital hut. James felt his fingers curling into a branch of the tree. Again the twisting within him. *Well? He had told her over and over again to marry Harrington, to get the hell out of the territory.*

But she hadn't left. And now he prayed for her safety. And *twisted* with the damned awful hunger and wanting and jealousy.

He forced himself to slip to the ground with Wildcat. She was safe for the time being, not riding with Warren.

"I will kill him! I will find a way to kill him!" Wildcat said savagely.

"But not in the fort," James murmured.

Wildcat looked at him sadly. "Not at the fort."

They found their horses where they had been tethered deeper in the brush, mounted them bareback, and rode inland. James looked back, shaking off an uneasy feeling. Fort Deliverance stood strong beneath the rising sun. Still, he would ride far distant from it, he told himself.

He did not accompany Wildcat toward the hammock where Osceola had taken up his temporary residence. He rode to a place deep along a trail by a small lake he had known as a boy. Where pines carpeted the ground. Where, as yet, peace could be found.

And solitude.

From the whites . . .

From the Seminoles.

And the world torn between them.

Warren had been gone no more than twenty-four hours before Katy sought out Teela in the hospital.

"My dear, General Jesup has given word that you're to travel out with Captain Mayerling tomorrow. He and his company are riding north to St. Augustine, and there will be a ship there, the *Bonne Brianne,* to take you straight home to Charleston."

So soon! Teela thought with a moment's panic. So soon! She *had* wanted to go, she reminded herself. Ever since she had seen Otter's work, she had felt exhausted,

weary, unable to keep living on hope. She had wanted to leave this place of death and disease and torment behind.

She had told Joshua she wanted to go, and Joshua had made her feelings known to Jesup. And Jesup was going to explain to both her father and young John Harrington that he had insisted that she leave.

"Oh, Teela, you've been such a sweet friend. And I do love you dearly and will just miss you so terribly!" Kathy said, offering her a firm hug. "But, my dear, though some of the men do love you, too, there are those still angry with your sympathies for the enemy. Home will be the best place for you."

Home. She loved Charleston. Charleston was beautiful. She would always love Charleston.

But it was so far away.

And here . . .

James was here. Somewhere. The man who didn't really want her. Her soul was here, her being was here. Watching, waiting, always in a tempest.

She couldn't go.

She had to go.

"How wonderful," she told Katy. She tried to smile. Yes, she was going home. Far, far away. Maybe she would see things differently while walking along the Battery, where everything was beautiful and civilized and manicured.

Maybe at home she could nurse her wounded heart and soul. Learn to forget him. She hadn't heard a word from him, about him, in so very long. He might have even forgotten her name.

"Teela?" Katy asked worriedly.

"Katy, you're a dear. I'm going to miss you so very much, too. And I will pray for you, daily. I guess I'd best—pack," she said. She started to hurry from the hospital, then hesitated, turning back. "Mayerling . . . Captain Mayerling? Isn't he . . . ?"

"A tremendous Indian fighter, my dear! He's taken down entire villages. Indeed, he's cleared out entire

hammocks for the military! A brave and dedicated man. You'll be safe with him."

Safe ...

Yes, safe. She would pray the ride went swiftly. Mayerling was very much like her stepfather; in fact, he would surely have been her stepfather's choice as an escort for her. He had indeed killed many Indians. Young ones. Women. His men boasted of their exploits. Other soldiers—even fierce Indian fighters among them—whispered of his brutality.

It didn't matter. She had made the decision to go. Warren was not here to stop her. She would ride in the morning, be gone by evening's tide.

James slept without really sleeping, dozed while listening.

In the night he heard the bird's cry that wasn't a bird's cry.

He rose quickly, moving from the hidden shelter of the hootie he had built by the lake. He returned the cry and waited.

A second later, he heard a horse moving through the brush. He strode forward to greet Wildcat.

"I have come thinking myself a fool. Yet a fool who is a friend to one who I believe would give his life for his people, no matter who those people be."

James nodded, acknowledging the compliment. "What has happened?"

"Within the next hour a party is due to leave from Fort Deliverance. Captain Mayerling will be leading the party."

Mayerling. Despised among all braves. Otter would surely be moving like the wind if there was any opportunity to reach the man.

"How many in his party?" James asked.

"Two companies. Fifty, sixty men."

"Otter will massacre them," James said softly. His heart was cold. The men were doomed. He felt a sense of bereavement and pity, yet one of justice as well. May-

erling deserved death. He collected ears from the infant Indian children he killed. Yet some men would surely travel with him who would not deserve their fate.

"Your red-haired witch is riding with them," Wildcat said.

James stared at him, cold to the bone.

Then he said no more, racing back to his bay. He hadn't a single second to spare.

It was difficult to say good-bye to Katy, more so to say farewell to Joshua Brandeis. She never realized just how deeply he felt for her until he held her close, a hug good-bye. One that lasted just a few precious seconds too long.

She had never realized, either, just what he meant to her. The pity was that she loved him as a friend. A good friend, a best friend, one she would love for life.

Captain Mayerling was impatient to be under way, his words polite as he urged her to mount up for the ride.

"Dawn's breakin', Miss Warren. We'd best be on our way. The men and me will have a long enough ride back with supplies this evening."

Joshua released her. "You want to come back, you write now, eh?"

"Of course."

"I shouldn't allow you to come back. No man in his right mind should allow you to come back. I'm grateful as all hell that you're leaving."

She smiled. "Thank you!"

His smile deepened. He kissed her on the forehead, then spun her about, setting her up on her horse, a handsome black cavalry gelding that would be returning that evening along with the men.

The gates to the fort opened. She rode out in the center of the men. They walked their horses in silence. Dreary hour after dreary hour. She closed her eyes. Sweat trickled down her back. The landscape seemed to stretch on endlessly. The silence was heavy and oppressive. . . .

All at once, the most ungodly screeching seemed to tear the very air, ripping apart the silence.

"Attack!" someone shouted.

"Dismount! Battle formation!" Mayerling ordered. The words had barely left his lips when the sound of gunfire exploded around them.

Mayerling fell dead from his horse.

Again gunfire exploded, ricocheting through the air, so loud it was unbearable.

Her horse reared. She fought to steady it. Men leapt down from their mounts, taking shelter behind the trees that lined the road and copse from where the first fire of the ambush had come.

More shouts exploded. War cries whooped out, a cacophony of voices as the Indians burst upon them. So many of them! Turbaned, bare-headed, most of them half naked, armed with rifles, knives, bows and arrows . . .

Her horse suddenly went down. Shrieking, Teela slipped free from her mount, rolling before she was crushed. She tried to rise.

And then she saw a brave rushing for her. She had no weapon! She ducked down for a handful of dirt, threw it into his eyes, started to run.

Screams filled the air. She tripped over a body. She shrieked in panic, nearly falling upon a brave in the very act of stripping the scalp from a young, blond, and thankfully dead, soldier.

She turned back. The brave was closing in on her.

"No!" she gasped, racing harder.

A hand fell upon her, spinning her around. She barely saw the man at first. All that she saw was the knife and the trail of crimson blood that dripped in a stream from its razor-honed edge. . . .

The carnage taking place in the copse was horrible. James had seen battle before, more often than he had wanted. He had tasted blood and steel and fear. But these soldiers had already been bested; those who were not dead would die soon, and blessedly. He couldn't

even spare a thought for those dying such wretched deaths. He could only pray that Teela was not yet among them. As he rode more deeply into the scene of battle, he desperately searched for her.

He saw her across the copse. She'd been backed up to an old, half-fallen cypress tree. She stared up at the knife about to spill her blood, sever her life. She stared at the warrior about to slay her with hot defiance. Her hair streamed in its fiery splendor down her back, her eyes glittered in contempt for her attacker, never defeat. She was white, so very white, and startlingly beautiful here in these bloody surroundings, her features so delicate, chin so high. In those few brief seconds in which he saw her, the whole of his body seemed to constrict and knot with a burning fever. He hated her, wanted her, feared for her. Felt he would die without her, knew he could never have her. Because of this. This carnage. Even if he could save her life, they must never meet again.

The knife was plunging toward her.

Otter. Otter was about to kill her. Otter, who had forgotten his promise.

James reined in his pony and shouted in Otter's first spoken language, the Hitichi of the Mikasukee. "Otter, stop! By your word! Her death will mean yours!"

Not only did Otter pause in his act of murder, but the whole of the glade seemed to still as James dismounted swiftly, and strode toward Otter. The cries of victory and triumph and *massacre* went silent.

Teela did not seem to recognize that rescue was at hand. He heard her shout in fury.

"Bastard!"

Otter still had his hands in her hair. She didn't seem to care. She offered the brave a savage kick against belly and groin.

A good, solid kick. It must have been, because Otter cried out furiously in pain.

Damn her! Whatever influence James might have borne over Otter, he held no more. Otter had already

caught her arm and swung her back around. In a matter
of seconds Otter's blood-drenched knife would fall with
full force into her heart.

James catapulted across the clearing in the road, heedless of the dead that lay strewn upon the ground between them. There would be no reasoning with Otter;
James's only hope was his superior strength.

Before that blade could fall.

James cried out again, a cry of warning and of fury,
then pitted himself against Otter, catching the warrior's
muscled arm, the one that held the knife, and wrenched
it back with all his strength, causing Otter to spin. Enraged, Otter wrenched free, raising his knife again with
deadly intent against James. He leapt at Otter, bearing
him down to the ground beneath him. His fingers wound
around Otter's wrist. He slammed Otter's arm and hand
against the earth until the knife fell free from his fingers.
Otter stared at him with a deadly hatred. "You'd kill
me for the white woman, for Warren's daughter? Your
brains, your pride, lie in your cock, traitor!"

James sat up swiftly, hurtling the knife away. The
world around them had come back to life. Braves again
gathered rings from the fingers of the fallen, food from
their haversacks. "I'm not killing you, Otter. And you'll
not interfere with the white woman again."

Otter continued to stare up at him. James had no
choice but to leap to his feet, disdaining Otter. And go
for Teela.

Sweet *Jesu*! She had risen from the cypress and run
and was now halfway across the copse, racing back along
the trail. He shouted to her, then realized he did so in
the Hitichi he had spoken with Otter. It didn't matter.
He would terrify her now as much as any other warrior
here—yet it was imperative that he get her away from
here as quickly as possible, before his own position could
be forgotten by Otter's warriors, before they both went
down in a rain of carnage.

She deserved to be terrified. His fury at her rose along
with his fear that they might not make it out alive.

The running speed he had never fully appreciated became his greatest asset that day. He all but flew after her, winding his fingers into the skeins of vibrant red hair that flared behind her, the hair she had so nearly lost to Otter's lust for vengeance against Warren. She shrieked, still trying to fight, flailing, kicking, pummeling. He dragged her down to the earth, desperate to make her not just see him but obey him.

Swearing beneath his breath, he straddled her, catching her wild-flying fists, pinning her wrists above her head with one hand. She continued to twist and writhe with a savage energy that threatened to defy his strength. He swept the tangle of hair from her face, staring down at her. She was gasping for breath to scream again, yet the scream did not come to her lips.

She stared at him, closed her eyes, lay still and trembling.

"Look at me," he ordered curtly.

She did. Her eyes flew open, filled with ice and hatred. It had been a long time since they had met face to face. A lifetime in this hell that was the world between them.

"So you are a part of a war party now," she stated coolly. "Kill me, then, and have done with it! Slaughter me, slice me to ribbons, as your people have done with these men."

"It was a fair fight!" he countered angrily. Was it? He didn't know, he hadn't been there. There was no fair fight left to be had here. She knew that. She knew what the battle was here, knew that women and children died on both sides.

She had merely never been under attack before herself. Feeling death's whisper against her cheek.

"It was an ambush!" she spat at him.

He felt a coldness in his heart. She had been living in her world. Living among the soldiers. Attending dances, sipping champagne. Well, she belonged in her world, he told himself with all the contempt he could muster. But he meant still to force the truth of everything that went on here down her throat. "The captain leading this party

ordered the direct annihilation of two entire tribes, Miss
Warren, men, women, and children. Babes still within
their mothers' wombs. Yet you say these soldiers should
have been shown mercy?"

"I know that there is none within you! There is no
mercy to be found in this wretched hell, I am well aware,
so do whatever you will! End it!"

He leaned closer to her, longing to shake her, make
her see, make her realize . . .

What? He wasn't a murderer. Yet he was a part of
these people now stripping fallen bodies. He gritted his
teeth, arching a taunting brow to her. "End it? But we
do so enjoy torturing a good victim!" And how had she
become such a victim? She should have been at Cimarron, safe. She should have listened to him.

"What were you doing with these men?" he demanded. His words were incredibly harsh, he knew.
They had to be. She wasn't answering him. Shaking inwardly and praying not to show her any of his own fear,
he shouted the question again, "What were you doing
with these men?"

"Leaving!"

His heart slammed like a rock against his chest. "For
where?" he demanded.

"Charleston."

Charleston! Charleston! Damn her, now she was running home, when running was deadly! He'd told her to
go home before, but she'd defied him, stayed. Seeped
into his very blood, obsessed him, until . . .

He leapt to his feet, reaching down for her. She was
already trying to rise, trying to run from him again. Incredulously, he reached for her, slamming her with a
savage force against his body, determined to let her realize they still faced danger.

"Fool! You will not be going anywhere now!"

"You're the one who has always told me to leave!"
she reminded him fiercely. "You'd have thrown me off
your precious land were it possible. You *told* me to
go—"

"And you didn't listen."

"I was trying—"

"Apparently, you didn't listen in time," he snapped. "Leave my side now and you are dead, Miss Warren, don't you see that?"

A scream suddenly split the air. A scream that came from a white man not quite dead as a piece of scalp was sliced cleanly from his head.

Teela trembled in his arms even as her eyes continued to defy him. Her eyes glittered with a fresh fever. Tears. She was trying so hard not to shed them.

James called out in his own Muskogee, not looking around, keeping his eyes on Teela. "Warren's daughter is my captive; I am taking her now!" He caught her firmly by the upper arm, aware that he didn't dare loosen his grasp for an instant, yet aware that she could too easily see the tragedy strewn on the ground around them. "Don't look down and don't look back!" he ordered sharply.

Thankfully, he had managed to keep the bay, a gelding raised at Cimarron, well enough fed that the horse was a good and decent mount, able to carry them both swiftly from the scene of the carnage.

Still, he offered his horse little mercy, forcing it at reckless speeds over the trails, across marsh, through the bush. He wanted to put as much distance between them and the massacre as quickly as possible.

He didn't speak to her, didn't slow his gait, until they had traveled to his shelter within the hammock. There he dismounted, setting her quickly down before him.

She stared at him, very stiff and straight. *Regal.* The perfect white southern lady. Without blinking, she turned coolly from him, walking to the water.

He was grateful that she was alive.

He was furious that she had been nearly killed. Furious that he still shook with fear, furious that he had nearly been too late.

"So you were leaving," he drawled contemptuously. "Going back to graceful drawing rooms, charming com-

pany, and the elegance appropriate to such a well-bred young lady."

"I wasn't trying to go back to anything," she replied, perfectly composed.

He wasn't going to have it. She had nearly died. She was a fool, and she needed to be shaken until she realized what a dangerous little fool she was.

"You were just trying to leave this barbaric wilderness?" he taunted.

She spun around, staring at him. He wished that her eyes weren't so brilliant, her skin so silken white, her hair such a tantalizing shade of pure fire. "I was trying to leave the wretched battles and the horror and the—death! Your friend meant to slit my throat!"

Yes! Otter would have gladly killed her. A knife seemed to be slicing into him. "I'd have killed him very slowly had he done so."

"How reassuring! I could have cheered on your efforts from heaven."

"Or hell!" he said, eyes narrowing. Then his fury seemed to erupt within him. "Why did you leave my brother's house?"

"I had no choice."

"Jarrett would never have cast you out."

"I had no choice!"

Defiant. Still defiant. Stubborn and fighting to the end. He could best white enemies, red enemies. He could not best her.

Again his fury erupted within him. He strode to her. She tried to back away, but there was nowhere for her to run. He set his hands upon her, not knowing what he meant to do, wanting to shake her. Fire seemed to rip and tear throughout him. Heated iron, bolting, bending, twisting. He clutched her hand, dragged it against his bare chest. Words spewed venomously from his lips. "You left Cimarron, but not for home then, when you could have sailed right out of Tampa Bay. You forged across the territory! What then? Did sense come to you at last? Did you run from the war?" he demanded

harshly. "Or did you run from *this*? Bronze flesh, copper flesh, *red* flesh?"

She wrenched her hand away with such vigor he couldn't stop her.

"I'm not afraid of you!" she cried out. "I'm not afraid of you, you—"

"You should have been afraid! You should have been afraid a long time ago. You should have run back to your *civilized* Charleston drawing room the second you set foot in this territory. Damn you, you should have gone away then!"

"Go to hell!"

"I think I shall get there soon enough," he snapped back quickly, his temper soaring again. He didn't know quite what he was doing, but he was suddenly touching her again. Touching her. The anger was hunger, gnawing at his soul, eating away at his loins. His fury was passion. He didn't know what it was about her, what so obsessed him. He knew that he had watched her through the windows of her life long enough. His torment would come to an end for this night.

He set his hands upon her shoulders, backing her along the riverbank until she was forced against an old, gnarled cypress. His whisper was as hot against her as the tempest raged within him. "Weren't you sufficiently warned that there was a war on here? Didn't you hear that we pillaged, robbed, raped, ravished, and murdered? That red men ran free in a savage land? Didn't you hear? Or didn't it matter? Was it tantalizing to play with an Indian boy? Touch, and back away, before you get burned?"

"Anyone who touches you is burned!" she spat at him. "Burned by your hatred, your passion, your bitterness. Anyone is burned—"

He could bear no more. His fingers dug bitingly into her shoulders, a promise there would be no escape from him now. "Then, my love," he warned her, *"feel the fire!"*

And it was a blaze, wretched, demanding, ruthless, that filled him. With any sanity he'd never be so rough. But

sanity was lost. The rapacious hunger in his blood seized hold. He touched her, and fabric split and tore. He ground his lips down upon her mouth, tasting, questing, searching, demanding. Her hands were against his chest. He fought the violence within himself. She writhed and kicked, slammed her fists against him. He didn't care, couldn't care. He swept her up and cast her down upon the soft, damp earth, carpeted there by a bed of pines. He hated her. Hated himself. Hungered all the more.

He straddled her, caught her wrists. And she ceased to struggle. She stared at him, eyes liquid and glittering with fury.

He eased his hold from her wrists.

Her hands did not move against him again.

The tempest, the passion, stayed with him. Yet his fury suddenly seemed lost on the gentle breeze that swept around them. Her hair was a pool of fire against the green earth. Her flesh was absurdly beautiful against the rich and verdant ground. Theirs was a hell neither had created; it was an inferno that ignited the instant they had first set eyes on each other. There was no explaining it, and no denying it.

"What in God's name am I going to do with you?" he whispered.

And he touched her. Touched the rise of her breast, the hardened nipple, the fullness of the mound.

He nearly cried aloud. Desire shot through him like rifle fire. The sweetness of touching her was almost unbearable. His lips found hers again, and there was no protest to be found there. . . .

"Bastard!" she whispered.

Yes. Indeed.

"Perhaps. But tell me to leave you be. Say it with your eloquent words, and mean it with your soul!"

"Bastard!"

"I know, I know," he agreed, shuddering with the feel of her, the wanting.

He threaded his fingers through her hair, found her lips. Found more of her, inhaling the scent of her,

breathing her in, tasting her. His lips traveled everywhere, teased, hungered, teased, tasted. Ruthlessness filled him again, but ruthlessness tempered now by tenderness, by the desire to evoke within her a hunger to match his own. Her soft cries increased the desperation of his urgency and desire. There was no intimacy he would spare her, needing more and more of her. Nothing would deter him. Nothing but ...

She cried out suddenly, fighting him again. Yet fighting him because of the sensations exploding within her, sensations she longed to deny. Ruthless again, he took that moment to thrust deeply within her, sinking into a field of ecstasy with the simple act, shuddering before feeling the maelstrom seize hold of him. She'd been in his dreams too long. Haunting his sleep, taunting his days. Now she was his, encompassed in his arms. She touched him. Held him. Moved with him. He felt as explosive as a cannon, charged with a desperate, urgent desire, so glad to hold her, wanting to caress her forever, so damned on fire that he could not hold back the bursting climax rocketing from him. Into her. Again, again, until he was empty and she was filled.

He lay back, half ecstatic, half ashamed.

She stirred beside him, ripping her hair from beneath him. She tried to gather the pieces of her dress together—impossible. She cast them aside, rose naked like a goddess, and walked to the water. He rose restlessly and followed her. Stooped down to gather the water up in her hands, she would not look his way. "Feel the fire!" she whispered softly. "I am well burned!"

Shame constricted within him, along with the haunting jealousy he had not been able to help but feel when he had watched her within the fort. "You should have known better than to play with an Indian boy from the very beginning."

She stared at him. "I never played," she said with dignity, and rose again. She walked away from him, staring down at her destroyed clothing. "It will be a cold night."

A damned cold night, he thought. He stood, walking back to her. "I will warm you through it. In the morning we'll worry about something for you to wear." He'd be damned if he'd let her hear any kind of apology in his voice.

"I don't intend to stay the night," she informed him in her most regal tone.

The hell she wasn't staying. And the hell with her tone.

"You wanted to play the game. It is well under way. You didn't run to your drawing room soon enough. Now, Miss Warren, you will be my guest."

"Prisoner, so it seems."

"Whatever, you will stay."

She stood there stubbornly. With an impatient burst of violence, he swept her up from where she stood. He carried her to his small shelter in the woods, setting her down without much gentleness, silently damning her all the while. She wouldn't leave when he had told her to do so. When she might have done so safely. She had played her game. And now that game was so well and deeply engaged, she was going to have to see it through.

She shivered, and he set one of the fur blankets around her. He realized that he had taken her from the road, from near death, and all but raped her. Staring into her eyes, wanting her, hating her, refusing to believe that he loved her, he offered her a drink of water from a leather gourd. She accepted it in silence, drinking, then told him, "You'll never keep me if I choose to take my chances and leave. I came from a drawing room, but I've learned your jungle well."

What had he done to deserve her amidst this jungle of red and white, right and wrong? If she tried too hard to get away from her only salvation within the deadly terrain, he might as well kill her himself and get it over with!

"A challenge? Then let me assure you, if it is my choice, you'll never escape me."

"Damn you—"

"Teela, would you escape me to meet another brave

anxious for the beauty of your hair—ripped away along with your scalp?"

"I'd escape you to find freedom from this travesty. Not all Seminoles are barbarians—"

"What a kind observation, Miss Warren," he commented. He could feel anger growing within him again.

"Nor are you any more a Seminole that you are a white man! Don't tell me about the bronze of your flesh—even your mother carries white blood in her veins, indeed, you are actually more white than Indian—"

"Teela, one drop of Indian blood suddenly turns the color of a mans' flesh, and you are worldly enough to know that it is so. Look at my face, and you know that I am Indian."

"I look at your face and know that you are a creation of two worlds!"

"Then know this—life has made me Indian in my heart, and you must not forget it."

Was he angry that she was *not* Indian? Could not be part of his world? He wondered if it was so.

"Life is making you cruel—"

His temper exploded. "Enough, Teela. Enough for tonight!" he warned her.

Surely, she saw that he was frayed and weary. She gritted her teeth hard, her eyes glittered with fury. But she said nothing more. She turned her back on him and lay down in silence.

He stared at her back. At the soft white flesh rising above the fur. At the tangle of red hair streaming around her.

Leave her! Walk away! he commanded himself.

Tonight, he might as well will the moon to fall from the heavens.

He lay down beside her and took her firmly into his arms.

He couldn't have her, couldn't have her . . .

All the more reason to hold her, possess her, while he could. Feel her nakedness against him. Cherish it.

Chapter 19

Whir Teela awoke, it was barely dawn.

The colors filtering through the trees, cypress, pine, and moss-laden oak, were both delicate and striking. Just as the sun set with majestic palette, it rose in splendor as well. Shades of gold and pink and mauve entered the sky, in hues both soft and vivid. Light dazzled through tree limbs, catching little dust motes that rode upon the air. Dew covered much of the earth, creating a diamond pattern against it. Morning kept the insects at bay. In the distance an elaborate spider web spanned two branches, as dazzling with morning's moisture as if it were decorated with thousands upon thousands of precious jewels. The air was sweetly cool, clean, kissed with a breath of freshness. The sun would rise soon, hot and punishing, but for the moment the morning was completely and without doubt glorious beyond measure.

Morning . . .

She was awakening in a savage territory where the colors of morning and night were equally fed with the crimson of spilled blood. She had set out yesterday with over fifty soldiers. Every one of them must surely lie dead. She should be dead herself.

She half rose to discover that James had apparently awakened some time before her. He was dressed in a pair of form-hugging cotton trousers, probably homespun out of Cimarron, and his doeskin boots. Leaning against a structure pole of the hootie, he chewed a blade of grass, studying her reflectively.

She sat up uneasily, dragging the blanket of furs with her, meeting his gaze.

"Sleep well?" he inquired politely.

"Remarkably so. Amazingly so," she added, her eyes faltering, "for someone who saw so many murdered not twenty-four hours ago."

He made an impatient sound, tossing down the blade of grass. Three long strides brought him down beside her, balanced on one knee, his eyes intense as they challenged hers. "What did you call it when Mayerling went into Indian villages? War?"

"I called it murder as well, for that is what it was! That you all massacre one another with vicious brutality does not make it right for anyone! Don't defend those warriors who want my hair because of my father's actions. They are no better than he is!" she informed him heatedly.

He arched a brow at her slowly. "Perhaps not," he said. "Perhaps not. Except that you must remember, the military has come here to remove or exterminate the Seminoles. We've never assumed to remove or exterminate the entire white race."

She rolled away from him, frightened by passion and fury that seemed so alive within him still. "I'm sorry. If you wish to blame me for the war, I'm just too tired to listen."

She was startled when the blanket of furs was suddenly ripped from her, leaving her naked and shivering on the bare ground. She was instantly very awake, leaping to her feet, quite ready to do battle with him again.

"Tired, Miss Warren?" he inquired incredulously. "But you chose to stay here—"

"I was trying to leave when I was so nearly murdered yesterday!" she reminded him.

"Ah, but too late. I warned you time after time to go. I told you to stay at my brother's house. I do vividly recall stumbling upon you on a battlefield and warning you to keep out of the warfare! Did you ever heed a word I said? Alas, no. So here you are now, my prisoner,

preferable, I do pray, to being a hairless corpse on the trail. But, my dear Miss Warren, you may be too *tired* to direct a servant after a Charleston soiree. Seminole prisoners are never too *tired* to pay heed to their captors."

The morning air was damp and cool. He knew her as no other human being on earth, and she had certainly stood her ground often enough with pride. But she was both cold and humiliated at the moment, and very resentful of the fact that he frequently didn't even seem to consider that they were the same species.

"Go to hell, Mr. James-Running-Bear-McKenzie. Fill the air, the water, sea, space, fill it all with your violence and mockery and cruelty. You can't force me to listen, you—"

"Coffee," he snapped suddenly.

"What?"

"Coffee. Our women awaken and work, Miss Warren. Always. There is something to do. There has always been work, of course, but since your people came it is a harder life than ever our women lead. Preparing what food they can gather, what little can be grown, what can be hunted. And when the Seminoles are forced to run, the women pack what little they possess and carry it on their backs. They are forced to fight. To practice infanticide."

"What has this to do with coffee?"

"I'd like some."

"Good for you."

A strangled sound escaped her because he was suddenly all but on top of her. He'd captured a wrist, drawn her close. His eyes seemed like twin blades of steely fire, about to slice cleanly through her.

"You're a prisoner, Miss Warren. Ah, but you can't. appreciate that luxury. We used to take prisoners. We didn't seek to slay all women and children. We brought them back with us. Some grew to stay among the Seminole by choice. They learned our ways. Some even came to love their captors, and discover that they were not as

savage as they might have imagined. In fact, many realized they had seen more viciousness and savagery in
some of the finest drawing rooms in their own nation."

"Let go of me."

"I shall have to, won't I, if you're to make the
coffee?"

"Isn't coffee a white man's luxury?"

"If so, we have been trading for it for a very long
time, and I am a spoiled man in many things, and like
coffee for breakfast. The basic structure for the fire is
to the left of the shelter; the river water is fresh and
sweet, and you will find the rest of the fixings in the
haversack to the rear of the hootie."

"So you say!" she hissed, ripping free her hand from
his grip. She was shaking from more than the cold. This
time yesterday she had thought never to see him again.
Now he stood just inches from her, his bare chest brushing her naked flesh. She told herself that she absolutely
hated him for his judgment and mockery; yet again, he
had not failed her when her life had been in the gravest
jeopardy. Nor did such complex emotions matter under
circumstances such as these, for just his proximity was
enough to make her heart race, thunder with such speed
and fury against her chest that he must surely see its
beat beneath the white wall of her flesh. "I won't make
you coffee!" she cried.

He pulled her flush against him. His fingers splayed
into her hair at either side of her head. His lips found
hers with heat and fever and force, his hands then sliding
through the length of her hair, over her shoulders, down
to her buttocks, cupping them. She tried to draw her fists
between them. Her fingers pressed against the muscled
barrier of his chest. He drew her down to her knees,
whispering against her lips.

"I don't want coffee anymore," he informed her. She
was pressed down. To the earth. The morning-fresh
scent of it filled her. His scent swept into her, a part of
him, his warmth, his vitality.

"Wait! I will make coffee!" she began desperately.

But his hands were all over her, his lips, his teeth. "Always too late, Teela," he told her. "You ran for home when it was too late. You chose to obey me when it was far too late."

Too late . . .

She had dreamed of him, night after lonely night. Longed for him, longed for this. His touch on her. She hadn't imagined the moss- and pine-strewn earth as her bed, the sky was her canopy. The raw, rough feel of dirt against her back, the golden streaks of the sun shining down with an ever greater brightness on her nakedness. Hadn't imagined how wild it could be, how lonely in a deep green glade, how she might hear the ripple of the nearby water one second and nothing but the heavy tenor of his breathing the next. He touched her everywhere. Leaves rustled beneath him. She twisted to elude him, to avoid complete surrender. To no avail. His teeth gnawed gently at her nipple as his tongue bathed it. "I make—very good coffee!" she gasped, clinging to his head, trying to dig her fingers into his hair. Stop him. Have more of him. Love him. Be free of him.

"But you do this better!" he hissed softly, rising above her.

She whispered the word no. Surely, she did. But he didn't hear her. And she didn't mean it. Her legs were parted; he was within her. The rising sun touched her flesh with a wicked heat that nearly matched that of his ardor. Again different sensations caught and filled her. The flight of a bird far above their heads, the increasing intensity of the sun. The feel of his hands on her hips, rough, urgent, his kiss, his stroke, the earth beneath them, soft, cushioned by the moisture of the nearby river, and hard cradling her against the momentum of their rhythm. Then all blended together, and it seemed that the sun's rays had exploded inside her, liquid gold, warming and filling her body, radiating throughout it. She blinked, and the sun was still overhead. He was beside her, his weight eased from her, the scent and feel of him still touching her.

He rose abruptly, walked naked to the river, and plunged into it, walking and then swimming into the depths. She crossed her arms over her chest and looked up at the uncanny blueness of the sky. How was it possible to know such ecstasy and misery at one time? To long to be with him. To hurt and ache inside and feel so wretchedly hopeless?

A moment later, he was standing over her, river water dripping from his flesh.

"You need clothing," he told her abruptly.

She arched a brow at him. "Imagine! Perhaps you should have thought of that last night, Mr. McKenzie!"

"Ah, but Miss Warren. I hadn't seen you in some time. Foolish me. I had completely underestimated the enemy."

"The enemy?" she challenged furiously, leaping to her feet. "Enemy! As if I might have brought any of this about, as if I ever attempted to seduce or flatter you, as if—"

He caught her, drawing her close, laying a hand across her mouth, yet doing so gently. "You are the enemy, Miss Warren, because you don't know your own strength. Nor do you recognize my weaknesses." The words, so softly, almost tenderly spoken, brought a string of tears to her eyes. Half sobbing, she laid her head against his chest. He held her, fingers gently moving through her hair. His body was wet and very warm, rippling with muscle. It was oddly comforting to be there, leaning against him, held against him, both naked and somehow vulnerable beneath the endlessly blue sky in a place so devoid of other men and women and creature comforts that it might have been the first design of Eden.

He lifted her chin, kissed her lips gently.

"I'll make us some coffee," he said huskily.

"I don't mind making coffee."

"I'll build the fire."

"I'll get the water."

In a few minutes, coffee was nearly on. He had expertly stoked a cooking fire within a circle of rocks. His

coffeepot was, indeed, of European design. His coffee, however, was chicory, very strong and somewhat bitter. She sat by his side, looked longingly at the river as he hunkered down and set the pot on a wire-mesh camp stove above the flame.

"Want to go in?" he asked.

"Is it safe?" she asked nervously.

"Only a few alligators," he said.

She shivered violently.

He smiled, looking downward. "Quite honestly, there's no guarantee that 'gators will not be in any Florida waterway, but they are surely scarce here. And actually," he added, "you're not natural pray for a 'gator. He prefers birds and small mammals. With most wild creatures, you keep your distance, they'll keep theirs." He cocked his head. "Perhaps that's something you should have learned by now."

She smiled. "Are you, then, a wild creature?"

"Haven't you made that determination, Miss Warren?"

She shook her head slowly, gravely. "I reserve my judgment until I have weighed all that I have seen as fairly as I may."

He lowered his head. She thought that he smiled ruefully to himself.

"Want me to protect you from the wild things in the water?"

"Would you?"

"Yes."

"Are you afraid of the water?"

"No."

"Do you swim?"

She hesitated. "A little. Years ago, when I was very young, my father used to take me to the creek by my home. It's been awhile."

"You'll remember."

"You'll come with me?"

He nodded, reached for her hand, and drew her along with him.

It was wonderful. The water was so beautifully clear and refreshing. Fed by underwater springs, James told her. She could see beneath it, shake out her hair beneath it, plummet down and rise up. At first she stayed near James, not venturing out where the water was deep. But she did remember, and it was wonderful to swim. She wanted to explore, to feel the coolness of the water, the heat of the sun. She didn't think that she had ever felt such a sense of freedom.

And she was a captive. So she had been told.

James, surely far more accustomed to such sweet and natural freedom, tired of the water more quickly than she. "Come in!" he called her.

Treading water, she smiled and shook her head.

"Miss Warren!"

"No!"

She dived under again. She nearly shrieked, inhaling a lungful of water, when she felt something tug her foot. She kicked madly for the surface, and when she broke through it, she spun to see that it had been James.

She might have remembered how to swim, but he was an expert at it. "I called you to come out!" he snapped.

"And I wasn't ready!"

"You forget that I am the captor here, and you my prisoner."

"A pity, then, for prisoners must attempt escape at all costs," she said, still treading water.

"And if there was danger in the water?"

She arched a brow. He was lying. "What, sir, you now resort to scare tactics?"

He smiled. "Look down."

She looked. Good God, he wasn't lying. There were two massive creatures swimming beneath him. She shrieked, throwing herself at him, though to what avail she didn't know, for he was treading water as well. Indeed, her impetus sent them both hurtling downward, right toward the monstrous animals.

"Get out, get out!" she cried, but he was laughing, holding her close in his arms, treading the water for

them both. She hadn't seen him laugh so easily in a long time. No, she hadn't seen him really laugh so ever before. He was changed, entirely. He was a young man. A very handsome one. The curve of his smile was completely charming. Her heart slammed against her chest. So monsters were about to eat them. It was all right, because James was smiling, and no monster could come upon them that was a greater evil than the warfare that stretched before them.

"You've never seen them before?" he queried.

"Sea monsters? No! Why aren't you moving? Don't you care in the least—"

"Tara never mentioned them to you? Why, she is crazy about the beasts."

"I'm beginning to think that you're all mad beasts!"

He arched a brow but still smiled. "They're sea cows, as gentle as can be, and just like 'gators, they inhabit many of our waters. They're rather like ... well, they're mammals. They're like dolphins."

Teela shuddered. "Damned ugly dolphins!" she whispered vehemently.

"All right, my love, so perhaps they're more like cows in appearance, big and squat and hardly graceful. Never fear them, though. They wouldn't dream of feasting on any kind of meat, and certainly not human flesh."

He had leaned back, a strong and accomplished swimmer, able to backstroke with her weight half atop his chest, her arms still clinging around his neck. As he moved, she tentatively ducked her head into the water, watching the sea cows swim on by. There was a mother and a baby, so it seemed. Swimming together, oddly graceful despite their funny faces and heavy bodies. The mother was a good eight to ten feet long, mottled gray. The baby was perhaps four feet and a slightly softer color.

Teela surfaced, lying her head against his chest, feeling the ripple and movement of his muscles as he swam toward the shore.

"How odd," she said softly.

"What is odd?"

"That it can be so hard to tell sometimes by appearance what to fear—and what to trust."

"Fear everything," he warned her. "Trust no one."

"You trust your brother."

"That's different. He's my blood."

"White blood."

"Teela—"

"You're lucky."

"I'm lucky?"

She nodded earnestly. "You share that blood and something very special with your brother. I never had that with anyone. I loved my father, and he died so young. I loved my mother, and I lost her, too. Then I had Michael Warren."

He had reached a point of the river where he was standing, she realized, but he still leaned back, holding her. He smoothed back a piece of her wet hair. "Perhaps you don't realize, Miss Warren, how quickly you have made friends here."

"Friends . . . ?"

"Both my brother and Tara adore you. Robert Trent would defy the wind for you, and young Harrington is head over heels. Joshua Brandeis as well. Of course, the later three would certainly desire much more of you than friendship . . ." His voice trailed away, a slightly bitter note to it once again. He shrugged. "Unless, of course—"

"Don't you dare accuse me—"

"Accuse you? I've told you to save us all grief and marry Harrington!"

She tried to kick away from him; his hold around her tightened, his arms enveloping her. Then suddenly he was whispering fiercely, words tumbling out with passion and fever. "Listen to me, and listen to me well. Don't ever think that I don't desire you more than anything in all the world, or that I do not dream of holding you in my arms, feeling, breathing the sweetness of your flesh when you are away. Don't think I don't long to kill any

man when I watch you dance with him, laugh with him.
The jealousy in my heart and blood is like something
alive and dark and terrible, ready to riot, tear me apart.
Yet I say to you with all truth that yes, I wish you to wed
Harrington, because I wish life, peace, and happiness for
you. And God, yes, sometimes I'm bitter, so sorry, so
damned sorry that I can't say, yes, my father was a white
man, a rich white man. I can't buy my place in the white
world and turn my back on these people. They are mine.
It is their plight, my plight. My world is starvation, and
yours is a night dining on fine china to the sweet sounds
of violins. Mine is running, yours is dancing. Mine is the
rough earth, while yours is a feather bed. You cannot
survive without your world. I *must* survive without it.''

She pulled back from him, amazed at his words.
Amazed at his fever. He had almost said that he cared
for her. That he wanted her. For more than just the
passing of a frantic night, a fleeting, heated passion. She
stared at him, at the emotion in his eyes, the harsh,
rugged beauty of his features, and she wanted to cry out
with an agony greater than death. ''And what if I cannot
survive without *you*?'' she asked.

He pulled her close again, shuddering fiercely, holding
her. He held her for the longest time, and she was grateful for the river, glad of the water that drenched them
both, for it would hide the silent, damp tears that
streamed down her face.

''You can and must survive without me.''

''What is survival if the soul perishes?''

''I had thought my soul had perished long ago,'' he
informed her very softly.

''James—''

''Have you ever made love in the water?'' he whispered to her suddenly.

His words angered her, shattering the closeness of the
past moments. She felt as if she was choking. She tried
to free herself from his hold. ''My God, James, you
would know!'' she cried. ''You would know!''

''Shh! Shh!'' he whispered, and he was laughing again,

she realized, and when she met his gaze, there was a tenderness in his eyes unlike any he had offered her before.

"Damn you!" she hissed, but with no conviction.

"Since we've not shared the pleasure ..." he murmured. He kissed her. Long and deeply. The water felt chill. Her body seemed ablaze.

He began to make love to her in the water.

They drank the strong, hickory coffee. He clothed her in one of his large cotton shirts.

He caught fish for their dinner. She learned to skin and debone it, and cook it over the open fire. He talked about being a boy and visiting Charleston, where Jarrett's mother's family had hailed from. She told him how the city had changed.

Night began to fall. They sat on the riverbank and watched the sunset. Watched the colors in silence, felt the breeze touch them while the golden orb of sun flattened and stretched out, spreading tenacles in bright red, orange, yellow ... then a softer crimson, a mauve.

Darkness blanketed the landscape. Coolness seeped in along the river. He built up the fire, and they sat before it. He taught her a few words in Muskogee and then Hitichi, explaining how the languages differed, how white men had labeled the Creeks for the bodies of water they lived along. She told him how she had come to love medicine, what a thrill it was to treat a man and see him heal. She caught him watching her intently over the campfire, and she flushed and told him, "Any man, James. I love to see any man heal, be he white, red, or black."

He nodded, reached across the campfire, and kissed her. Then he rose, sweeping her up, carrying her to their makeshift bed within the crude hootie. He made love to her again, his desire never sated, just newly awakened as he learned each new smile she could offer him.

There was a war on. Hundreds had died, she had nearly perished. She hadn't even the clothes that had

been on her back. She lay in the wilderness, without
even solid walls around her.

She had never been happier in all her life.

In the middle of the night she awoke slowly. So slowly.
He had been arousing her, awaking her, his finger stroking down her spine. His lips, tongue, following it its
wake. He rolled her swiftly, his kiss suddenly searingly
intimate. She caught her breath, crying out a soft plea,
shuddering with the hot sweetness that soared through
her as he entered her. Moving. Oh, Lord. Moving slowly,
more swiftly . . .

Dimly, she heard the cry of a bird, and realized that
dawn was nearly upon them.

Again, the bird.

"What's that?" she whispered, suddenly pressing
against him.

"Nothing!" he muttered, but he paused. He hesitated,
then stood. The moon had risen. Naked, slick, shimmering
in its glow, he walked down to the water. He stood there
for a moment, as striking as some pagan god in the mystical light of moon with the sun just beginning to touch the
horizon. Then he turned, disappearing into the brush.

Teela shivered, pulling the furs around her. Birds cried
again. She listened intently, frightened that she would
hear some rustling in the brush. She heard nothing.

She gasped as she felt a hand upon her shoulder, spinning with alarm. It was James. She hadn't begun to hear
him return from behind her.

"What is it?" she demanded anxiously.

"Nothing," he told her.

"But what—"

"Nothing!" he repeated firmly, pressing her down.
Covering her with his body and warmth and strength.
Sexuality and seduction.

When he moved again within her, something was different. He made love with an even greater passion.
Reckless, almost ruthless. He held her with a greater
fervor. A greater urgency.

It seemed that he would never let her go.

* * *

Major General Joseph M. Hernandez stood quietly by his tent. A hundred and seventy men had set up bivouac in the ruins of Dunlawton Plantation. Night was falling. Peaceful time, pretty time. He loved dusk, the soft coating of shadow that added a muted beauty to his surroundings.

He was a Floridian, and did not mind his duty here in the territory. Of Hispanic descent, he had a fine, subtle sense of humor and a liking for humanity in general. He had befriended many of the Indians, and was often torn with pity for them. He knew the enemy he fought, and often wondered if the war could possibly ever end.

"General!"

John, a young aide-de-camp, approached him quickly across the overgrown lawn of the once beautiful plantation. He saluted quickly, and Hernandez saluted in return.

"We've gone with the Negro, sir, and spotted the Indian camp. It appears easily assailable now that it is discovered."

"Ah!" Hernandez nodded. Well, if the Seminoles did not suffer enough from the whites, they had their own numbers and rebellious Negroes to deal with as well. They were here tonight because a servant to the Mikasukee chief, King Philip, had grown weary of life in the scrub. Actually, it was the man's wife who had grown weary. Life was increasingly burdensome among the Indians. They were constantly on the run. Seeking poorer and poorer shelter. Seeking more and more desperately for any food to still their hunger, that of their children, their servants.

King Philip's man had promised to lead the whites to the chief's camp. And now he had done so.

"Sir?" John said.

Hernandez sighed deeply. "Ready the men. We will surround the camp, watch our enemy, attack by first light."

"Sir!" John acknowledged.

The order to march was sounded.

The dusk was too quickly gone. They marched by darkness, finding their positions around the Indian camp by midnight. He split his troops, ordering groups of volunteers to encircle the encampment on three sides. His regulars remained mounted, ready to ride in at first light.

No dog barked, no guard called out. Deep in the hammocks, too often the Indians slept with no guard. It had long been their way. The battle tactics of the whites were not easily accepted or realized, even when it brought terrible destruction upon the Indians.

By the first faint light of dawn, Hernandez gave the order for the troops to attack.

No alarm ever sounded. The soldiers ran over the encampment.

There was no battle. None of the Indians was slain, only one escaped, the rest were captured. There had been no chance to fight under the circumstances, and the Indians had known it. They were scarcely dressed; they'd scant time to pick up weapons.

"Royalty!" a soldier called, guffawing loudly. Shouts went up. Hostile cries from the Indians, jeers from some of the men.

Hernandez came forward, brushing past an army surgeon, Dr. Motte, who seemed ready as well to snicker at the sight of the man before him.

The Indian was not large in stature; indeed, he was covered in dirt, for he had run, probably for his weapons, and been dragged down. He was naked as a jaybird, except for the small breech clout covering his loins.

"A dirty king at that, eh, General?"

Hernandez, a striking, imposing man, turned with distaste to see who had called out. He didn't judge the Seminoles; he didn't judge his own men. They'd seen too much of disease and grisly death. He turned back to the man who, naked and dirty and not large at all, still managed to stand with tremendous pride before him.

"King Philip?" Hernandez said.

The Indian nodded in acknowledgment. Interpreters

stood by, but the *mico* had apparently understood his name.

"You are my prisoner, sir. Perhaps things will go better for you if you send out for your followers. Have them come in. Talk with us."

The interpreter repeated his words. Philip stared at him. Hernandez thought he smiled. Philip spoke in his own tongue to one of his people at his side.

"King Philip will send out runners for his allies."

"Tell him to bring in his son, Coacoochee. Known to the white men as Wildcat."

Philip again appeared to be smiling. He said something to a man at his side.

"What was it?" Hernandez asked John softly. He had learned many words himself in the Indian tongues, but John had a gift for language and spoke Philip's language fluently.

"He said, sir, indeed, he will send for the 'Wildcat.' And he says that white men should take grave care. He cannot know what manner of creature will come once a wildcat is summoned."

Hernandez nodded, acknowledging Philip's importance. He turned on his heel, aware that the night wasn't over. Another captive, called Tomoka Jon, had promised to lead them to another camp.

He should have been glad, proud of his leadership, proud of his troops. In all the time they had battled so far, he had just made one of the most important captures ever, that of King Philip. The more leaders they brought in, the more they would break the resistance.

He had Philip. And Philip could bring him Wildcat. And other wild denizens of the forest as well perhaps. Smart, dangerous creatures. Like an Alligator—or a Running Bear.

He felt weary, not elated.

The Indians, it seemed, were far wiser than many of their white enemies realized.

Wildcats and other creatures of the forest simply could

not be kept in captivity. They couldn't be tamed, and they couldn't be chained.

God alone knew what blood and fur might fly when they were accosted.

Chapter 20

The days passed strangely for Teela and James, as if time had somehow stopped within the copse, gone still. It had not, of course. Beyond the green shade of their hammock, the world, and the war, were going on. But here, for the time, it didn't touch them.

At first James seemed somewhat subdued, brooding. And almost determined to make Teela see that she couldn't endure the hardships of life in the hammock.

He told her that they had nothing to eat; she said that she wasn't hungry. He found roots that could be ground for a starch stew or porridge; she learned to grind roots. He told her that the Seminoles always kept a sofkee pot going, so that any visitor or man or woman within the tribe might eat when he or she was hungry. He told her Seminole women served their men.

She told him she wasn't Seminole.

Two mornings she was wretchedly sick, and determined he wouldn't realize it. He did see it, damned himself, and collected some wild berries and some squash and potatoes from an abandoned plantation. He killed a rabbit, which she annoyingly and expertly prepared over a spit, according to his directions.

His temper eased. His brooding gave way to a simple thoughtfulness.

And finally, in the privacy of the copse, they managed to cease being white and Indian, and simply be.

James didn't mention what he was going to do with her; Teela didn't ask. They swam, they fished, they lay in the sun, they slept beneath the moonlight. They made

love at any hour. They saw no one, they wished to see no one.

The best times, Teela thought, were those when the sun was setting. When the sky was etched in magenta, when cranes and egrets streaked across the heavens and came to rest upon gnarled roots by the water. Sometimes then James lay propped against the trunk of a fallen cypress, and she lay curled within his arms, and they both watched the sky and talked. One day when they had spent nearly a week in their haven, there had been rain, and the sun was just beginning to fall with an extraordinary beauty. Teela told him about Lilly, about how her mother had thought that marriage to Michael Warren would be so wonderful, fitting, and proper. Lilly believed with her dying breath that Warren had been a fine father for Teela. "I don't think she ever loved him. I think she loved my real father, but then . . ."

"Then?" James queried.

Teela shrugged. "Well, marriages are often arranged in Charleston. She'd known most of her life she was going to marry my father. I used to love to dream about them, though. To imagine that he had been the great love of my mother's life, that they'd shared a passion beyond bounds. Children want to believe those things, though, don't you think?"

"Sometimes they're true. In that, I was lucky. I know that my father adored my mother." He hesitated a moment. "He was willing to give up everything for her, not that she asked him to."

"She must miss him."

"She has missed him a long time," he said softly, his hand moving gently over her arm as he spoke. "He was quite a man, my father. When Jarrett's mother died, he grieved terribly until he found a new interest in life. Indian culture. He was intrigued, fascinated, by other cultures and people. He was twice blessed. He met my mother, and she adored him, and Jarrett." He smiled ruefully. "At times, I believe, she is actually more fond of Jarrett than me. I accused her so once, in good

humor, really, and she told me that she'd had Jarrett longer than me."

Teela laughed. "Jealous little ruffian, eh?"

He smiled, shaking his head. "Mary has a tremendous capacity for love. She might still marry again, who can say? She was sixteen when I was born, and gives the appearance of a young woman even now. She has mourned Father a long time and I imagine—" He broke off suddenly.

"What?"

"She might indeed marry again. If any men are left alive to marry when this is over."

Teela drew slightly away from him. "I don't want to talk about *this*."

He hiked his weight up, half leaning over her. His eyes were grave. "Eventually, we're going to have to talk about what we're going to do."

"We could stay here," she said stubbornly.

"Not forever."

"Why not forever?"

"Warren will hunt us down and you know it. And though I honestly wouldn't mind a chance to rip him to shreds, he'd kill so many others in the process of finding you that their lives would be on our conscience."

"So what will you do?" she demanded.

"I don't know yet," he said evasively.

"Go back to war," she accused him.

"And have you a better suggestion?"

"Yes! Quit fighting, live at Cimarron with your brother and your daughter, and—"

"Trade my life for my honor and the debt I owe my mother and her people?"

"What about the debt you owe your father, your brother, your friends?"

"They are not threatened with extermination."

"You've said you will not raid plantations—"

"And I will not, you know that."

"Then walk away from the war!"

"Do you think it will be so simple now?"

"What do you mean?"

"Never mind."

"Damn it, James—"

"Never mind!"

"You need to explain yourself and listen to me in return. The war will eventually be lost. The army will come, and come again in droves."

"Mark my words, Teela, you are wrong. This war will not be lost. One Indian standing firm can defeat a dozen exhausted soldiers, hungry, weary, and riddled with disease."

"The Seminoles are hungry, and many have died of malaria and measles."

"Teela—"

"James, if you just—"

"Stop."

"But I—"

"Enough!"

Enough, enough! He spoke, and she was supposed to obey.

She startled him by leaping up, her hands on her hips, looking like a very feminine pirate in his white cotton shirt, tied at her waist with a dyed red band of rawhide. She glared at him through narrowed eyes. "*Enough! Enough!* What is that, Mr. McKenzie, your favorite word? Order? Command, rather, I should say! Well then, you're damned right. I've had *enough*!"

She spun away from him, the wild length of her hair flying behind her. Shoulders straight, head high, her posture suddenly again that of the well-bred southern lady she was, she stalked away from him.

He watched her for a moment, vexed. Then he smiled slowly, because her appearance was so at odds with her bearing. His shirt chastely covered her shoulders, back, and rump, but there stopped, revealing the slim and delicious length of her legs. Her carriage was prim; her movement was unbearably evocative. He watched her another moment, making her barefoot way a good distance from him along the water. Where she was going

he didn't know. That she was never going to reach her point of destination was a dead certainty.

He closed his eyes briefly. Their time was limited. He knew it well. It seemed they'd found a hidden paradise. But Wildcat had always known this place. Jarrett knew it as well; they had sometimes come across the territory as children; they had come for conferences; they had celebrated the Green Corn Dance with other tribes and factions. They had played here, a refuge for them then, a refuge for them now. Luckily, only those he trusted completely—whites and Seminoles—did know of this place.

Wildcat knew he was here. He had come briefly in the night to tell James that Otter had conceded Running Bear's right to the woman. She would be safe from Otter in the future. Otter was pleased that his attack had been so perfectly planned. Only a few soldiers had escaped the slaughter. Wildcat had spoken very quickly, warning James that white soldiers were rumored to be in vast numbers all around St. Augustine. Though James was safe from Otter, he had best take care on all other fronts.

Wildcat was a strange friend for James. No one, not even Osceola, was more determined to dig in. He could battle and kill without blinking and speak his mind clearly no matter what the opposition or consequence. He was a man of integrity who could also keep completely quiet when necessary, and in the bonds of friendship he could be utterly trusted.

So much for Otter and Wildcat.

He didn't need thoughts of either man to warn him anew that his time in this strange haven was limited.

She was still walking. With such dignity. Yet still, she . . . swayed. She was so angry, aloof, disdainful, proud . . . Delectable.

He rose swiftly, agile, silent. It was true that his silent speed was uncanny.

Yet she heard him. In the split second before he

caught up with her, tackled her, and brought them both down to the earth.

"Enough!" she shouted to him, gasping for air, struggling furiously against his hold. "Enough, enough, enough—"

"Enough!" he agreed, his fingers lacing with hers, forcing them against the damp earth.

Yet as his body straddled hers and his lips silenced any further argument, he realized with a sinking feeling of anguish that it would never, ever be enough.

They had to talk with the white men. Another parley. The events taking place recently demanded that it be so.

Staring into the fire, seated before it, Osceola thought these things with a great deal of pain in his heart.

Yes. He had to talk. The children were starving. The women were bones. The warriors themselves were little more than skeletons. Some temporary truce must be made.

If he went in to talk, he realized, he might never walk away again. He had done things the whites did not understand and would never forgive. He had waged the war against them that they had waged against him and his people.

He was interrupted in his weary thoughts by the sudden arrival of Otter. The warrior stalked with his typical fury to stand before the fire opposite Osceola.

Osceola refused to acknowledge him, so Otter sat before him.

"We need Running Bear. Now," Otter told Osceola. "That he fought me I will accept, for I challenged him to do so. That he took a white woman whose scalp might now hang from my rifle, I accept, for he fought for her. I have granted his right to her, sworn her safety from me. But he stays deep in the hammock now when he is needed. He stays with the white woman, forgetting us. You know where he is. Tell me. I will go for him now."

Osceola looked up at Otter. Yes, he knew where Running Bear had gone. Wildcat had been to see him very

early one morning, before the dawn had begun to brighten the sky. They had spoken briefly. Running Bear had the problem now of the white woman, but he trusted Osceola, and Osceola would not betray that trust.

Wildcat could not go to Running Bear again. Wildcat had felt he had no choice when his father's messenger had come to tell him that the whites had demanded King Philip bring in his son or perhaps face the hangman's noose. So Wildcat, a fierce warrior they needed badly, was a captive of the whites.

But there were others who could be trusted to summon Running Bear. Despite Otter's words of honor, Osceola could not trust Otter with directions to the secret copse.

Osceola was suddenly very tired.

There were days when he could rise and feel as well as he ever had, days when it seemed that strength and sun and life came with swift energy to his limbs. Then there were times when he believed that he dreamed those days, for some mornings when he woke, he could almost imagine that death slept atop him like some dark, blanketing form. As it did so often lately, Osceola's mind drifted back in memory.

Wild Orchid had been so beautiful then. The best that three shades of men had to offer. Her skin was deeper than copper, her eyes darker then black. Her hair was like the wing of a raven, curling beautifully from her Negro heritage while her white blood softened her features. He had warned her often enough when they had been young to keep clear of the soldiers, but she had loved life. Loved to move, to dance, to run, and so, long before his run-in with Wiley Thompson that had become so well-known, he had become enemies with the man. Because Wild Orchid had come too close to the whites, and she had been seized as a runaway slave. It hadn't mattered that he had explained the beautiful mulatto was his wife. She had been taken from him, and he hadn't had the strength or the power then to fight and demand that she be returned to him. He had been able

to do nothing but follow behind through the bush as the soldiers had taken her, chained, to St. Augustine. All along the way he had looked for a chance to attack the whites and rescue her. They had been too strong. He had all but wept with fury and frustration. Then he had waited for word of her sale, and he had learned that she had been stripped down on the block and sold to a gaunt-faced white man who intended to take her to a plantation near Tallahassee. They had laughed while she stood on the block. They had commented on what fine sport she would make in a white man's bed, how lush and erotic her flesh would appear against the whiteness of cotton sheets.

He had been sickened, knowing then that to wage a war would mean sure death for him and so many others. They hadn't planned as yet. They hadn't gathered rifles and gunpowder. They were too weak. Yet even as he waited just south of St. Augustine, desperately plotting and planning, he had heard a woman's joyous cry, shouting his name in greeting. And through the brush she had come running to him. Behind her, leading the pony she had ridden, were the McKenzies. Running Bear and his white brother. They had known, they had heard of the injustice, and they had gone to the overseer and persuaded the licentious bastard to sell her to them. At an exorbitant price, Osceola was certain, but neither brother would ever comment on it.

Now neither of his wives was so very young or fragile, but neither had he forgotten what that first hunger and passion of love could be, denying all reason and logic. Wild Orchid had been precious to him all these years, as had Morning Dew. He loved his children by both wives; he knew the strength and support of his family, all begun by love.

He could not deny James McKenzie his passion. Especially, he thought with a certain humor, since he had seen the red-haired woman himself.

"You will leave him be one more night," Osceola said. "Let him watch the sun go down in his hammock one

more time, see the colors streak the horizon, feel the kiss of the dew upon his flesh with the coming of the dawn."

"Osceola, you forget the events that have taken place! We need him—"

"One more night will not change the war, not the history of our world or theirs. I will send for him myself come the morning," Osceola said.

He would let McKenzie have one more sweet taste of his savage paradise before the world exploded upon them all.

General Thomas Sydney Jesup sat at his desk, studying again the war orders from Secretary of War Joel Poinsett. He closed his eyes morosely, damning his Florida duty. In fact, for the moment, damning the military altogether.

Let them come down from their high horses in Washington! he thought angrily. They had ignored him. Ignored his plea that they leave the Seminoles alone. Let them flee south. Live out their pathetic, starving lives in the no-man's land that filled so damned much of the mosquito-infested peninsula.

He was a military man, a hard-core soldier. He had come to Florida from battling the Creeks, and he knew how to fight Indians. If he had ever said anything negative regarding any of his predecessors as to their stint of duty as commanders in Florida, he had let it be well-known that he retracted such statements. This was hell. A war that couldn't be won. He had quickly, painfully learned that the Seminoles could split their numbers and disappear into the terrain while his men floundered in hammock and swamp. He had come expecting to round up the Seminoles with all speed, and send them west to live. Poinsett was an able man, an incredibly able man, in Jesup's opinion. But Jesup damned him just the same. Poinsett had left him no choice but to exterminate the Indians.

Jesup sighed, running his fingers through his white hair. His bitterness extended toward the enemies. Before

the escape in June of the nearly seven hundred Indians from the center at Tampa, he had believed he had broken the resistance, that his war was all but over. But then those seven hundred had disappeared, with the wily Osceola at the head of it, or so it seemed.

He slammed a fist against the table. The Indians deserved no decency on his part. They knew nothing of any code of honor. They were slippery, cunning, treacherous.

If he had to use treachery against them in return, then so be it.

He set aside the missive from the secretary of war. He picked up his quill and began to pen the orders he would give in turn to General Hernandez.

His hand shook as he wrote. He set his quill down. And still his hand shook. A chill fell over him. He shook it off. He refused to admit that his ill feelings might forebode the damning consequences of his own actions, setting the cry of treachery upon himself for his lifetime, and all history yet to come.

The day had been a good one. They'd awakened to a powder blue sky, puffs of clouds moving across it. Teela had been ecstatic to catch a fish herself, spearing it through with lightning speed. He'd skinned it, they cooked it and ate it with nuts and fruit.

Now they played in the river. Teela had become an excellent swimmer. The water was filled with an abundance of sea cows, and Teela took great pleasure in them. She'd even decided that they weren't ugly anymore. There were adorable, as charming as otters, as gentle as puppies.

"There!" she cried to James suddenly.

"Where, what?" he asked, turning.

She dove beneath the surface, caught his foot, dunked him thoroughly, then swam away with a practiced speed that startled even him. He sputtered to the surface. "Playing with fire again, eh, my love?" he shouted, swimming hard to pursue her. Damn. She was getting good. She reached the bank and raced out of the water,

laughing and shrieking. He followed her. Despite the
fact that she was a quick learner and swam very well
indeed now, she hadn't a chance against him on dry land.
Yet even as he sped after her, he suddenly ground to a
dead halt, staring past her to the entrance of the secluded copse.

There was a rider there, a very old black man on a
gaunt gray mare. It was difficult to determine which was
more pathetically thin, the man or the horse.

Osceola's old servant, Riley, had come for him, he
realized, the air all but sucked out of him with the
knowledge that the days he had clung to so desperately
had come to an end. That Riley had come already indicated trouble, for if things were normal, Wildcat would
have been the one to come.

Teela had been looking back at James as she ran. Still
laughing, she whirled around and shrieked in sudden terror as she nearly crashed into the black man who had
dismounted from a horse. James found motion again,
running swiftly enough to be there when she backed
away from Riley, trembling. Perhaps Riley was a startling visage. He dressed in buckskin trousers and a white
man's shirt. A turban of bright cotton and egret plumes
sat atop his dark head and cascaded down his back. It
was a magnificent headdress, a gift from Osceola to a
faithful servant. It made him appear, however, to be
nearly seven feet tall.

James wound his arms around Teela, then eased her
behind him. Her hands set upon his hips, the fullness of
her naked body pressed against him as if he were a barrier of steel.

"Riley," he said quietly. "Teela, it's all right. It's
Riley. He offers us no harm."

She was shaking still, but it occurred to him then just
how greatly she trusted him.

"Don't be afraid," he said softly.

"I'm not afraid. I'm—I'm naked James."

"Riley will take his clothes off, too, if you want."

She slammed a fist against his back.

"Riley, have you something there Miss Warren might wear?" he asked.

Riley nodded gravely, tossing a satchel he carried down to James.

"Real clothing," James muttered, bending down to open it. Teela quickly ducked down behind him. In the bundle he found a full, flared indigo-dyed skirt and a colorful pullover blouse. He turned and offered both to Teela, who scrambled into the items quickly and awkwardly, refusing to rise behind him until she was dressed.

"Coffee, Riley?" James suggested. His breeches were back by the cypress log, and it didn't seem that Riley had brought anything for him.

"Coffee would be fine fittin', Master James," Riley said. The old man's usage of both the Muskogee and Hitichi languages was fluent, but he had always addressed James by his English name and in the English tongue.

"Well, let's all come along, then, shall we?" James said, starting back to his pants and their shelter.

"Did you come alone?" Teela asked him.

"I did, Miss Warren."

"How did you know where we were?" Teela demanded.

"Osceola knows this place. Wildcat came before and talked to James. We knew where James would be when the time came."

James winced, stiffening his back for a moment.

"Wildcat was already here?" Teela asked sweetly. "And we didn't know?"

James found his breeches and scrambled into them. When he turned, old Riley was grinning and Teela looked flushed. "Master James, he knew. He knew."

Teela turned her stare on James. Accusingly. He brushed past her to get water for the coffeepot. "We always knew that our time here was limited," he told her.

She followed him to the water. "Your friend, this Wildcat, was the bird, right?" she demanded in a furious

whisper. "I was, we were—" she sputtered. "And he was there!"

He sighed. "Wildcat was discreet. Since he did rather interrupt us in the middle of something."

"Bastard!" she hissed.

"He has seen far more," James said with a shrug. "Besides, it was dark."

She started to shove him. He caught her hand and warned her harshly, "Teela, he came, he went. He didn't mean to interrupt. He came to tell me we were completely safe from Otter. Now, my love, you behave, or I'll have to paddle you black and blue to keep my standing—and perhaps my life—among the people. Riley is a good man but a damned talkative one."

He didn't give her a chance to obey or disobey, keeping one hand and a firm grip upon her arm and another on the coffeepot as he rose and headed back toward the hootie. Old Riley had already laid out some of the delicacies he had brought them, smoked deer meat and cornmeal cakes. Dragging Teela with him, James quickly had the chicory coffee going. As the fire lapped beneath the pot, James asked Riley, "What news?"

"Soldiers seized all of King Philip's camp. King Philip was betrayed by his servant, whose woman was unhappy." Riley paused to glance at Teela, silently warning against the evils of female influence. "Wildcat has gone in to the whites for his father's sake. There is to be more talk. Osceola has sent messages to General Jesup, and General Jesup has said that there will be a meeting again. Running Bear, Coa Hadjo will speak for Osceola, but Osceola has asked that you accompany him and the others when they meet."

James bowed his head. "He knows that I will come."

Riley hesitated. He looked at Teela again. "Osceola says that you must know there is talk that you are the most dangerous of all Indians, a white Indian."

"Why this talk?" James demanded, frowning.

"The white soldier, Warren, has said that you planned

the murder of many men in order to steal his daughter. Warren says that you should be hanged."

Teela gasped, horrified. "He is a liar!"

"There are many who will believe his lies," James said quietly.

"But I'll tell them all that he's a liar—" Teela began.

"Tell them what you will," James said. "Some men will believe you, and some will not."

"Then you can't go in with Osceola!" Teela said. "James, you must stay hidden!" she insisted fervently.

"I have to go."

"You cannot! You—"

"Teela!" he warned her, his voice low and grating, a harsh command that she stop.

Riley said, "You can keep your camp here until morning. Then Osceola asks that you meet with him tomorrow, behind the soldiers' road that leads to the east."

James nodded. "That will be fine."

"That will not be fine—" Teela began.

James clamped a hand over her mouth, dragging her hard against his chest. "That will be fine," he repeated.

Old Riley poured himself coffee and rose. "I will sleep behind the copse," he told James. James nodded. Teela was fighting like a scalded wildcat against his hold. He gave her a firm shake, not daring to release her until Riley had made his way from the copse.

"You can't go! You can't go!" she told him, tears blinding her eyes.

He stared down at her, not replying. "You can't, you can't, you can't!" she said, slamming her fists against his chest, beating him, pummeling him. He didn't stop her. She kept it up until her blows were soft, until her words were sobs.

"We've a last sunset," he told her.

"You can't go. You can't—"

He hushed her with a slow, tender, heartbreaking kiss.

Yet as darkness came, she was the one to refuse tenderness. To hold him fiercely. Make love with a wild, wicked, violent abandon.

But with sobs, not words. Now her very violence brought her to exhaustion. When at last she slept next to him, he cast a fur around his shoulders and left the copse, coming to Riley.

Awake, resting against an oak, Riley smiled grimly, as if he'd expected James.

"I must make arrangements for Teela. Osceola knows this."

"Osceola has sent word to Jarrett McKenzie, and he and the young soldier Harrington will come for your woman."

James nodded, feeling a twist like a knife in his abdomen. "Sleep, Riley," he told the old man.

He returned to the hootie and stared down at Teela. Her cheeks were liquid with tears. Her hair was a fan around her, beautiful in the moon glow, red, radiant. She was almost ivory in her whiteness, her naked body as perfect as porcelain. He lay down beside her, intending to let her sleep.

But their last sunset had already fallen.

He woke her. Silenced her words, her protests. Made love tenderly, fiercely, tenderly . . .

Indeed, their sunset was gone.

And dawn was coming. A red dawn. A bloodred dawn.

Chapter 21

Teela was subdued during the ride early the next morning.

She kept her distance from him at first, and he thought that she was feeling ill again. He didn't attempt to comfort, though he worried at the many deadly diseases she might fall prey to. No matter what emotions and desires tore at his heart, it was not just necessary but good that she was going to be back in his brother's care. Harrison's care, even. Out of the territory, with any luck!

She swam without him, using sand for soap as he had shown her, and dressed without a word in the strange new outfit Riley had brought her. He longed to seize hold of her, defy the bleak future. He turned away. He couldn't hold her tightly enough to change the future. He braced himself as he did so, wondering if this was the last time he would ever see her. A million different things could go wrong. Osceola's parley could turn into a desperate battle. Warren might have already made arrangements for Running Bear to be seized and hanged upon first sight. Yes, Teela was best far removed from him. There was nothing that she could do.

"Teela! Come along!" he told her when she hesitated by the water, watching the sun rise. She turned back to him. Her hair was as soft as angel's wings, floating freely down her back, its exotic color wildly at odds with that silky softness. Her eyes were brilliant, beautiful. She lowered her lashes, though, and came to him. Riley had mounted. James put his hands on Teela's waist to lift

her atop his bay. She caught hold of his shoulders, eyes blazing into his. "Don't go!" she whispered.

He held still for a moment, wishing with all his heart that he could oblige her, very nearly doing so.

Despite the fact that they were riding double, they made good time, both Riley and James knowing the land so well. The sun rose swiftly, but it was a beautiful day, just kissed by a hint of the coming of fall. The trees dappled green light over their heads. They made their way through swamp and pine barrens.

Toward noon, James paused, seeing that the trail had recently been used. His brother was near, he was certain. He felt Teela jump when he let out his bird's cry, a perfect imitation of a loon. Jarrett McKenzie came riding out of the bush toward them. He was accompanied by Robert Trent and a few of his plantation men, including some of the Indians who had long worked for him.

He didn't dare speak to Teela. He dismounted from the bay. Jarrett dismounted from his horse as well, and the brothers greeted each other in the pathway with an affection neither man made any attempt to hide, embracing, then stepping back at last.

"My daughter?" James asked.

"Sends her love. She is very well."

"Let's walk for a moment, shall we?" James asked. Jarrett nodded in agreement, and the two turned, heads lowered in private conversation.

"I hear Warren has stated that I was behind the attack on the companies out of Fort Deliverance."

Jarrett nodded grimly. "The good news is that General Jesup and most sane commanders know you too well. They don't believe the story. Also, as you must know now, King Philip and his people were taken, and then a group of Yuchis—Blue Snake and Yuchi Billy among them. Philip sent for Wildcat, and Wildcat is a prisoner now as well."

"Yes, I know."

"Wildcat has told the generals in quite disdainful terms that they are fools. That Warren's daughter would

have been dead for simply wearing his name were it not for your interference."

"Well, that's good, for it seems Osceola has arranged a meeting with the military."

"Yes. Some speculate that he has agreed to meet so that he can discover some way to rescue Philip and the others. Jesup has not forgotten the seven hundred men Osceola freed in June."

James shook his head. "He has moments when he is strong, but he is sick. Really sick. I don't think that the military commanders realize just how sick he is."

"That may be. I hope that the next meeting will bring peace, but I feel uneasy about it."

"What do you know?"

"Nothing—I am no longer trusted by our military friends."

"I'm sorry."

"Don't be. We are both at a loss in this war."

James nodded, turning toward Jarrett, extending a hand to his brother. Jarrett gripped it. "Thank you," James told him.

Jarrett shook his head. "There is nothing to thank me for. We are both our father's sons. Perhaps the time will come again when we can be like a normal family. I pray for it. I hold your property against that time. I beg you to take care, and live to let us touch that time again."

James grinned, nodded. He glanced toward Teela.

"Take care of her. It's a heavy burden I set on you, I know, but please try to keep her out of trouble."

Jarrett hesitated. "I think I can do so. Tara is in St. Augustine with the children. We've taken a house there for the fall and winter so that I can, perhaps, be nearer the present theaters of operation and step in if I am needed. It's my understanding that Osceola's council is going to be set not far from Fort Peyton, just seven miles south of the city. I'll be near." He hesitated. "John Harrington is stationed at Fort Peyton at the moment. I'm hoping he'll prevent any confrontation that might occur once Warren rides back into the picture."

"Where is Warren now?"

"Still in the interior, south of us now, I believe. Hunting down more women and children. If he follows his orders, he should not come around to hound us at least for a few months."

"That's a relief," James murmured, glancing back toward Teela again. She looked so stoic, seated atop the bay. She would probably remain so, as still and silent as a statue, even if Robert approached her. James lowered his head, glad. Robert was one of the best men James knew. He had the ability to make anyone feel at ease, to draw out conversation, even laughter, when there was none to be drawn.

He looked back up at his brother. "Jarrett, you have to give me one promise."

"What's that?"

"You don't risk your life for mine."

"James—"

James set up a hand. "If things go badly, interfere only if I ask you to do so. Things are more deadly now than ever before. My association with you could bring daggers into your back from your white friends, as could your influence on my part hurt me among the people at this time. I beg of you, don't interfere now. If you can help me at any time, and safely so, I won't hesitate to call, I swear it, big brother. Now, I want your word."

Jarrett, dark eyes somber and unhappy, hesitated. "James, these are difficult times—"

"Your word, big brother. White Tiger."

Still Jarrett hesitated. "My word," he agreed grimly at last.

"Take Teela to safety. Send her away. Make her marry Harrington if that is what it will take."

Jarrett crossed his arms over his chest, arching a brow at James. "How many things have you managed to make that woman do, little brother?"

James smiled slowly. "Well, a very few. The key is never to let her know that there are any weaknesses in men.

"Hell, if it comes to it, drug her. Drag her down an aisle rolled in a blanket if need be. Just keep her from harm. Perhaps you can put her on a ship out of St. Augustine. That was what she intended to do when she was traveling north before Otter's band attacked the group. That would be best. Try to make her leave. Please."

"My word again. I will do my best."

"Thank you."

"But . . ." Jarrett began.

"But what?" James asked, crossing his arms over his chest as he stared at his brother warily.

"Well, you have chosen this life."

"I didn't choose anything. I was born with this!"

"And which parent would you rather not have had?"

"Neither, of course—"

"You could build a plantation on the land you own right outside Cimarron."

"Under these circumstances—"

"Right. You cannot refuse to be part of this. So therefore you choose to be a part of it. Perhaps she has chosen the same."

"Well, she can't. She's got to go, dammit."

Jarrett lowered his head, lifted his hands.

"She could be risking her fool life."

"Some people choose to do so."

James let out a growl of irritation.

"Jarrett—"

"I will do my best. My word."

James inhaled deeply. "Thank you."

"You do something for me. Your word," Jarrett said.

"What is that?"

"Keep yourself safe."

James smiled, nodded. "That's it, I guess."

"Another good-bye."

They turned in unison, heading back toward the others and the horses. James went straight to Teela, lifting her down from the bay. The warmth of her body fell against his, slid against it as he lowered her to her feet. Her eyes were on his, glittering. She drew her hands

from his shoulders even as he set her down. Jarrett cleared his throat discreetly. He, Robert, and his men moved ahead in the clearing, followed by old Riley. For a moment they were alone in the strange peacefulness of the clearing.

"You're not going to ask me not to go again?" he inquired.

She shook her head. "You've already made the decision. What does it matter what I say? You're going."

He nodded. "Jarrett will get you to St. Augustine. You were ready to leave the territory. Now you must go."

"Must I?"

"You said yourself that it was your course of action to leave the territory when Otter and his band attacked you and the soldiers."

"Yes, but . . . so much has changed."

"I told you to go—"

"You've also told me to marry John Harrington."

"Teela, dammit, don't argue with me—"

"Why? Everything in your life must be so neat and tidy. It's time to go to war again, so you put Teela away, you cannot play with her any longer."

He suddenly couldn't bear the parting, or that glitter, cold and disdainful, that had come into her eyes. He wanted to shake her. He drew her hard into his arms, pressed his lips to hers one last time, determined to taste and remember. He wanted her to feel his fury and his anger, know the harshness, feel again that what she had said herself was true—his bitterness made him a fire, a fire that burned others . . .

When he released her, she was shaking. Her lips were swollen and red. Her eyes were alive with a blaze of their own. "Yes, damn you, I'm done playing with you!" he snapped.

He didn't dare look at her again. He leapt, an Indian, bareback, up on his bay.

And rode away from her as quickly as he could.

*　　*　　*

With Jarrett and his men, as with James, it was possible to move very quickly through the landscape.

Jarrett was exceptionally eager to do so. Their small party was heavily armed, and if Osceola was still wielding any power, they were safe, but he wasn't eager to take any chances.

The men were incredibly polite to Teela, constantly solicitous. She was grateful. James's last stinging words remained in her heart. He did not mean them, she told herself. She had taunted him into them. But throughout the day she was chilled to the bone. She felt the pain of losing him as she might feel the pain had some piece of her been cut away. The worst of it was that she was so afraid he would be killed. He was a strong man. But no man was stronger than a bullet. Yes, he could probably best a number of soldiers, but if her stepfather came against him, he could command more and more soldiers. No one could stand up to battle forever. Any man could be tricked, fall prey to treachery.

They rode very late and made no fire that night. Jarrett didn't want to attract parties of either Indians or soldiers. He was hoping to bring her into St. Augustine quietly, and give them all time to adapt before she was forced to talk to any of her father's friends in the military.

When they did stop, Jarrett and Robert created a bed for her from a tarp and blankets, with a saddle for a pillow. Jarrett sat down beside her, leaned against an old oak, his rifle at his side. "You can sleep," he told her. "You'll be safe, I promise."

"I have no fear with you or James," she assured him.

He was quiet a few moments, then said, "Teela, this war is going to go on and on. I see no hope for a solution. If new boundaries are created, the settlers will overstep them again. The Indians will send out their hunting parties when the food in their poor sections runs scarce. Many of the generals think they can stop the war by capturing the chiefs. There will be more chiefs. Young warriors will grow to cunning leaders."

"Why are you telling me this? These things I already know," she said softly.

"Because I know your intentions regarding my brother now, Teela. You are in love with him. With no prejudices and no reservations. But you shouldn't be. The world will not allow what lies in your heart. You need to sail away as you were going to do. Forget everything and everyone here."

Teela sat up, hugging her knees to her chest. "You have told me my intentions—or what I feel at least. Now tell me about your brother. He saved my life. I never planned what I feel. I'm like the arrow of a compass, ever pointing north, and he is north. And when I'm with him, I cannot give a damn about the rest of the world. Yet, sometimes, it is as if he has come to dinner at your house, enjoyed the fullness of a meal, the feel of soft white sheets against his flesh—and then ridden away, needing no more. He can be brutal—"

"James has hurt you?" Jarrett queried, his voice gruff.

She shook her head. "Only with his words. So tell me, where is the truth in him?"

"The truth, Teela, is that he is obsessed with you. But he knows what I have told you is the real truth—this war could go on forever."

"He loves you and Tara and his daughter. You all love him in return. So—"

"We all know that he could be killed any day. We accept that in our hearts. Do you, Teela?"

She lowered her head. "He has told me to leave, or marry John Harrington. Does he mean it?"

"If you were to marry Harrington, he would probably want to slash Harrington's throat and have you drawn and quartered. But yes, he means it."

She lay back down, tears stinging her eyes, and not wanting Jarrett to see them. She was startled when she felt a soft shifting of her hair from her face, and felt a very light, paternal kiss on her forehead. "He wants you to marry Harrington because he loves you, little fool," he said softly. And that was all. He sat back against his

tree, his rifle at the ready. The night breeze moved very gently around her, and she slept for the few hours left before first dawn.

They were back on the road incredibly early. They were not far from the city of St. Augustine, but Jarrett wanted to slip in before most of the citizenry awoke. Teela had never been to the city, but even in Charleston she had heard stories about it and the Spaniards who had founded it. They had always been seeking gold and the fountain of youth Ponce de Leon had been promised by the early Indian tribes, decimated now, that he had found within the peninsula. The architecture was charming, old government buildings with balconies and arches interspersed with more modern dwellings, some in wood, some in masonry. She did not look long, though, for as they passed through an old cemetery, Jarrett pointed out the giant Castillo de San Marcos, Fort Marion, rising off a spit of land against the water. "Let's not run into soldiers now!" he told her, and they hurried down the streets to the old Spanish house he and Tara had taken.

Once they arrived, it was wonderful for Teela to see Tara, Jennifer, and little Ian McKenzie again. Wonderful, even, to soak in a very hot tub, sip sherry, wrap up in a soft cotton nightgown provided by her hostess.

It had been a hard ride, and she was exhausted.

But she was glad of Tara's company after her bath. Glad to have Tara by her. She was brought a rich red steak with corn and a fruit garnish, and she had to admit that the dinner was absolutely delicious. When she finished eating, she was still weary, but content to sit back in a heavy upholstered chair and have Tara brush the snarls out of her hair.

"Newspaper reporters may soon be after you," Tara warned her. "Anything to do with Indian abduction and captivity always intrigues readers."

"I wasn't abducted! Surely, Tara—"

"I know that, of course. But that's my point. You should speak with a reporter. Let him know that James

McKenzie saved your life. It's amazing what sway public opinion can sometimes have over the army."

Teela swung around, catching Tara's hand and meeting her gaze. "Is James in greater danger because of me?"

Tara sighed. "Well, he is an outlaw at the moment, most certainly. But it is not because of you. It is because Warren is a treacherous liar. If you'll allow me, I can see to it that you speak to the right person. Warren's lies will be disarmed. You should do so soon, before your ship leaves."

"My ship?"

"Well, you were returning to Charleston?"

Teela swallowed hard. "I—I'm not ready now."

"But perhaps you should," Tara suggested softly.

Teela shook her head stubbornly. "I've caused trouble for James, but now perhaps I can change that."

"And what are you going to do? Run out and shoot down both the Indians and the army?"

"I'm going to give your reporter the story," she said firmly.

"And when your father does come out of the interior, he'll do something horrible to you."

"I can't go—yet. Please, don't you be against me, too."

"No one is against you. I just think that maybe, for both you and James, it would be best if you did go home soon."

Teela felt something bubbling in her stomach. She leapt up, biting her lower lip.

"What—?" Tara said with alarm.

"The chamber pot!" Teela said. Tara found it in the nick of time. Spasms seized Teela until she was weak. She soaked her face and hands in the fresh water Tara brought her.

"Are you all right now?"

"The food was delicious, too good. I don't think I could handle so much so soon. I shouldn't have wolfed it down like that."

Tara looked at her strangely.

"You should try to get some sleep. We'll talk again in the morning."

Tara left her. Teela had never felt more drained or exhausted. She curled up on the soft four-poster bed in the room with its clean white sheets. She slept.

Tara came downstairs and went into the library of their rented home. It was quite a wonderful place, built in the mid-1600s by a wealthy don for his beloved bride. There was a beautiful mantel hewn from the same coquina shell they had used to build the fort. It was still owned by one of the don's descendents, a charming man with a Spanish name and an English accent, since his family had retained ownership through the years when the territory had passed from the Spaniards to the English, back to the Spaniards, and on to the Americans. He'd been happy to offer the home to a family, just as Tara had been happy to come to the Atlantic side of the territory. She found St. Augustine to be charming, a mixture of the cultures that had passed its way. There were well-stocked general stores, and there was the military base at the ancient fortress, rising on the horizon with a tremendous magnificence. It hadn't actually ever withstood any attacks. Perhaps it was too foreboding to attack.

The city was long established, filled with many languages, the social elite of different cultures, military, slaves, free blacks, even Indians—remnants of decimated tribes and those who had simply embraced white ways.

Jarrett had suggested that they come for a change of scenery and a bit of a social scene throughout the fall and winter. Tara knew, of course, that he didn't give a damn about scenery or society. He had come because he feared for his brother, and seemed to think that he could be of greater help here.

As she walked across the tiled floor of the library, he looked up from the ledger he had before him on the heavy old Spanish desk. "Is she settled?"

Tara nodded. "Sleeping by now, I think. She was very tired."

"There are a number of ships stopping in Charleston that leave here soon."

"There will always be ships leaving St. Augustine," she murmured, perching on a corner of his desk. "She's going to speak with a reporter."

Jarrett folded his arms across his chest and leaned back in his chair, watching his wife. "Two men escaped that slaughter. Both of them told reporters that James McKenzie was not the leader of the band that attacked them. Warren's story was surely a better one."

"But not the truth."

"Lies often catch the public imagination."

"But Teela will be able to make a better story of it, I'm quite certain."

"But should she?" Jarrett murmured, looking out the window. They could see the water from the house, a very blue inlet of the Atlantic.

"My God, of course—"

"Then Warren will tear her to ribbons."

"Jarrett, he won't dare. It will be done before anyone sees him again. And then she can be gone."

"She doesn't want to go."

"Well, she may not have a choice!"

"Are you ready to drag her, kicking and screaming, onto a ship?" she asked him. Then she smiled slightly. "Never mind, what a question! There's very little I put past you, my love, in the pursuit of right as you see it. But I'm warning you, she won't go otherwise."

Jarrett sighed with exasperation. "Then what? Shall I send for Harrington? Should we insist she marry the poor fellow if she's so determined to remain? Harrington would probably become a groom with the greatest pleasure, but would it be fair?"

Tara looked down at the desk. "No, I don't think that sending for Harrington would be a good idea at this point. Jarrett, she's sick."

"With what? Should we quarantine her? Get her away from the children as quickly as possible?"

"No, no. She hasn't a fever or the like. She's—sick. To her stomach."

Jarrett tapped a finger upon his desk thoughtfully. "Oh, dear. I think she was ill along the way as well. She refused, of course, to let me see that she felt poorly in the least. She's determined that she will forge through the territory without a complaint, come what may."

"You don't understand," Tara murmured.

"My love, I understand this situation far more than I wish! Tara wants to stay near my brother no matter what, and though he covets her pathetically, he wants her gone! Perhaps she really should marry John, then—"

"Jarrett, trust me, you don't understand!" Tara repeated. She leapt off the desk and came around, kneeling beside him and taking his hands in hers. She had that strange half smile on her face that meant that men didn't really ever understand anything.

He smiled in return, a brow arched. "What is it, Tara?"

"She can't marry Harrington."

"Tara, Warren remains her guardian—"

"Jarrett, she's expecting."

"Expecting what?"

"Oh, my God. A baby!"

He felt like an idiot. He simply hadn't been prepared for a bomb to be thrown in what was already a dangerous battleground.

"Oh, good God!" he groaned. He clutched his wife's hands more tightly. "How can you possibly tell? I mean, you can't possibly know this for fact. He didn't rescue her from that slaughter in the woods that long ago—"

"It must have happened back in June. When he slipped back to our house after the massive escape of the Indians from near Fort Brooke. Remember the day of the skirmish down the river, when Teela met Harrington and Brandeis and James came back that night?"

"Yes, I remember the night. It was the last time I had seen him until today. But just because she's been sick—"

"Jarrett, I was just in the room with her. While she was bathing."

"Yes?" He arched a brow suspiciously.

"She's changed."

"You were looking at another woman that closely?"

She made a fist of her hand and slammed it on his knee. "Jarrett! I didn't need to stare!"

"Oh, God!" he repeated. He stared at his wife. "James doesn't know."

"I don't think Teela even knows."

An ink dark brow rose on his forehead once again. This time, he realized, he was probably giving her the male look that indicated women were far less than sane and never rational in the least.

"I didn't know for the longest time about Ian," she reminded him. "You get caught up in life, in the worries from day to day—and she has certainly had enough going on around her! Time goes by—and she's been living under such strange circumstances."

Jarrett reached into the bottom desk drawer for a brandy bottle and glasses.

"She doesn't know, but you're certain."

"I've had a baby. I know the signs." She counted on her fingers for a moment, showing him. "Middle of June, end of September. Mark my words. It will be evident to all of us very soon."

Jarrett was about to pour the liquid into a glass, then brought the bottle to his mouth instead. Tara took it from him. "You might share!" she admonished.

He took the bottle from her, poured an equal amount into both glasses. "Sorry, my love," he said, and raised his snifter to her.

Tara picked up her glass. "Thank you, McKenzie."

"Well, congratulations, we are about to become an aunt and uncle once again."

Tara clinked her glass to his, but didn't sip from it. "Indeed, my love, congratulations. Oh, dear Lord! We

will need no longer worry about Major Warren. He will die of rage and apoplexy upon receipt of the news."

"We can only hope. But now, Tara McKenzie, since you are so certain about this impending event, when do you think we should share the information with the happy mother-to-be upstairs? And then, for the love of God, where do we go from there?"

"I'm not sure," Tara murmured. She glanced up at him, setting her snifter down on the desk and pushing it from her.

"What now? You did just insist I share."

"Yes, but actually, it doesn't go down well at all. I haven't been feeling quite as robust myself the last several weeks."

"Tara," he began frowning, "are you trying to tell me—"

"Yes, I am," she said. She looked up at him, smiling ruefully. "If nothing else, these cousins will be very close in age."

Jarrett scooped up his wife, set her upon his lap, and held her very tenderly. "I am delighted, of course," he said huskily. "Ian is still so young—"

"He, too, will be close with his new brother or sister."

Jarrett smiled, breathing in the scent of her, cherishing the moment they shared. "Have I told you recently that I love you more than anything in the world?"

"Actually, you are quite wonderful, and say such things at least once a month, and not always in the absolute heat of passion," she teased him.

"Alas, you remain a vixen!" he sighed with mock despair. "Hmm. Now our lives are made easier. We need only hide Teela until March. We can say that we have become the proud parents of twins, the war can go, and those nearest and dearest to us can continue running around the bush."

"We've one little difficulty with that scenario," Tara said, contentedly leaning against him.

"What's that?"

"Your brother can be amazingly like you. He has your

father's eyes. But no one will mistake his child for ours, because the baby will have Indian blood."

"Well," Jarrett mused, "maybe it will not be such a bad thing if Warren dies of apoplexy after all."

She smiled again, closing her eyes, glad to be with him. "God forgive me for saying this, but it's quite a pity that he will surely not do something so convenient for us all any time soon!"

"So what do we do?" Jarrett asked softly, his whisper against the golden softness of her hair.

"Pray."

"For Warren's death? Does God answer such prayers?"

"If he knows Warren, perhaps!"

Chapter 22

Osceola had a look of the spirit about him when he met James. He was seated on one of his war ponies, and he was dressed in full, splendid array with a plumed turban, red leggings, colorful shirt, and fringed jacket. Coa Hadjo, a subchief and wise man for Osceola's band, was close at his side while a half-dozen near-naked warriors surrounded him

"Thank you for coming when I have called you."

"I'm anxious to hear what news you have, what parley you wish to make."

"We will talk at our council," Osceola told him, leading the way along the trail. They moved swiftly across high ground, then plowed more slowly through the marsh, disappearing through the dense brush that flanked the swamps until they reached a pine barren. There the warriors were greeted quietly by the women and some of the boys not quite ready for warfare. Their horses were taken, food was brought, and they sat cross-legged before an open fire built in a clearing.

"You know what has happened?" Osceola asked him.

James nodded. "All of King Philip's people have been taken. A Yuchi village was invaded right after, and Blue Snake and Yuchi Billy were seized along with others. Wildcat has gone in to the whites as his father sent for him, and is now a prisoner as well."

"Word has been sent to General Jesup that we will parley again," Coa Hadjo told James.

"I am very tired, but also wary," Osceola said. "Coa Hadjo will speak for me when we go for our talks with

the whites. But you must be another set of eyes and ears for me. You must help me understand the white men's words, see what really lies beneath them."

"I will be happy to be with you, Osceola. What do you seek to gain from your council with the military?"

Osceola lifted his hands. "I have not wished to rob the whites. I have never sought to massacre their women and children, though I do not deny that they have died. I have always sought true boundaries. I want to draw lines again. I want to let the whites live in peace, and I want my people to be left to live in peace."

"There is speculation among the whites that you wish to see their strength and learn what you can about how and where they are keeping Wildcat, Philip, Blue Snake, and the others prisoner."

Coa Hadjo and Osceola exchanged glances. Coa Hadjo shrugged. "Men always talk to gain new information."

James grinned. "That is true."

"I seek no battle, Running Bear. That I swear to you by the Great Spirit."

"I have never doubted Osceola's word."

Osceola stood. He seemed to tremble as he did so, and his color was ashen. James and the others stood quickly as well. "Thank you for being among us," Osceola told him briefly.

"I am glad to be with a friend," James replied, but as he watched the war chief, he was worried. Osceola had looked well during the day; he looked as if he was ill again by night.

He left them, and the others moved away, except for Coa Hadjo, a power in his own right, who watched James.

"In truth, what do you think of these new talks, Running Bear?" Coa Hadjo demanded.

James sighed. "I think that men have talked and talked. And that most of the talk has been lies. From both sides," he added sadly.

"What truth is there except that which each man sees in his own heart?" Coa Hadjo asked him.

"Osceola is gravely ill," James said flatly.

"And very, very tired," Coa Hadjo added.

"And what does that mean?" James asked him.

"It means he tires of war," Coa Hadjo said. "Good night, Running Bear. I have never feared for my own safety. I am glad to speak for myself, and for Osceola. But I am glad that you will be with us as well."

James nodded in acknowledgment. Coa Hadjo went his own way. James stared at the fire, then went to find the shelter he had been provided there in the barrens. It was a simple platform raised above the ground a few feet, covered with cabbage palm. The air was cool circulating in and around it. Being elevated, it protected the inhabitants from the creatures that preyed upon the ground at night.

He lay down, weary. He closed his eyes. And all that he could think was that she was gone. He had slept so well beside her. He had felt her warmth, her fire, her heat. Now there was cold and loneliness. He wanted to cry out in the night. He wanted to close his eyes, sleep and dream.

And in his dream there would be no war, nothing savage, and nothing civilized, and nothing red or white. The sky would be alight with a brilliant red dawn, and she would be laughing, running to him, and when he captured her, and spun her beneath the sun, he would never need to let her go again. . . .

He tossed, cold, stiff, uncomfortable.

It was a dream.

Just a dream. And in this wretched world it could never come true.

There was no way to hide the fact that Teela Warren was with the McKenzies, in their home. Teela was very anxious to set the papers straight about her capture and so-called kidnapping. At Jarrett's suggestion, certain of the reporters from Florida and the nation who had swept

down upon St. Augustine to cover the Indian wars were invited to the house. Both Tara and Jarrett were with her when the five invited interviewed her.

She was amazingly composed and relaxed, relating her story from the moment she had left Fort Deliverance to the time of her capture.

"That anyone has accused James McKenzie of any evil or treachery in this entire affair is pathetic and laughable," she informed them. "He saved my life."

Thomason, of a Washington paper, demanded, "But what of your captivity, Miss Warren? You were seized by a savage and held against your will—"

"My brother-in-law is not a savage!" Tara interrupted, as fierce as a terrier.

"I'm sorry, Mr. and Mrs. McKenzie," Thomason said hastily, stroking his white-bearded chin. "What I meant is, there was a certain time in which you were kept in the bush. Was no danger, no offense forced upon you? What will your fiancé think and feel? Have you spoken with Lieutenant Harrison since your ordeal?"

"John Harrison and James McKenzie are the best of friends. I know that John will be grateful, as will anyone who is pleased to see me still alive, that James came to my rescue. Sir, I cannot even condemn Otter, the chief who so craved my death, because his own family was cruelly murdered in this war."

"Preposterous!" the heavily jowled fellow from St. Augustine muttered.

Teela rose. "Sir, if you find the truth preposterous, there is nothing else I have to say. Now, if you will all forgive me ..."

She didn't care if they did or didn't. She was suddenly exhausted. She turned and headed for the stairs. She was incredibly grateful for Jarrett McKenzie's stern admonition that the men were now to leave his residence.

In her room, she stretched out on the bed. She could hear the reporters talking among themselves outside the house, nearly below her window.

"It's disgusting! A decent woman would be horrified

by all that has occurred—" one man began. Evans, from an Atlanta paper.

"Ah, but through history they tend to fall under the influence of their captors," another man asserted.

"Gentlemen!" It was Thomason speaking. "You're forgetting that the man involved is a McKenzie, half white, brother to one of the most influential man in the state. Both have been highly respected for years; they have both acted as negotiators often enough in this sad fracas."

"What, are you an injun lover, too, Thomason?" Teela was sure it was that vile Evans speaking again.

"There is right and wrong, my friends. And I have seen right and wrong on both sides of this affair. You tell me, sir, would it be better if young Miss Warren was today a dead woman yet a *decent* corpse? Her life was saved, quite simply. That is the story, the way I will print it."

"Ah, but it isn't what Warren believes. The half-breed McKenzie is one powerful buck, so rumor has it. Warren believes his daughter feels a fascination for this man. Perhaps he slaughtered the troops, yet she gave him promises of wicked pleasure if he should spare her!" Evans theorized. He would have spoken again when Teela heard something like a choking sound. And it was Jarrett's voice she heard next.

"May I suggest, sir, that if you wish to discuss *my brother* in such slanderous terms, you do so far from my home. Otherwise, I might be the one to give you some very savage behavior to condemn within your text!"

"Mr. McKenzie, you're hurting me—" Evans gasped out.

"Indeed. Get off my property before I kill you!"

Teela heard a door slam. A scurrying. And then ... blessed quiet. She rolled over, heartsick, wondering how she could feel so exhausted when she had slept so deeply the night before.

There was a tapping on her door. She sat up, trying to straighten the damage she had done to her pinned hair by lying upon it. "Come in!"

It was Tara with a tea tray in her hands. She set it on

the morning table by the window. "You did very well," Tara assured her.

Teela sighed. "I heard them talking afterward. It didn't really matter what I said. They all have their pre-conceived notions."

"No, you spoke very well." She paused reflectively, pouring the tea. "You were very good. Jarrett let his temper get the best of him. No matter, he's been accused of everything in the world already. Come over here now. You must eat something."

"Oh, Tara, thank you so much, but I'm just not hungry."

Tara sighed, looking at her in perplexity. "Teela, you are actually losing weight."

"Am I?"

"You must come eat."

"But—"

"Oh, you little fool!" Tara cried at last in exasperation. "Don't you want a healthy child?"

Teela felt a sudden surge of energy and bounded to her feet, staring at Tara. "What?"

"The most casual of observers will soon notice your condition, and yet you have not considered the possibility yourself!"

She had not. Oh, God. Sweet Jesus, she had not. Why not?

She had been so busy. Men had been dying. She had patched them up. She had lain awake nights at Fort Deliverance, praying that she would not get word that James McKenzie, *Running Bear,* was dead. Praying that she would not find him maimed and dying on the operating table. And then . . .

"Teela?" she dimly heard Tara's cry.

But that was all. She was spared any more of the initial shock and trauma of the revelation.

The room misted to shades of red and gray.

And she saw no more.

A strange period of peace and inactivity settled over Osceola and his warriors as the time passed before the

agreed-upon date for the parley. James worried more
and more about Osceola. The chief had days when he
looked fit and well, and days when chills and fever seized
him. He liked to talk during those periods about his
boyhood, about the life he had spent, always fighting, so
it had seemed.

"They think that I have waged a war against their
people," Osceola told him. "The whites—they think that
I have wished to kill them all, as they have wished to
rid the land of us. They are wrong. I fought and I killed
just so that we could have our piece of this great land.
I know what the white newspapers tell people. I know
that there are those in the great cities who consider this
a battle against a people they would rip from their heart-
land, their blood land. And there are those who say the
whites have more right to this peninsula than we do,
that we *Seminoles* are new here. Yes, I am Creek, yes,
many of my brothers are what *they* call Creek. But we
have come here now in waves for well over a hundred
years. We have shed our blood here; we have fed the
land here with it. I have always fought only to stay, only
for our right to the land we have bled upon for our
heritage. There are many among your father's people I
have called friend. Young John Graham, your brother,
others in the military. If only they could make a treaty
and keep it!"

James stared at the fire without replying. But Osceola
smiled. "Many of them have said that I cannot keep a
treaty. That I make promises, come for the white food
and supplies, and then run again. Sometimes I have done
so. I could not watch my children starve."

James looked at him. "I am uneasy about this parley
to come."

"Why?"

He shrugged. "I don't know. I feel it. Like we feel the
footsteps of others when they are near. Like a scent on
the wind. I fear for you."

Osceola was quiet for several long seconds. "The parley will take place. I am resigned."

* * *

The date came. Osceola, Coa Hadjo, many of the others, were dressed in their finery for the talks that would take place.

The army was coming to the Indians. In a copse not far from Fort Peyton, Osceola and his warriors raised a huge white flag above their camp.

James had dressed neither to suit his Indian heritage nor his white, but chose his usual dark breeches, cotton shirt, strip of red fabric around his head to keep his hair from his eyes.

He was on his way to find Osceola when he heard the cry of a bird.

One he had not expected. He answered in kind.

Jarrett stepped from the foliage but beckoned to him. "Follow me out some. The soldiers are coming here even as we speak."

James quickly did as his brother bade him. He almost felt as if they were boys again, running wildly through the forests and marshes, learning, laughing. Jarrett had taught him to hunt, to fish. Through their mothers they had differed. Through their love of their land, they had forged a bond deeper than blood.

They were older now. Jarrett was gasping somewhat as he paused next to an old oak. "General Hernandez left St. Augustine early this morning for the parley. Jesup will not be with him; he is so nervous that he awaits the results at Fort Peyton. Altogether Hernandez will have a force of nearly two hundred and fifty well-armed men. James, this is not to be a talk. Jesup believes that Osceola has betrayed him again and again. He plans to capture him under a flag of truce. You shouldn't be here. Teela has given a statement to the newspapers—"

"Teela is still in the territory?"

"She is safe, she lives with us, and Harrington has been the best of friends, escorting her about town so that they can be seen together. There is more about Teela that I must tell you, but pay heed to me about this first. Most men believe that you are the noble if

half-savage negotiator you have been throughout the conflict, but there are those still eager to hang anyone associated with any attacks on whites."

"Do they plan on hanging Osceola?" James asked.

"No, there is no such talk. The Indians are to be escorted to Fort Marion. You know, the old Castillo de San Marcos." Even as Jarrett spoke, James became alarmingly aware of motion on the trails near them. He dragged Jarrett down low beside him as they watched the mounted men of Hernandez's force riding by on the trail nearest them.

"Jarrett, I've got to go back."

"You'll be imprisoned with the others by association."

"Perhaps. And perhaps I will speak for myself and clear my name before your military friends. Jarrett, all I know is that I must be with Osceola now. He—"

"He what?"

"I think he's dying. I have to go. If I need you, I swear, I will send for you. If not, brother, I have to pave my own way in this world. You must get out of here before you are condemned as a traitor for coming to me!"

"Wait! I have to tell you—"

The more horses that rode by, the more James worried. For his brother now, not himself. He turned, ready to run back the way he had come. "Go!" he commanded his brother, and disappeared back into the bush himself.

He ran harder than he had come. Too late. He slipped through the back of the copse even as the first of the military men entered the Indian camp with its high-flying white flag. There was nothing that he could do.

He stood back in uneasy silence, watching as the white soldiers came around them. General Hernandez was at the head of the delegation. As Jarrett had told him, General Jesup was not among the soldiers. James studied the uniforms of the men around Jesup. There were Florida mounted men with him, dragoons on foot.

Scents on the wind . . .

He suddenly knew that they were completely sur-

rounded by white military, just as his brother had warned. There was nothing that he could say or do; any cry of alarm on his part now would bring all the white guns blazing against them before the Indians had a chance to raise their own weapons. He saw that Osceola seemed to be choking. He went forward with Coa Hadjo at his side. General Hernandez stepped forward with his black interpreter at his side. He greeted Osceola and Coa Hadjo with all courtesy, then said, "I thought there would be more of your number among you. Where are Alligator, Micanopy, Jumper, and Cloud?"

"Ill," Coa Hadjo said. "Disease—the spotted disease, measles—has laid many of our people low."

Hernandez saw James then, arms folded over his chest, watching. He nodded in acknowledgment, flushing. Hernandez was a good man, James thought. In the quick glance Hernandez had cast him, he thought he saw many things. It was true that this was pure treachery. Jesup had planned it; Hernandez disagreed with it. He was following his orders.

"I am your friend," Hernandez said. "Tell me, why have you come to talk?"

"For the good of all," Coa Hadjo replied.

"Why?"

"We have had word from King Philip through the messenger of his son, Wildcat."

"Have you come to surrender to me?"

"No, that was not our intent. We had not understood that we should do so. We have kept our peace during the summer."

"Ah, but there have been incidents—"

"Ah, friend! Not by us. We have sought peace. Just as the generals have not always been able to control the slaughters by the farmers settling the land, neither can we always control a renegade warrior."

"Have you brought back stolen property!"

Here Coa Hadjo hesitated. "We have brought in the negroes many call their property."

Again Hernandez looked conflicted. "I wish you all

well," he said. The words were repeated by the interpreter. "But we have so often been deceived. I am afraid
that you must now come with me. I will promise that you
will be treated well. Here, I have brought Blue Snake of
the Yuchis to speak with you. He will tell you that you
must come with me."

Blue Snake, his leathered face weary, stepped from
out of the soldiers and came forward. "General Hernandez, it was not my understanding that any who spoke
would be seized."

Hernandez looked surprised at Blue Snake's defiance.
He made a movement, the slightest movement. The
troops that surrounded them surged forward.

The trap was sprung.

Every single warrior saw what James had seen. Though
they carried rifles, they could not get off a shot before they
would all be mown down like corn in autumn.

James looked at Osceola. His expression was unread-
able. Hernandez continued to speak with them. It was
to be as Jarrett said. They were to march the seven miles
to St. Augustine to the fort there. They would be well
treated. They wouldn't be harmed or killed.

Osceola and two others were brought horses. James,
his arms still crossed over his chest, watched the proceedings until Hernandez rode to where he stood.

"It was treachery," James said quietly.

"It was necessary."

"You seized a man who is already a legendary chief
while he waited under a white flag of truce."

"And I shall live to rue the day, surely," Hernandez
said wearily. "I can excuse nothing to you, James. I am
sick myself with what we have done, yet I see that Jesup
believed he had no choice. He thinks if he can stop
Osceola, he can stop the war."

"He won't stop the war. He will create a martyr."

"God forgive me, I just pray to stop the bloodshed
for a while. James, I say again, I can offer no excuse. I
can but give you a chance to slip into the woods if you
so desire."

OFFICIAL RULES

1. NO PURCHASE NECESSARY TO ENTER OR WIN A PRIZE. To enter the SEE HOW FAR A GOOD BOOK CAN TAKE YOU SWEEPSTAKES, complete this official entry form (original or photocopy), or, on a 3" x 5" piece of paper, print your name and complete address. Mail your entry to: SEE HOW FAR A GOOD BOOK CAN TAKE YOU SWEEPSTAKES, P.O. Box 8012, Grand Rapids, MN, 55745-8012. Enter as often as you wish, but mail each entry in a separate envelope. All entries must be received by November 29, 1996, to be eligible. Not responsible for illegible entries, lost or misdirected mail.

2. Winners will be selected from all valid entries in a random drawing on or about December 31, 1996, by Marden-Kane, Inc., an independent judging organization whose decisions are final and binding. Odds of winning are dependent upon the number of entries received. Winners will be notified by mail and may be required to execute an affidavit of eligibility and release which must be returned within 14 days of notification or an alternate winner will be selected.

3. One (1) Grand Prize winner will receive 25,000 American Airlines AAdvantage miles. Approximate retail value: $500.00. Five (5) First Place winners will receive 10,000 American Airlines AAdvantage miles. Approximate retail value: $200.00. Ten (10) Second Place winners will receive 3,000 American Airlines AAdvantage miles. Approximate retail value: $60.00. Thirty (30) Third place winners will receive 1,000 American Airlines AAdvantage miles. Approximate retail value: $20.00. Approximate retail value of all prizes: $2,700.00.

4. Sweepstakes open to residents of the U.S. and Canada except employees and the immediate families of Penguin USA, American Airlines, its affiliated companies, advertising and promotion agencies. Void in the Province of Quebec and wherever else prohibited by law. All Federal, State, Local, and Provincial laws apply. Taxes, if any, are the sole responsibility of the prize winners. Canadian winners will be required to answer an arithmetical skill testing question administered by mail. Winners consent to the use of their name and/or photos or likenesses for advertising purposes without additional compensation (except where prohibited). No substitution of prizes is permitted. All prizes are nontransferable.

5. American Airlines may find it necessary to change AAdvantage program rules, regulations, travel awards, and special offers at any time, impacting, for example, participant affiliations, rules for earning mileage and blackout dates and limited seating for travel awards. American Airlines reserves the right to end the AAdvantage program with six months notice. AAdvantage travel awards, mileage accrual, and special offers subject to government regulations.

6. Winners agree that the sponsor, its affiliates, and their agencies and employees are not liable for injuries, loss, or damage of any kind resulting from participation or from the acceptance or use of the prize awarded.

7. For the names of the major prize winners, send a self-addressed, stamped envelope after December 31, 1996, to: SEE HOW FAR A GOOD BOOK CAN TAKE YOU SWEEPSTAKES WINNERS, P.O. Box 714, Sayreville, NJ 08871-0714.

Penguin USA • Mass Market
375 Hudson Street, New York, N.Y. 10014

Printed in the USA

American Airlines and AAdvantage are registered trademarks of American Airlines, Inc.

- What type of story do you prefer?

    a: Very sexy   b: Sweet, less explicit
    c: Light and humorous   d: More emotionally intense
    e: Dealing with darker issues f: Other

- What kind of covers do you prefer?

    a: Illustrating both hero and heroine   b: Hero alone
    c: No people (art only)   d: Other_____

- What other genres do you like to read (circle all that apply)

    Mystery   Medical Thrillers   Science Fiction
    Suspense   Fantasy   Self-help
    Classics   General Fiction   Legal Thrillers
    Historical Fiction

- Who is your favorite author, and why?_____
  _____

- What magazines do you like to read? (circle all that apply)

    a: *People*   b: *Time/Newsweek*
    c: *Entertainment Weekly*   d: *Romantic Times*
    e: *Star*   f: *National Enquirer*
    g: *Cosmopolitan*   h: *Woman's Day*
    i: *Ladies' Home Journal*   j: *Redbook*
    k: Other:_____

- In which region of the United States do you reside?

    a: Northeast   b: Midatlantic   c: South
    d: Midwest   e: Mountain   f: Southwest
    g: Pacific Coast

- What is your age group/sex?   a: Female   b: Male

    a: under 18   b: 19-25   c: 26-30   d: 31-35   e: 36-40
    f: 41-45   g: 46-50   h: 51-55   i: 56-60   j: Over 60

- What is your marital status?

    a: Married   b: Single   c: No longer married

- What is your current level of education?

    a: High school   b: College Degree
    c: Graduate Degree   d: Other: _____

- Do you receive the TOPAZ *Romantic Liaisons* newsletter, a quarterly newsletter with the latest information on Topaz books and authors?

    YES   NO

  If not, would you like to?   YES   NO

  Fill in the address where you would like your free gift to be sent:

  Name: _____

  Address: _____

  City:_____Zip Code: _____

  You should receive your free gift in 6 to 8 weeks.
  Please send the completed survey to:

Penguin USA•Mass Market
Dept. TS
375 Hudson St.
New York, NY 10014

WE NEED YOUR HELP

To continue to bring you quality romance
that meets your personal expectations,
we at TOPAZ books want to hear from you.
Help us by filling out this questionnaire, and in exchange
we will give you a **free gift** as a token of our gratitude.

- Is this the first TOPAZ book you've purchased? (circle one)

  YES   NO

  The title and author of this book is: _____

- If this was not the first TOPAZ book you've purchased, how many have
  you bought in the past year?

  a: 0 - 5   b 6 - 10   c: more than 10   d: more than 20

- How many romances in total did you buy in the past year?

  a: 0 - 5   b: 6 - 10   c: more than 10   d: more than 20 ____

- How would you rate your overall satisfaction with this book?

  a: Excellent   b: Good   c: Fair   d: Poor

- What was the main reason you bought this book?

  a: It is a TOPAZ novel, and I know that TOPAZ stands
     for quality romance fiction
  b: I liked the cover
  c: The story-line intrigued me
  d: I love this author
  e: I really liked the setting
  f: I love the cover models
  g: Other: _____

- Where did you buy this TOPAZ novel?

  a: Bookstore   b: Airport   c: Warehouse Club
  d: Department Store   e: Supermarket   f: Drugstore
  g: Other: _____

- Did you pay the full cover price for this TOPAZ novel? (circle one)

  YES   NO
  If you did not, what price did you pay? _____

- Who are your favorite TOPAZ authors? (Please list)

- How did you first hear about TOPAZ books?

  a: I saw the books in a bookstore
  b: I saw the TOPAZ Man on TV or at a signing
  c: A friend told me about TOPAZ
  d: I saw an advertisement in_____magazine
  e: Other: _____

- What type of romance do you generally prefer?

  a: Historical   b: Contemporary
  c: Romantic Suspense   d: Paranormal (time travel,
     futuristic, vampires, ghosts, warlocks, etc.)
  d: Regency   e: Other: _____

- What historical settings do you prefer?

  a: England   b: Regency England   c: Scotland
  e: Ireland   f: America   g: Western Americana
  h: American Indian   i: Other: _____